THE NIGHT
WE MET

THE NIGHT
WE MET

Rob Byrnes

KENSINGTON BOOKS
http://www.kensingtonbooks.com

KENSINGTON BOOKS are published by

Kensington Publishing Corp.
850 Third Avenue
New York, NY 10022

All Kensington titles, imprints and distributed lines are available at special quantity discounts for bulk purchases for sales promotion, premiums, fund-raising, educational or institutional use.

Special book excerpts or customized printings can also be created to fit specific needs. For details, write or phone the office of the Kensington Special Sales Manager: Kensington Publishing Corp., 850 Third Avenue, New York, NY 10022, Attn. Special Sales Department. Phone: 1-800-221-2647.

Kensington and the K logo Reg. U.S. Pat. & TM Off.

Library of Congress Card Catalogue Number: 2001099266
ISBN 0-7582-0193-1

First Printing: September 2002
10 9 8 7 6 5 4 3 2 1

Printed in the United States of America

Acknowledgments

They say that writing is a solitary activity. True enough. But getting it right is a group effort.

So I thank my editor, John Scognamiglio, for his wise counsel. Thanks, too, to Douglas Mendini and John Masiello at Kensington Publishing, as well as to my agent, Katherine Fausset at the Watkins/ Loomis Agency.

Not to mention Alan Boyce, Nurmi Husa, Illyse Kaplan, Mick LaMarca, Jeff Marks, Alanna Martin, Denise Murphy McGraw, Joyce Moye, and Shaun Terry. They—along with many members of CompuServe's Literary and Writers forums—were valuable resources and, best of all, honest critics.

John L. Myers and Margaret Campbell . . . where would I be without them? Still stuck on Chapter 3, I suppose. Their early friendship and encouragement not only sustained me but helped me treat writing as a craft, not a hobby.

Three real pros also gave me their valuable time and insight: authors Diana Gabaldon and Rabih Alameddine, and my Publishing Jungle tour guide, Robert Riger. I hope I've let them know what they mean to me, because it can't be put into words.

Penultimately, I want to thank three talented people who spent an incredible amount of time working with me to make sure my ellipses had three dots, my extra *than*s were stricken, there were no breaks in continuity, and I cut down on my dialogue tags: K. D. Santineau, Elise Skidmore, and the great Bonnee Pierson. They were sharp-eyed, creative, and I love them to death. If I were straight and a Mormon, I'd marry them.

Finally, I would like to dedicate this book to the one person whose faith in me has never wavered, even when mine has. Thank you, Lynette Kelly. You may have saved my life; you certainly saved my soul.

THE NIGHT
WE MET

1

Life Before Frank . . .
And Why I Particularly Hate Nicholas Hafner

The first thing you should know is that I'm a romantic. I've tried to become another jaded, cynical New Yorker, but I've failed. Yes, I live in the real world and have all the problems that come with it, but that's never seemed to dampen the visions of romance that live in my head, where Bogie and Bergman always have Paris, Fred and Ginger sweep across my cerebellum, and, if I'm not dating Mr. Right, he's waiting around the corner, just as the cliché promises.

And I like the trappings of romance: cards and flowers; champagne and strawberries; long walks with a lover on warm beaches under blue, cloudless skies as our Golden Lab romps in the surf . . . Reality has tried but failed to beat the saccharine out of me. Those illusions of romance live deep inside me.

The second thing you should know is that Webster's offers several definitions of the word *romantic*, including "having no basis in fact," which is sort of the yin to the yang of passionate love. But that's an easy definition to overlook when Fred and Ginger are distracting you.

And I've had my share of distractions. Take Ted Langhorne, for example.

I had already lived in Manhattan for fifteen years before I met Ted, after moving from Allentown, Pennsylvania, to realize my dreams of going to New York University, finding a pack of cool homosexual friends to run with, and becoming one of the preeminent literary voices of my generation.

Of course, those were dreams. In reality, I did manage to graduate from NYU, and I did manage to befriend a number of homosexuals, although no one who was known far and wide as "cool." But the closest I came to becoming the literary voice of my generation was when my bosses at Palmer/Midkiff/Carlyle Publishing, Inc., let me dip into the slush pile—that's what we in the business call the heaps of unsolicited and largely unreadable manuscripts that arrive in our offices, day in and day out—to see if I could find the literary needle in the haystack that would launch me as the Maxwell Perkins of the 1990s. That needle didn't exist, of course, because if it did, someone else with more ambition and a sharper eye for talent would have found it long before I did. But still, I could dream . . .

And then came Ted.

Ted was an accountant, and he acted like I expected an accountant to act, which doesn't mean that he was boring, but . . . Well, let's just say that he was more *adult* than any of my other friends. More *mature*. More . . . well, yes, *boring;* but boring in a good way. And after fifteen years in New York City—years that spanned the end of my teens, all of my twenties, my early thirties, Reagan and Clinton, AIDS and Mad Cow Disease, disco and house music, cocaine and Ecstasy, and about eighty-nine managers of the New York Yankees—I was ready for boring in a good way.

And, of course, we met cute.

"Hey," he said, approaching me as I stood alone, back to the wall of a Greenwich Village bar late one Friday night. "Aren't you a friend of John's?"

"I know a lot of Johns," I replied dryly.

"I thought so," he said and flashed a dazzling, inviting smile. "Can I buy you a beer?"

Okay, I know . . . not exactly *Love Story.* But, since it *did* work out at the time, it still sort of counts as a romantic, love-at-first-sight kind of meeting. In my mind, at least.

He was tall and handsome, thick chestnut brown hair framing a wholesome face that belied his true age, which I later learned was forty. I didn't have to touch him to know his body was taut and muscular, although I discreetly did, anyway. And those eyes—piercing green, flecked with brown. I instinctively knew their color, even though I defy anyone to ascertain the color of someone's eyes in a dimly lit bar.

"I love your eyes," I told him a few beers later.

"Contacts," he replied.

In retrospect, I know that was the moment I should have run away. That was the moment when Ted Langhorne had first shown me his basic lack of understanding of the illusions of romance. That was the moment when Ted Langhorne had revealed that deep inside the soul of this accountant was . . . another accountant.

But the moment passed. For those of us who still believe in the illusions of romance, they always do.

That night we went back to his apartment in Chelsea. He showed me his view—the apartment building across the street—and, after some idle conversation, he showed me that taut and muscular body. I put it to good use.

"So, what do you do?" he asked later as we lay entwined on his bed.

"Editorial assistant at Palmer/Midkiff/Carlyle. Ever hear of them?"

He hadn't. Given PMC's relatively small size in the era of increasingly large publishing houses, that wasn't especially surprising.

"It doesn't matter. It's probably time for me to move on with my life. I'm not getting anywhere."

"Is that what you want to do for a career?"

"No," I confessed, a bit embarrassed, because he was about to become one of the few people in the world to know my dream. "I want to be a writer. But . . . no luck so far."

"Why?"

"Writer's block. A decade's worth of writer's block."

Ted persisted, and I finally confessed to ninety-seven pages of an uncompleted semiautobiographical manuscript about a young man's coming of age in Allentown hidden in a desk drawer back at my apartment.

He said he wanted to read it.

"You don't have to do that," I said. "I'll have sex with you again even if you *don't* read it."

And I did. But late the next morning, while we were still in bed wrapped in each other's arms, my hand gently caressing his broad, smooth chest, he asked, "So, when do I get to read your novel?"

"Are you serious?"

"Yeah. I want to read it. You said that it's semiautobiographical, right? Well, I want to see what you're all about."

And if I was already starting to fall in love, that pushed me over the edge.

Ted, too, seemed to accept the inevitability of our relationship. We'd only known each other for hours, but we both seemed to instinctively know we were meant to be together forever.

We didn't need to discuss whether or not he'd follow me home the next morning. Of course he did. Together Forever had its roots in Together the Next Day, after all, so there'd been no question about it.

We took the subway to West Eighty-sixth Street, then walked the short block to Amsterdam Avenue, where my bland building anchored one corner of the intersection. We passed under a weathered green canopy jutting from the grimy brick facade and entered the lobby. The elderly doorman nodded vacantly as we passed.

"Top-notch security here, huh?" said Ted as we walked into the tiny elevator.

I pushed the button for my floor. "Nothing but the best for me."

We reached the seventh floor and I ushered him into my apartment, slightly embarrassed when I realized I'd left newspapers and dirty laundry strewn throughout the room that served jointly as living room, dining room, and, for the most part, kitchen.

"Sorry for the mess," I apologized, hurriedly collecting an armful of the previous week's discarded clothes from the faded couch angled in the middle of the room. I opened the door to the bed-sized bedroom and tossed them out of sight.

"Nice place," he said, looking around and choosing to ignore the disarrayed bookshelves, fraying furniture, dying plants, and worn hardwood floors. "A little cramped, but livable. Which is more than you can say for most apartments in Manhattan."

I hunted through the refrigerator for a couple of Cokes. "I used to have an apartment in the Village, but I got tired of living in a rabbit warren. This place might be small, but it's a palace compared to that place."

"There are just too many people in this city," he called back.

When I returned with the Cokes, Ted was gazing out the window.

"Not much of a view, I'm afraid," I said.

"One of the paradoxes of living in New York City. There are a lot of great views, but you need a lot of money to get one. The rest of us get to look at other apartment buildings."

I handed him his Coke. "Sometimes you sound like you don't like it here."

"I survive. But one of these days, Iowa, here I come."

"Iowa?"

"Or Ohio . . . Utah . . ."

"Why?" I asked. "Do you want to get back to the land? Or do you just want to live in a state with four letters?"

He smiled and waited for a blaring car horn to stop. "I wouldn't mind a little peace and quiet in my life."

"But you can't leave New York," I told him. "I don't think there are any gay people in Iowa."

Still framed in the window, Ted leaned forward slightly. "I can see the entrance to your subway station down on Broadway."

"Really?" I already knew that and didn't care, but I used it as an excuse to press up against him in the window.

He felt my body rub against his and turned slightly to kiss me. When he did, his striking green eyes—and, to me, they would always be his *eyes*, not his contact lenses—narrowed to slits, and he moaned softly.

We stood there, framed in the window, for several long minutes.

"I think you've got something to show me," he finally said softly.

"Mmm-hmmm," I purred. I took a step back and, in one swift and very practiced motion, unsnapped my top button, unzipped my fly, and slid down my briefs. My semierection spilled out.

He laughed. "That isn't exactly what I meant. I was talking about your book."

"Oh . . ." I said, embarrassed.

"But . . ." He trailed off as his mouth moved down my torso. "This is good, too."

Half an hour later we were both sprawled on the couch, naked, sweaty, and more than a little sticky. That's when he said, "Now, about that book . . ."

Without disentangling myself from him, I blindly reached behind me and patted my hand around until I felt my desk. Then, still operating through sense of touch, I moved my hand around until I felt a drawer handle, slid it open, and pulled out the too-thin manila envelope.

"Voilà," I said. *"Allentown Blues,.* Chapters one through seven. And please don't laugh at me."

Ted took the envelope from me and slid the ninety-seven neatly printed pages of manuscript out of it—along with the title page, which simply read *"Allentown Blues* by Andrew Westlake"—before tossing the envelope to the floor. Then he started reading.

He was on page twelve or so when I felt myself starting to nod off. I decided to let myself go, exhausted from our lovemaking, and delighted my body was entwined with his. And when I woke up, he was done.

"So?" I craned my neck to see his face. "What did you think?"

He smiled. "Why don't you finish it?"

"First, tell me what you think."

He started stroking my hair. "Well, it's very funny. I love your dialogue."

"Uh-oh. I feel a 'but' coming on."

"The only 'but' is that you left me hanging. I want to know what happens to Grant. Does he come out of the closet in Allentown? Does he escape to New York?"

"I don't know," I answered truthfully. "Grant hasn't decided yet."

"What do you mean?"

"I mean that, when I started writing, I had everything plotted out. But the more I wrote, the more the characters started taking on lives of their own. That's why I put the book away. I don't know what should happen next. They haven't decided."

"I don't get it," he said with a self-conscious laugh. "Maybe I don't understand how the creative mind works."

There. I had a second warning. I had another chance to run away, screaming. Sure, he was intelligent and beautiful and sexy and gave a great blow job. But he didn't understand the illusions of romance and he didn't understand why I couldn't just force my literary creations to follow a one-dimensional plot outline.

But, like the first warning, I ignored it. Just as I would ignore all the subsequent warnings. Hundreds of them.

Intellectually, of course, I knew I was in love. But the intensity of the emotion caught me by surprise. I realized that I was beginning to formulate my thoughts using a "What would Ted do?" construct, and his verbal distinctions found their way into my words. Some days, I would catch myself staring into the cracked bathroom mirror, wondering what there was about the person staring back that an incredibly beautiful and fascinating man like Ted could possibly find to love.

I forced myself to confess that, yes, I was a good-looking man. The wear and tear I had put on my body hadn't caught up with it yet. I still had a full head of naturally brown hair with occasional golden highlights, and my skin still had a healthy glow, although admittedly, Oil of Olay played its part. Good fortune and good genetics had provided me with a healthy physique while sparing me the rigors of the gym.

But still, I was no Ted.

Ted's love should have made me feel good about myself, but instead it consumed me in self-doubt. I felt unworthy of his attention and affection.

That irony didn't escape me.

I got over it. Mostly.

Three months later, when his lease was up, Ted moved into my apartment on the Upper West Side at Eighty-sixth and Amsterdam, which consequently became a lot more cramped. But I didn't mind, because I was in love and we were acting out the ritual of domestic bliss.

Six days after Ted moved in, I presented him with a carefully wrapped final draft of the manuscript for *Allentown Blues*.

"You did it!"

"I did it," I replied, quite proud of myself and thrilled I'd made him proud of me. "Grant finally told me what he wanted to do with his life."

"And what's that?"

My finger softly traced a line from his forehead down the bridge of his nose. "He decided to move to Manhattan and meet a nice accountant."

On the following Monday, I walked into the offices of David R. Carlyle IV, who was the black sheep son of David R. Carlyle III, who was one of the founders of Palmer/Midkiff/Carlyle. That was enough to keep him in a lot of money and entitle him to the position of senior editor, which in David's case was more or less a part-time position.

Although he was quite a bit older, David was the closest thing I had to a social acquaintance at PMC for many of the same reasons that he was the black sheep of his family. He was unapologeti-cally—sometimes flamboyantly—gay, he loved to spend money, and he often acted as if he considered PMC little more than a place to hang out between parties and pick up a paycheck.

In short, he was my kind of guy . . . but with more money. A *lot* more money.

"Andrew," he gushed when he saw me. His wide, pink face broke into a smile. "Good to see you. And how are things with you and your accountant? Ted, isn't it?"

"I'm in love," I replied without thinking twice.

"Good for you." He fussed around his office. "God, look at this place. Dust an inch thick. And nobody's been watering my plants."

"Can't get good help nowadays."

"Don't I know it," he said before he brightened and added con-spiratorially, "Well, that's not totally true. I met the cutest young thing the other night. I think he'd make an excellent house boy."

"Can he dust?" I asked, raising an eyebrow.

He threw his hands in the air with a dramatic flourish. "Perish the thought! I certainly wouldn't want him to get dirty." He fussed some more and motioned for me to take a seat. "So, what can I do for you? Have you finally had it with PMC? Are you here to tell me you're quitting?"

"Of course not."

"God, I wish *I* could," he snapped. "But I suppose it's good for me to have a place to go that gets me off the streets for a few hours every week. So . . . if you're not quitting, and I *know* you're not here to do something foolish like ask for a raise, what can I do for you?"

Without a word, I handed him my manuscript. He took it from me as if it were breakable and glanced at the title page.

"'*Allentown Blues* by Andrew Westlake,'" he read, settling his over-stuffed frame into an overstuffed chair. Then he glanced up and jokingly asked, "Any relation?"

"I thought I'd give PMC the first crack at it."

"Why not? Our slush pile is as good as anyone else's." He slipped me a quick and somewhat indulgent smile. "I'll read it myself, Andrew. But"—and now his voice slid into a deeper octave, which was, I presumed, supposed to connote professionalism —"I hope you understand that we can't publish it just because you work here."

"I understand."

"Good."

"But remember," I said, as I rose to leave, "I know where you live."

One week later, just as I was reaching the point where I thought I was going to be rejected, David Carlyle called me.

"I'm sorry it took me so long to finish your book," he said, "but I took it with me to Fire Island and I didn't have as much free time as I'd expected. *Please* don't ask me about that lovely German boy who was dominating my time."

"So, what's the verdict?" I asked, hoping to bypass a self-indulgent soft-core account of his week in Cherry Grove.

"You're on. I thought it was delightful. A little light, but delightful."

"Light?"

"When PMC has published novels in the gay genre in the past, we've tried to look for things with poignancy. I loved *Allentown Blues*, but I wouldn't exactly call it poignant. It's just a fun read."

"Actually," I said defensively, "I think there *were* some poignant parts in the book."

"Whatever," he said, not particularly caring what I thought was in my novel. "I've already talked to some of the other senior editors—you know, the ones who have the same title as I do but with the authority to actually *do* something around here—and I've convinced them that we should publish it. We'll let the readers decide if they think it's appropriately poignant or not."

Ten months later, *Allentown Blues* was in the bookstores.

Well, not *all* the bookstores. It was in gay bookstores, and one or two copies sometimes found their way into the Barnes & Noble superstore on Upper Broadway, but I suspect that's mostly because Ted and I made periodic anonymous calls to ask if they had it in stock.

The $7500 advance I received from PMC—the only money I

made off *Allentown Blues*, by the way—paid for a one-week vacation for two in Key West and reduced a few credit card balances. And then it was back to the day-to-day drudgery of life in Manhattan.

Time seemed to pass at an alarming rate. One night I met Ted, the next night we had moved in together, the next night my book was published, the next night we were in Key West, the next night we were celebrating our first anniversary, the next night we were in a mall in Jersey City and I decided that I'd show Ted the new art book I'd helped edit and . . .

"Let's go," he said abruptly, grabbing my arm and pulling me toward the front of the store.

"What's the matter?" I asked, returning the book to the shelf.

"Nothing. I just want to go."

He dragged me to Sears—such a *Ted* store—and pretended to look at stereo equipment.

"So, what was that all about?" I asked. "Does Waldenbooks bring back some repressed childhood memories or something?"

"No," he said unconvincingly. "I just wanted to leave."

"Okay. Fine." I joined him in pretending to look at stereo equipment for a few minutes, then told him I had to find the rest room. When I was out of sight, I backtracked and took the escalator down to the lower level.

Back at Waldenbooks, I found the spot in the store that had troubled Ted. I didn't see anything. All that was there was . . .

. . . the discount bin.

With about ten copies of *Allentown Blues*, all bearing a huge Waldenbooks label that told the world that this book that PMC had published just a few short months earlier, with a retail price of $23, could now be theirs for only $2.95.

"No," I gasped.

A middle-aged woman who'd been scanning a copy of the dust jacket, trying to decide if my novel was worth her $2.95, glanced at me. Then she glanced at my picture on the dust jacket, then back at my face, trying to tell if the pitiful failed author of this discounted book could possibly be the same pitifully moaning customer standing next to her in a mall in Jersey City.

"I'm sorry," said Ted, who was suddenly behind me. Oblivious to the fact that we were in a Waldenbooks in Jersey City, he wrapped a muscular arm protectively and lovingly around my chest. "I didn't want you to see this."

"I'm a failure," I said.

"Don't say that. All those people who didn't buy your book are the ones who lost out."

"I love you. You say the nicest things."

The middle-aged woman, for some reason unfazed by our affection, held the book open to my photograph on the dust jacket and asked, "Is this you?"

"No," I said and walked away.

We had dinner at the food court.

"I'm a failure," I said again.

"So, what are you gonna do about it?"

I drew little designs in ketchup with a french fry, trying to decide what I was going to do about it. "I guess I'll just resign myself to the fact that I'm not a writer. I am and will always be a slave boy at PMC."

"I've got a better idea. Why don't you write another novel?"

"No way. It's too much work to go through just for humiliation."

And suddenly that middle-aged woman from Waldenbooks was there. "I *knew* it was you," she said too loudly. A few other food court patrons turned to see what was going on. "You're Andrew Westlake!"

"Yes," I confessed.

"I'm sorry about bothering you at the bookstore," she said, still too loudly and without bothering to apologize for bothering me at the food court. "It's just that I never met a real author before." She opened her Waldenbooks bag and produced her marked-down copy of *Allentown Blues*. "Would you autograph this for me?"

Three teenage girls sitting at a neighboring table with several plates of the food court version of Chinese took note.

"You write a book, mister?" one asked.

The middle-aged woman proudly held up her copy of *Allentown Blues* for the girls—and several other patrons—to see. "He wrote this." Then she flipped to the dust jacket photograph and said, "See? That's him. That's Andrew Westlake."

"Cool," said one of the girls.

The woman set the book down again and told me her name, so I wrote, *To Marlene Birrell . . . Suddenly, you're my number-one fan! Enjoy the book! Best wishes, Andrew Westlake.*

We took the train back to Manhattan, then another one back to the Upper West Side, but it wasn't until we walked through the front door that Ted said, "So, when are you going to start your *next* novel?"

"Oh, please," I said, dismissing him but at least smiling now.

As he unbuttoned my shirt, he said, "Hey, now you've got a real, live fan. If you don't write another novel, Marlene Birrell will be very disappointed in you." He stopped, then added, "So will I."

A few months later, Ted and I were enjoying a Sunday afternoon in late May, lying on a blanket in Central Park.

"Look at them," I said, watching a young couple squabbling from a distance. "Wouldn't you like to know their story?"

"Not particularly."

I rolled over and looked at him. "What's the matter? You sound distracted."

He glanced at me, then trained his eyes somewhere else. "I guess I'm just a little tired."

I tossed a playful punch at his shoulder. "Come on. We're in Central Park, the people-watching capital of the world. Let's people-watch!"

"That's what I'm doing," he replied dully. "I'm watching people. What else is there to do?"

I scanned the park, found the squabbling couple again, then pointed them out to Ted. "Here, let me show you how to people-watch. It's an art, and this will help unlock your creative side. Now, you see that man and woman over there, arguing?"

Ted grunted.

"Well, I think she's just told him she's pregnant. But he's only twenty-two, and he doesn't want to be tied down with a wife and a baby when he's so young. So now he's trying to convince her to have an abortion, but she ... she ... uh ... she's a devout Catholic, so she refuses to do it. And that's why they're arguing."

I turned and looked at Ted. He wasn't looking at me *or* the young couple.

"So, what do you think they're arguing about?" I asked him. "What kind of story can you come up with?"

He turned and finally looked me in the eye. "I think they're fighting because she's trying to force him to make up stories about the people they're watching in the park."

Some of us, I suppose, are cursed by our delusions of creativity. But some people are cursed by their lack of creativity.

And Ted was one of those people.

My second book was *The Brewster Mall,* which had a few gay characters—well, it *did* involve a huge retail shopping complex, after all—but was mostly a humorous story about the intermingled lives and loves at a mall not unlike the one in Jersey City. It even had a Waldenbooks where the philistine manager loaded the discount bins with the works of Ernest Hemingway and F. Scott Fitzgerald.

David Carlyle still thought a little more poignancy couldn't hurt, but—especially since it was mostly about "those drab, colorless little heterosexual people"—it was acceptable and PMC would publish it. I got another $7500 advance.

The dedication read, *"To Ted, who made me write this book, so blame him."*

David arranged for me to sign copies of *The Brewster Mall* at that mall in Jersey City. In the spirit of the book, the Waldenbooks manager set up a discount bin full of marked-down classics.

I sold an entire three copies of *The Brewster Mall,* including one to Marlene Birrell. Waldenbooks sold out of $1.95 copies of Faulkner and Salinger. And the guy who managed the Arby's in the food court was pissed off because he thought I'd libeled him. It wasn't one of my better nights.

It was a long ride back to Manhattan, made bearable only because I knew that when it came to an end, I'd see Ted. And after two years, seven months, and one day, our relationship felt as fresh as ever. I was still very much in love.

I unlocked the apartment door. It was dark inside.

"Ted?" I called out. There was no reply.

I shrugged it off. Outside of tax season, Ted didn't work late very often. But there *were* occasional nights. If he had decided to stop somewhere for a beer, who was I to begrudge him?

I tapped the play-back button on the answering machine and listened as I poured myself a stiff drink.

Beep. "Hello, dear, it's David. Please call me when you get back from New Jersey. I want to make sure you escaped alive and that you're still wearing natural fibers. Oh, yes, I also want to know if you sold enough books to make my company enough money so I can finally retire and move away from this godawful city. Love you." Beep.

I sat down on the couch with my scotch and water and called David back. He answered on the first ring.

"*Three* books?" he said unhappily. "Oh, Andrew . . ."

"What can I say? They bought Faulkner and Salinger and passed me over."

"But Faulkner and Salinger are dead, and you were sitting right there. And you're so stunning, how could they have missed you?"

"Damned if I know. But I have news for you: Salinger's not dead."

"He's not on PMC's list, so he's dead to me."

I laughed, spitting up a trickle of scotch that ran down my chin. "Ah, damn."

"Excuse me?"

"Sorry," I said, looking around for a napkin or paper towel. "I dribbled."

"Well, a day in New Jersey will do that to you," David said, and he started to launch into some new ideas he had to publicize the book.

In the meantime, I found a paper towel. I was about to wipe my chin when I realized there was writing on it.

Ted's handwriting.

Written with a felt-tip pen, which had bled into the towel and made the words almost illegible.

And it started: *"Dear Andrew . . . I'm sorry—"*

If I strained, I could read it:

> *Dear Andrew . . . I'm sorry, but I can't go on with our relationship. I've tried to tell you in person, but you've been so busy with your book that we haven't been able to talk. Again, I'm sorry, but I need more out of life than what we have, and I've met someone I think can give me what I feel is missing. I took some of my stuff. Maybe we can talk later. Good luck with your book and your life . . . Ted.*

"Andrew?"

"Huh?" I was still too stunned to react. "I'm sorry, David, I didn't hear what you were saying."

"That's because I haven't said anything in thirty seconds. I've just been sitting here, listening to you whimper. Are you all right?"

"I—I—I don't know."

"What's wrong? You sound horrible."

"It's Ted." I started to feel the haze lifting as the reality of his words sank in. "He's . . . he's . . ." The tears forced themselves out slowly, and I sank back into the couch.

"Oh, God," mumbled David, his deeply concerned voice still coming through the phone that was now tucked somewhere near my neck. "Is he all right? He's not *dead,* is he?"

"He—he—he left me." My voice was hollow.

The phone fell to the couch, but I heard David's distant voice. "I'll come over."

A while later, I managed to get off the couch long enough to tell the doorman to let David into the apartment building. I really just wanted to be alone with my grief, but I suppose it was good that he came over, if for no other reason than to finally hang up the phone.

"You'll be all right," he assured me in a hushed voice, repeatedly stroking my back as I choked back sobs, curled up in the closest imitation of the fetal position that a thirty-five-year-old man can achieve.

"I loved him," I moaned between convulsions.

"You'll get the last laugh when you win the Pulitzer Prize. The men will be beating your door down then."

Somehow I managed to control myself long enough to turn to him and say, "David, you're really not making me feel any better about this."

In the days to come, I found out that what Ted needed more of out of life was packaged in the twenty-three-year-old body of Nicholas Hafner—Nicky to his friends—which meant that I would always consider it a point of honor to call him Nicholas.

Nicholas Hafner was a twink with double-pierced ears who aspired to design windows for a living. He was, at that time, merely an *apprentice* window designer.

My mortal enemy was an apprentice window designer. No, not just an apprentice window designer—an apprentice window designer who bleached his hair.

Why couldn't Ted have found himself a nice doctor?

*   *   *

After Ted left, I did a lot of moping. I didn't leave my apartment for the first week. I spent most of the time sitting perched in the window overlooking Eighty-sixth Street, watching the appropriately gray skies and rain. And sighing. And straining to look toward Broadway to see if his was one of the faces coming out of the subway station, having come to his senses and decided to return home, where he knew I'd forgive him after some brief histrionics.

But, of course, his face never emerged from the subway station. He was gone. He was the property of Nicholas Hafner, the twenty-three-year-old apprentice window designer with double-pierced ears, bleached hair, and absolutely no commitment to anything deeper than keeping ahead of the curve on the latest styles and music. And since I couldn't really hate Ted, no matter how hard I tried, I came to double-hate Nicholas, even though we'd never met.

If I found any consolation, it was in the knowledge that one day one of them would hurt the other just as Ted had hurt me. Superficial Nicholas would probably discover it was no longer fashionable to shack up with older accountants, and he'd dump Ted for the latest in boyfriend chic. Or Ted would discover that Nicholas—who danced each weekend until five in the morning and was decades away from developing an ability to settle down—wouldn't and couldn't offer him the domesticity he craved.

That was my consolation. But when it happened, if it happened, it would be down the road. Right now, Ted and Nicholas were lovers; they were having fun, having sex, and having each other. They were going to dinner parties and clubs and movies. They were living their lives.

I was sighing and sobbing and watching the rain. And the subway entrance.

David Carlyle called me occasionally, but I seldom bothered to pick up the telephone. I hadn't been going to work, and although David covered for me, as the week wore on and his sympathy waned, he subtly warned me it might be in my best interests to "snap out of it and come back to earth one of these days." In an effort to lift my spirits, he told me—well, actually, he told my answering machine—that sales of *The Brewster Mall* were running much better than expected, which I knew was a lie because I'd personally seen how the book was selling and doubted there was more than one Marlene Birrell in the world.

Denise Hanrahan also called. She was probably my closest friend left in New York City, since I'd lost all my other friends when I'd coupled up with Ted and shut out the rest of the world. I usually picked up for her.

Even though Ted had just ripped my heart out and filled the empty cavity with lead, Denise always had a way of besting me in depressing, tragic boyfriend stories. I mean, at least *I* didn't consider it a disaster to find out my boyfriend was gay. In a bizarre way, it was almost therapeutic to hear her tales of the horrid heterosexual and allegedly heterosexual men of New York. The Germans call it *Schadenfreude*—taking pleasure in the pain of another.

And between the passage of time and Denise's horror stories, I at last reached the point where I was able to leave the apartment. Which was good, because my appetite was coming back and I desperately needed groceries.

My first day out on the street was also the first day in several weeks that the sky cleared, treating New Yorkers to a warm and sunny September afternoon. I spent it walking; walking through the Upper West Side, walking through Central Park . . . I considered, but rejected, taking the subway down to Greenwich Village; that excursion was squelched because that was where that no-good bastard Ted and his twink boy toy were now living, and I was afraid it would encourage the stalkerlike impulses I was trying to fight back.

It was only when I stopped, after several hours of walking, that I realized I hadn't seen a thing. I was sleepwalking, that's all. Exercise for the emotionally dead. And now I was on the east side of Central Park, tired and far from home.

So . . .

"Andrew! What a pleasant surprise!" said David, after he told his doorman to allow me up to his apartment. "Holding up okay?"

"Well, I'm out of that damned apartment," I said. "That's progress."

David lived in an apartment perched high above Fifth Avenue with a panoramic view of Central Park. You probably know the names of most of his neighbors from the society columns, or *People*, or at least the Page Six column in the New York *Post*. On the few occasions I'd been here before, I usually stood slack-jawed, gaping at the grandeur. The wide-open living room, broken up only by a small grouping of chairs, couches, and end tables surrounding an oak entertainment center; the expensive collection of artwork tastefully displayed on the walls; the terrace overlooking the park; the bookshelves lined with dust-free first editions . . .

But today I was sleepwalking, so I simply slumped on one of his couches and stared at the floor.

Each year, David selected a new color theme and had the apartment completely redecorated. Recently, he'd entered what we at PMC jokingly called—behind his back, of course—his Blue Period. With the exception of the woodwork and the always-polished-but-seldom-played Mason and Hamlin grand piano tucked in one corner of the living room, everything—the walls, the furniture, even the carpet—was a shade of blue.

How appropriate. So was I.

He poured a couple of vodka and tonics. "Well, now that you're ambulatory again, I hope you'll be able to join us at Palmer/Midkiff/Carlyle. We've missed you."

"Sorry. But I'm snapping out of it."

"That's what you've got to keep doing, dear. Keep moving. You know . . . life goes on, you'll find someone else, and all those other tired clichés."

"I guess. But it still hurts."

"It's supposed to hurt," he said, still mixing. "When it stops hurting, you'll be as emotionally dead as half the other gay men in this town, and you'll lose your creativity and therefore your livelihood. Then you'll have to work as a waiter, and the last thing we need in this city is another emotionally dead gay waiter. So let it hurt, Andrew. Let it hurt for me." He handed me my drink, moved near to me, and almost whispered, "I saw him last night."

"Ted?" I heard myself ask breathlessly. "Where?"

"Walking. In the Village. Alone." His voice fell low, and he added, "And he didn't look happy."

"Did he look depressed?" I asked with too much eagerness, because if he did, then maybe the affair with Nicholas had already fizzled.

"Uh . . . not particularly."

My heart sank. "That's just the way Ted usually looks. Sort of blank."

"Yes, but he didn't look ecstatic!" said David, as if this was proof of something. Which it wasn't.

"I'm sure he's had an ecstatic look on his face more than a few times over the past week." I felt the pain begin to well up again.

David slumped down into a chair, clearly not wanting to probe any deeper into emotional topics that we both knew were basically unavoidable.

In an effort to change the course of the conversation, David asked, "Are you writing again?"

I almost laughed at the silliness of his question. Couldn't he see that I was totally absorbed in my own misery?

"I haven't exactly felt creative recently," I said bitterly. "Who can write with all of this shit going on?"

"Maybe the writing will help you work through it." Apparently, David was under the assumption that his accidental role in life as the scion of the founder of a publishing empire qualified him as an expert in the therapeutic applications of writing. "And who knows? Maybe this experience will make you a better writer. Maybe it'll give you more depth."

"Excuse me?" It sounded to me as if I was getting a little un-needed and unsolicited armchair criticism. "What's wrong with my depth?"

"Don't take it the wrong way, Andrew. Don't be so touchy. I mean, we *have* had this conversation before. I just thought maybe this Ted thing would . . . well, you have to admit your style is a little light."

"It's supposed to be light. I like writing humorous, enjoyable books. I'm not Ayn Rand."

"Of course you're not, dear. People *buy* her books. Maybe that should tell you something."

"I'm sorry you're not happy with my sales. But I don't know what else I can do."

"I'm just thinking about you," David said. "Do you want to be re-membered as insubstantial?"

I threw up my hands. "Listen, David, I'm really not in the mood for this conversation. Why don't we just drop it? You don't like my books—"

"I didn't say that!"

"And I'm not in the mood for your criticism. So, let's just agree to disagree."

"Fine. All I was trying to do was point out that there could be a positive aspect to Ted leaving you."

"Let's drop it," I said again, regretting my visit.

After we stopped discussing Ted and my writing style, we quickly discovered that we didn't really have anything to talk about. Not that evening. Every conversation seemed to wind around itself and come back to touch on Ted. The fall social events, vacation plans, the price of lumber in Estonia . . . Ted managed to work himself into every facet of life.

Falling in love is easy enough. Why does falling out of love have to be so hard?

"You need to find yourself a new man," said Denise Hanrahan a few weeks later as we killed time over coffee. It was early October, and noticeably colder. "It's been a month, Drew, and he's not coming back."

"Easier said than done. But it seems like all the good men in this city are married or straight."

"Oh? I hadn't noticed."

Denise grimaced at her own remark. It had been bad enough when she'd learned her boyfriend Carlo was gay—or, as he claimed, bisexual—a few years earlier, but when Perry came out to her the following year after their fourth date, she claimed she was swearing off the men of Manhattan forever.

I knew the feeling.

Love wasn't playing fair with either of us, of course, but it was especially unfair to her. At thirty-five, Denise could still pass for ten years younger. She was attractive, fit, a sparkling conversationalist, and an undyingly loyal friend. Her only problem was that she couldn't attract the attention of heterosexual men . . . which, as a heterosexual woman, she considered to be a big problem. Spending a lot of time with me probably didn't help, of course.

"It took me so long to find Ted," I said. "It took years. I mean, you've known me for fifteen years. How many men have you known that I was serious about?"

"So, it'll take you some time," she said, pulling back a loose ribbon of wavy dark hair. "What's your rush? There are a lot of single people, and they aren't throwing themselves in front of the subway.

Take your time. And let's face it, I know you *think* the good one got away, but how good was he if he dropped you overnight for a kid?"

I stirred my coffee distractedly, recognizing that her logic made far more sense than my emotions. She was right. How could I be moping about Ted, glorifying the memory of our relationship, when the bastard didn't even have the decency to give me a proper good-bye? Just a few short sentences bleeding into a paper towel, which, instead of throwing it out as I should have done, I still kept in a safe place and treated like it was the Declaration of Independence.

I tossed a few dollars on the coffee shop counter. "Let's move."

"Where are we moving to?"

"To resolution."

With Denise in tow, I went home and found the paper towel, opened the window, and let it flutter down to West Eighty-sixth Street, seven stories below.

"Good for you, Drew," she said, sitting with me in the window, watching it waft along in the breeze.

"Yeah," I said. "Good for me." But I was distracted because I thought I saw someone who looked like Ted emerging from the subway station.

It wasn't him, of course, and I'll spare you the suspense and reveal right now that Ted never returned to our apartment. But this story isn't about me and Ted. Ted is over. Ted is the past. The only reason I've written about Ted is to give you some perspective.

This story is about what came after Ted. And that wasn't very pretty, either.

2

The Hottest Passes in New York . . . Dude!!

David Carlyle and I had always been friendly in a distant sort of way, but, in the weeks after Ted left me, a stronger bond developed between us. I think a number of factors brought us together, especially the Ted crisis and the fact that, even though I wasn't exactly climbing the bestseller lists, I was now a twice-published author and therefore slightly closer to belonging in David's social circle than the average editorial assistant at PMC.

For his part, it soon became apparent to me that David Carlyle needed a real friend. Because once you stripped away his exotic and largely apocryphal tales of weekends with David Geffen, dinners at Gracie Mansion, AIDS benefits with Elizabeth Taylor, and sexual encounters with countless German boys, Filipino boys, Japanese boys, Swedish boys, Mexican boys, Thai boys, Greek boys, Turkish boys, and a particularly deranged threesome with an Israeli boy and a Palestinian boy, the sad reality was that David Carlyle was fifty-five years old, overweight, effeminate, and, for all his money, pretty damned lonely.

So, there we were, a lonely, successful older man and a lonely, less-successful, slightly younger man who had no interest in each other beyond mutual entertainment and passing time. It was kismet; how could we have avoided becoming close friends?

In recognition and acceptance of this fate, we started bonding and doing the kinds of things friends do with each other when they're gay and platonic. Like shopping and gossiping and eating at trendy restaurants and singing at Greenwich Village piano bars.

In fact, we were on our way to dinner in the Village one day after I finally more or less accepted that Ted was history when David said something that started the course of events that would change my life forever.

"Guess what?" he said. "I've just heard about the event of the season!"

"You say that about fifteen times every season."

"That's just rhetoric. This time I mean it. There's a new club opening, and guess which night they're having a private grand opening party? *And* guess who snagged a couple of the hottest passes in gay New York?"

"I give up," I said without even trying to guess.

"Well, *I've* got the passes." With a flourish, he pulled two black and pink squares out of his pocket.

"I sort of assumed that. So, what night is the party?"

"Halloween!" he squealed. "Don't you just love it?"

Halloween. A night beloved by people everywhere who want to put on costumes and masks and cloak themselves in anonymity. And, I had to admit, a hell of a good night to open a gay nightclub.

"It's going to be called Benedick's," he continued as we walked down Christopher Street, with the sincere excitement over something as common as a club opening most men his age had lost decades ago. "They've got this huge old building over on West Street they've been pouring money into. It'll be fantastic. And, Andrew, there are only five hundred of these passes. This is going to be a *very* exclusive crowd."

"Sounds good," I said noncommittally. I just couldn't bring myself to join in with David's overheated enthusiasm. Between us, hadn't we seen hundreds of nightclubs come and go over our years in the city?

"Good? This is *great!* I don't think you realize how *exclusive* this place is going to be. No riffraff; just the brightest, wittiest, cutest, and studliest."

The question had to be asked. "Then how come we got invited? Or have we just been notched up in the 'studliest' category?"

"You're doing okay for your age," he said with a laugh. "A bit too old for me, but you're not falling apart yet." He returned to my question. "We got them because I'm on *all* the best lists. I can't even begin to tell you how many things I get invited to. Openings, benefits . . . Most of them are very tiring. I don't even bother opening half the envelopes that come in the mail."

"Then why are you inviting me? Aren't there going to be any eighteen-year-old Armenian sailors in port that night?"

He glared at me unpleasantly. "If you'd rather not go . . ."

"Sorry."

He brightened again. "I'm inviting you for three reasons. First, because I've come to enjoy your company despite your puzzling habit of biting the hand that feeds you. Second, because I'm hoping that an appearance by the author of *Allentown Blues* and *The Brewster Mall* might generate a little interest and publicity and help make both of us some money. And third, because maybe you'll meet your next lover there."

"That's very noble of you."

"Nobility has nothing to do with it. If you meet a nice upstanding white-collar man, maybe you'll stop moping and rediscover your muse. Then you can write me a best-seller."

I realized with a jolt that we were heading toward Ted and Nicky's love nest, so I gently took hold of David's arm and guided him around a corner. He never even seemed to notice.

"This place is going to be great!"

"Who owns it? Who's Benedict?"

"Bene*dick*," he corrected.

"Oh. Now I understand."

"No, you don't," he said, shaking his head. "Benedick. Remember your Shakespeare? *Much Ado About Nothing?* Although I can't be sure there's not an intentional double entendre at work."

"Classy. There's nothing like a bunch of Shakespeare-quoting homosexuals in spandex dancing to Madonna to give me hope for the future of our sexuality. And anyway, wasn't Benedick straight?"

"As far as I'm concerned, the jury is still out. Remember, he was a confirmed bachelor in the beginning of *Much Ado About Nothing . . .*"

"And almost a married man at the end," I pointed out.

"Details," he snorted. "Even Oscar Wilde was a married man. Maybe you're still too bitter to go out in public."

We stopped to window-shop in front of an antique dealer's store and, as we peered in the dusty window, David recited, " 'Sigh no more ladies, sigh no more/Men were deceivers ever . . .' "

"Excuse me?"

"*Much Ado About Nothing.* I *think* I recited it correctly, although I'll be damned if I can remember the context. Do you understand the theme of Benedick's any better now?"

"If this is known as a gay club with gay patrons, where's the deceit? This isn't the Nineteen-fifties."

He rolled his eyes at my naïveté. "Trust me, Andrew. See who's there on Halloween, then watch the society columns for the next few weeks and watch them all pop up escorting blue-haired dowagers to weddings and charity balls. I think you'll see that deceit is still alive and well."

We continued our walk, admiring the well-preserved town houses lining the eerily quiet streets. And as we walked, I asked David again who was bankrolling Benedick's.

"I don't know. I think it's owned by some corporation they've thrown together for this. Barry Blackburn is promoting parties there, but he's the only one I know who's involved in the venture."

"I hate Barry Blackburn," I pointed out, although I could barely remember why. Something to do with us both competing for the same man ten years ago or so. He won; I hated him.

"I know. But you'll probably never see him, so don't worry about it."

"What if he's in costume and I don't recognize him, and I accidentally pick him up?"

"I see you've got your creative imagination back up and running. And speaking of that, we've only got two weeks to come up with some stunning costumes! An event like this is see and be seen, and we have to be seen at our best. I want to be ravishing!"

"Do you want the front end of the horse or the back end?"

David's imagination was flowing now. "I see us going as French aristocracy. Or pirates."

"Nothing with too much makeup. It makes me break out."

"Well, you're a sorry excuse for a faggot!" he shot back.

"Ain't I, though?"

David stopped so abruptly I walked into him. When I looked up, I saw why he'd stopped. There, directly across the street but not seeing us, were Ted and a twink I presumed to be Nicholas.

Strangely, despite the fact that I was obsessed with Ted and had been for several years, it was Nicholas I noticed first. But then again, he was hard to miss. He was very young, very cute, very thin, and very, very bleached. His hair, stripped of almost all of its natural color, looked almost white.

"Um . . ." David fumbled for something to say, coming up with, "Let's go the other way, Andrew."

"No, I'm fine," I said, and was a bit surprised that I almost meant it. "Small city, huh?"

"*Far* too small."

Seeing Ted after all these weeks didn't have the jarring effect I feared it would. Seeing Ted with Nicholas didn't even pierce my heart. But I did realize I was transfixed; I couldn't take my eyes off them.

"Was Ted that animated when he was around me?" I asked David.

"Nothing animates a man like coming home to a twenty-three-year-old body," was his wistful reply.

We watched them window-shop, talk, and laugh for several minutes from across the street. They didn't move far; we didn't move at all. And then Ted turned and spotted us.

"Uh-oh," said David. "Our cover's been blown."

Playing it casually, I waved and called out, "Hi, Ted." He—no, *they*—waved back. Then, horror of horrors, they started to cross the street toward us. I froze a smile on my face and David let out a long moan under his breath.

And then they were in front of us, within easy striking—or strangling—distance.

"How have you been, Andrew?" Ted asked. I said I was okay, which was more or less true, but nevertheless was the only thing to say. One never admits to one's ex-lover that one's been devastated.

"Hi," said Nicholas. "I'm Nicky."

No, you're not. You are and will always be Nicholas.

But I said nothing, of course. Instead, I bit my lip and gamely shook his hand, as did David.

"So, what's going on?" asked Ted. He was clearly uncomfortable, his fidgeting hands jammed deep in the pockets of his baggy khakis.

"Nothing," I replied sadly.

"Oh, come on!" said David, bursting in between us and grabbing Ted by the elbow. "Guess what we've got?"

"What?"

Again, the black and pink squares emerged from David's pocket. "Only the hottest passes in New York!"

"Oh, my God!" gasped Nicholas. "I've *seen* those. Aren't those passes to the Halloween party at Benedict's?"

"Bene*dick*'s," mumbled David. "One and the same."

"Let me see them, dude," said Nicholas.

David gingerly handed the passes to Nicholas, who treated them as if they were holy relics.

"What's Benedict's?" asked Ted, and I was very happy to be farther ahead of the curve than him on the news of the newest, hottest club in town.

"Bene*dick*'s," I said, and was greeted with an approving wink from David. "It's a new club, opening on Halloween." I said this as if I'd known about it forever. "Those passes are for a very exclusive grand opening party."

"It'll redefine the meaning of the word *exclusive*," added David.

"We'll give you five hundred bucks for them," said Nicholas.

"What?" shouted Ted. "You don't have that kind of money!"

"I'll pay you back," said Nicholas without shame.

"It doesn't matter," said David. "They're not for sale. And I don't think the people at Benedick's would ever forgive me if I started trading their passes on the black market."

"A thousand dollars, dude!" offered Nicholas, in the true spirit of a person who can't handle or doesn't understand money and the relative value of club passes.

"Nicky!" snapped Ted. "Stop trying to spend my money like that!"

David took the passes out of the young boy's hand and slipped them back into his pocket. "Sorry, but it'll be open to the public the following night." Then, after glancing at his watch, he added, "I didn't realize how late it was. We've got to get going, Andrew!"

We said our good-byes and left them standing curbside, Ted staring at Nicholas and Nicholas staring at the pocket where David had stashed the passes.

When we turned the corner, David said, "And *that's* how you handle the ex-lover and his new boyfriend."

"I'll give you a billion dollars for those passes, dude!!" I screamed, and we dissolved into hysterical laughter as we slumped onto someone's front stoop. "*A zillion!!* Please! C'mon, dude!! Please!"

"He certainly picked himself a young man of substance. And that hair! What an interesting shade!"

At dinner, David planned our costumes for Halloween. I tried to contribute but spent most of my time trying to think of a way to drown Nicholas in the Hudson River without anybody knowing I did it. Finally, I decided that it was impossible. That's the problem with premeditated murder; the person who did it can't help but become a suspect.

David watched me over the rim of his wineglass. "Can I ask you a question?"

"Sure."

"Why do you keep dropping cauliflower in your gravy and holding it under with your fork? Are you afraid that, if it floats back to the surface, it'll scream for help?"

Oh. I *was* doing that, wasn't I? I was committing the premeditated murder of cauliflower. And unless I killed the witnesses—David and Randy, "our server for the evening"—I'd become the prime suspect. Since I didn't have enough gravy to kill them both, I speared the cauliflower and rescued it.

David nodded approvingly at my rescue effort. "So, what do *you* think about the costumes? Drag?"

"I don't do drag. I've managed to live in this city for almost eighteen years as an openly gay man without ever dressing in women's clothing, and I'm not about to start now."

"But your features are so fine. I think you'd be devastating."

"No."

"I've never seen you undressed. Are you hairy?"

"No. But it doesn't matter because—"

"In that case, you could go strapless. Oh, this *is* exciting!"

"No."

"I think you should be a brunette. If we find the right hair color, it'll bring out your eyes."

"No."

"And just a touch of makeup—"

"No."

* * *

The cab dropped us off in front of a nondescript former warehouse on West Street, marked only with a huge neon *B* and a line of people waiting to get in. We were at Benedick's, it was finally Halloween, and David had just spent the past three hours repeatedly assuring me that I was a dead ringer for Demi Moore, if she were five foot-eleven without heels.

"I hate you," I muttered as he paid the driver. "And you don't look a *thing* like Bruce Willis."

"I most certainly do," he replied, although except for the receding hairline, he most certainly didn't.

"Okay. You *do* look like Bruce Willis. *After* he's gained about forty pounds, aged fifteen years, and totally fagged out."

"You're just upset because you've discovered the joys of drag so late in life." He took my elbow and guided me toward the entrance. "And remember, try to keep your voice at a higher level. You sound like a man."

"I *am* a man."

He smiled. "In your dreams."

At the entrance, David presented the beefy bouncer with the passes. He looked us over carefully.

"You know this is a queer club, right?" he asked, looking directly at me.

"Speak to the man," David commanded.

I came up with a voice out of my normal register, a hybrid of Southern belle and Lauren Bacall. "Why do you think this place is so queer?"

The bouncer still stared at me, unsure. So David, still playing Henry Higgins, said, "Now, speak in Andrew's voice."

I gave him an uncomprehending look and stuck with my Belle Bacall voice. "Who's Andrew?"

"Sorry," said the bouncer, moving to block the door. "I don't know where you got the passes, but this place is open tonight for gay men only."

Gay men only. I recognized that as one of Barry Blackburn's themes, the periodic and controversial "Boys Need A Safe Place" parties that I'd always managed to avoid in the past. I mentally added misogyny to the list of Barry Blackburn's sins.

"Oh, for Chrissake . . ." muttered David, less concerned with the political correctness of the situation. "Okay, Andrew, you've shown the world you can pass as a woman. Now would you knock it off? I'd like to get inside."

No longer entertained, the bouncer moved us off to the side to admit a leather version of the Lone Ranger and Tonto. When the door closed again, he said, "Please move it somewhere else, folks."

"I'm a man," I confessed to him in my normal voice, but he still blocked the door.

"Andrew," said David, growing more annoyed than the bouncer, "since this man doesn't believe your voice anymore, show him your dick."

I hoisted up my skirt, pushed aside my garter, pulled my panties slightly to the side, and exposed one testicle.

"You're pretty convincing," admitted the bouncer, somewhat embarrassed, as he ushered us in the door.

"Thanks . . . I think."

"Told you so," whispered David.

"Shut up," I growled.

Inside, Benedick's was lavish, gaudy, and an exaggeration of everything good and bad about gay nightclubs. The voice of Grace Jones—who was rumored to be making an appearance later that night, gay icons being the only apparent exception to Barry Blackburn's no-girls-allowed rule—throbbed over the speakers as hundreds of New York City's brightest, wittiest, cutest, and studliest men gyrated on the huge dance floor. Hundreds of other men crowded the bar and ringed the dance floor, drinks in hand, watching the dancers do what they wouldn't or couldn't do and hoping someone would try to pick them up.

And everyone was in some semblance of a costume: soldiers, sailors, police officers, firefighters, cowboys, Indian chiefs, Roman emperors, Greek gods, hard hats, a lot of masks, and an awful lot of awful drag. It was a theme park for fetishes; every fantasy was represented, although not always by fantasy men.

David went off to "buy a girl a drink," and his space next to me was immediately filled.

"You're the best-looking woman in the place," said an older, balding *faux* police officer. "Mind if I frisk you?"

"Sorry, no thanks," I replied in my Belle Bacall voice. Just because I'd let David talk me into this costume didn't mean I was going to help trolls fulfill their fantasies. "I'm here with someone."

"I've got handcuffs." He patted the cuffs dangling from his belt, then leaned closer to me and added, almost inaudibly, "And I've got a hose I can beat you with."

Oh, please. I'd been here less than ten minutes and already wanted to go home and take a shower.

Still Belle Bacall, I sweetly said, "Thanks, but . . ."

He smiled and nodded downward. I glanced down to see the tip of his penis poking out from his fly, then looked him sternly in the eye.

"Fuck off or I'll rip it out by the roots and shove it up your ass," I said, this time as Andrew Westlake. Shaken, he stuffed it back in his fly and moved away.

"Wasn't that Paul Musso?" asked David, who was suddenly there with my drink.

"Who?"

"The cop."

"I don't know who the fuck it was," I replied, in a surly mood. "But I wish he'd go back to the Port Authority Bus Terminal where he belongs."

David nodded his head. "Yes, that would be Paul Musso."

We made a circuit of the club. David ran into a number of his A-list acquaintances and pointed out several young men on the dance floor whom he allegedly had slept with, all conveniently too far away from us to be engaged in conversation.

I, of course, knew no one, although a towering black drag queen did approach to tell me, "You look fabulous, darling. You're a natural."

"That's me," said Belle Bacall. "I'm all woman."

"You sort of look like Demi Moore," said the drag queen as she departed.

David smiled smugly.

After an hour I had to go to the bathroom. I excused myself to "powder my nose" and left David chatting with the president of a major record label, who was dressed as a pimp.

I walked in the direction of what I presumed to be the men's room, but once I passed through a set of doors and into near darkness, I realized I'd made a mistake. When I heard the doors latch behind me and I was trapped in *total* darkness, I realized I'd made a *big* mistake.

"Great," I muttered, out of character, as I fruitlessly tried to open the locked doors.

So there I was—my first time in drag, let alone heels—standing on the wrong side of the door in an unlit, locked corridor of a converted warehouse now hosting what would hopefully become the hottest gay dance club in the world, lost and really having to take a leak.

What was a poor girl to do?

After my eyes adjusted to the darkness, I saw faint light at a far end of the corridor. I took a few steps, bumped into a cardboard box hidden in the dark, lost my balance in the heels, and fell over.

"I *hate* David Carlyle," I growled through gritted teeth as I picked myself up off the floor. I slipped off the high heels and carried them with me, walking carefully as I navigated toward the light.

When I reached the end of the corridor, I saw that the light was coming from a small room around the corner. In stocking feet, I walked gracelessly to it.

"I'm lost," I announced, back in character, as I entered the room. It was an office, and the only person in there was a handsome young man with bright brown eyes, sipping coffee and reading the *Daily News* as a Marlboro Light sat burning almost to the filter in an ashtray that desperately needed to be emptied.

"You're not supposed to be back here," he said cautiously. His hand reached for something under the desk.

"I'm sorry, but I walked through the door down there"—I pointed back down the dark corridor—"and it locked behind me."

His brow furrowed under a thick overhang of curly black hair. "That door's supposed to be locked."

"Well, it wasn't. Anyway, I'm just looking for the bathroom."

"I'll show you." He relaxed his grip on whatever was under his desk.

When he stood up, I gasped and almost collapsed in character, an overheated Southern belle with an attack of the vapors. The handsome face sat on top of a six-foot frame, and muscles bulged from his wide shoulders through his narrow hips and down his powerful legs wrapped tightly in denim.

Almost speechless, I followed him as he flicked fluorescent lights on and led me through the catacomb of halls, which were the non-public places inside Benedick's. Although lost, I paid no attention to the path we were taking. After all, I didn't intend to ever be locked in this corridor again and, more importantly, I was too busy watching his ass sway back and forth in front of me as he led me to the bathroom.

"Here you go," he said, finally stopping at a door. "Now, to get back in the club, you just go through here." He opened the door slightly, and the loud sounds of late seventies disco poured through. "Hey, pretty packed," he said, surveying the crowd.

"Yes, it is," I replied as Belle Bacall. "You've got a nice place here. Are you the manager?"

"The *owner*." He gave me a broad smile and extended his hand. "I'm Frank DiBenedetto."

"I'm—" Oh, why not? I took his hand. "Belle Bacall. Nice to meet you."

The smile never left his face. If anything, it grew broader. He was adorable. "No. Nice to meet *you*. I hope I'll see you here again, Belle. Hey—Bacall? You any relation?"

"Uh . . . no." For some obscure reason, I decided giving him my freshly coined drag name was as far down this road as I wanted to travel.

"Yeah, well . . ." Still smiling, he glanced shyly at the floor but didn't move. When he looked back at me, his brown eyes fixed on mine and he swallowed nervously. Which made me swallow nervously, too.

From the other side of the door, the final notes of one song segued effortlessly into the lush opening notes of the Bee Gees' "How Deep Is Your Love."

Frank swallowed hard again. "Um . . . Would you like to dance?"

I laughed. "Here? Back here? Really?"

"I mean, if you don't want to, it's all right. It's just, well . . . I sort of feel like I'm missing my own party."

"Well, we can't have that. Yeah, sure, I'd love to dance."

So, he wrapped those thick arms gently around me, taking care to not appear overly familiar. I took hold of his shoulders and we swayed slowly to the music for several minutes, not talking but occasionally smiling self-consciously when we caught each other's glances.

When the music ended, we let go and backed a step away. Ever the gentleman, Frank bowed slightly. "Thank you for the dance."

"Thank *you*."

It looked like he was about to say something else but couldn't find the words. Instead, he settled for, "I suppose I should get back to work."

Awkwardly, I said, "Well, it was nice meeting you, Frank. And I hope to see you again soon."

He looked up at me. "You know, you look a little bit like Demi Moore?"

Under my light makeup, I blushed, although I wasn't sure if I was blushing from the compliment or from the fact that I was embarrassed to be complimented on looking like a woman. I mumbled a little "thank you" and left it at that.

He shuffled for a second, then said, "I'm gonna go lock that door so no one else wanders back here." Then he paused again, adding, with a hopeful tone in his voice, "I'll see you later."

And with that, he turned and walked away, flicking lights off as he vanished down the corridor, giving me only the slightest glimpse of his perfect butt as it disappeared into the darkness.

The sign on the bathroom door said WOMEN.

But . . . No, he *had* to have known. I mean, this was a gay dance club, right? And didn't the bouncer explicitly tell us that no *real* women were allowed to enter? And he *was* the owner, after all, so wouldn't he know the policy?

He must. So, he must have known I was a man dressed as a woman. Which meant that Frank—sweet, handsome, muscular Frank; Frank with the broad, enticing smile and curly black hair and the cutest little butt on the planet; Frank who slow-danced with me and held me in his arms—wasn't flirting with Belle Bacall or Demi Moore. He was flirting with Andrew Westlake.

As if to prove something to myself, I peed standing up.

"*Where* have you been?" David asked when I returned. "Whole countries have had time to go to the bathroom while you were gone. Pee shy?"

"I was lost," I replied. "And then I was found." I leaned close to him. "I think I'm in love."

He grimaced and mumbled unpleasantly. "That didn't take long. Who's the lucky man?"

"His name is Frank. He owns the place."

More unpleasantness from David. "Andrew, you cannot date a man who owns a gay dance club. They're all into drugs and other illegal activities, they all screw anything that moves, and they all end up going into bankruptcy within three or four months. Now, *what's* his name?"

"Frank," I replied, dismissing his disapproval. "Frank DiBen— DiBendenna—Di—I don't know, something like that."

He waved a dismissive hand at me. "Great. You don't even know his last name, but you're in love. You know what that means, don't you? It means you'll go home with him tonight and he'll screw you and you'll never hear from him again."

"Are you jealous?" I asked, amused.

He was distinctly *not* amused. "Trust me, Andrew. I know how these people are. And what was that last name again? Something Italian? He's probably in the Mafia."

"What do they have? A gay auxiliary?"

He sighed. "I've been around for a long time, and I remember well how the Mafia used to own all the gay bars. It still owns a lot of them. They made a lot of money off us, Andrew, and they still make a lot of money off us."

"I didn't think homosexuals were supposed to stereotype other people. Don't we get stereotyped enough ourselves?"

"There's a certain amount of truth behind every stereotype. Considering the fact that you're a gay man wearing a dress, I think you should recognize that."

"Hi, David," said a familiar voice hidden behind a leather mask, interrupting my friend at the end of his tirade.

David squinted, as did I, until the masked man said, "It's Barry."

"Barry *Blackburn!*" gushed David. Apparently, he was going to make me pay for Frank by cozying up to my bitter enemy. "God, it's been a long time! How have you been?"

"Great." Barry removed the mask to reveal his pinched face and freshly frosted, unnaturally blond hair. "I'm promoting this place, y'know."

"I heard," said David. "Congratulations. This is quite an opening."

"We're happy. Tomorrow night's the real test, though. Then we'll see how the common man likes it." He turned to me and held out his hand. "Hi. Barry Blackburn."

I reluctantly took his hand and forced a smile. "Belle Bacall."

David rolled his eyes.

"You look a little bit like Demi Moore," said Barry.

David rolled his eyes again and decided to end the charade. "You remember Andrew Westlake, don't you?"

Now it was Barry's turn to squint. He dropped my hand when he realized it was me. "Hello, Andrew."

"Barry," I acknowledged, equally cold.

David chose to punish me for what he felt was my heart's poor choice in men by talking interminably with the evil Barry Blackburn. After a few minutes of their conversation, I moved a few steps away. After five more minutes, I moved several feet away. And some time around the fifteenth minute, I moved to the other side of the club.

I was leaning on the bar, minding my own business, when I heard a voice say, "Well, hello there."

When I turned, I saw it was Paul Musso, the balding trollish cop wannabe with the occasionally unconcealed nightstick.

"Go away," I told him with irritation, making a point of not looking at him . . . especially below the waist.

"I'd really like to take you home," he said. "It would really be hot. I'd fuck you so hard you'd be begging for more—"

That was all I heard.

It was time to leave, and *not* with Paul Musso. And, for that matter, *not* with that meddlesome, Barry Blackburn–schmoozing David Carlyle, either. I left a full drink behind on the bar and headed for the exit.

Halloween might have been a great night to open a nightclub, but as I walked out the exit and onto West Street, I realized it was a very bad night to find a cab. Earlier that night, the annual Halloween Parade had flooded Greenwich Village with tens of thousands of revelers. At this hour, any cab driver who had the slightest interest in picking up fares would be several long blocks east, hovering around Sheridan Square, rather than cruising the rundown outskirts of the Village.

So I started walking. I was half a block away when I realized someone was following me.

Ordinarily, that wouldn't faze me. Up to that point, I'd lived in Manhattan for the better part of two decades without incident. But tonight wasn't an ordinary night. Tonight, I was wearing a skirt and a wig and stockings and heels. Tonight, I was Belle Bacall, walking unescorted through a neighborhood that had a tendency to be a bit rough. Tonight, I was a potential rape victim . . . at least until my panties were torn off, at which point I would become a potential rape *and* bashing *and* castration *and* murder victim.

So, I tried to remember what every woman in every woman-in-jeopardy movie had done when she heard footsteps approaching. I started to walk faster.

Behind me, I heard the other set of footsteps quicken their pace.

I was about to break into a sprint when I heard a voice call out, "Belle!"

That stopped me. I turned.

It was Frank. With an ear-to-ear smile. "I'm sorry," he said, jogging up to me. "I didn't mean to scare you. I was just leaving and saw you leave, so I thought . . ." He trailed off and glanced shyly at the sidewalk.

"You'll never know how glad I am it's you," I said breathlessly, slipping instinctively into Belle's voice.

That dazzling smile widened at what he perceived as a compliment, and since I meant it in part as a compliment, I decided not to add that I was also glad it was him because he wasn't a rapist/basher/castrator/murderer. Unless one listened to David Carlyle.

"Wanna go get something to eat?" he asked. "There's this diner a few blocks from here—"

A diner—a brightly lit, very public diner—was probably the last place I should have gone with Frank. It was one thing to do drag in a dark club with strobe lights, alcohol, and hundreds of other distractions; it was quite another to sit in an overlit booth with stubble trying to poke through minimal makeup.

But there we were, Belle Bacall and Frank DiBenedetto, sipping coffee and talking in Frank's favorite diner. I took some consolation from the fact that there was some drag there far worse than mine, and even more consolation from the belief that actual women wore some of it.

Frank and I didn't talk about anything too deep or important. We just skipped along the surface of small talk. It was over in half an hour.

"I gotta get home." He waved for the check. "I'm exhausted. Getting Benedick's ready for the opening was a lot harder than I thought it would be."

"How come you didn't join the party?"

He shook his head. "Not really my crowd."

"Mine, either," I confessed.

He paid and we walked outside. "I'll hail you a cab. Where are you going?"

"Upper West Side."

"No kidding? Me, too. We can share."

Traffic was light, so the cab sliced through Manhattan. We were closing in on Frank's apartment on West Seventy-second Street near Central Park when he gave me a boyish smile. "Can I have your home phone number?"

"Sure," I said with a laugh, and I scrawled it out on a slip of paper. "Promise to call?"

"Promise." He pocketed the phone number. The cab slowed as we approached his building, and he added, "And when I call you, you can tell me what your real name is."

"Don't I look like a Belle Bacall?"

"*Nobody* looks like a Belle Bacall." He handed the cabbie a handful of crumpled bills, then leaned over and gave me a kiss on the lips, which wasn't as passionate as it was forceful.

"Good night," he whispered.

"It'll be a much better night when I get out of this wig and dress," I replied, and the voice of Andrew Westlake slipped out.

He smiled, closed the door, and, as the cab started its sixteen-block trip to my apartment, did a double take.

And that's when it hit me. Despite the fact that he had no reason whatsoever to think that I was a woman, he did.

Frank didn't call the next day.

Neither did David.

But Denise came over.

"You did *what?*" she asked, stunned, sitting amid the scattered and discarded sections of the Sunday *Times* that littered my apartment.

I was embarrassed, but reasoned that confession was good for the soul, so I said it again. "I accidentally tried to pick up a straight man."

She folded her arms and kicked at the Real Estate section for a few seconds. "Aren't there enough gay men out there for you? Why do you have to try to ruin things for the rest of us? Some of us *want* straight men to stay straight. Some of us *need* straight men to stay straight. And I'm not even talking about propagating the species, Drew. Gay men aren't the only people who like to have sex, you know!"

"Sorry." I flopped down next to her on the couch. "If it's any consolation, I don't think my efforts to convert him were successful. And anyway, how was *I* supposed to know he was straight? He owns a gay nightclub, after all." I had a thought. "Maybe I could introduce the two of you."

"Oh, that would work." Her voice dripped with sarcasm. "Hi, I'm Denise Hanrahan and I'm a friend of Betty Bacall!"

"Belle," I corrected her.

"Like it matters. I really don't feel like meeting any guys who are trying to find out whether or not I have a penis before they'll talk to me. Face it, Drew, you've traumatized one of the few remaining single heterosexual men in New York. He'll probably become a priest."

I tossed the Business section off the couch and uncovered a pillow. Denise ducked as I swung my legs around until they came to rest, propped on the back of the couch behind her head.

"This is all Ted's fault," I said. "If he hadn't left me, I never would have been there last night. And now I've made a fool out of myself."

She wrapped one of her hands delicately around my left leg. "Oh, it wasn't all bad. Even if I *am* mad at you. At least you found someone who made you feel like you could fall in love again."

"He's *straight*," I playfully moaned, burying my head in the pillow.

"It happens. No one knows why—maybe it's heredity, or maybe it's upbringing—but sometimes it just happens."

I laughed, and she joined in. And we spent the rest of the afternoon watching football on television and calling Barnes & Noble to see if they had copies of *The Brewster Mall* in stock.

The passage of thirty-four hours had mellowed David when I finally saw him at work the next day.

"At least you discovered you're very convincing as a woman," he said after I told him about my night with Frank.

"I'm never doing drag again."

"Demi Moore will be relieved."

*   *   *

When I got home, there were a few messages waiting for me on my answering machine.

Beep. "Hi, Drew, it's me," said Denise's voice. "A bunch of us from work are going to see *Rent* on Wednesday night and we have two extra tickets. If you want one, give me a call. Talk to you soon." Beep.

Beep. "This call is for Andrew Westlake. My name is Tom Percy and I'm with Citibank. I'm calling about your Visa bill. Please return my call at your earliest opportunity. I can be reached at . . ." Beep.

Beep. "Uh . . . I'm not sure who I'm looking for, but . . . uh . . . my name is Frank DiBenedetto and . . . uh . . . I think we met Saturday night at . . . uh . . . my club." He laughed self-consciously. "I'm looking for Belle Bacall . . . I guess . . . Uh . . . Anyway, call me at the club if you get a chance. The number is . . ."

I played the message over and over again, listening to his voice. The soundtrack in my head played "How Deep Is Your Love" as accompaniment.

3

My Life as a Man Again, and What I Did With It

I saw no reason why I shouldn't be calm.

After all, he was just a man, and I'd called hundreds of men in my life, perhaps thousands, for the sole purpose of arranging a date or a more informal sexual liaison.

And *I* was a man now, too. The wig, the dress, the high heels, the stockings, the makeup, and all the other paraphernalia needed to turn me into Belle Bacall were stashed in a Macy's bag in the back of my closet, where they would spend the rest of eternity, never again to see the light of day. Never ever ever.

But when I dialed the phone number, my entire body shook and my mouth went dry.

"Benedick's." An uninterested voice answered the phone.

"Frank?" I squeaked in response.

"Who?"

I took a few quick deep breaths, closed my eyes, and tried to calm down. "Is this Frank?"

"No."

"Well, I'm trying to reach Frank."

"Frank who?"

"DiBenedetto." My tongue twisted over the name.

"I'm not sure if he's here. Who's calling?"

I swallowed hard and almost said "Belle Bacall," but, since my one-time drag experience was in the past, I told him, "Andrew Westlake."

"Let me check." I heard the receiver roughly set down.

I waited for five minutes or so until he returned, listening to the dance music in the background.

"He's not here," he said finally.

"Well, can I leave—?"

The guy at Benedick's hung up on me.

I dug out my to-that-point-unused copy of the Manhattan white pages and looked up DiBenedetto. There were three Franks, but none of them lived on West Seventy-second Street. There were also two *F*s; I called both the numbers, and both phones were answered by annoyed women who claimed that no Franks lived there.

So I called Denise. After I begged off on her spare theater tickets and excitedly told her about Frank's message, she said, "This is just too weird. Maybe you should let this thing drop."

"But he called. He knows I'm a man and he called."

"He's *straight*. God knows what sick thing he's got planned. Take my advice: If you don't want to end up getting screwed by some guy who likes to get off with men wearing dresses, forget about him! Take a cold shower or something."

"But—"

"*Andrew* . . ." she said, which I knew was a warning, because she always called me Drew except when she was pissed off at me. "Take a cold shower."

The shower wasn't cold, but it served its purpose. The warm stream of water steamed the romantic illusions out of my brain, and the loud hiss as the water sprayed the tub sealed me off from the outside world. Within minutes, Frank became a dim memory, huddled with Ted somewhere on the outer reaches of recall with other momentary pleasant memories of my past.

Fifteen minutes later—feeling refreshed, relaxed, and, most importantly, over it—I dried off, wrapped the towel around my waist, and padded barefoot across the worn hardwood floor through the living room into the kitchen. I found a water glass and a bottle of scotch and decided to indulge myself with a pleasant after-shower alcoholic buzz. I brought the bottle and glass back into the living room and made room for myself by tossing what was left of the Sunday *Times* off the couch.

The first few sips went down rough, but I was soon rewarded with a warm feeling of peace and goodwill toward men and the firm belief that nothing that had happened on Halloween at Benedick's mattered, because I was still a relatively attractive thirty-five-year-old published author and someday my prince would come, even if he wasn't destined to be Ted or Frank.

And then, as I stretched out on the couch only moments away from achieving complete inner peace, I saw a flickering red light out of the corner of my eye.

The answering machine.

The phone, I assumed, had rung while I was sealed in my showery cocoon. I debated internally whether or not to play the message back. It wasn't going to be Frank; Frank had already passed on his chance to talk to me. And it wasn't going to be Ted calling to tell me he'd come to his senses and wanted to return. And I really didn't feel like talking to Denise or David, and especially not the guy from Citibank who was calling about my overextended Visa card.

On the other hand, I *was* in the mood to get some *good* news; say, that a previously unknown relative had died and left me a substantial inheritance. Or that Hollywood wanted to option *The Brewster Mall.*

Curiosity and optimism won out. I tapped the playback button.

Beep. "Uh . . . Andrew Westlake? Uh . . . this is"—again came the self-conscious laugh—"this is Frank DiBenedetto. Sorry I didn't take your call before . . . I didn't know who you were. But I looked up your number in the phone book and it matched, so you must be . . . uh . . . you know, Belle. Anyway, I'm gonna be here at the club for a while, so come down. If you want. Uh . . . you know where the office is, I guess. Bye." Beep.

Ten minutes later, I was running down the steps to the subway platform at the corner of West Eighty-sixth Street and Broadway.

Even though it was Monday night, it still cost me ten dollars to get into Benedick's. And once I was inside, I was able to estimate that the club must have raked in an entire three hundred dollars or so in cover charges that night. You do the math.

I stopped at the bar and bought a Miller Lite; then, heart

pounding, I made my way to the almost-hidden door that led to the dark corridor, off of which was the office. And the women's rest room.

He was sitting behind the desk, exactly like he'd been when I first met him: the *Daily News* open on the desk, the Marlboro Light burning in the overflowing ashtray. He looked up at me and instinctively reached under the desk. "You're not allowed back here. This is private."

My hands were shaking. "I was invited."

He looked at me, squinted, then tentatively asked, "Andy?"

I nodded, beaming. "I prefer Andrew. Or Drew."

He relaxed his grip under the desk and folded his arms across his chest. That smile from the other night was missing as he closely examined my face, replaced with a quizzical, confused expression.

"I . . . uh . . . I guess I look a little different when I'm not wearing a dress, huh?" I babbled nervously as my smile flickered away.

And, for his part, he seemed nervous, too. "You look like a man," he said finally.

"I don't . . . uh . . . I never dressed in drag before. I let myself get talked into it."

"You looked good," he said, still without a smile. "A little like Demi Moore."

"So you said. But I'm still not doing it again."

We awkwardly looked across the small room at each other. He was as beautiful as I remembered, but much less approachable without the smile. And while I didn't know what he thought about me, I felt that the lack of a smile said it all. Still, I *had* gone through the effort of running down to the Village on a Monday night, so I felt owed some kind of explanation.

"Why did you want me to come down?"

He shrugged. "I dunno."

I didn't say anything in response. I just looked at him with a steady yet unintimidating gaze. Finally, he said, "I wasn't going to call. You sort of surprised me when you talked like a man as I was getting out of the cab."

"I thought you knew."

"Yeah." A small piece of his smile finally slipped across his face. "I guess I should've, huh? But I'm new to all this."

"Everybody here that night was male. They almost didn't let me in because the bouncer thought I was a real woman. That's why I thought—"

He held up a hand to stop me. "I didn't make the rules, and I guess I didn't know the rules. I just own the place; I've hired people to manage it and promote it. I mean, I don't know all this gay stuff."

Again, silence fell between us. I noticed his forehead was beaded with sweat, which was causing one of the ringlets in his curly black hair to slowly unravel over his brow. And, at that moment, as I stood there entranced by his uncurling curl and his nervous vulnerability, I was even more sorry he was heterosexual and unattainable.

"You know this place is gay, don't you?" I finally asked, worried Barry Blackburn and his crowd had totally put one over on poor, naive Frank.

He laughed, and the smile again made a brief appearance. "It would be hard to miss that. Yeah, of course I know it. That was part of my business plan. But I thought girls—*real* girls . . . I mean . . . uh . . . *straight* girls—I thought they sometimes went to gay bars. You know, to dance and hang out without worrying that some asshole's gonna hit on them."

"Well, you should have a talk with Barry Blackburn. I think he's afraid of women."

"I guess so."

Okay, that was out of the way. Now it was time to talk about me.

"So, if I surprised you—and I'm sorry about that, by the way—why did you call?"

He looked at the floor and swallowed hard a few times. When his eyes returned to me, there was a new sadness in them. But he quickly recovered. "I don't know. I guess it's because you were such a great-looking woman . . ."

Oh, God, Denise was right. All Frank wanted was for me to put on the wig and dress while he fucked me. I turned and started to leave.

"I felt this kind of, um, *bond* between us," he said quickly, rushing to get the words out as I walked back into the corridor. "We seemed to connect on a deeper level. I mean, when we danced . . ."

I turned back and bitterly said, "I'm not what you want, Frank. I'm not a woman. I don't dress like a woman and I don't act like a woman and I'm not going to get fucked around by straight men like a woman. There are already too many *gay* men screwing around with my head. They don't need company."

My triumphant, defiant, scene-stealing speech over, I spun on my heel and started to march down the hall.

He caught me before I reached the women's rest room.

We were back at the diner, drinking coffee and eating french fries covered in gravy. He apologized for giving me the wrong impression, so I apologized for making a scene, although I was fully prepared to make another one.

"What I meant to say," he said, "is I felt like there was something between us as two *people*. Not just as a guy and a girl. But it took me until this afternoon to sort it out."

"So, what's that mean? Any way you look at it, we're still two men, and that means we've got the same equipment. I really don't get the impression that that's what you're interested in."

He shrugged. "I don't know what it means, and I don't know how to work it out. There must be . . . I don't know."

I started to laugh.

"What?"

"This is perfect. I couldn't have written it any better. I finally find the man of my dreams, and he's straight. And you finally meet that special someone, and he's a gay man. And short of a sex-change operation—and don't even *think* of suggesting it—there's nothing we can do about it."

He leaned back in the booth and frowned. After a long pause he said, "I've got something to tell you. Something else. I have a fiancée."

I barely looked up from my coffee. "Great. Another insurmountable complication."

"I don't love her."

I didn't respond. I just watched him as he put his elbows on the table and ran a hand through his hair, then across his face until it fell to rest in a position that shaded his eyes.

"I don't love her," he said again, but this time he was almost inaudible.

I told myself not to get drawn into Frank's personal psychodrama but couldn't help asking, "So, why are you marrying her?"

His hand didn't move from its position, but he started slowly massaging his brow as he said, in a voice still just above a whisper, "Family stuff. It's just something I have to do."

"Like an arranged marriage? That's kind of old-fashioned, isn't it?"

"It's not really like that," he said, still massaging his brow. "It's just . . . I have to do it."

Of course.

I liked Frank, I really did. Maybe there were even the first flickers of love for him somewhere deep inside me. But the last person I wanted to get involved with was an emotionally damaged straight boy who didn't know what he wanted, who he wanted, or why he wanted it. I tossed my napkin on the table.

"It's been a real experience, Frank. But I'd better get home."

His free hand darted across the table and wrapped itself around my wrist. "Don't go."

"Frank . . ."

He looked at me with plaintive eyes. I noticed they were misting over.

"Frank . . ." I gently tried to free my wrist.

"I've told you something about me," he said sadly. "Don't go yet. Tell me something about you."

"Why?"

"Because I want to know."

He was so pitiful that, despite all the very obvious warning signs, I couldn't bring myself to do the sensible thing and get up and leave. I settled back in the booth and leaned forward, mirroring his posture.

"Okay. I'm thirty-five. My parents have both been dead for years, and I was an only child, so I'm all alone in this hard, cruel world. Still, I've survived. I've written two books that almost nobody has read. I thought I found the love of my life a few years ago, but he dumped me in September. So now I'm back on the market, and I'm not real happy about it. Is that enough for you?"

"Sorry to hear about your parents," he said softly. "I lost my mother ten years ago, so I know what it's like."

"Yeah, well . . ." I shrugged. "It happens to everyone eventually. That's why we have to make the most out of the time we have, right?"

"Right."

"So, what about you?"

"Not much to tell. I'm twenty-nine years old and I dread turning thirty. Every penny I've ever earned is invested in the bar."

"*And* you're engaged."

"Yeah. *And* I'm engaged. But can we talk about something else? What about the book you wrote?"

"Two books, actually. Have you heard of *The Brewster Mall?*"

He shook his head.

"Well, in that case, I'm sure you haven't heard of *Allentown Blues.* That was my obligatory gay coming-of-age novel, but apparently nobody gives a damn about gay people coming of age in Allentown, Pennsylvania."

"Cool," said Frank, surprisingly excited to learn about my novels. "Is Allentown where you're from?"

"I barely remember anymore. It was a long, long time ago."

"So, what's the deal with this guy who dumped you?" he asked. "He was gay, right?"

I laughed. "I make it my policy to only date other gay men. Life is complicated enough."

That, at least, got a smile out of him.

"His name was—*is*—Ted. He's an accountant. And let's just say our personalities were apparently too far apart for us to be able to compensate for it with great sex. I like to look at things and let my imagination run wild, and he likes to look at things and see the bottom line." I paused and sipped my coffee. "It could have been partly my fault, I suppose. Maybe I didn't add up for him when he got to the bottom line. Although I'll be damned if I know what kind of bottom line he sees in—"

I stopped myself, unable to miss the bitter edge creeping into my voice, but not soon enough. Frank looked at me expectantly. When it was clear I wasn't going to finish the sentence without prompting, he asked, "Sees in *what?*"

I tried to shake away the bitterness. "Let's just say he didn't leave me for another accountant, okay?"

"He left you for someone else?"

"Yeah," I confessed, letting the bitterness spew forth. "A twenty-three-year-old bleached bimbo." I sighed. "Maybe Ted was going through a midlife crisis."

Frank's hand reached across the table and cautiously patted my arm. "I'm sorry."

"Me, too."

At that point, neither of us felt like talking anymore. We split the check and once again shared a cab to our respective apartments, but, exhausted from our emotional tour de force, we barely spoke.

When we stopped at his apartment, he said, "I hope you don't mind, but I think I'm gonna pass on a good-night kiss tonight."

I smiled for his benefit, but the minute the cab pulled away from the curb, it left my face.

When I called her at four in the morning, Denise wasn't very happy with me.

"*Why* are you calling me in the middle of the night?" she asked.

"Can't we just think of this as very early in the morning?"

"*Andrew* . . ."

"Sorry," I said contritely. "But I can't sleep."

"*I* can," was her terse reply. When I didn't respond, she resigned. "Okay, what's wrong?"

I didn't want to tell her, because I knew that I was asking for a lecture. But I'd dialed the phone and let it ring and gone this far, so . . .

"I went to see Frank tonight."

"Who?" she started to ask with a yawn, until the fog lifted and she snapped awake, screaming, "Oh, God, Drew! You didn't! Please, tell me you didn't!"

"I did. He called me, and I went down to Benedick's to meet him."

"With your dress on?"

"No. I'm back to living life as a man. And anyway, after we got reintroduced, we talked."

"Oh, Drew . . ."

"I know . . ." I mumbled apologetically, then added, "He's confused."

"*He's* confused?! Hell, *I'm* confused! What the hell were you—? *Of course* he's confused! Is this some kind of late-breaking bulletin to you? There's something wrong with him, and there's something even more wrong with you if you—*Oh, God!* You didn't sleep with him, did you?"

"No. My perfect record of not having sex with heterosexuals is unbroken."

"Thank God for small favors."

"We just talked. I think he's doubting his sexuality."

"Drew . . ."

"I don't know what the deal is, but he's supposed to marry this woman he says he doesn't love."

"Drew . . ."

"I don't know what to do . . ."

"Drew . . ."

"I mean, I should at least help him get out of this engagement, right?"

"Drew . . ."

"It's not like he loves her."

"Drew . . ."

"And I don't even care if he stays straight. I'm sure that we can just be friends."

"Drew . . ."

"I mean, I'd expect a friend to stop *me* from marrying someone *I* didn't love."

"Drew . . ."

"How can I stand back and let him ruin his life? What kind of friend would I be?"

"*Andrew!!!*"

Denise's scream finally caught my attention.

"Are you listening to yourself?" she asked harshly. "Have you heard a word that you're saying? *I'm* your friend, Andrew, and *I'm* telling you to stay away from him! He's not your friend, and you don't have to save his life."

"But—"

"He's just another screwed-up person in New York City. One of about seven million." Her tone softened. "Listen, Drew, you're just a little bit vulnerable right now. But trust me: In a few months, you'll be amazed that you ever *thought* about getting involved in this guy's life. Put this behind you."

"But—"

"He's not your type, Drew. Maybe he liked you when he thought you were a woman, but you're *not* a woman. So, get some sleep and stop thinking about this guy. Let him solve his own problems."

I hated her logic. It always made so much sense, and yet it never quite worked for me.

I brewed a pot of coffee and didn't sleep a wink the rest of the night.

It rained on Tuesday. I watched it start to drizzle as the sun rose, and watched it intensify into a heavy downpour just before I had to leave for work. It was appropriate.

Fortunately, I had enough work to do at PMC to keep me busy for most of the day, which kept my mind more or less off Frank. In fact, for two full hours in the late morning, while I tried to deal with a particularly difficult writer with some real raw talent but a reluctance to have her rough edges smoothed out by someone as low down the food chain as me, I don't think I thought about Frank at all. And that was good.

In the late afternoon, the lack of sleep caught up with me. While it made me groggy and cranky, it also further minimized my feelings about Frank. And that was good, too.

"Leaving so soon?" asked David, who was uncharacteristically wandering through the offices as I prepared to make my early getaway.

"Yeah. I didn't get much sleep last night."

He leered. "Do tell."

"You don't want to know," I said truthfully. "Anyway, I think I'm over it."

A flicker of recognition crossed his face, and he said disapprovingly, "You *didn't!*"

"Didn't what?" I asked innocently, but it didn't work. He just stood there, arms folded, waiting for my answer, and I wondered how he was able to read my mind.

Finally, he asked, "Did you go back to Benedick's?"

"Yeah. But I'm over it."

"Did you sleep with him?"

"No."

"Don't. Take my word for it. Don't." And with that, he left.

I slept on the couch until eleven o'clock; to the point, that is, where it was almost time to wake up so I could go to bed again. The ringing telephone woke me up.

It was Frank.

I let him leave a message, and held a pillow over my head so I wouldn't listen.

And then it was one o'clock, and I was still on the couch, and I couldn't fall asleep again, and so I decided to listen to the message.

"It's Frank. It's around eleven o'clock on Tuesday night. Just wanted to tell you that I read *Allentown Blues*. It's really good. Anyway, I'm at the club, if you want to call me."

"Don't," said David, who was suddenly sitting next to me on the couch.

"But—"

"Don't," said Denise, on the other side of me.

And then, just as suddenly, they were gone.

"Don't," I repeated to myself.

I did.

"Benedick's."

"Can I speak to Frank DiBenedetto?"

"I'm not sure if he's here. Let me check. Who's calling?"

"Andrew Westlake. He's expecting my call."

A few moments later, Frank was on the line.

"I didn't think you were going to call," he said. "If you called two minutes later, you would've missed me. What's up?"

"Sorry I missed your call, but I was sleeping," I lied. "I was awake most of last night."

"I didn't get much sleep, either. But I did manage to find your book."

"How? It's been out of the stores for a long time."

"You know that new bookstore on Fifth? Hanover's?"

Know it? He was only talking about the newest and second-largest bookstore in Manhattan. But Hanover's didn't even carry *The Brewster Mall,* so I knew that it wouldn't stock old copies of the already-discounted and discontinued *Allentown Blues.*

"I've got connections there," he explained. "They can get things for me."

"Tell them to put *The Brewster Mall* in the window, then."

"Actually, I want to talk to you about that," he said. "Can I come over?"

Huh?

No, I told myself. Say no. Because all he's doing is satisfying his own curiosity at the expense of my own mental well-being. Besides, David and Denise are my friends, and they look out for my best interests, and they don't approve of this. So that means that this isn't healthy. Frank should sort out his own problems without destroying me. Just because he spent twenty-three dollars and maybe seven hours of his life reading *Allentown Blues* doesn't mean that I owe him anything.

But . . . he had connections with Hanover's! And they had a huge display window!

And it was Frank!

And maybe David and Denise didn't always know what was best for me, anyway.

"Don't," said David and Denise in unison, bracketing me on the couch.

I gave him my address, ignoring my friends until they disappeared again.

"I'm leaving right now. Give me twenty minutes."

That gave me just enough time to shower, shave, and throw on some fresh clothes.

And then he was there.

He entered the apartment warily, taking tentative steps as he scanned the living room. It occurred to me that this was probably the first time Frank had ever knowingly walked into the apartment of a homosexual. I imagined that he felt much more secure in a relatively public place like Benedick's, especially since he seemed to spend all his time holed up in the private office off the back hallway.

But now it was just the two of us. And we were on my home turf.

"Can I get you a drink?"

"What do you have?" His voice was soft and hesitant.

"Anything you want. As long as it's Miller Lite or scotch."

"Beer is fine."

I grabbed two bottles from the refrigerator as he sat, tellingly, not on the couch but in a chair, where he could be assured that I wouldn't violate his personal space. I handed him his beer and picked a spot on the couch that respected his distance.

"Nice place," he said, as he now surveyed the room with less wariness. He spotted a print on the wall. "Hockney?"

"Yup," I said, nodding. "Hockney prints are de rigueur for Upper West Side apartments. Hadn't you heard?"

He fell into silence, staring vacantly at the David Hockney print as he absently scratched at the label on the beer bottle. Part of me wanted to break the mood and plunge us into conversation; the other part of me wanted to just sit and watch him.

And so I let him stare for a few moments, until he finally turned his gaze on me. "I really liked *Allentown Blues.* It was—I dunno . . . It was kind of . . . uh . . . God, I can't think of the word I want. But . . . It really felt *personal.* Like I was getting this intimate glimpse into your life."

"I guess you were. I mean, I changed some things, of course. But basically it was all about me."

"*Poignant!*" he said suddenly, snapping his fingers. "That's the word I was looking for."

Oh, dear . . . I tried to conjure up the images of Denise and David, but they were nowhere to be found. Frank was sitting six feet away from me, using just the right words, and I was defenseless.

"*Poignant?*" I asked him, not sure if I could trust what I heard.

He looked uncomfortable. "Isn't that the right word?"

"Yes!" I said, surprised to hear myself shout. I turned my voice down a few decibels. "It's just that I don't think I've ever heard anyone call it that before. Except me. Not even Ted"— when I said his name I felt a twinge somewhere deep inside me —"called it *poignant.*"

That broad smile swept across his face. "Well, it was. And I really enjoyed it. I can't wait to read the mall book."

I waved a dismissive hand. "Even *I* don't think *The Brewster Mall* is *poignant.* It's just fun." Which reminded me. "Of course, that doesn't mean it shouldn't be displayed in Hanover's window."

He didn't seem to mind that I lunged right into business.

"I think it can be arranged." His smile flickered for just an instant, as if he was trying to remember all the strings that come attached to promises. Then, out of the blue, he asked, "Did you always know you were gay? Like Grant in the book?"

"Did you always know you were straight?" I replied, too glibly and maybe too defensively. He just looked at me blankly, the smile fading away, so I continued. "Yeah, I did. As soon as I graduated from high school, I couldn't wait to get out of Allentown and come to New York. This was a wild town then."

"I thought it still was."

"Not like then," I said, digging back in my memory to my early days in Manhattan. "At least, not for me. Maybe it's just that I'm getting older. But I think AIDS has changed things a lot. I moved to New York before anyone knew any better, and . . . well . . . things have changed."

His brow creased and he awkwardly asked, "Are you . . . um . . . okay?"

"Yeah. But just because I was lucky, not because I was a Boy Scout."

"Did you know a lot of people—?"

I interrupted him tersely. "I don't want to talk about this right now."

"Sorry." He returned his eyes to the Hockney print.

And I gave myself another lecture. Oh, good. This poor, confused, beautiful guy walks into my life, and even if he *is* straight, he wants to be friends and he may be able to help me sell a few more books. And just because he asks a few obvious questions to help educate himself about gay people in general and me as an individual, I cut him off. Open up to him, dammit!

"A lot," I said quietly, this time obeying the lesson of my lecture.

"Huh?"

"I've lost a lot of friends."

He looked at me, and then at the floor, mumbling an apology for asking in the first place.

"Don't apologize. It's just that it can be difficult to talk about."

"I know that feeling," he said, still staring at the floor. "Not about AIDS . . . but about other things."

"Like?"

"Things." He finally lifted up his head and looked me in the eye. I thought he was about to open up—maybe *he* did, too—but all he did was mutter "Things" one more time.

We sat there, looking at each other across six of the eleven feet of my living room, not speaking for the longest time, studying each other.

He broke the spell with a laugh and shook his head. "I must be fuckin' crazy."

"Why's that?" I asked, holding back from joining in his laughter.

"I'm—You're . . . Ah, geez . . . We're not—I mean . . . It's just—crazy!"

I allowed myself a small smile. "Yeah, I guess it is."

He stood and stretched his well-proportioned frame, still laughing and shaking his head, and set his barely touched beer bottle on the coffee table.

"I gotta get home. I'm sorry I kept you up so late."

"No problem," I said, playing along. "I'm glad you came over. And thanks for your help with Hanover's."

"I liked your book. I wouldn't have offered to do it if I didn't."

I walked him to the front door and was just starting to turn the knob when he stopped me by putting his hand over mine.

"I want to be friends," he said softly, his face very close to mine. "I really like you. Uh . . . as a guy."

"Friends," I agreed. "And I promise I'll stay a guy."

His eyes never left mine, but his hand, still over mine, started to turn the doorknob. When we heard the click of the latch, he released it and shook his head again. "I must be crazy . . ."

"What?"

The Frank smile returned, this time just six inches from me. And then, although the smile began to slip away, his face was five inches from mine. Four inches . . . three inches . . . two . . .

Oh, God.

Ohhhhh . . .

And the amazing thing—the thing that once again kept me up most of the night playing the scene over and over again in my head—is that *Frank* was the one who took the initiative and kissed *me*.

And that Frank kissed me on the lips.

And that Frank let the kiss linger.

And that Frank slipped me his tongue.

"Don't tell me. I distinctly do *not* want to know." That was how David Carlyle greeted me as I dragged my ragged body into the offices of PMC the next morning, a half-hour late for work despite the fact that I'd barely slept since 1:00 A.M.

Four or five hours of sleep over the previous two nights had left me a mental and physical wreck. Deep, dark semicircles were etched under my bloodshot eyes, my skin was ashen, my back ached, my posture sagged from exhaustion, and my brain activity faded in and out like bad television reception.

And despite David's protest to the contrary, he did want to

know, which is why he followed me as I hauled my broken body through the office to my cubicle. He waited until I slumped in my chair before he spoke again.

"I think you were better off when you were heartbroken and miserable. Please tell me that you've just been very sick, and that this Frank fellow hasn't been the cause of all this."

I leaned back in my chair and focused my tired eyes on David. "I know that you've got a problem with him, but . . ."

"*Oh!*" he exclaimed as his suspicions were confirmed, throwing his arms wildly like a two-year-old in mid-tantrum and attracting the attention of at least half the people in the office. "You're just too much, you know that? Just because Ted left you doesn't mean you have to—Good Lord, Andrew! Have you lost your mind?"

"He's not anything like you think he is," I said, feebly trying to defend Frank even though I wasn't quite sure *what* he was really like. "He's just a nice guy."

Exasperated, David sputtered and threw his arms around some more, unable to verbalize his disgust with me, Frank, and the whole situation. Finally, he calmed down enough to say, "You have a bright future as a writer, Andrew. I'll admit that I was a bit skeptical at first, but I'm warming up to the reality of your talents. Good things are starting to happen to *The Brewster Mall* and, if we can keep things rolling, maybe your next book will be your breakout novel. But I'm not sure it's worth the trouble if you're going to throw everything away on some low-life nightclub owner who's just screwing around with your head! I might as well just go back to my office right this minute and call Hanover's and tell them not to waste their precious window space on you!"

With that, David stormed away from my cubicle. It took a few seconds for his individual words to filter down into my brain and reform themselves into sentences, but when they did, a second wind whipped through my body.

"Hanover's?" I gasped to myself, before I leapt out of my chair and chased through the office after David. "Did you say Hanover's?"

He was almost to the elevators. Calmly, he turned and nodded. "They called this morning. Apparently, someone over there read *The Brewster Mall* and thought it was fabulous, so they want to help promote it. At no cost to PMC, either, which thrills me to no end."

"But that's—that's—*Frank* did that!!" I said too loudly.

David frowned at my comment and pushed the elevator call button.

"Last night he came over and said he'd read *Allentown Blues,* and he told me he knew people at Hanover's who could get me a window display for *The Brewster Mall.*"

David raised one eyebrow, not quite believing me but not quite dismissing me, either.

"It's *true,* David," I said, almost begging him to believe me.

A *ding* announced the arrival of the elevator. In parting, David simply said, "Maybe it *is* true, although the thought of this Frank being able to read much beyond pornography is a stretch for me. But if it is, then it only reconfirms what I've been telling you: Stay away from him." Those last words of warning were delivered through clenched teeth.

"But—"

David stepped into the elevator. "We'll discuss this later."

"David Carlyle is so bizarre," I said when Denise answered her phone. "Wouldn't you think that he'd be overjoyed to have one of his authors in Hanover's window?"

"Uh . . . yeah," she replied, but there was no commitment in her voice. "So, what's the problem?"

"He's upset because Frank made the arrangements to get me the window."

At the mention of Frank's name, Denise sighed deeply.

"Oh, Drew," she moaned. "Not Frank again."

"Do you think David has some kind of crush on me or something? I mean, that would explain why he hates Frank so much . . ."

"I've never met Frank, but I don't think he's any good for you, either." I could tell from her voice that she instinctively knew that our friendship had advanced to a slightly different level, even if she didn't know the details of the kiss. "And, no, I don't have a crush on you, loverboy. It just sounds like a really bad situation."

"You'd like him if you met him."

"Well, I doubt that will happen, so—"

"Do you still have those extra tickets to *Rent* tonight?"

Denise was silent for a long time. Finally, and without answering me, she asked, "Why?"

"I thought it would be a nice gesture to take Frank out. To thank him for getting me in the window."

"Drew—"

"Do you still have the tickets?"

She exhaled unhappily into the mouthpiece of her phone while she tried to think of a way to avoid the situation without having to eat one-hundred-fifty dollars in theater tickets. Finally, realizing she had been beaten, she mumbled, "I'll meet you in front of the theater at seven-thirty."

Of course, I made the arrangements without talking to Frank, and without even knowing how to get in touch with him during the day. I called Benedick's, but, not unexpectedly, there was no answer. So . . .

"Hanover's. How may I help you?"

I was quickly connected to the manager's office, where a tired-sounding woman answered the phone. I explained who I was—she had never heard of me; so much for the concept of instant fame through a window display—then asked her if she had a daytime phone number for Frank DiBenedetto.

"Who?"

"Frank DiBenedetto." I repeated the name slowly. "He has some kind of connection to your bookstore. If you ask around, I'm sure someone there knows him."

"Sorry," she said crisply. "I don't know him. Let me take your name and number, and I'll check around."

A half-hour later, the phone rang on my desk.

"You Westlake?" asked a gruff male voice. I said I was. "Why are you looking for DiBenedetto?"

"I . . . uh . . . lost his home phone number." I was a bit frightened by his tone. "And I need to get in touch with him this afternoon."

"So, why'd you call here?"

"He said he knew people there. You see, yesterday he told me that he had talked to someone at Hanover's about promoting my book in the window and—"

"Oh." The gruffness in his voice hardened. "You're talkin' about *Frankie*. Frank *Junior,* that is."

"I guess so."

"Why do you want him?"

"We're friends. Listen, I just need—"

"Friends who don't have each other's phone numbers?"

"I lost it. Listen, I just need to call him because I have theater tickets for tonight and I thought he'd like to go."

"*Theater* tickets?" The man at Hanover's didn't sound impressed. In fact, it's fair to say that he sounded contemptuous.

"Can I just get—"

"All right. Hold on a sec." He set down his phone. A few moments later he was back on the line with Frankie's home phone number.

Just before our conversation ended, he said, "You tell Frankie that Paulie Macarini tells him to have a nice time at the theater." With that, he snickered and hung up on me.

As for the name Paulie Macarini, well . . . it was a name I would hear again.

When I finally reached him, *Frankie* thought that taking a night off from Benedick's sounded like a great idea. And I was pleasantly surprised that he seemed to have no embarrassment about the previous evening's extended good-night kiss.

Granted, we didn't talk about it. But part of me was fully prepared for him to dodge me altogether, or feebly offer up the boy-was-I-drunk-last-night defense.

But, no, even though the subject of the kiss didn't come up, he didn't dodge, evade, avoid, or lie. He sounded happy to hear from me and easily agreed to meet me outside the theater at seven-thirty.

At seven-fifteen, I was the first one to arrive. I was bundled warmly against an icy wind that picked up speed as it rolled south down Seventh Avenue and into the theater district, where it rounded the corner onto Forty-first Street and swept past me as I huddled in front of the Nederlander Theatre. It was still almost an hour before the curtain would go up, so I stood with my back pressed against the building, almost alone on the sidewalk that soon would be crowded with theatergoers and theatergoer-gawking tourists, trying to retain as much body heat as I could.

Slowly, as the minutes crept past, a sparse crowd of people began assembling with me on the sidewalk, blocking at least some of the wind. Some paid for their tickets at the box office then milled around on the sidewalk, waiting for the doors to open so they could get out of the cold. Others, like me, stood waiting for their companions. And yet others just stood there, hands pressed deep in the pockets of their coats, staring at the marquee and the patrons and vicariously drinking in the Broadway theater experience.

Frank's cab arrived at seven-thirty on the nose, and I was greeting him when the cab hauling Denise and two of her friends from work pulled to the curb behind it.

"It's about time," I said, shivering. "Let's go inside before I freeze to death."

"We *said* seven-thirty," said Denise, who then motioned to her co-workers. "Do you remember Jenny and Paula?"

"Yeah, hi," I said, not really remembering them. It was my turn, so I put my hand on Frank's shoulder. "And this is Frank."

"Hello," said Denise distantly, with a forced smile.

"Nice to meet you," said Frank, ignoring or oblivious to Denise's antipathy as he offered her his hand. She gave it one abbreviated shake, then quickly returned her hand to her pocket.

I slipped Denise cash for my tickets, and she walked to the line at the box office window, dragging Jenny and Paula with her.

"I'm sorry about Denise," I said. "I think she's been having a bad day."

"That's okay," he said. "I'm not one of those people who believe that you can't change first impressions." He laughed. "If I was, then I'd still think of you as a woman."

At one point during the performance, as two male cast members sang of covering each other with one thousand kisses, I bravely reached over and squeezed Frank's elbow.

He grinned.

On the other side of me, I heard Denise hiss a muted, *"Andrew!"*

I ignored her and squeezed Frank's biceps, as the actors sang of finding a new lease on life through love.

Of course, I already knew that one of the lovers would die later in the show, but I had a knack for ignoring such fine points.

All that mattered was the illusion of romance. Whether the illusion was on the stage or part of my very real life didn't matter very much. I was flexible.

4

The Place Where John Lennon Got Whacked, and Why I Should Care

There are over seven million people in New York City, and one and a half million of us live within Manhattan's twenty-two square miles. That means that the island of Manhattan has more residents than several states, all living in a space roughly 2 percent the size of the state of Rhode Island. And that's before you start adding the millions of tourists, visitors, businesspeople, and commuters who come into Manhattan on a daily basis.

Is it any wonder that we get a little crazy?

What's more, and perhaps unfairly, Manhattan is known throughout the world for the isolation of its residents from each other's lives. The part-myth/part-reality is that, although we live crammed into towering apartment buildings and in neighborhoods teeming with other people, side by side and one on top of another, we seldom see each other, meet each other, or make any kind of physical or emotional connection with each other.

It's just faceless human being after faceless human being after faceless human being, the way I imagine that people in the hinterlands see tree after tree after tree or corn stalk after corn stalk after corn stalk; all different in some small way, but not different enough to bother noting.

For example, I had lived in my apartment at Amsterdam Avenue and West Eighty-sixth Street for five years, but I couldn't begin to tell you what anyone in my building looked like, except for some of the doormen, including my neighbors on the seventh floor. And I was the rule for Manhattan, not the exception.

If you want a neighborhood or a community, then you go to New York's outer boroughs or the vast world beyond their borders.

If you never want to see the same person twice, welcome to Manhattan.

So, given all that—given the crowded, impersonal, simply overwhelming nature of Manhattan—why was it that the first people I saw when we walked into the lobby of the Nederlander Theatre at the end of the musical were Ted and Nicholas?

Why didn't they both disappear into the Manhattan scenery like everyone else did?

"Fancy meeting *you* here," said Ted, spotting me moments after I spotted him and tried without success to hide behind Denise.

"I remember *you*," said his bleach-headed twink, showing none of the shame appropriate for a homewrecker. "How was the party at Benedict's the other night?"

"Bene*dick*'s," I growled softly, adding, "It was fine."

Ted greeted Denise, who barely acknowledged him, and then asked, "Enjoy the show?"

"Yeah," I mumbled as I pretended to glance at my watch. "Well, we gotta go."

That's when I heard Frank ask Nicholas, "Have you been to Benedick's?"

"Noooo," he drawled, trying to be boyishly charming by fluttering his eyelashes at Frank, which to me looked perfectly ridiculous. Then he tossed a glance at Ted. "*Some*body's been too busy to go. And when he's free, he'd rather go to the *theatah*."

"Sorry for trying to expand your mind," Ted chided Nicholas quietly.

"Benedick's is gonna be the place to be this Friday night," said Frank, picking the wrong time to drum up business, and with the wrong potential customers at that. "Barry Blackburn has this big drag show scheduled. RuPaul is supposed to be a judge."

"Oh, good, Drew!" Denise chirped cheerfully into my ear. "Maybe Betty Bacall will be there, too."

"It's *Belle*. And she *won't* be there."

Well, *this* was turning out to be a fun conversation, full of all my favorites: Ted, Nicholas, Barry Blackburn, Belle Bacall . . . could it get any worse? I took Denise's arm with one hand and Frank's arm with the other and prepared to lead them into the night.

"By the way, since it doesn't seem that Andrew is going to introduce us," Frank said to Ted, ignoring my tug on his arm, "I'm Frank. I own Benedick's."

"Hi, Frank. I'm Ted. And this"—he nodded at the twink—"is Nicky."

I glanced at Frank and saw by his tightened features and the crimson flush that crossed his face at the mention of Ted's name that he remembered. He remembered that Ted was the man who broke my heart. And for a moment, I thought Frank was going to avenge my honor, right there in the lobby of the Nederlander Theatre.

But it passed, and Frank's face soon betrayed no trace of hostility. He listened briefly to Nicholas babble about what all the other twinks thought about RuPaul and Benedick's, then patted first Ted and then Nicholas on the shoulder, saying simply, "Nice to meet you both."

We left them behind, and I hoped that they would blend back into the anonymity of Manhattan and become two more faceless human beings.

No such luck, although that would be through no fault of their own.

Denise, Jenny, and Paula went their separate ways, and I let Frank convince me to go with him to Benedick's.

Our cab was turning onto the West Side Highway a few blocks from the theater when he said, "So that was Ted."

"Yup. I'm afraid so."

"And the other one?"

"Nicholas," I said with a sigh. "The boy he left me for."

"Hmmmph. I thought so." Frank slid down in the seat and stared out the window at the lights of New Jersey across the Hudson River. He didn't say anything for a few blocks, until, "What's his last name?"

"Why?"

"Just curious. I was wondering if we've met before."

"Langhorne," I answered, not satisfied with his answer but seeing no reason to protect Ted's privacy. Frank didn't say another word until we reached Benedick's

The club was modestly busy when we walked through the doors and, because I was with Frank, I didn't have to pay the cover charge. I followed him to the bar closest to the entrance and we ordered a couple of beers.

"Now, this Ted . . ." he said haltingly. "What's he do again?"

"He breaks hearts," I replied dryly.

"No, no," said Frank. "I mean for a living."

"Oh. He's an accountant. Why?"

"Don't worry." He flashed a brief smile for my benefit. "I'm not gonna hire him or anything. I was just curious . . . wondering about what your life was like before I met you."

"Then maybe I should write a sequel to *Allentown Blues*. God knows I've got enough new material."

"Where's he live?" Frank asked.

"Huh?"

"Ted. Where's he live?"

"On Bedford." I was growing tired of talking about Ted. "In the Village. Why?"

"Just curious," he again answered, and then he mercifully dropped his line of questioning, because I had no interest in discussing Ted any further.

When our beers arrived, Frank said to the bartender, "Thanks, Greg. Hey . . . is Vince around?"

"Want me to call him?" the bartender asked.

"Yeah," said Frank, sending the bartender on his way.

"Who's Vince?" I asked.

"Just business." It was clear that was as detailed an answer as I was going to get. He sipped his beer in silence for a while, then tilted his head and looked at me. "Y'know, I had a *really* good time tonight. I can't remember the last time I saw a show. Don't take this the wrong way, but most of the people I hang around with think Broadway's kind of gay."

I raised an eyebrow.

"No offense," he said defensively.

"Frank, I don't know how to tell you this, but you're sitting in a gay bar." I added, sotto voce, "And you kissed a gay man last night."

He paused for a second, then nervously asked, "Did you say anything to anyone? About last night?"

I laughed. "No, Frank. That's just between the two of us."

"I think it's better that way."

"Yeah," I answered, without conviction. "Whatever."

"Not that I—not that I'm saying that there's anything wrong . . . I mean . . . Oh, damn . . ."

I decided to let him off the hook. "Don't worry about it. I know that, deep down, you like girls. I'm just an . . . *exception.* And I know that nothing is going to happen between us."

"Yeah." He turned his gaze to the liquor bottles displayed behind the bar so that he wouldn't have to look at me.

"And," I heard myself saying, before I could stop it, "I know that you're gonna get married."

At that, his head snapped around violently and he fixed a hard stare on me.

"I don't wanna talk about that," he said, barely moving his lips. "I already told you that I don't love her. But I've got to do it. And that's got nothing to do with you and me. Just stay out of it."

"Sorry. But if you don't love her—"

"Stay out of it," he said again. This time, if possible, more harshly than before.

And then Greg the bartender was there, telling Frank, "Vince is on his way. Give him ten."

"Okay. Tell him I'll be in the office."

Frank slid off his bar stool and took a step toward the door that led to the hallway that led to the office. I started to follow him, but he turned and coldly said, "You stay here. I'll be back in a little while."

"Maybe I should just leave." I wished that I had said that back at the theater, because there was something about *this* Frank that was far different than the Frank I was afraid I was falling in love with.

"No. I think it'd be best if you waited for me to get back. I just have to make a few phone calls and meet with this guy. Then I'll come out."

"Oh," I said, and decided to make light of things by adding, "You're coming out tonight?"

"Huh? Yeah, like I said. I'll be out after I meet with this guy."

"I meant . . ." Belatedly realizing that some people just aren't meant to understand gay points of reference, I stopped. "Never mind."

So Frank left and I sat at the bar, sipping a beer or two or three for the next half hour and paying no attention to the comings or goings of any of the other patrons, which is how I managed to miss the entrance of a tall thug with a jagged scar across his cheek, and his exit a few minutes later.

When Frank finally returned, he simply said, "Let's go."

"Where?"

"We're going to the diner." It was less an answer than an order.

"But I'm not hungry."

"Then you'll have coffee."

"But—"

He grabbed my elbow, practically dragging me off the stool, and I realized that further protests would be in vain. I was going to go to the diner, whether I liked it or not. Obediently, I followed him to the door and we walked the several blocks to the diner quickly and in silence.

"Is something going on?" I asked, after we were seated in a booth.

"No," he said, not looking at me. "I just wanted something to eat. What time is it?"

I glanced at my watch. "A few minutes before twelve."

"*How many* minutes before twelve?"

"Three. Why? Do we have a train to catch or something?"

Before he could answer—if, that is, he intended to answer me—the waitress approached and took our orders. After I ordered my coffee, poor, starving, absolutely-had-to-go-to-the-diner-right-that-very-instant Frank ordered coffee and an entire bagel.

"Will that be all?" asked the waitress.

"Yeah, *will* that be all?" I asked Frank. This exercise in control was beginning to annoy me.

"I'm set," Frank said, answering her and ignoring me. Then he peered at the waitress's name tag. "Oh, your name's Celia. That's a pretty name."

"Thank you," she said, smiling, as she left to place the order for Frank's sumptuous feast.

When she was gone, Frank asked, "Is it midnight yet?"

Again, I glanced at my watch. "Another minute. Why?"

He didn't answer me, but leaned across the table and quietly said, "I really like you, Andrew."

I thought there was a *but* coming, but there wasn't. It was an *and,* as in, "And I want us to be good friends."

I leaned over the table myself to get slightly closer to him. "I like you, too, Frank. And I'm sure that we can just be friends."

It was Frank's turn again. He looked troubled and his voice dropped to a near whisper. "If we're gonna be friends, I've got to ask you to do me a favor."

"What?"

"There are some things that you don't want to ask, okay?"

"The fiancée?"

"That's one. And there are some others. Just—just kind of follow your instincts, and if you think you shouldn't ask, then don't."

"Gotcha," I said, as I leaned back again, although I had no idea *what* he was talking about.

Frank relaxed and sat back in his seat as Celia arrived with our coffee.

"Cream and sugar are on the table," she said, setting the cups in front of us.

Frank picked up his cup and thanked her. Seconds later, the cup fell out of his hands, glancing off the edge of the table and smashing on the tile floor. Celia jumped back, narrowly avoiding the geyser of coffee that erupted from the broken cup on impact. And everywhere in the diner, heads swiveled in our direction.

"I am *so* embarrassed," said Frank, grabbing his napkin and dabbing ineffectually at the stream of coffee that ran across the floor. "I am *so* embarrassed."

"Don't worry about it," said Celia, who politely pushed him and his soaked paper napkin away from the mess. "Let me grab a mop."

When Celia went to get the mop, Frank settled back into the booth.

"Accidents happen," I said, doing my part to try to ease his embarrassment.

"Yeah," he said calmly, almost to himself, and I noticed that he didn't look the least bit embarrassed. "They do."

Celia returned, cleaned up the spilled coffee and shards of the cup, and quipped for probably the thousandth time in her waitressing career, "That's why we don't put out the good china." She replaced Frank's coffee and left us alone again. Frank dawdled over his coffee and bagel for a while, and we made innocent small talk until a muted chirping sound interrupted us.

"That's me." He pulled a beeper out of his jacket pocket. "Excuse me for a minute."

He used the pay phone and was back moments later with a slightly satisfied smile on his face.

"Business never sleeps, huh?" I said.

"Not mine." He caught Celia's eye, waved to her, and asked for the check.

Frank apologized to Celia two more times, once when she brought us our check and again by leaving her a twenty-dollar tip.

"Uh . . . I don't think you're the first person who's ever broken a coffee cup here," I said.

"I want her to remember us."

After we left the diner, as we stood out in the cold wind on the sidewalk, I suggested to Frank that we share a cab back to the Upper West Side.

"I have to go back to the club," he said apologetically, patting the slight bulge of the beeper in his pocket.

"The place can't run itself for a night?"

He chuckled. "C'mon. It's only been open for a few days. Just because we got a liquor license and unlocked the doors doesn't mean that I can leave it alone. Not yet, at least."

"Too bad," I said, inching my way out on a limb by adding, "I was going to invite you in for a nightcap."

He smiled and shook his head, and the combined effect was unreadable, somewhere between "Oh, you dope, stop making a fool of yourself" and "Maybe if you ask again . . ."

"Good night, Andrew," he said finally, taking my right hand in both of his and clasping it firmly. "I had a great time tonight. Maybe I'll call you tomorrow, okay?"

Well . . . at least I finally got a decent night's sleep.

The next morning I took the subway one stop past my usual station and walked a few blocks out of my way to Fifth Avenue.

Hanover's Book Store wouldn't be open for another hour, but the window gates had already been rolled back up. I squinted at the displays in the row of windows lining Fifth Avenue but only saw the same old authors and the same old books set out to entice impulse buyers and window shoppers. Stephen King's latest; Jackie Collins's latest; a new collection of shorts by Garrison Keillor; the new unauthorized joint biography of Arnold Schwarzenegger and Maria Shriver; Doris Kearns Goodwin; Diana Gabaldon; Tom Clancy; Nelson DeMille . . .

I was about to leave, my anticipation unrewarded, when I thought I caught a familiar sight out of the corner of my eye. I strained against the glare of the sun off the plate-glass window and, sure enough, saw the cover of *The Brewster Mall* in the hands of a store employee just as he was about to set the book on a wooden prop in the window.

And then he took away a Tom Clancy book. No, not just *one* Tom Clancy book . . . *all* the Tom Clancy books! One by one, as I stood in slack-jawed witness, he removed copies of the New York *Times* number-five best-seller from that valuable window space and then, when Clancy was gone, replaced the entire display with copies of *The Brewster Mall.* By Andrew Westlake. Me.

I decided that it was going to be a wonderful day.

I was wrong once again.

"Good morning, Andrew," said David Carlyle stiffly when I arrived at PMC. He was waiting for me at my cubicle.

"Great news," I said, beaming. "*The Brewster Mall* is in Hanover's window!"

"Oh, good," he said without enthusiasm. "I hope the police are as thrilled with the news as you are."

"Huh?" I hated it when David decided to get cryptic with me.

He took me by the arm and began to escort me to the elevator. "A Detective Brogan and a Detective Mueller are here to see you in my office."

"Huh?"

"I'd tell you more if I knew more, but they don't want to talk to me. And so far, they haven't cracked under my interrogation."

We took the elevator up one floor to David's office, which gave me enough time to formulate a mental picture of Brogan and Mueller. Brogan would be a middle-aged, weather-beaten, ruddy-faced, borderline alcoholic whose first love was walking the beat; someday he would drink himself to death. Mueller would be the younger, professional up-and-comer with a college degree and a lot of ambition; in ten years, he would be chief of police.

When we reached the reception area outside David's office there were, indeed, two detectives. But not *my* detectives.

They introduced themselves. Brogan wasn't a ruddy-faced Irishman; he was a middle-aged black man. Mueller was both the younger *and* ruddy-faced one . . . and also a woman.

"Thanks for seeing us, Mr. Westlake," said Brogan, extending a hand.

"I didn't really think I had a choice," I replied, while I readjusted my imagination to conform to reality. "Is something wrong?"

"We'd just like to ask you a few questions," said Brogan, who then turned to David and asked, "Can we use your private office?"

"Can I sit in?" asked David in reply. "Andrew is a friend, as well as an employee here."

Brogan looked at Mueller, Mueller looked at Brogan, they both shrugged, and then Brogan said, "Fine with us, if it's okay with Mr. Westlake."

"Yeah, sure," I said, in a bit of a confused daze.

The four of us went into David's office, and he closed the door behind us.

"Do you know why we're here?" asked Brogan, settling into an overstuffed armchair and pulling a notepad out of his pocket.

"No."

"Do you know a Theodore Langhorne?"

"Ted? Yes."

"When was the last time you saw Mr. Langhorne?"

"Did something happen to Ted?" Fear began to well inside me. What could it have been? There were so many crazy things that could happen on the streets of Manhattan that any number of possibilities immediately presented themselves. A violent street crime? A gay-bashing? An out-of-control cab barreling down the sidewalk on Christopher Street?

"Just answer the question," said Mueller, finally joining our conversation and refocusing my thoughts.

I obeyed. "I saw Ted last night. At a play."

"Were you together?"

"No. I ran into him in the lobby."

"Did you fight?" Brogan asked, taking over the questioning.

"No. In fact, we had a very cordial conversation. Why?"

Brogan jotted a few notes, then looked at me. "*How* do you know Mr. Langhorne?"

I looked at David, who simply shrugged, so I steeled my gaze and looked Brogan in the eye. "We used to be lovers."

Brogan didn't flinch. He just jotted a few more notes.

It was, apparently, now Mueller's turn again. "Bad breakup?"

"Me and Ted? Uh . . . it was . . . it was *painful* for me. But that was a few months ago, so I'm over it."

"Good," said Mueller, with a slight smile. "By the way, I want you to feel comfortable with me and Detective Brogan, okay? We've both put in our time in the Village and Chelsea, and we've both also gone through every kind of sensitivity training that the NYPD has. We're not gonna pass any kind of judgment, and we're comfortable with gay people. Okay?"

"Okay," I said, mirroring her slight, crooked smile.

"Is the touchy-feely stuff over?" asked Brogan sourly, leveling a contemptuous gaze at his colleague. "We've got a criminal investigation to conduct here."

"What exactly happened?" I asked, and then, remembering that Ted did my taxes for me when we were together, the possibility that he had been ripping off the IRS crossed my mind. "Is Ted in trouble?"

"Where were you at around midnight last night?" Brogan asked, ignoring me.

"Midnight?" My mind raced, but I kept drawing a blank until I remembered Frank dropping his coffee at the diner. "At midnight, I was at the Seventh Avenue Diner with a friend."

"Seventh Avenue?" Brogan asked again, still taking notes. "In the Village?"

"Yeah."

"That's near Mr. Langhorne's apartment on Bedford Street, isn't it?"

"Yeah. Sort of."

"In fact, you could have walked from the diner to his apartment in five or six minutes, couldn't you?"

"Yeah . . ." That was the precise moment when I realized that Ted wasn't in trouble with the law . . . but for some reason, *I* was. "Wait a minute!" I started to get out of my chair. "What the hell is this all about?"

Mueller's hand came to rest on my shoulder and she gently

eased me back into the chair. "Relax, Andy. We're just asking a few questions."

"It's not *Andy.* It's *Andrew.*"

"Oh, right. I forgot that a lot of you guys like to use your full names."

"Did you learn that in sensitivity training?" sniped David from the sidelines.

Brogan ignored him. "Mr. Westlake . . . *Andrew* . . . we're investigating an assault on Mr. Langhorne that occurred at midnight last night in his apartment."

"Oh, God." I reflexively brought my hands to my face. Suddenly everything seemed even more confusing and frightening, all the more so because *I* was being questioned. "Is Ted all right?"

Brogan shook his head. "Well, he was beaten up pretty badly, but he'll be all right. He'll have to stay at St. Vincent's for a few days, though."

"Sorry for bothering you here at work," said Mueller, shrugging apologetically in turn at me, then David. "But your name didn't come up until this morning. Mr. Langhorne was pretty traumatized and drugged up, so the doctors asked us to hold off last night."

"You certainly don't think that Andrew had anything to do with this, do you?" asked David. "He's *not* a violent person."

"Do I need a lawyer?" I asked, sinking deeper into that dazed shock. "I think I need a lawyer."

"Does he need a lawyer?" asked David.

"We're not here to do anything but ask a few questions," said Brogan. "Nobody's accusing Andrew of anything."

"Well . . . Except Ted Langhorne," said Mueller, before Brogan cut her off with another nasty stare.

"*Ted* is accusing *Andrew* of this crime?" asked David, genuinely aghast. "That's absurd!"

"What about Nicholas?" I asked. "Maybe *he* did it!"

"Who?" asked Mueller.

"Nicholas. Nicholas Hafner. He's Ted's boyfriend."

"Oh, Nicky!" said Mueller. I didn't want to be paranoid, but it sounded to me like she said his name with far too much affection. "Oh, no, we checked, and he was out all night. We have three hundred witnesses. A kid like that, well, people remember. Anyway, Langhorne was pretty clear that his assailant mentioned your name."

Brogan picked up his notepad and flipped back a few pages.

"Whoever did this to Langhorne claimed, according to Langhorne, and I quote, 'This is for what you did to Andrew Westlake.' Unquote."

David was right; this *was* absurd. I decided on the spot to get a lawyer before there were any more questions, but not before I gave them my ironclad alibi once again.

"Last night, at midnight, I was at the diner. I got there a few minutes before midnight, and I didn't leave until after twelve-thirty. And if you want to check my story out, just ask the friend I was with. And the waitress . . . uh . . . I can't remember her name, but my friend dropped his coffee cup on the floor, so I'm sure she'll remember us." I faltered briefly at those words; something about them rekindled a vague memory. "Now, until I have a lawyer, I don't think I should answer any more questions."

"Okay." Brogan snapped his notepad shut. "Fair enough. Hopefully, you won't be hearing from us."

The detectives were almost out the door when Mueller stopped. "By the way, what's your friend's name, and how can we reach him—or is it a her?—to verify your story?"

"It's—"

"That's enough for now, Andrew," said David, clamping the palm of his hand over my mouth. "Save it for when you have a lawyer."

"But—"

"I said to save it." To the detectives, he said, "Check his story out with the waitress, and if you need more information about any of Andrew's friends, you can contact him again."

Brogan and Mueller shrugged, thanked David for his hospitality, and left.

When he was sure they were gone, David turned to me. "You're not going to pleasantly surprise me and tell me that you were at the diner with Denise, are you?"

"I was with Frank," I said, confirming his suspicions.

David flopped into the chair behind his desk. "We have to have a talk."

"But Frank can help back me up."

"Let me tell you something about your friend Frank. I've been asking around about him. You'd better sit down."

I sat. David leaned into his desk and closed his eyes, then took a manicured hand and rubbed them. He kept rubbing as he spoke.

"Frank DiBenedetto is the son of Frank DiBenedetto Senior—"

"Yeah, I know," I said, interrupting him. "Frank's a junior."

"Well, apparently, like father, like son. Frank DiBenedetto Senior is the number-two man in the Stendardi organized crime family. I think they call him the underboss."

"Huh?"

David's eyes opened, then narrowed, and with mounting anger he said, "Don't you read the newspapers? Jesus Christ, Andrew, Frank DiBenedetto is one of the highest-ranking men in the New York Mafia!"

"What do they call him?" I asked, with more sarcasm than I knew I had any right to be throwing around. "Frank the Hammer? Frank the Enforcer?"

"Frank DiBenedetto the Elder isn't the kind of man who needs a silly nickname. He's the kind of person who *gives* people silly nicknames. Although I suppose he'd be proud to be known as 'Frank the Guy Who Killed the Homosexual Who Was Fooling Around With His Son,' if you want to push him."

"But—but—" Well, *that* certainly threw me off track. The only response I could think of was a very weak, "How do you know he's in the mob?"

He threw his hands in the air and snapped with disgust, "How do I know? I know because I asked around. And because I *read!* The newspaper doesn't stop at the book reviews, you know. Goddammit, Andrew, you've gotten yourself involved with some very dangerous people! That bar is probably nothing more than another way for the Stendardi Family to launder money!" He stopped and took a few deep breaths to calm himself down. "My God, you are so naive!! I wanted to have this conversation before anything like this happened, but I was hoping you'd come to your senses without my assistance."

"Wait a minute. You don't think that I had something to do with whatever happened to Ted, do you?"

"I'm sure you didn't. I'm not so sure that your friend Frank didn't. In fact, I'd bet on it."

"But . . . Well, what about Hanover's? Are you gonna tell me that the Mafia is running a bookstore, too?"

"I think the more appropriate term would be *using*. And yes, for your information, it's pretty well established in publishing circles that Hanover's has a lot of mob money in it. That's why I wasn't as enthusiastic as you were about going into Hanover's window. And I certainly never would have paid for it." When I didn't immediately respond, he added, "It's perfect for their purposes, Andrew. With the volume of sales, books constantly being ordered and returned from hundreds of different publishers and distributors, high overhead costs, large amounts of money tied up in stock, sales . . . It's a paper trail nightmare, and it's just the sort of thing that the mob can use to their advantage. As far as they're concerned, Hanover's doesn't need to make money, any more than Benedick's needs to make money. The purpose of those so-called 'legitimate' businesses is to launder the money they make illegally." He paused. "Why can't you just sleep with someone at Barnes & Noble, like everyone else?"

I wanted to get angry with him . . . to defend Frank and Frank's family—lowercase *f* family, that is—and Frank's honor and Frank's bar and Frank's good heart and Frank's innocence. But . . .

But.

That word said it all. One simple three-letter word that kept winding its way through my head and touching on all the doubts I still had about Frank. The secrecy about his fiancée and his life . . . the way he warned me not to ask too many questions . . . his easy access to Hanover's . . . the strange way he acted at the bar and the diner the night before . . . even the ambiguity of our relationship. None of it made sense.

And then that unsettling phrase, "I'm sure she'll remember us," popped into my head again. But this time it wasn't my voice speaking to Brogan and Mueller. This time I very clearly heard Frank's voice saying, "I want her to remember us," as he left the waitress a twenty-dollar tip. And things started to make sense to me. Frightening, dreadful sense, but sense nonetheless.

"Where are you going?" asked David, as I headed for the door.

"St. Vincent's. I have to see Ted."

"Andrew, I have to warn you that that's not a very smart thing to do. In case you've forgotten already, the police have taken an interest in all of this."

"But I want to hear it from Ted's own lips before I start jumping to conclusions."

He followed me to the doorway. "And what do you intend to do when he confirms what the police said?"

"I don't know," I answered truthfully, hoping that I wouldn't reach that point.

When I found Ted's hospital room, he was sleeping, so I stood at the foot of his bed for several minutes, taking in the sight of the beaten body and coming to terms with the fact that it belonged to Ted. His jaw, naturally square and strong, was swollen and badly bruised, and the flesh on the right side of his face was mottled. His right arm was in traction, a fresh white cast encasing it from elbow to wrist.

But I was prepared for the bruised face and broken arm. I *wasn't* prepared for the overall effect of seeing Ted, sleeping fitfully despite the painkillers, weak and suffering and seeming to wither before my eyes in that hospital bed. The beating seemed to have atrophied his entire body. He was no longer the healthy, vigorous, and masculine man standing in the lobby of the Nederlander Theatre only thirteen hours earlier, the man I had loved and lived with and vacationed with and made love to. Despite the swelling, he now looked painfully small and fragile.

I set the bunch of dyed carnations I had bought on the street corner outside the hospital on the bed next to him and whispered in his ear, "Ted?"

"Mmmph," he groaned, moving his head slightly but not quite coming to.

I tried again, a little louder. "Ted?"

This time, his head rolled against the pillow with a bit more energy and his eyes flickered open. They scanned the room for a second until they found me.

"Hi, Ted," I said gently, nervously picking up the flowers. "It's me. Andrew." I held out the flowers. "I brought these for you."

His eyes blinked a few times, then started to bulge as the pupils dilated. From somewhere deep inside him, a low groan started to rise up through his throat until it escaped through his swollen lips.

"No, Ted," I said, pleading with him to stay calm, holding up my hands as if to prove I was harmless. "I'm just here to see how you are. It's okay! It's just me!"

But Ted wouldn't, or couldn't, halt that semi-scream. It grew in volume as he rocked violently back and forth in the bed, trying to free his helpless arm.

I was trying to explain once again that I meant him no harm when Nicholas, carrying his own bouquet of flowers, walked into the room. "What are *you* doing here!"

"I—I just heard and I wanted—"

"'Just heard,'" Nicholas sneered with contempt. He grabbed my flowers by the petals and threw them to the floor as he shouted, "Get out of here!! Get out or I'll call Security!"

"But I—I didn't—I don't—"

"Get out!" Nicholas continued to scream in a high-pitched, nasal voice, gesturing wildly at the door as Ted's terrified moan continued to build in volume.

I decided to give up. I obviously wasn't going to win any humanitarian awards on this particular morning. I carefully stepped over the dark red petals that now littered the floor and left the room.

For what it was worth, I now had an answer to my question. Even if it wasn't the answer I wanted.

I found a pay phone on the street and called Frank's apartment.

"I have to see you," I said, without bothering to identify myself.

"Come by the club tonight," he replied groggily. It was clear that he was still in bed.

"No," I said, with as much assertiveness as I could bring to my voice. "I have to see you *now.*"

"Well . . ."

"Frank, don't play games with me. There's something we've got to talk about."

"Okay." I heard the sound of his sheets shifting. "Can you call me later this afternoon?"

"No. We have to do this now."

"What's the problem?"

"Ted Langhorne."

There was a long silence on his end of the line, and although I was tempted to fill the void, I held my tongue and let the tension build. Finally, he caved in.

"Give me half an hour."

"Where should I meet you?"

"Come to my apartment."

I hung up without saying good-bye and called David.

When he picked up the call, he said, "I hear that you saw Ted."

"How'd you hear that?"

"I just got off the phone with your friends Brogan and Mueller. They try to follow up whenever the prime suspect in an assault case goes to the hospital to terrorize the victim."

"I didn't terrorize Ted."

His voice was so heavy with judgment, I was surprised it could pass through the phone lines. "I *told* you not to go to St. Vincent's, dear. And you're not making this any easier on either of us. Please just come back to work, get rid of Frank, and leave the criminal acts to the criminals and the policework to the police. We'll all live longer that way. Now, where are you?"

"I'll be back to work in a while," I said, intentionally ignoring him. "I've just got one more little thing—"

"Andrew."

"But—"

"Andrew! For once in your miserable life, would you shut up and listen to me? You're digging yourself into a big hole, young man. And I'm not going to let you—"

I hung up on him and set off for the subway station.

I reached the oversized lobby of Frank's building—The Mercer—forty minutes after my call to him. The uniformed doorman ushered me to a black marble bench while he called upstairs for Frank's permission to let me into the building. When he got off the phone he said, "Mr. DiBenedetto is in twelve-twenty. The elevators are straight ahead and to the right."

I found the bank of elevators and took one up to the twelfth floor. When the doors opened, I stepped into a lavishly decorated hallway that put the simple, threadbare carpet in the hallway of my own building to shame. A carefully preserved antique writing desk and several overstuffed chairs were placed in a recess next to the elevators, and the walls were lined with decorative mirrors and richly detailed woodwork. I was most definitely out of my league.

I found 1220 and checked my profile in a mirror, taking care to push back a stray hair before knocking.

Seconds later, the door opened a crack and Frank's left eye and nose were visible.

"Did you come alone?"

"Of course."

The door swung open. "Come on inside."

I took a few steps into the small entryway and avoided looking at him, seeing only enough of him to know that he was freshly out of the shower and was every bit as beautiful in sweatpants and a ribbed tee with a damp towel slung over his shoulder as he was when he was fully dressed. I glanced at the walls, the ceiling, the floor . . . anywhere but at him. I was afraid that if our eyes met, I'd lose my determination to confront him.

I heard him close and lock the door behind me, then felt one of his hands gently grab hold of my shoulder.

"Do we have a problem?" he asked.

"Yeah," I said, looking, appropriately enough, at his closet doors. "I want to know what happened to Ted."

He didn't say anything. He just stood behind me, with his hand gently caressing my shoulder.

"I said . . ." I began, fighting back the strong urge to fall into his arms.

"I heard you." His hand let go of my shoulder and patted my back. "Let's go into the living room."

My entire apartment could have fit neatly within Frank's living room, with plenty of room to spare. An immaculate pale gray carpet, still showing the recent imprint of a vacuum cleaner, stretched out before me for fifty feet until it met the opposite wall, where a series of tall windows opened out onto a northern exposure under the fourteen-foot ceiling. The room was minimally if tastefully furnished, centered on the side nearest the front door around a black sectional sofa arranged around a glass-topped coffee table and, on the opposite side, around a solid dining table and even more solid hutch.

I couldn't help but admire the room. Hell, even David Carlyle would have been impressed. But still, it only served to stir up more questions in my mind. How could a twenty-nine-year-old who's supposedly sunk all his money into getting a club off the ground afford to live in a place like this?

"C'mere." He took my arm and led me to the window. "Take a look at this view."

I did. To the right, I could see a broad section of Central Park. Across the street was the Dakota, home to many of New York's rich and famous. It was a much better view than my slight glimpse of the subway entrance at Eighty-sixth and Broadway.

"See down there?" he asked, pointing at the Dakota.

"Yeah, I know. It's the Dakota."

"No, no." He jabbed his finger a few times for emphasis. "The driveway down there. That's where John Lennon got whacked."

Whacked? Well, *that* brought me back to reality. I spun around. "What happened to Ted last night?"

He took his eyes off the spot where John Lennon got whacked and trained them on me. "You tell me."

I wasn't in the mood to play games with him and made that clear in my voice. "Jesus Christ, Frank. Do you know what you've done?"

"Hey!" He raised a cautionary hand. "Don't blaspheme."

I felt control over my temper disappear and stormed around Frank's living room. "Don't blaspheme?! You had someone almost beaten to death, and *you're* telling *me* not to blaspheme?!! Jesus Christ!!! Jesus *fucking* Christ!!!"

"Hey!" he warned me again. "Stop that!"

But I was powerless to stop. I kept ranting, stringing together profanities and the names of every religious figure I could think of in a mindless, offensive, and mostly unintelligible stream of consciousness until, finally, I was too tired to continue and I wilted onto the couch, simmering wordlessly.

When my outburst was over, Frank looked at me from across the room and calmly, if unhappily, asked, "Are you through?"

I closed my eyes tightly and doubled over as the vision of Ted, at the same time swollen and withered in that bed in St. Vincent's Hospital, came rushing back to me. My voice sounded dead as I said, "I saw him, Frank. I saw him in the hospital. Oh, God . . . he's a mess. Why?"

"I told you, there are things you don't want to ask about."

I opened my eyes to erase the image of Ted. Across the room, Frank was leaning against a wall, studying the floor, rubbing his bare feet against each other nervously.

"Well, now this involves me, and I have to get some answers. The police came by to see me this morning. I'm involved in this, whether you like it or not."

At the mention of the police, he sighed deeply and looked off to some distant part of the room. "I did it for you, okay? I couldn't stand the thought that he hurt you like he did."

"So, that's why you asked all the questions about Ted." Everything was coming into sharp focus. "His last name . . . where he lived . . . and I gave you everything you needed to track him down."

"Yeah," he said, still not looking at me.

"And the scene in the diner . . . the coffee, the big tip . . . You wanted to make sure the waitress would remember exactly where we were when Ted was getting the crap beaten out of him, huh? So no one could say that either of us did it?"

"Yeah."

I shook my head and almost blasphemed once again but caught myself. Instead, in measured tones, I said, "The problem is that the guy you got to beat up Ted mentioned my name. He told Ted, 'This is for what you did to Andrew Westlake,' or something like that. So now the police *know* that there's a connection to me."

"Ah, shit." He finally looked at me. "I'm sorry, Andrew. I'm real sorry. It's just that Vince has this thing about letting people know the reason they're getting beat up. I should've told him to keep it to himself."

"No." I surprised myself with my calmness, which almost seemed out of place with the subject we were discussing. "I think you're still missing the point. You shouldn't have had Ted beaten up in the first place. No matter what he did to me."

Frank started to walk slowly across the room toward me, his head bowed in appropriate contrition. When he reached the couch, he held both his hands out to me. "It won't happen again. I'm sorry, but I . . . I . . ." He stopped and turned his head upward, struggling for words.

I took his hands in mine, then clasped all four together. Slowly his body started to sink down, until he was kneeling in front of me. And then, attracted like magnets, we both began to bend toward each other. He stopped himself when our faces were just inches apart and whispered, "I can't stand the thought of anyone hurting you."

And then our lips met. His hands broke free of mine and moved to my shoulders, and I felt him pulling me tightly against him. In turn, I knocked the damp towel off his shoulder as I wrapped my own arms around his hard, warm body, one hand bracing the back of his neck while the other found a shoulder blade to grab and pull toward me. And the kiss—for this was a single, prolonged kiss— grew even more passionate. His lips pressed feverishly into mine as our tongues probed deeply into each other's mouth. I felt my body start to melt into his; my skin scratch against his stubble; my penis start to stir . . .

And then Frank pulled away, and as suddenly as it had started, it was over.

"What am I doing?" he asked himself aloud, leaning away. "I— I—I'm sorry. I don't know what came over me. I mean . . . I *like* you and everything, but I'm not gay. So, we shouldn't do that."

I exhaled and slumped against the back of the couch, feeling the simultaneous effects of stimulation and rejection. Frank stood and nervously took a few steps back from the danger zone. "Okay, so I guess I should level with you about things."

"I *know* that you're straight," I said with boredom, even though I was being provided with ample evidence to reinforce my distinct doubts.

"I wasn't talking about that." He blushed slightly. "I meant about this, uh, *incident* last night."

"Oh." I wasn't really sure if I wanted to go through this anymore.

He absentmindedly ruffled his thick, curly hair with one hand and paced as he continued. "Did the cops tell you about my old man?"

"No. They don't know anything about you or your involvement. I didn't say a word about you." Then, playing dumb, I asked, "So, what about your father?"

"He's kind of involved in . . . um . . . some . . . um . . . *things.*"

"Things?"

"Things," he said again, pausing before adding, "Things that aren't necessarily considered totally legal."

"Oh," I decided to put an end to the charade. "So, what you're trying to tell me is that your father is in the Mafia."

His gut instinct was to deny it, but apparently he no longer felt the need to lie to me and fought it back, because his response came out as, "Nnnn . . . kind of."

"And are *you* in the Mafia?"

"*No!!!*" he said emphatically, without looking at me. "You've got to believe me!" When I didn't say anything, he added, "I mean, sure, I know some people. Like Vince. But only through my father."

He walked to the window. Despite the disgust I felt for this entire situation, I still caught myself watching his butt as he swaggered across the room, then admiring the rest of his body as he stood silhouetted in the light.

He stared out the window and held his pose for a short time before continuing. "I admit that my old man's money paid for the bar and this apartment, so I guess you could say that I haven't exactly gone out of my way to get out of the business. Not that it's all that easy, y'know."

Great. In less than four hours, I had gone from being a happy-go-lucky rising young writer to becoming a suspect in a brutal beating and a confidante to a young Mafioso. Regretfully, I decided that it was time to nip this friendship or relationship—or whatever it was—in the bud. Cute butt be damned.

"I've got to get back to work, Frank," I said as I rose from the couch.

"Will you call me later?" he asked softly, turning his face from the window.

"No." I startled myself with the harsh tone of resolution in my voice.

He turned again and looked out the window. "I see."

As I walked to the door, I glanced over my shoulder to see if he was following me . . . to beg me to stay . . . to promise to reform . . . to give up a life of crime and violence and run away with me to a small Midwestern town where no one would ever find us . . .

But he wasn't. It was only when I finally reached the door that I heard his voice, so muted that I almost missed it.

"Andrew?"

"Yeah?" I turned to face him.

"I'm . . . I'm sorry. For everything."

He was still looking out the window, so I couldn't see his face. But I saw that his shoulders were quivering.

"Are you okay?"

He turned slowly, and I saw that his face was streaked with tears. With a husky voice he said, "I'll be all right. I guess I really fucked things up, huh?"

Common sense told me that I should simply agree with him and leave, and never set eyes on him again. David and Denise would have certainly concurred. So would Brogan and Mueller. And Ted and Nicholas. And everyone else in the world, with the possible exception of Barry Blackburn.

Which is why I surprised even myself when I found myself slowly crossing the room, walking toward him, saying nothing harsher than, "Don't ever do that again."

"I did it for you."

"I know. But I can take care of myself."

He wiped the back of his hand across his wet eyes. "I don't know why I'm crying like this. I don't understand it. I shouldn't feel this way. I mean, you're a guy, and . . . well . . ."

"*I* understand it, Frank. And I think you do, too."

I put an arm around his shoulder and gently tucked his head against mine. I felt his hot breath against my neck as he asked, "Do you think I'm gay?"

"I guess the important question is, do you think you're gay? Maybe somewhere down deep inside of you, in a place you're afraid to acknowledge exists?"

"I don't know." His arms wrapped around me. "I never thought so before. But . . ." His voice trailed off, and I felt his tears dampen the side of my face.

I held him, rocking gently. "I hate to bring up one of those things I'm not supposed to mention, but if you want any help getting out of your engagement . . . well, I'll do whatever I can to help you sort out all this confusion. I mean, you said you didn't love her, right?"

"Right. But I still have to marry her."

"I don't understand. Just cancel the wedding."

"It's not that easy. Anna—that's her name—is the daughter of Tommy Franco."

"Who?"

He pulled his head back and looked at me with incomprehension. It was the same look that David had given me when he realized that I had never heard of Frank DiBenedetto Senior and the Stendardi family.

"Tommy Franco," he said again, slowly. "Crazy Tommy Franco. You never heard of him?"

I shrugged.

"Tommy Franco's a top *capo* in the Morelle organization. There's been a lot of bad blood over the years between Franco's family and the Stendardi organization, and this wedding is supposed to link the families."

"So, let me get this straight," I said, shaking my head in disbelief.

"You've got to marry this woman—a woman you don't love—so that two Mafia families will stop shooting each other?"

"Basically." He slipped out of my arms. "Also, they're thinking that if they can bring the families together, they'll have dominance of the—uh—business in the New York City area." He grabbed a tissue off an end table and dabbed at his red eyes, then said, "Wait here a minute."

Frank went into another room, and while he was gone all I could do was ask myself, once again, why I didn't leave when I'd had the chance to remain ignorant of the details.

When he returned, he was clutching a three-day-old copy of the New York *Post*. "Here," he said, opening the paper and pointing to a headline. "See what this is all about?"

The headline read BROOKLYN MAN DEAD IN BREWING MOB WAR.

"That was one of our guys." He pointed at the grainy black-and-white photograph of the recently deceased Brooklyn Man, not seeming to notice when I jerked my head at his use of the word *our*. "Things are starting to fall apart between the families. If I don't marry Anna, this city could blow up. Especially now that we're engaged. If I don't go through with it, Tommy Franco's gonna take it as a sign of disrespect. Do you understand why I have to marry her now?"

He folded the *Post* and wandered into the other room, returning almost immediately with a pack of cigarettes and a lighter clutched in one hand.

"I'm trying to cut down, but this seems like a good time." He fished a cigarette out of the pack and quickly lit it before he thought to ask, "Do you mind?"

"No," I replied, and reached for the pack. "In fact, I think I'll join you."

He handed me the lighter. "I didn't know you smoked."

"I quit five years ago. But cigarettes were made for moments like these."

My first drag off a cigarette in five years—well, technically only four years and ten months, but why be picky at a time like this?—was harsh but instantly rewarding, making my head spin in a pleasant way, as opposed to the unpleasant head-spinning I'd been experiencing for the previous several hours. The bunched-up muscles in my back and neck began to relax, and—at Frank's nod—I willingly followed him over to the dining table and took a seat across from him.

"So, what am I gonna do?" he asked me.

"I don't know. That's quite a choice you have: get married or be responsible for a mob war. This is sort of out of my field of expertise."

"And what if I'm gay? I mean, what if I'm really attracted to *you?*"

"I can't answer that for you," I said, trying to brush away a mental image of me as a mob wife. "That's something you have to answer for yourself."

"Yeah." He tapped his cigarette on the edge of the ashtray. "I'm just so . . . so . . . confused."

I started to take another drag off my cigarette but choked on the smoke. Apparently, the fun was over, so I snuffed it out. Then I got up and walked back over to the window, leaving Frank behind to brood alone at the table.

What was I doing? Everything—including my friends and my own common sense—was underscoring the obvious. I had no business being involved with Frank and Frank's world. I didn't understand it, I wasn't prepared on an emotional level to help him find his way out of the closet, and I didn't have any answers for him.

All I had was that visceral attraction to him that overwhelmed me, and some vague belief that love could conquer all, although I wasn't sure if it could conquer gunfire from semiautomatic weapons.

I looked out the window at the Dakota, to the spot where John Lennon got whacked. The crime scene was just outside one of the Upper West Side's most expensive addresses, seemingly out of place with its distinctive, eerie spires casting shadows across the generic neighboring apartment buildings. The crime victim was one of the world's best-known singers and songwriters, only forty when he was killed by one of those crazed fans who seem to pop up every few years.

It was violence, yes, but it was violence on an outsized scale. John Lennon had money, fame, prestige, respect, peace of mind, and the right address, none of which could stop one small, insignificant, deranged man from gunning him down in the shadows of those spires. And all of it happened thirty yards across the street and twelve stories below this window, where Frank and I were discussing routine mob murders, beaten accountants, dangerous men with absurd nicknames, and a marriage of convenience.

People walked by the murder scene—men and women, young and old, all races and nationalities and socioeconomic classes . . . All I could do was look at them and wonder, which one was a psychopath? Which one was going to wheel around, produce an AK-47 from under his or her coat, and start shooting at this window? Which one was going to beat up a gay accountant? Which one was going to try to push me in front of a subway train, not as an act of deranged admiration but as an act of anonymous brutality?

I didn't hear Frank approach, but I felt his presence behind me before he touched me. Then his arms delicately wrapped around me and he pressed his body into mine, nuzzling his head against my shoulder.

"I'll understand if you want to cut out," he said. "This whole situation's a mess, and it's wrong for me to drag you into it." Then he paused, and when his comments were met with silence, asked, "What are you thinking about?"

That's when I finally realized that the visceral attraction had won out over common sense. Which, I suppose, is the way that true romance is supposed to work.

I laughed lightly. "I was just thinking about John Lennon. He had everything, you know? Everything. And then it was gone, for no reason at all." I arched my neck to see his face. "That just goes to show that we don't have total control over our destinies. Even if we think we're safe—if we're rich and famous and happy and have a dozen people watching our backsides—something can come from out of left field and end it all."

"So, what are you trying to say?"

Still in his embrace, I slid my body around so that I was facing him. "I guess I'm trying to tell you that there aren't any safe answers . . . there aren't any magic bullets . . ." I faltered. Maybe that was the wrong term to use. But Frank seemed unfazed, so I continued. "If there aren't any guarantees—for *either* of us—then maybe we should take a chance."

"Together?"

"I'm not going anywhere. We'll find a way to get you out of this."

He smiled. It was the old ear-to-ear smile, the one that had first captivated me at the bar, dimpling his cheeks and squinting his eyes. He didn't say anything; he just pressed his lips against mine and kissed me, first gently and then with increasing passion. And I kissed back.

And then, quite slowly and quite unexpectedly, we melted to the floor still locked in that embrace, until we were lying side by side on the pale gray carpet. He slid my tie from around my neck and undid a few buttons on my shirt. I rolled him over on his back and slid his T-shirt up over his shoulders, exposing a flat, rippling abdomen and chiseled chest covered with dark curls.

I leaned over and gently stroked his chest, feeling the hair bristle beneath my fingers, and moved the gold crucifix he wore on a chain around his neck out of the way, reasoning that if there *was* a God, there was no sense further antagonizing Him in the wake of my extended bout of blasphemy. Then I discarded my own shirt and slid a leg over him, so that I was straddling his stomach. Beneath me, I felt his warm body shudder from nervousness and anticipation.

"Are you okay?" I asked tenderly.

He didn't answer but, smiling slightly, reached up and traced an unsteady finger across the left side of my chest until it came to rest briefly on my nipple, lingered for a moment, then followed a barely existent narrow trail of hair from my chest down my abdomen until it vanished under my belt.

"I'd like to try it," he said, straining to get the words out of his dry mouth.

I leaned forward until my stomach and chest pressed down hard on his warm body and I could feel the intense heat and stiffness under his sweatpants grind into my groin. My mouth reached his and, as we kissed, I moved a hand to the elastic band of his sweatpants, slipping it inside and then deeper until I felt his rigid penis.

At my touch, he trembled and his lips went dry. My free hand stroked his brow and I murmured a reassuring, "Relax."

"I'm okay," he whispered in a wavering voice.

I rose to my knees and pulled my pants and briefs down around my thighs. His eyes traveled immediately to my erection, and it occurred to me that this was almost certainly the first time Frank had ever seen another man's erect penis in real life. I took satisfaction in the fact that it was mine.

Then, without prompting, he arched his back and lifted his midsection off the carpet, and I gracefully slid his sweatpants down to his knees. I stopped only briefly when I realized that, as outsized as everything else was about Frank—his family, his apartment, his money, his problems, and his mysteries—his endowment was, to be charitable, just average.

And even *that* made him more attractive to me. It made him less intimidating and more human.

I glanced up at his face. His eyes were closed and his facial muscles were tensed. Again, I reassured him. Again, I asked him if he was all right. And again, he said that he wanted to do it.

And so, for the next hour or so, we did. And if I was already in love with Frank, I fell even deeper in love. I fell in love with the feel of his body . . . its taste . . . the curves of his muscles . . . the spot where he was ticklish under his scrotum . . .

And gradually, as Frank got used to the feel of a man's body entwined with his, he started to relax and participate. For a few brief moments he even took the more active role, during which he inexpertly took my erection into his mouth and raked his teeth over it, then yanked it with such force that I would have pulled away from him if I hadn't forced myself to remember that this was his first time, and it was with me, and therefore it was a privilege to be bitten and yanked by him.

Eventually, and with almost no warning, he ejaculated, sending a warm, almost clear, stream of semen across his stomach and chest. Kneeling over him, I came a short time later, and my own flow mixed with his, matting down the curls and streaking his bare skin.

It was only then that I noticed that his eyes were tearing over. I stretched down next to him and asked, "Are you okay?"

He turned his head to look at me and smiled. "It was great, Andrew. It was great."

I kissed him, pressing my bare skin against his. "I guess this means that now you're a 'made man.' "

He giggled and rolled his head from side to side, then, with a bit more darkness to his voice, said, "Oh, shit. What am I gonna do?"

"We'll be all right."

That's not what I was thinking, of course. I was thinking that if rich and famous people like John Lennon can get whacked for no reason, it could happen to me.

Frank's eyes were closed. I rolled my head onto his chest and listened to his heartbeat. It was the only sound in the room.

In fact, it was the only sound in the room for another five minutes . . .

Until it was interrupted by the scraping of a key in the front door lock.

5

Lawyers and Mobsters and Cops . . . and Me

So there I was, lying naked on Frank's living room floor. With Frank, who was also naked. And, even if there hadn't been any physical evidence that we had just had sex, which there was in abundance, no one in the world was going to believe that we were just getting in a few minutes of innocent Greco-Roman wrestling.

But still, neither of us panicked at the sound of the key in the lock. We just lay there, on the floor, naked, listening . . . almost as if it wasn't happening to us, but rather to characters in a movie we were only half-watching.

It wasn't until we actually heard the doorknob turn that the re-alization that someone was about to walk into the living room hit us. And by then it was too late.

Everything seemed to happen in slow motion. The door took forever to swing open, she took forever to walk into the entryway, and Frank took forever to whisper a drawn-out and barely audible "Anna" into my ear as a small, dark, attractive woman with big breasts and bigger hair finally came into full view.

And, of course, since we could see her, she could also see us, which she did before the front door was shut, which occurred with the same tension-inducing slow motion as it had opened, until it latched with a reverberating thud.

That's when everything started to speed up . . . most specifically my heart rate and blood pressure.

Anna Franco—the daughter of Crazy Tommy Franco, who, it was safe to assume, was a homicidal sociopath—stood in the entry-way and stared at the sight of two naked men who had very obviously just had sex, one of whom was her fiancé. In a harsh Outer Borough accent, she flatly asked, "What's goin' on here?"

It wasn't a very good question, since it was blatantly obvious what had been going on, but I'm sure that if I were in her place, I would have asked it, too. Theoretically, I suppose there was an outside chance that what seemed so obvious could have had a satisfactory and innocent explanation, although *I* couldn't imagine what that explanation could possibly be. Possibly something involving extra-terrestrials and probes.

Frank clearly was having no better luck than I was in coming up with a good response. So, we all just looked at each other for what seemed like hours.

I glanced at Frank. His wide-open brown eyes and sweat-beaded brow gave him the appearance of a trapped animal that had lost its ability to fight back. It was, I assumed, an appearance I shared.

Anna, though, stood calmly and coolly, taking everything in. Except when she subtly shifted her weight from one leg to the other or absentmindedly stroked the handle of the purse that was slung over her shoulder, only her eyes moved.

Finally, after what seemed like weeks, she spoke. "Are you some kind of *faggot*, Frank?"

Well, at least she got straight to the point.

"Anna . . ." His voice was raspy and soft, as if fear had rendered him almost mute. "I can explain . . ."

No, he couldn't, I thought.

"No, you can't," she said.

She stood there, arms folded, with a continuing calm that I would have thought unimaginable under the circumstances, until it suddenly occurred to me that she probably had the same icy control over her emotions that her father had when he was about to eviscerate someone and hang him on a meat hook. I did not find comfort in that thought.

"This is great," she said with a sneer, her emotions still under that icy control. "It's bad enough that I gotta marry you, but now I find out that you're a faggot. This is friggin' great."

"I'm *not* a faggot," Frank said harshly and instinctively, finally finding his voice, as if Anna had merely walked into the room and caught him listening to the original cast recording of *My Fair Lady* instead of laying naked, covered with semen, with another man.

"Oh. Then that's one ugly growth your girlfriend's got between her legs, Frankie."

I really didn't want the attention, so I tucked the ugly growth between my legs.

She stood there in the entryway for a few more seconds, still taking in the view, then—with a flip of her jet black hair—walked into the living room and tossed her purse onto the couch.

"The least you could do is cover up." We both obeyed, reaching for our clothes. It was an easy decision. At that point, I would have obeyed any command from her. I reasoned that I *might* stand an outside chance of living longer if I did.

She sat down on the couch and continued to watch us with a disconcerting dispassion as we hurriedly dressed. When I was almost done, missing only my tie and shoes, I quietly said to Frank, "Maybe I should go."

"You ain't goin' nowhere," Anna said, glaring at me. Frank—clearly stunned into speechlessness—stood wide-eyed and silent. "Who are you?"

It *did* occur to me that "Barry Blackburn" would have been an appropriate response, but I couldn't bring myself to lie to her because, deep down, I was afraid of what she'd do if she caught me lying. I imagined that it would be neither pretty nor painless. So, I settled for semi-anonymity. "Andrew."

"Andrew *who?*" She wasn't going to let me off that easily.

"W-w-w . . ." I took a deep breath and tried to concentrate on my last name, and finally was able to nervously utter, "Westlake."

She rolled her eyes, shook her head, and hardened her sneer into a frown. "The writer, huh? You're the guy who wrote that book Frank was reading?"

I nodded and she rolled her eyes again, then leveled her frown at Frank. "I shoulda known that something was wrong when I caught you reading a book. You are *such* an asshole, Frankie. You gotta go and use *my* father's store to sell your friggin' boyfriend's book. Unbelievable!"

"He's not my boyfriend," said Frank. "He's just . . . a *friend*."

That wasn't really something I wanted to hear, but under the cir-

cumstances, I tried to understand. Anna, however, felt no such
obligation. She almost seemed to take delight in prodding him.

"You suck dick with *all* of your friends, Frankie?"

That knocked any remaining wind out of him. He sank into a
chair and buried his face in his hands, surrendering to Anna's sarcasm and ceding total control over the situation to her and, to a far
lesser degree, me.

"Listen," I said to her, as I realized that—with Frank out of the
picture—my powers of persuasion would likely be the only thing
standing between Anna's spitefulness and a particularly grisly
death. "I think you should know that he's never done anything like
this before."

"Oh." Her quiet tone fooled me into a momentary belief that
maybe—*just maybe*—Frank and I still had a chance of living through
the weekend, until she continued. "Imagine my luck, walking in on
the two of you on the one and only occasion when you had sex.
Whaddaya think the odds are? Maybe it's a sign or something.
Today must be my lucky day. Maybe I should play the lot-
tery . . ."

"Well, it's true."

"Yeah, yeah, yeah." She dismissed me with a wave of her hand.
"How stupid do I look?"

Well, I obviously wasn't going to touch that comment. Plus, I
wasn't about to assume that she was the least bit stupid. Truly stupid people were most likely the ones who thought that her attrac-
tiveness and crude edges were an open invitation for them to take
advantage of her. She probably chewed up and spit out people like
that. And I didn't want to be chewed up and spit out.

So I said nothing more than, "You two have things to work out,
so I should go."

"You're part of the things we have to work out, so you're gonna
stay." Anna Franco made it clear that that part of the discussion was
closed. She paused, then ominously added, "*So far,* I'm not mad.
But you don't want to make me mad, Andrew. Trust me on this."

Oh, I did. I did, indeed. Obediently, I sat down and awaited her
next instructions.

She was quiet for a while, moving her eyes back and forth between me and Frank, snorting with contempt. I felt my chest tighten
at one point when she reached into her purse, but it was a nail

file—not a handgun—that she fished out. I was fairly confident that Frank and I could handle her if she tried to use it as a weapon.

"You really screwed up, Frankie," she said, now looking at her fingernails as the file sharpened them and mercifully not looking at either one of us. "I wasn't crazy about this wedding thing, and I know you weren't, either . . . Of course, now I know *why* you didn't want to get married. But I figured that we could both go through with it to try keep the peace, y'know? People have made bigger sacrifices. We coulda made it workable for us . . . made arrangements." She looked up at him. "You know what I mean, right? *Arrangements?* It's not like I don't know how to take care of myself." Her gaze traveled back to her nails. "But that ain't gonna happen now. I'm not gonna marry a homo. The Franco family name will not be humiliated. That's all I need, for everyone to be saying, 'Oh, there's Anna DiBenedetto, the one who's married to the fag.'" She paused again, and looked up from her nails. "No, that ain't gonna happen, Frankie."

Frank didn't quite take his head out of his hands, but rather peered over his fingers. "So, what are we gonna do? How do we *not* get married?"

She didn't answer him right away, but finished filing her nails. It was only after she dropped the file back into her purse that she once again fixed Frank with a serious stare. "Here's what *you're* gonna do, Frank. You're gonna break up with me."

"But, you know what'll happen then. The Morelles and the Stendardis . . ."

"I got news for you, Frankie. Everybody wants to be on top—*your* father, *my* father, all the rest of 'em—so there's *never* gonna be peace and harmony. All of 'em are just gonna keep trying to climb over everyone else, and it doesn't really matter if there's one big family or seven hundred little families. You and me getting married isn't gonna stop one person from getting killed. The best it's gonna do is delay things for a while. Make for a little temporary peace. But some day, everything will go back to normal." She laughed. "Who fed you that we'll-all-live-in-harmony line of bullshit, anyway? Your father? And you believed it? He probably just wanted to marry you off 'cause he figured out you were a fag and he didn't want anyone to know."

"You gonna tell anyone about this?" Frank asked nervously, gesturing at me. He seemed to be relieved to hear that, in Anna's opinion, he was absolved of responsibility for any future mob wars.

Anna stood and picked up her purse, letting Frank dangle for a moment. "You're gonna break up with me to go out with another girl. Maybe some people—like my father—will want to ice you, but I'll make sure you're protected. But *please* notice that I said *girl*, not *guy*. If I so much as hear about you even *speaking* to someone that even *looks* gay outside of your bar, I'm gonna tell. I'm gonna tell if I hear about anything going on *in* that bar, too. And trust me, I *will* hear about it if that happens." She paused briefly, letting her first set of instructions sink in, before continuing. "Then, after a while, you're gonna leave town. I don't friggin' care what you do with your dick after that, unless word gets back to New York, in which case I'm gonna tell everyone what I saw here today. And the first one I'm gonna tell is my father." An evil grin crossed her face as she added, "The second one I'll tell is *your* father . . ."

With that, she tossed her purse back over her shoulder and walked to the front door. Frank finally moved, standing and taking a few tentative steps to follow her, but she turned and said, "Don't bother. I can see my way out."

And then she was gone.

In her wake, we were statues: Frank standing . . . me sitting . . . neither of us moving or speaking . . . both of us watching the door and silently praying for the sudden appearance of a time machine that could take us back a half hour.

"Well," said Frank, when it became clear that the time machine wasn't going to materialize, "all in all, I think that went pretty well."

"Huh?" I said, incredulously. "What was it exactly that went well? I must have missed it."

Frank talked as he walked to the bedroom, and continued as he returned with his cigarettes.

"Let's put it this way, it could have been a lot worse. She could've called her father right away, for instance. Or—I dunno—she could've shot us right here on the spot."

"Okay. By those standards, it went well. I guess it's a good thing that our executions have been delayed. But still . . . what are we going to do? She made it pretty clear that she's not going to let us see each other."

"I don't know . . . I don't know." He slipped a cigarette out of the pack and played with it absently, until—in one sudden motion—he popped it into his mouth and lit it. I thought about joining him, then—prompted by the bitter taste that lingered in my mouth from the earlier cigarette—thought better of it.

For the next several minutes, Frank and I restlessly paced the living room in silence, urging ourselves to come up with a feasible solution to our disastrous problem. Occasionally, a thought would cross my mind, but Frank quickly quashed each one without bothering to go into details that I agreed were best left unsaid.

"We could change our names . . ."

"It's not that easy."

"We could move away . . ."

"It's not that easy."

"We could change our names *and* move away . . ."

"It's not that easy."

Finally, he stopped pacing.

"What?" I asked expectantly, hoping against hope that he had come up with an idea.

No such luck, though. He simply shrugged. "I guess we've got to do what she says. I've got to dump her for another girl and stay away from you."

"But—but—"

"There's no other way, Andrew." He slipped an arm around my waist. "I'm sorry."

Deep down inside me, I knew he was right. But I also knew that I was in love, and I had already made my peace with the sidewalk outside the Dakota, and I couldn't bring myself to give him up so easily. A thousand protests welled up inside me, but I couldn't find the words to articulate any of them, because none of them recognized the stark, cruel reality of our situation . . . the reality that the slightest misstep would almost certainly have very ugly consequences for both of us.

His arm dropped from my waist and he quietly moved across the room, away from me, not glancing back.

"I guess I'm gonna have to dig out my little black book," he said with a sad smile, once he was safely distanced from my physical presence. "If I'm gonna cheat on Anna, I'm gonna have to find someone—a girl—to cheat with."

I let out a sigh and turned to the window. Outside, the Dakota no longer called to me to pursue true love, no matter what risks were involved. Now, it just looked cold and forbidding.

"Wanna help me pick the girl?"

"No."

But then I was struck by an idea . . . a wonderful, exhilarating idea. "Wait a minute, Frank! Yes! I *will* help you pick out the girl!"

"No."

"But, Denise—"

"No."

"But—"

"*No!*" She screamed the word that time, punctuating her refusal by hanging up on me.

I had called Denise the moment I finally returned to my cubicle at the office, prioritizing the call to her above the stack of messages from David Carlyle demanding that I see him IMMEDIATELY. I gave her only the sketchiest of details—well, perhaps it would be more accurate to say that I gave her *no* details. I conveniently failed to mention Ted's beating or Anna's interruption or the police or anything other than the fact that Frank needed to date another woman in order to break off his engagement. But Denise remained unmoved. She made it clear that she was not going to pretend to date Frank DiBenedetto, no matter how much I begged, pleaded, or whined.

I decided to wait until that evening to ask her again.

Almost immediately after she hung up on me, I heard David loudly clear his throat behind me. "Which syllable in the word *immediately* don't you understand?"

"Sorry," I said, spinning my chair around to face him.

He was extremely unhappy with me, and underscored his unhappiness by picking up and sifting through the pile of messages he had left for me, tossing them one by one back on my desk.

"This has been a very bad day at PMC," he said, as the last of the messages fluttered onto my blotter. "I've got an author on a book tour—Glenda Vassar—who thinks she's having a nervous breakdown. Two of our authors have announced that they're signing with other publishers, a fact that I had to read about in *Publishers Weekly*. One of our major distributors is having union problems.

And—oh!—did I forget to mention that one of our editorial assistants has been missing for most of the day? It seems that he's decided to cavort with mobsters instead of doing his job. But I suppose that's okay, because there'd hardly be any room for him in the office, what with the place being full of police officers all day."

"I can explain," I said, even though I couldn't.

David looked around at the occupants of the other cubicles, all of whom were listening to us while they pretended not to, giving the normally noisy office a strangely muted atmosphere.

Then, in a quieter voice, not wanting to continue to air too much of my dirty laundry in front of my co-workers, he said, "I want to see you in my office in five minutes."

Five minutes later, I was sitting across the desk from David. As usual, it was cluttered with papers and copies of several freshly printed books, which gave me something to look at as I tried to avoid eye contact with him. David, on the other hand, stared at me, searching for something, then scowled. "You had sex with him, didn't you?"

I was prepared for an interrogation but not for that. Surprised, it didn't even occur to me to deny it. "How can you tell?"

"I can just tell." He shook his head unpleasantly. "It's a sad wisdom that comes with age. That was a big mistake, Andrew."

David didn't know how wrong—and right—he was.

"I hate to act like your surrogate father," he continued, "but it's become quite clear over the past few days that someone has to baby-sit you. Your judgment and self-control have disappeared altogether."

I started to protest. "Well, I don't think that's . . ."

He held up a hand to stop me. "It's not just because you've become obsessed with a gangster. It's not just because you're placing yourself in the middle of an all-out mob war. It's not just because your actions have already led to a near-fatal beating and God knows what else. Now you—*personally*—are in serious trouble with the police."

"But I didn't do anything!" I tried my best to affect innocence. Which—considering the fact that I *was* innocent—should have sounded more convincing.

"I know that you didn't do anything. But the police aren't as convinced as I am that you're a naive fool, rather than a dangerous criminal. Look at this from their perspective, Andrew. Ted was badly beaten, and there are indications that you're his assailant. You do, after all, have a motive. And then, what did you do? Against my strong recommendation, I might add. You went to his hospital room, which reasonable people could interpret as an attempt to intimidate him. And finally, after you were chased out of the hospital by his boyfriend—your rival—you didn't return to work for several hours, even though you knew that the police wanted to talk to you."

David paused for a moment; then, after burrowing through the new releases on his desk, he found what he was looking for and slid a newly published crime novel across the desk at me. "Read this. It's Margaret Campbell's latest mystery. It's very good . . . and it'll make PMC a ton of money. It's all about a person who's being relentlessly pursued by the police, who are convinced that he's a killer based upon a slew of circumstantial evidence."

"That's all this is, David. Circumstantial evidence. And weak circumstantial evidence, at that."

"Ah." He pressed his index finger against his lower lip. "That's why this book is so ingenious. Margaret's put an unexpected twist in her story." He leaned toward me and dropped his voice. "Her protagonist actually committed the crime."

"But I didn't commit any crime."

He picked up the book and displayed it. "Margaret's book is what real policework is all about, Andrew. Ninety-nine percent of the time, the circumstantial evidence doesn't lead to an innocent person . . . it leads to the perpetrator. And the guiltier—and stupider—you act, the more convinced the police will be that you were responsible for Ted's beating." He placed the book on my side of the desk. "Read it."

I picked it up and set it in my lap.

"Good boy. Now, since I hope I've convinced you that you have some very real problems, let's see if we can figure out what to do about them."

"What about the police?"

"Well, of course, I think you should tell them everything you know. But I know that you won't, so I won't insist. Frankly, that only leaves us with one option: We're going to have to get you a good lawyer."

"I can't afford a lawyer. Let alone a good one."

"You can't afford *not* to have a lawyer. Not now. I'll call Max Abraham—he's my lawyer—this afternoon and arrange a meeting for you."

"Max Abraham!" I gasped. "Isn't he a little bit . . ."

"Exclusive? Yes, he is. But because he and I are friends, I'm sure he'll be willing to take you on."

"Well, yes, he *is* exclusive. But I'm more concerned with how *expensive* he is. I can't afford . . ."

He stopped me. "Don't worry about the money. It's covered."

I shrugged to indicate my uncomfortable agreement with the relationship. If David wanted to retain Max Abraham for me, who was I to object? However, I still had a big question.

"What about the police?"

"At this point, now that you've done everything but stencil the words 'Please Arrest Me: I'm Guilty' across your forehead, I'd recommend that you not call them until you've had an opportunity to consult with Max."

David nodded, indicating that I was dismissed. He was angry, but I couldn't help noticing that he seemed to be getting a bit of enjoyment out of serving in loco parentis to me, the wayward son.

Acknowledging his dismissal, I rose from the chair, then asked him, "Is there anything else?"

"No. Not now. I'll phone down when I hear from Max."

"Okay, then," I said as I headed out the door. "See you later . . . Dad."

I didn't have to look back to know that the expression on his face was conflicted between exasperation and indulgence.

Two hours later, I met with Max Abraham.

I had heard of him, of course. Everyone who knew anything about the rich and famous and their legal problems knew of Max Abraham's reputation.

Max Abraham was a legal jack-of-all-trades. While that also made him a master of none, giving him a broad but relatively shallow range of legal knowledge, it also provided him with enough knowledge that, when coupled with a sharp, retentive mind and unlimited access to a myriad of experts and their expertise who could shore him up whenever he was out of his league, made him one of Manhattan's quintessential power lawyers.

He had made his name in the late seventies and early eighties, using his legal, business, and society contacts—he was a regular at Studio 54 when it was firmly at the center of New York's social life, and an intimate of celebrities, politicians, and business leaders—to get in on the ground floor of Wall Street's emerging flamboyance, then watched his career and reputation skyrocket with the stock market. But, while the stock market leveled off or dipped from time to time, Abraham's career never veered from its upward trajectory. After all, there were legal fees to collect in an overheated economy, and there were legal fees to collect when corporations, banks, and arbitrageurs went bust.

Max Abraham was made for the 1980s every bit as much as the 1980s were made for Max Abraham. And the nineties were treating him quite nicely, too.

Although his specialty—as much as he could call anything a *specialty*—was corporate and tax law, he had learned something that too many of his corporate clients had failed to learn, to their great regret when they later filed for bankruptcy: Diversity was the key to success. Therefore, Max Abraham's clients and cases were varied. The only things they seemed to have in common were that they were always in the news and they always garnered media attention for Abraham. Wall Street financiers who cheated on their taxes . . . congressmen on the take . . . victims of terrorist attacks . . . spoiled rich kids who took innocent lives . . . Max Abraham had his hands in a little bit of everything, and everything those hands touched turned into even more publicity and, therefore, even more money.

Of course, there's publicity and there's good publicity, and by the mid-eighties, the other partners in the stodgy white-shoe law firm he'd been associated with since 1968—before he started indulging himself with flamboyance and self-promotion—decided that Max Abraham was a little too colorful for their black-and-white firm. The buyout offer they made to him was extraordinarily generous, but he sued them anyway and ended up almost doubling it. To add insult to the injuries of his former partners, he opened an office directly across Lexington Avenue from them and, in his first year, almost equaled the old firm's revenues.

In short, Max Abraham was a very good lawyer. A *very* good lawyer.

Still, I approached the meeting with trepidation because, to the best of my knowledge, he was not known for discretion. Everything about his reputation was outsized and showy, and I felt no great need to see my name on the cover of the New York tabloids . . . especially since I was now certainly on Anna Franco's enemies list.

I wanted a very good lawyer. But I also desperately wanted to keep everything quiet.

And that's why my stomach was doing somersaults as I sat in his reception area late in the afternoon of the worst day of my life, idly flipping through a year-old copy of *Newsweek* and trying to ignore the copy of Margaret Campbell's book, *The Duct Tape Murder,* which was tucked out of sight in the folds of my coat.

The reception area was appropriately gaudy, and matched Max Abraham's reputation. There was something to look at everywhere my eyes wandered, although there wasn't always something *pleasant* to look at. The mismatched, though expensive, furniture cried out for an interior decorator to coordinate its confused mishmash of woods and styles, and the array of citations lining the walls—many of which seemed to be dubious honors from even more dubious organizations—were apparently framed in whatever do-it-yourself frame was on sale at the pharmacy on the week they were awarded.

Max Abraham was clearly the type of person who believed that each piece of expensive furniture went with every other piece of expensive furniture, and that frames serve a strictly functional purpose. He was certainly heterosexual.

In the middle of all this decorative chaos sat Abraham's bleached-blond secretary, perched at an ugly, yet practical, gray metal desk which was, if possible, even more out of place than the rest of the furniture. The effect was akin to that of an armored tank parked in the middle of an improbable forest made up of competing pine, maple, oak, chestnut, and cherry trees . . . with cheap frames hanging on them, of course.

I was spared further exposure to the reception area when, at our appointed time, Abraham promptly appeared at the door to his private office.

"Mr. Westlake?"

I nodded.

"Won't you step into my office?"

I was somewhat taken aback by how much older and quieter he looked, in contrast to the television and newspaper images I'd seen. Thick black eyebrows and thinning salt-and-pepper hair framed his somber face, and a dark suit added gravitas to an already grave countenance. Since I was expecting him to be something like an extremely affluent used-car pitchman, I took that as a good sign.

I grabbed my coat and the book, and he led me into his office. I was pleased to note that someone with taste and a sense of color coordination had been there before me. In this room, the wood was all a dark brown oak, which complemented a burgundy carpet. The walls, papered with a subtle and dignified pattern on off-white, served as the background for a number of tastefully framed awards and photographs. I tried not to stare, but I couldn't help noticing photographs of Max Abraham with Jacqueline Kennedy Onassis, Max Abraham with Golda Meir, and Max Abraham with the Pope displayed prominently.

"Nice office," I said, meaning it.

"Thank you." He brushed a thin strand of graying hair off his brow and moved behind his desk, motioning for me to take a chair. "Not quite my taste, but my wife insists on dignity. She's horrified by the reception area."

"Hmmph," I mumbled noncommittally.

"So, can I call you Andrew?" he asked, which seemed an odd formality, given our disparate social standing. I told him he could, and he told me to call him Max.

"In a bit of trouble, huh? Why don't you tell me about it."

And so, reasoning that my lawyer was the one person I shouldn't hold back with, I told him everything. My adventures as Belle Bacall brought a slight smile to his lips . . . my subsequent infatuation with Frank, whose family ties needed no explanation to him, brought a gently chiding "tsk" . . . Ted's beating brought one arched eyebrow . . . and, as I related my adventures of earlier in the day, his face became a mask of deep concern.

And that was *before* I mentioned Anna's interruption. Which, of course, I did.

"Ho-boy," he muttered, closing his eyes as I told him about Anna's ultimatum.

"Bad, huh?"

His eyes opened and he again swept his hair from his brow. "You could say that, Andrew. You sure managed to land in the middle of some deep trouble."

"But can you get me out of it?"

He drummed his fingers on the desktop, studying them with his eyes . . . thinking. When he finally spoke, he chose his words carefully.

"The first thing you're going to have to accept is that Frank DiBenedetto Junior is off-limits to you from now on. Don't go near him and don't call him . . . and don't let him come near you or call you. Every single problem you've got is only going to get worse if you're seen with him. If the police don't find out and ID you as a mob associate first, you can bet your life that Tommy Franco or his daughter will find out about the two of you. And if *they* don't get you, then Frank DiBenedetto Senior probably will. Take my advice, Andrew. Right now, they're all probably watching you, and they're all waiting for you to make one mistake."

"Okay."

"Now, about this beating . . ."

"I didn't do it," I said, too quickly and too defensively.

"I know that," he said calmly, doing his best to reassure me. "But you know who did. And if Ted Langhorne for some reason didn't actually see his assailant . . . or thinks that you hired someone to beat him up . . . or decides to lie and say that it was you, you've got a big problem."

"But I've got an alibi!" I was momentarily surprised to hear how guilty those words could sound, even when spoken by an innocent man.

"Well, you do and you don't. You told them, 'I was in the diner at such-and-such a time,' right?" I nodded. "Well, they're going to check and find out that's the truth . . . but they're also going to find out that someone else was there with you, and then they're going to want to know who that other fellow was. And you can't tell them, can you? Because if you do, you're going to bring attention to DiBenedetto and the rest of the mob, and that would be a very bad thing to do. So you're going to have to have a lapse of memory when they ask you who you were in the diner with. In all fairness, though, I have to point out to you that the police don't tend to view that sort of forgetfulness very innocently. In fact, I think it's fair to say that it will move you straight to the top of their list of suspects, if you're not there already . . . which you probably are."

I felt sick. As Max Abraham was brilliantly pointing out, there was no easy way out of this mess. In fact, it was starting to occur to me that my best bet for survival might be to confess to Ted's beating and hide out in prison for a few years until things blew over.

"So, what should I do?" I hoped that he would see more options than I did, and not recommend confessing.

"First and foremost, stay away from DiBenedetto. Next, now that I've already recommended what you should tell the police, I'm going to strongly advise you not to say anything to them unless I'm present."

He rose, signaling an end to our meeting. As I gathered up my coat and the book, he smiled. "Third, get a good night's sleep. You're going to need it."

I gave him a wan smile and was about to leave when he stopped me.

"Is that the new Margaret Campbell book?" he asked, spotting *The Duct Tape Murder* poking out of my pocket.

"Yeah."

"I saw the review in the *Times*. It sounds pretty good. I heard that she wrote it all from the perspective of a guilty man." He paused, then uncomfortably added, "Uh . . . I hope that wasn't a spoiler for you."

"No, I knew that. But what happens at the end? Do the police catch up with him?"

He placed a hand on my back, gently escorting me toward the door. "Does it matter? It's just fiction."

I shrugged and shuffled out of his office.

Fiction, indeed.

David Carlyle and Max Abraham had both advised me that the absolute last thing I should ever do again in my life was to contact Frank. But that was easy for them to say; they weren't in love with him.

I walked home through the crisp air and surprisingly quiet city streets. Given the amount of work that was piling up on my desk, I should have hailed a cab and returned to the office, but—in light of Max Abraham's highly sought-after legal advice—I needed some time to think for myself.

Even in my darkest days—for instance, when Ted left me—I've taken pride in seeing myself through crises and working things out. And this was a crisis in which a lot of things needed to be worked out.

Intellectually, I realized that there was nothing right about my relationship—or whatever it was—with Frank. It made no sense. He was the son of a mobster, recently engaged to the daughter of another mobster. If he wasn't just dabbling in homosexuality, he was certainly deep in the closet. He had repaid Ted's sin of the heart with disproportionate violence. My friends didn't approve. And on top of all of that, I had only known him for a few days.

Emotionally, though . . . Well, that was another story. On that level, Frank felt right, just as Ted had a few years earlier. Which I probably should have interpreted as a warning sign, but didn't.

I just couldn't get past the thought that, for all his negatives, Frank seemed to be a good fit for me. He had opened up to me, showing me his vulnerabilities. He had taken a genuine interest in me and, not incidentally, my work. I had been the first man he'd ever kissed, held, made love to . . .

And I couldn't deny that there was a measure of excitement being with Frank. Ted and so many other men before him had been safely predictable until the moment they left me, but no one would use those words to describe my relationship with Frank.

The question was, did we have any chance of making it as a couple? Or was Frank going to slip back into his closet before we had the opportunity?

When Max Abraham had told me to cease all contact with Frank, the first thing that ran through my head was that that would be impossible. So of course I was on the phone with him moments after letting myself into my apartment.

"Find me a woman yet?" he asked when he heard my voice.

"Not yet," I said, vividly remembering Denise's refusal of my perfectly reasonable request. "But I'm working on it."

"Get me a blonde."

"I don't know if we're in the position to be picky." I heard him mutter an agreement.

I had called Frank, fully intending to fill him in on my conversation with my lawyer, but—as I talked to him and felt comforted by the sound of his voice—I decided not to upset him with the expensive advice that I had already ignored. Instead, I tried to stay focused on us, together, and to block out the harsh reality that was bogging us down with every passing minute. That reality would be with us soon enough . . . as soon as we hung up our phones and were alone and apart once again.

We made small talk for a while, conspicuously avoiding any talk of Anna and Ted, until he started to close the conversation.

"I'd better get going. I should get down to the club."

"Oh, right."

"I don't think . . ." His voice faded off, then came back again. "I don't think it'd be a good idea for you to come down to Benedick's tonight."

"No," I agreed.

"I hope you don't mind . . ."

"No. Under the circumstances, I think I should keep my distance."

"Sorry," he said, genuinely apologetic. "But we'll . . . we'll get together soon."

"Sure." I felt the rapid onset of reality approaching.

We both said a quick, but sad, good-bye and hung up. I called Denise almost immediately.

"Oh, it's you," she said coldly when she heard my voice. "Are you calling to talk to me, or are you just pimping for another criminal? Gee, Andrew, do you think you could set me up with Charles Manson?"

"Knock it off. I'm sorry you were so put out that I asked for one little favor."

" 'Little favor.' You want me to be Mrs. Al Capone, and you consider it a 'little favor.' "

"Sorry."

She let my apology float for a moment until she halfheartedly accepted it. Then, she asked, "So, if you aren't calling to fix me up with your boyfriend, why *are* you calling? Could it be, perchance, that you called me just to talk, like we used to do in the days B.F.?"

"B.F.?"

"Before Frank. I've now found a new way to date things. B.F. signifies the historic time period when you and I had a close friendship and talked and did fun things, and A.F.—After Frank—signifies the current time period when I never hear from you unless you need something because you're too busy hanging out with the Goodfellas."

"Very nice. Is that any way to talk to your best friend?"

"Is that what I am? Well . . . okay, then. Why do you want to get together? To talk?"

"Yeah. I just need to talk to someone."

"Oh, thanks," she groaned.

I struggled to correct myself. "No, not 'someone.' You."

"That's better. Have you eaten yet?"

"No," I answered, realizing that at least some of the queasiness in my stomach was probably because I hadn't eaten all day. "How about dinner?"

"I thought you'd never ask. How about I meet you in half an hour at Renaldo's?"

I agreed to meet her.

No sooner had I hung up the phone than I heard a firm knock on my apartment door. Through the peephole, I saw a tall, well-dressed man in his mid-thirties with a fast-spreading case of male pattern baldness. In short, he looked like almost any of my fellow tenants.

"Yeah?" I asked, calling out through the closed door.

"I'm from down the hall." A very reasonable answer, considering that I knew none of my neighbors. "Someone dropped off a delivery for you."

I unlatched the dead bolt and unhooked the chain but barely had a chance to turn the knob when the door was kicked open. I reeled into the back of the couch as the man—mercifully alone, and even more mercifully burdened with a large and obviously heavy box—pushed into the apartment.

"You Westlake?" he asked harshly.

"Yeah," I said breathlessly, too terrified to try to lie. "That wasn't very neighborly. Which apartment did you say you lived in—?"

Without a word, he hurled the box at my chest. I tried to raise my arms to deflect it, but the box scored a direct hit, knocking the wind out of me and raising what in the morning would be a large, dark bruise. After it bounced off me, it fell to the floor and spilled its contents . . .

Roughly twenty copies of *The Brewster Mall.*

As I leaned against the back of the couch, in total confusion and more than a little terror, the man stepped back into the hall, leaned down and to the side, and produced yet another box. I cringed, but this time he merely dumped the contents of the second box—the same as the first box—on the floor.

"What's . . . ?" The pain from my chest when I tried to speak stopped me in mid-question, and I was afraid he had fractured a rib or two. I took a few shallow breaths to regain some lung capacity, then croaked out, "What's the matter? You don't like my book?"

He didn't try to mask his contempt. "Miss Franco don't like your fuckin' book, asshole. In fact, she don't like you. So, you're outta Hanover's, understand? They don't want your fuckin' book, and if I ever see you in there in person, I'll kick your ass. Got it, faggot?"

"But . . ."

"Nobody treats Miss Franco that way. Or else they answer to me."

So, this was it. The moment I had been dreading. The moment when the dam burst and my whole life was going to be destroyed by the flood. And all I could think to do was ask, "How'd you get past the doorman in the lobby?"

He rolled his eyes, sneered, and backed out into the hall, slamming the door behind him without an explanation. Not that I expected one.

Shaken, in pain, and scared, I sank to the floor and sat in the uneven heap of discarded copies of *The Brewster Mall.*

This had been a very bad day.

And the thought never even crossed my mind that the worst might be over.

As I was leaving the building to meet Denise, the doorman— usually surly, but smiling this evening—had the audacity to tip his hat, hold the door for me, and wish me a pleasant evening. Since my bruised chest and possible internal damage left me ill equipped to give him the tongue-lashing he so richly deserved for letting the goon into the building, I just waved him off and made a mental note to consider the bribe the goon probably gave him as his Christmas tip from me. If I was still living then, that is.

I slowly and painfully walked the block to Broadway, then three blocks north to Renaldo's, a shabby Old World Italian restaurant that thankfully hadn't become yet another sterilized chain like most of the other restaurants on that stretch of Broadway. In the not-so-distant past—B.F., if you will—Renaldo's had served as the neutral center of my friendship with Denise. It was four blocks from my apartment and two blocks from her apartment down West Eighty-ninth. And it had good food at low prices, low ceilings, casual ambiance, and a jukebox overflowing with Frank Sinatra records.

Denise was waiting for me when I walked in, casually sipping a glass of white wine at the long, nearly empty bar. Sinatra, of course, was singing in the background.

"Christ almighty," were the first alarmed words out of her mouth as I hobbled into Renaldo's. "What happened to you?"

I leaned against the bar, grabbing a few more of those precious shallow breaths that I was learning through painful experimentation were the only kind my chest and lungs would allow. Finally, I was able to talk, though each sentence required a few pauses for fresh air.

"Well . . . remember how I told you . . . that Frank needed to find . . . a new girlfriend . . . so he can dump Anna?"

"Yeeeeeah." She knew something was coming, and she already knew she didn't like it. "So, what does this have to do with you not being able to breathe?"

"Well, I sort of . . . forgot to tell you a few things. Anna . . . She walked in on me and Frank . . . this afternoon."

Her jaw dropped. "Oh, you didn't!"

I nodded.

"Oh, Andrew, you *idiot!*" She slapped her hand against her forehead and leaned forward until her nodding head was propped up by her arm against the bar. "I don't believe this!"

I let Denise continue with her series of head flips and eye rolls while I ordered a drink, then turned to her. "Well, it happened . . . and it can't be undone. Anyway, that's when she . . . gave Frank the ultimatum. That's why I called you."

"Oh, thanks a lot." I started to protest my good intentions, but she was on a sarcastic roll. "No, no, Andrew, I really mean it. Thanks for trying to put me in the middle of a Mafia shoot-out. Friends like you are hard to come by. I mean, isn't it every girl's dream to steal a mobster away from his psychotic mobster girlfriend?" She fluttered her eyelids. "Oh, I would have been so happy!"

"Are you through?" I asked sourly as my drink arrived. Gingerly, I slid myself up on a bar stool and managed to sit without too much pain.

"For now. To be continued."

"Good. Because I'm really not in the mood. The police want to talk to me . . . about Ted."

"*What* about Ted?"

Oops. I really hadn't wanted to tell her about Ted's beating . . . at least, not until I was in shape to physically defend myself. But now I had to tell her.

So I did. And, as I expected, she didn't take the news well.

"He didn't mean . . . for everything to blow up on me."

Denise was rapidly losing what little calm she had left. "This is . . . this is insane, Andrew! You've got to go to the police!"

"I can't," I wheezed. "Abraham says I shouldn't tell them anyth—"

"Abraham? Who's Abraham?"

"My lawyer."

"*Max* Abraham?"

"Yeah."

Her face displayed a variety of emotions, chief among them dismay. "Max-Abraham-the-Biggest-Lawyer-in-New-York? Are you telling me that you're in so much trouble that you have to hire Max Abraham to dig you out of it?"

"Well . . ." Well, I was, after all. "Sort of."

"Good God, Andrew. I don't believe this." She picked up her almost-full wineglass and drained it in one gulp, then waved for the bartender as she continued. "Okay, let me see if I've got everything. Frank's fiancée walked in on the two of you, the police think you beat up Ted, you retained Max Abraham—where are you getting the money for Abraham, by the way? He's not cheap."

"David. He's his lawyer."

"Oh, good. David Carlyle to the rescue. I guess that means a lifetime of indentured servitude to Palmer/Midkiff/Carlyle, huh?"

I shrugged. To me, *lifetime* was becoming a very ill-defined term.

"And, to top it all off, you got roughed up. By the way, are you finally going to tell me what that was all about?"

"Right after I got off the phone with you . . . someone came to my door. He was from Hanover's . . . Book Store . . . and he started throwing boxes of my books at me."

Denise surprised me by smiling.

"You're kidding, right?" she asked, unsure whether or not she should believe me. "A man didn't really come to your door and start throwing boxes of books at you, did he? I'm mean, that's just so . . . so . . . *bizarre!*"

"He did. But you have to understand . . . that Hanover's is a mob operation . . . and Crazy Tommy Franco—"

"Crazy Tommy Franco?"

"Yeah," I said. "Anna's father."

"Oh, good Lord . . ."

"Anyway, she must have gone back . . . and started spouting off about me and Frank . . . and that's why they pulled . . . all my books out of the store."

"Oh, good Lord . . ."

It was then that a sudden, frightening thought hit me. "That means . . . that Frank's in danger, too!"

My instinct—my *only* instinct—at that moment was to get word to Frank. I jumped off the bar stool too quickly and felt my chest constrict as a sharp pain shot through it. Gasping for air, I leaned against the bar.

"Andrew, what are you doing?"

Between painful breaths, I gasped, "I've . . . got to . . . get to . . . Frank . . ."

"You can't. It's too dangerous."

"But . . . if . . . Anna . . . told them . . ."

She put her arm around me and gently moved me back to the stool. As she did, I tucked my head into my shoulder, trying to stifle the pain in my chest.

And that's when I caught a glimpse of the book-throwing thug through Renaldo's front window, watching the front door of the restaurant from a bench on the traffic island between the northbound and southbound lanes of Broadway.

"Oh, God!" I jerked away from Denise.

"What is it?" She pulled back, afraid that she had hurt me.

"It's . . . it's him." I dug my fingernails into the bar, trying to stem the pain. "The guy who . . . who threw the books."

"Where?"

"On the bench . . ."

She stole a glance over her shoulder. "Which one?"

"The tall . . . balding guy . . . in the suit. Don't let him . . . see you. He must have . . . followed me . . ."

"I see him. Hmm. Not bad looking. He certainly doesn't look like a criminal." She turned back to me. "Are you sure he's the guy?"

"Yeah, that's the guy. What, do you think I'd just . . . throw open my door to John Gotti?"

"Take it easy. I just wanted to be sure."

"I've got . . . to get to Frank . . ."

"Stay here. He'll be fine. This is the sort of thing that's right up his alley. Guns, fistfights, flying cartons of books . . . Let Frank take care of himself."

"Call him." I grabbed a cocktail napkin and scrawled out the number to Benedick's. "Just call him . . . for me."

She bit her lower lip and looked at me, and I could tell that she found this assignment only slightly less offensive than she found the idea of dating Frank that afternoon. But seeing my evident pain, desperation, and fear, and looking once again at the thug watching me from halfway across Broadway, she grudgingly took the napkin and walked to the pay phone at the other end of the bar.

Less than a minute later she was back, with an unhappy yet resigned look on her face.

"They said he's not taking calls tonight."

"Oh, shit. Did you tell them . . . that it was important?"

She nodded.

"What am I going to do?"

"Calm down," she said gently. "You're just getting yourself all worked up. Frank will be all right."

"I've got to . . . let him know . . ."

She leaned toward me, closely examining my face.

"You're really starting to worry me." Then, she sighed deeply and shook her head. "I should really have my head examined. There's something almost as wrong with me as there is with you. I cannot believe what this Frank of yours is getting you—correction: *us*—into, but you better believe he's going to hear about it from me."

"What are you talking about?"

She grabbed her purse from the bar. "You really owe me for this one, Andrew."

"What?" I still didn't understand what she meant.

"Your wish came true. I'm going to Benedick's to see Frank. If I'm not back in forty-five minutes, call the police."

Without waiting for a response, she was out the door. She didn't look back as she stepped to the curb and hailed a cab.

As Denise climbed into the cab, I lost sight of the goon behind the passing traffic that filled the intersection. I started to panic, nearly convincing myself that he was following her, until the light changed and Broadway cleared. Then he was back in sight, still sitting on the bench on the traffic island.

I decided to wait an hour before I called the police, if it came to that. I knew how Manhattan traffic could be. And when the hour came and went, I added another fifteen minutes. I really didn't want to get the police involved if I could avoid it.

In any event, the bartender didn't seem to mind my somewhat distracted company and the goon certainly didn't seem to be going anywhere, so I leaned my aching body against the bar, sipped a few glasses of wine, and worried about Frank and Denise and what was going to become of me, as a Sinatra soundtrack appropriately accompanied my thoughts.

It was during this time, spent all alone in the deserted bar of a quiet restaurant, watched over by an underworld thug as I waited for Denise Hanrahan to return safely, that the out-of-control nature of my day started to sink in and I realized that I was no longer a normal person. Normal people didn't spend their days hiding from the police, having sex with the offspring of mob *capos*, and having cartons of books thrown at them by assailants. Normal people weren't confronted by the daughters of men with nicknames like Crazy Tommy, nor did they consult with Manhattan's most high-profile lawyer. Normal people didn't terrorize their ex-lovers in hospital rooms.

And normal people didn't entangle other normal people in their abnormal lives. But that's exactly what I was doing to Denise and, to a lesser extent, David. I was infecting them with my abnormality, pulling them into the undertow of my life just as surely as Frank had pulled me into the undertow of *his* life.

I glanced at the dusty clock over the dusty bar and realized that Denise's second fifteen-minute extension was drawing to a close.

When she breathlessly pushed the door open seconds later, we greeted each other with a delicate hug and sighs of wordless relief.

"Did you know," she said, as she flopped down on the stool next to me and signaled for the bartender, "that they didn't want to let me in because I'm a woman?"

"Barry Blackburn must have been holding another one of his Misogyny Nights," I said disappointedly. "So, you weren't able to get to Frank?"

She gave the bartender her order, letting me dangle for a moment, then smiled. "Of course I got to Frank! Betty Bacall's not the only drag queen in town, child!"

"It's Belle," I said by rote, before her words sunk in and I started to roar with laughter. "You told them—?"

She joined in, laughing and quite pleased with herself. "Uh-huh. Meet DeeDee Licious!"

Denise spread her arms out dramatically, then tilted her head forward in a silent bow as the bartender set down her drink.

"Well, as drag names go, it needs work."

"Says who? Belle Bacall?"

"Okay, okay. So, did you see Frank? Did you tell him?"

At the mention of Frank's name, she snapped back to reality. "Oh. Yes, I did."

"And . . . ?" I asked gently, trying to coax a few more words out of her.

She bit her lower lip and looked at the floor. It was one of her easy-to-read nervous habits, and it meant that she was about to confess a personal shortcoming. I decided to give her time—not *too much* time, but time—to unburden herself.

Finally, she said, "I hate to admit this"— which, of course, I already knew —"but I think I'm getting to like him. A little."

"Who?"

"Frank." Before I had a chance to comment on her turnaround, she rushed to add, "Oh, I'm still not exactly a fan of his, and I still hate what he's done to your life, but . . . I suppose I can see how someone could find him charming."

"Well, I'm surprised. What brought this on?"

"It started when he laughed when I told him how I convinced the bouncer that I was a man in drag. Then, when I told him what happened to you, well . . . he was so concerned. And it wasn't bullshit, Andrew. He was *really* concerned."

I should hope so, I thought, but left it unsaid. "I'm glad you got to see the real Frank the way I've come to see him. He's a really sweet guy."

"For a mobster," she added. "Speaking of which, the guy that's out there watching you is Paulie Macarini. They call him Big Paulie."

"I know that name," I said, searching my memory until I remembered where I had heard it. "He was the guy who answered the phone the other day at Hanover's, when I was looking for Frank's phone number. But how do *you* know who he is?"

She smiled slightly. "Frank told me."

"Huh?"

"We shared a cab uptown. I pointed out Big Paulie when we turned the corner."

"You mean—? Where is he?"

She glanced around the room, confirming that there were no eavesdroppers. "He's hiding out at my apartment right now."

"Well, let's go," I said impatiently as I pushed away from the bar.

She grabbed my elbow. "Not so fast, Andrew. I don't want that Big Paulie creep following you back to my apartment."

"Well . . ." She was right, of course. It seemed that everyone was right lately, other than me. "So, what do we do?"

"I have an idea," Denise said, and she started to whisper in my ear.

Big Paulie Macarini shadowed me back to my apartment building. After I was safely double-locked and bolted inside, I closed the blinds and peered out the corner of the window, easily spotting him leaning against a building across Amsterdam Avenue. Waiting for me.

Twenty-five minutes later I left my building, taking care to cross

the intersection of Eighty-sixth Street and Amsterdam Avenue opposite from where he had positioned himself, but otherwise taking
no special precautions. I casually walked down Eighty-sixth Street,
crossed Broadway, and proceeded two more blocks until I reached
the western edge of inhabited Manhattan at Riverside Drive, with
only an occasional glance over my shoulder—which is a natural
New York act of self-preservation—to make sure I wasn't being followed. I turned right, then briskly walked three short blocks to
Eighty-ninth Street, turned the corner at the yeshiva, and rang the
buzzer at the entrance to Denise's brownstone. She buzzed back,
and the door unlocked.

"You look good," she said when she greeted me at the door to
her apartment.

"Thanks. Worked like a charm."

Frank was sitting on the couch in Denise's sparsely furnished living room. When I walked into the apartment, he looked up at me
and smiled. It was that ear-to-ear smile, and I melted.

"Let me introduce you," Denise said, as she closed and bolted
her door. "Frank DiBenedetto, I'd like you to meet Belle Bacall."

"I didn't think I'd be seeing you in a dress again," he said, standing.

"Don't get used to it." I was already starting to peel off those
pieces of my costume that could be easily peeled off. "The good
news is that Big Paulie never noticed a thing."

As I continued performing my modified striptease, Denise grabbed
her purse. "Okay, I'm out of here. Don't wait up for me."

"Where are you going?"

"Hey! We're in the city that never sleeps, right? I've got options."
With that, she was out the door.

I looked at Frank. "So, I guess it's just us, huh?"

"Yeah."

My dress fell over my hips to the floor, and—despite the fact that
I knew I looked ridiculous in light makeup, a padded bra, and gym
shorts, standing in the middle of the living room with a dress around
my ankles—I leaned forward to kiss him.

"It's been a long day," I said quietly as we slid onto the couch,
gently holding each other. "Would you mind helping me unhook
my bra?"

"Not at all." He unhooked it, and once the bra was off, I covered
up with a T-shirt Denise had thoughtfully left for me, the thought-

fulness only tempered by my realization that the shirt was originally mine.

I smiled at him. "So . . . here we are again."

He didn't reply, but held one finger to his lips to silence me as he walked to Denise's CD player. With the touch of a button, the opening notes of "How Deep Is Your Love" came out of the speakers.

"May I have this dance?" he asked, offering his arm. And of course I said yes.

6

Adventures on the Other Side of the Point of No Return

Later, we kissed for a while; first gently and tentatively, then passionately and with urgency. I pulled him tight against me, feeling his cotton shirt crinkle against my now naked chest as my hands gripped his back. The stubble on his jaw scraped faintly against mine; his lips—at first, dry and tense—relaxed in time and became warm and moist.

"I like this," he said, smiling shyly.

"Well, if you liked *that* . . ." My hand groped for his zipper.

Frank let me start—I had his pants unzipped and was sliding my hand through the opening—but then he suddenly stopped me, grabbed my wrist, and nervously gasped, "No. Wait."

"What?" I tried my best to sound harmless and reassuring, rather than frustrated.

"I thought I heard something." His neck strained upward as he tried to find an out-of-place sound in the silence.

"I didn't hear anything. What are we listening for?"

"I don't know. But I don't want to get us killed." Well, *that* was a sobering and decidedly unromantic thought. "What if they know that we're here together?"

"They don't."

"But what if they do? What if you were followed? Or I was followed? Then what?"

"I'm sure we weren't followed." I started to inch my hand back up his thigh. "But if we were, then it's too late to worry about it now."

He brushed away my hand and stood, and I could only guess what thoughts were racing through his head. He did, after all, have far more experience than I did in these matters. As he paced the small room, he tried unsuccessfully to articulate his dark thoughts.

"This is . . . it's very dangerous," was one of his wordier comments.

"But we've crossed the point of no return. We crossed it when—" I almost said "I fell in love with you," but instead wisely said, "Anna walked in on us."

When, exactly, we had crossed the point of no return was largely academic, of course. The fact was that we *had* crossed it. Big Paul Macarini, probably still leaning against the storefront across Amsterdam Avenue from my apartment building, was clear evidence of that.

We had crossed it just as certainly as I had crossed the point where my feelings for Frank were more than an infatuation. It didn't matter to me that falling in love with him defied reason. Ted Langhorne and too many other men had been *reasonable* partners, and where were they now?

I watched him pace, full of raw energy, and knew that I was right to defy reason. Others might not understand, but they weren't there when Frank confronted urges he had long suppressed. They hadn't seen the expression on his face after his first experience with a man. They could only see Frank's façade; I had been invited inside.

The precise moment didn't matter. We had reached the point of no return, and we had crossed over.

He paced some more, then without a word, reached across me and turned off the reading lamp.

"Atmosphere?" I asked hopefully.

"I want it dark." There was an edge to his voice that strongly suggested his upbringing and the family business.

Frank made a sweep of the apartment and didn't stop until every light was extinguished. By the time he finished, the only illumination came from the streetlight outside, filtered through the battered wooden shutters, and when he crept up to the window overlooking West Eighty-ninth Street, I *did* briefly fear that he was going to shoot out that light, too. But instead, he stood off to the side of the window, searching the shadowy street for the tail we both hoped wasn't there.

"Do you see anyone?" I asked.

"No. But maybe I'm not supposed to."

"That Big Paulie guy didn't try to hide himself from me."

"That's the difference." He turned from the window and gave me an extraordinary, almost artistic, glimpse of his handsome face, half-hidden in the darkness. The pale light illuminated his cheekbones, as it hid the hollow beneath them in the shadows, and it sparkled off his bright eyes. "You were supposed to see him, so you'd be scared off. But with me . . . I don't think scaring me off is what they have in mind."

"*If* they're following you."

"Yeah," he replied, unconvinced. "If."

And so he stood at the side of the window, looking for something that neither of us knew was there but that, if it was, would be very bad.

And that didn't really put either of us in a lovemaking mood.

No matter how tense or nervous or excited or even horny a person is, there's only so much interest one can hold, sitting in the dark watching another person straining his eyes looking for something that isn't necessarily there. So after a while I fell asleep.

Frank was good enough to leave me a note on the coffee table, which I found when Denise woke me up on her return early the next morning.

" 'Can't stay,' " I read aloud. " 'I'll call you later.' "

"That's it?" She handed me a cup of coffee and a warm bagel, fresh from the shop a few blocks away on Broadway.

"No, there's more. He signed it 'F.' "

"F? Not even his full name?"

"Probably so it couldn't be traced back to him, in case it falls into the wrong hands." I shook my head. "Maybe I'm supposed to eat the note now that I've read it."

"Have a bagel instead. Supposedly, it's more nutritious. I'll just burn the note and scatter the ashes in Riverside Park on my way to work."

The longer I was awake, the more stiff and sore my body felt, and the more the residual pain from the assault the night before with a carton of my own books grew. The bruise on my chest was deceptively light in color, but I suspected that it would darken into a much more impressive and frightening shade of purple as the day went on.

"I can't believe I went through all this effort for nothing." I glanced at my Belle Bacall outfit arrayed neatly on a chair and tried to take my mind off the bruise.

"Well, at least I get the thrill of starting my day with a seminaked man on my couch," she said, and I noticed that she, too, was staring at the bruise. "That doesn't happen nearly often enough."

"Lucky you. So, what did you do with yourself last night?"

"I have a spare key to Paula's apartment, so I let myself in."

"She doesn't mind?"

"She's out of town for the week on . . ." Denise stopped abruptly. "Sometimes I talk too much."

"She's out of town for the entire week?" I asked, confirming Denise's worst fears. "If you'd let me borrow the key . . ."

"Oh, no, Drew. There's no way in hell that I'm gonna let you use Paula's apartment for your trysts. She'd never forgive me."

"But . . ."

"No!"

"Well, how about if you . . ."

"No!"

"But you don't even know what I was going to suggest."

"I don't care. All that's important is that I know you're up to no good, and I'm not going to be your coconspirator. Last night was a one-shot deal. Don't think I'm going to get in the habit of finding you places to have sex every night."

"But I didn't even get to have sex!"

"Welcome to the real world. The world in which everyone talks about having sex but no one actually gets to have it. Anyway, the way I see it, that's *your* problem, not mine." She glanced at the clock on the kitchen wall. "You'd better get dressed, loverboy. We're both gonna be late for work."

Twenty minutes later I was back in Belle Bacall drag and looking none the better for wear. Big Paulie, mercifully, was nowhere to be seen, which was a good thing, since Denise and I had rushed through my grooming ritual and I was counting on nothing but the grogginess of the hurried morning commuters to avoid detection.

As I had hoped, I made it back to my apartment building without receiving as much as a quizzical glance. The doorman—not the same one who had let Big Paulie into the building, but another one of no greater competence—simply pretended to recognize me and waved me in through the door. It was enough to make me seriously question the alleged increased safety benefits of living in a door-man building.

When I walked through my apartment door I almost fell over the scattered copies of *The Brewster Mall* that still littered the floor, and fear gripped me once again. This was serious business with serious people, and I had not only placed myself right in the middle of it, but I had also crossed the point of no return.

And I still didn't have the slightest idea what I was going to do about it.

When I finally got to work, it came as no surprise that David wanted to see me. Immediately, of course.

"So, tell me about your meeting with Max Abraham," was his greeting when I entered his office.

"He needs a decorator. What else do you want to know?"

"Oh, good!" he said dryly. "A smart-alecky comment! And here I was afraid that you might have started to recognize the severity of your situation and would no longer entertain me with your devil-may-care bon mots!"

"Okay, okay," I said, beaten down early in the first round by his sarcasm. "Basically, he told me everything you would expect him to tell me. Stay away from Frank, stay away from everyone who has ever met Frank, stay away from everything Frank's ever touched . . . He sounded exactly like you, as a matter of fact."

"Wise counsel from the grown-ups in your life. Of course, I'm sure that now that you've heard this advice from one of the nation's top criminal lawyers—instead of just me—you'll take it more seriously. Right?"

"Of course," I lied.

"Good. I'd hate to think that I was wasting money on Max Abraham's services. Now, let's move on to topic number two: Hanover's Book Store."

"What about Hanover's?" I asked, trying to play dumb.

He raised an eyebrow. "I'm surprised you don't know, because they called me this morning and insisted that they shipped all their copies of *The Brewster Mall* to your apartment last night."

"Oh." I had been caught. "That."

"That," he agreed, with a sigh. "They told me that they would *not* sell your book. Do you have any idea why? And do you have any idea why they shipped the books to the author's apartment, rather than the distributor?"

I shrugged. "My style's not for everyone."

"That's not a very satisfactory answer. But it's just as well. I don't like dirtying my hands with those kinds of people. And I don't like *you* dirtying your hands—or any other parts of your anatomy—with them, either."

Say what you will, but David was consistent.

Once out of David's earshot, I called Frank.

"Why didn't you wake me up when you left this morning?"

"I don't even think you could call it morning. It was the middle of the night. And you looked sort of . . . well, you looked cute sleeping, so I didn't want to disturb you."

Awww . . . He knew just the right words to use. And it wasn't lost on me that this was probably the first time that big, tough, possibly-in-the-Mafia Frank DiBenedetto had ever called another man cute.

"Thanks." I realized I was blushing. "We'll have to commandeer Denise's apartment and do it again some time soon."

He fell silent for a few moments. "Yeah, well . . . About that . . . um . . . I really like you, Andrew. I really do. But I don't know when we're gonna be able to get together again. I mean, your place is out, and my place is out. And even though I didn't actually see anyone outside Denise's place last night, I know that someone was there. I could feel it."

"Frank, you're just being paranoid. No one was there."

"Andrew, you're gonna have to trust me on this. Whether or not someone is out there in the shadows is one of the things I've been trained to know since I was a little boy. It's self-preservation. And I'm sure that someone knew I was in that apartment last night."

"I believe you." I hoped I sounded convincing. What I really meant, of course, was "I don't believe you, but it's not worth arguing about."

"Thanks. I feel awful about this crap with Anna and Hanover's, though. Maybe I can think of some way to make it up to you."

"Don't bother. You don't owe me anything."

"I think I do. If it wasn't for my meddling with Hanover's, you never would have gotten that display and none of this would have happened."

"I'm not so sure about that. Anyway, that's not the point. My work wasn't selling itself, and it certainly wouldn't have earned a window display on its own. God knows that PMC wouldn't have paid for the promotion. You're the one who did *me* the favor . . ." I rubbed the tender bruise. "Even if there were a few unpleasantries involved."

"Well, I want to do something to make things right by you," he said as we drew the conversation to an end. "I'll think of something."

I tossed out one more "You don't have to do that," and we hung up.

I made periodic calls to Denise throughout the afternoon, pleading for the use of her friend Paula's spare apartment, but she was remarkably unsympathetic to my situation. Whatever tender spots Frank had touched in her on the previous night had hardened in the light of the new day, and her comments about our relationship became increasingly negative as the afternoon progressed. I knew she was fully back to normal when—instead of Paula's apartment—I asked for the use of *her* apartment . . . and she hung up on me.

That's when I fully accepted that Frank and I were not going to be getting together that evening. Benedick's was out . . . my place was out . . . his place was out . . . Denise's was out . . . Paula's was out . . . We didn't have a "safe house," so we weren't going to be together.

That thought was depressing enough, but my afternoon grew even darker at five-fifteen when I spotted Detectives Brogan and Mueller winding their way through the office, en route to my cubicle.

"I'm not supposed to talk to you without my lawyer," I said, before either of them had a chance to speak.

"Maybe you should call him, then," said Brogan, "because we have some things to discuss."

"Are you taking me downtown?"

Brogan and Mueller glanced at each other and shrugged in unison.

"Why?" Mueller asked. "What's downtown?"

"Isn't that where—?" I stopped, realizing that I sounded stupid. They realized it, too.

"You've been watching too much television, kid," said Brogan. "We don't need to take you downtown to ask you questions. You're not being charged with anything. But I'd appreciate it if you would join Detective Mueller and myself at the precinct house to answer a few questions at your earliest convenience."

"I've got to call my lawyer."

"Of course," said Brogan. "And when can we expect to see you?"

"It'll depend on my lawyer."

"Good. Six-thirty it is, then." With that, Brogan and Mueller turned and walked away.

Fortunately, Max Abraham was free at six-thirty. Oh, he complained, of course, and I really didn't know exactly how to tell him that I wasn't the one who chose the time for the appointment, but he showed up nevertheless, looking crisp and alert, if a bit annoyed.

He asked me if there was anything new that he needed to know.

"Well . . . I did sort of run into Frank last night."

Abraham shook his head. "If you're not going to listen to my advice, you're going down. Do you understand? They'll find something—*anything*—and they won't let go of you until they've turned you inside out. Keep it up and they'll pin something on you, Andrew. They don't need to catch you with a smoking gun in your hand."

I was silent for a while, and we watched the clock slowly tick out the passing minutes. Finally, I said, "I suppose this is the wrong time to tell you that I was assaulted last night, right?"

"What?" he gasped, attracting the unwanted attention of a handful of loitering officers. He muted his voice. "When did this happen? Why didn't you call me?"

"I don't know. I just didn't think of it. Last night, this guy came to my door and hit me with a carton of books."

"Do you know his name?"

"Paulie something." I searched my memory for his last name. Max Abraham beat me to it.

"You're lucky that all you got was a carton of books thrown at you. Paulie Macarini—they call him Big Paulie—"

"Yeah, I know that. Frank told me."

"Please don't tell anyone else that, Andrew," he said, exasperated. "Big Paulie Macarini tends to solve his problems with bullets and garrotes, not boxes of books. He's an enforcer with the Morelle crime syndicate—the rival family to your buddy Frank's Mafia family—and he reports directly to Tommy Franco."

"Crazy Tommy," I said, nodding. "Anna's father."

"Exactly. But I wish you didn't know that. Anyway, Macarini's probably got a dozen hits to his name. Nothing that could ever be pinned on him, of course, but, well . . . people know. He's not the sort of man you want to mess around with, Andrew. Consider yourself lucky that he let you off with a warning. I suppose that's a sign that Anna Franco only wants you scared . . . not dead."

By the time Brogan and Mueller were ready for us, it was closer to six forty-five, and while the delay slightly increased Abraham's level of agitation, it almost sent me through the roof. This was one appointment I wanted to end before it started.

"Max Abraham," Mueller whispered to me under her breath as she led us into a dingy office decorated with nothing more than a battered metal desk, battered metal chairs, and a few dead flies. "I'm very impressed."

I didn't bother responding.

Brogan pulled out a thick file folder and idly thumbed through it until he found what he was looking for. "We were able to communicate with Ted Langhorne today, Andrew, and he gave us a much more thorough statement."

"I'm glad he's feeling better." Abraham stopped me from saying anything more by placing his hand on my forearm and clearing his throat. Brogan and Mueller gave us knowing looks.

"According to Langhorne, you definitely weren't the assailant. However, Langhorne reconfirmed that the assailant indicated that the beating was in retaliation for the way he treated you. Now, you've already told Detective Mueller and myself that you and Mr. Langhorne were involved in a sexual relationship—"

"It was a little bit more than a sexual relationship . . ." was all that I managed to get out before Abraham's hand again gripped my forearm.

"Sorry," said Brogan. "Let's just say a *relationship*. In any event, Mr. Langhorne ended it a few months ago, and you were upset. Is that correct?"

Abraham placed a preemptory grip on my forearm. "My client has no comment. May I see Mr. Langhorne's statement, as well as the notes you took when you initially interviewed Mr. Westlake?"

Unhappily, Brogan pulled the requested files out of his folder and handed them to Abraham. For the next several minutes, the room was silent as the lawyer reviewed them, until he finally handed them back. "You may continue."

"Thank you," said Brogan with a dash of contempt. "We checked out your alibi, and that waitress remembers you. But she said you were with a friend. A big tipper." Brogan leaned forward across the desk, staring directly into my eyes. I felt a chill. "Who was the big tipper, Andrew?"

I heard Abraham say, "My client has no comment" once again as he gripped my arm, but it never occurred to me to speak. Instead, I was transfixed by Brogan's watery, bloodshot, weary eyes staring deep into mine, and I thought, *He knows.*

"If Andrew would answer the question and clear up the confusion, I'm sure we could resolve things quickly," I heard Mueller tell Abraham, but it was little more than background noise. The real conversation was the telepathic interrogation between my eyes and Brogan's. His were wary, accusatory, and suspicious . . . but somewhere, deep inside, was the slightest bit of empathy and concern. Did he understand that I didn't belong here . . . that I had fallen into the deep end and was in way over my head?

And what were my eyes telling him? I was trying to project self-assurance, confidence, and innocence, but could he see the fear and the confusion?

Or did he just see guilt?

Brogan either found what he was looking for in my eyes or he gave up, because he abruptly pulled his gaze away from mine and returned to the folder.

"Mr. Langhorne was able to give us a rough description of his assailant," said Brogan as he pulled yet another sheet of paper out of the folder. "We had a sketch done. Now, I have to tell you that this is only a rough sketch, and we'll be talking to Mr. Langhorne again before we finish it up, but I thought that maybe, if you took a look, it would remind you of someone."

He slid the sketch across the desk. The crudely drawn face looking up at me was mercifully unfamiliar. The head was almost completely bald with pinched facial features. A prominent, jagged scar crossed one cheek. If I had seen this man, I would have remembered. And I would have been scared.

"I've never seen this man before," I said, ignoring Abraham's pulsing clench on my arm. "I have no idea who—or what—he is."

Brogan took the sketch back, then dug out another sheet of paper, and—without showing the paper to me—asked, "Do you know a man named Francis Anthony DiBenedetto?"

"Myclienthasnocomment," said Abraham too quickly, and his grip cut off the circulation in my arm.

"Hmm . . ." mumbled Brogan and Mueller in unison. They fell into silence again, drumming their fingers on the desktop for an interminably long time. I glanced at Abraham, who looked back at me sternly.

"The reason I asked," said Brogan finally, "is because the waitress at the diner identified DiBenedetto as the person you were with on the night that Langhorne was beaten."

"Perhaps she was mistaken," said Abraham. "Perhaps DiBenedetto was there with someone else, and she was confused. It could have just been a coincidence."

"Yeah," Brogan replied. "Maybe."

It was now apparently Mueller's turn. "Quite a bunch of coincidences," she said, her voice heavy with cynicism. "Here we've got a sketch of a guy who looks remarkably like a thug named Vince Castellano, who's known on the streets for telling people the reasons they're getting beaten—or killed—while he's beating them or killing them. Just like what happened to Ted Langhorne. And Vince Castellano works for Frank DiBenedetto Senior. Meanwhile, we've got a positive ID on Frank DiBenedetto Junior placing him at the diner just a few blocks away. That's another coincidence. Then we learn that that's the very same diner where Andrew Westlake was having a late-night snack . . . despite the fact that it's a half-hour subway ride from his apartment. That's *another* coincidence. And if it's *also* a coincidence that the waitress at the diner placed Andrew with DiBenedetto, well . . ."

The only thing running through my brain was those three little words that mean so much: I am doomed.

I felt hollow. I felt trapped.

I felt guilty.

"Is there anything else?" asked Abraham bluntly. "Because unless you're going to charge my client, I see no point in continuing with this."

Brogan threw his hands up. "Andrew is free to go at any time, Mr. Abraham. You know that. He hasn't been charged with anything. Yet."

Yet?

"Very well, then . . ." Abraham gathered his briefcase and coat, then helped me rise unsteadily from the chair. My mouth was dry. I couldn't concentrate on anything except for my very tentative, spur-of-the-moment plans to flee to some very remote location in Wyoming or the Dry Tortugas and live off the land for the rest of my life.

We said our good-byes—well, my lawyer said our good-byes for both of us, since I was falling into a stupor—and walked outside. I felt a bit weak, so Max Abraham helped steady me as I shuffled down the street to the nearest thoroughfare, then hailed a cab for me.

"Am I in a lot of trouble?" I asked him as I crawled into the cab.

"You're screwed," he said as he slammed the door shut.

Call me crazy, but—coming from one of New York City's preeminent defense attorneys—I didn't find a lot of encouragement in that comment.

This was my plan: I was going to lay low. For that night, at least. I would pick up the scattered copies of *The Brewster Mall* and stack them in a corner. Then I would hide from the world. I wouldn't call Frank. I wouldn't bother Denise. I wouldn't leave my apartment. I wouldn't open the door for anyone, even if I recognized the person through the peephole.

All I was going to do was sit at home—alone—and try to figure out some way to avoid prison. Or death. Especially death. Preferably both.

I was going to read some escapist fiction to take me away from my complex, all-too-real life. Maybe I'd read the new Margaret

Campbell novel, if I could bring myself to read a book written from the perspective of a guilty man.

And I was going to drink a bottle of wine or two or six to calm my nerves.

That was my plan.

But, of course, since it was *my* plan, it didn't work.

I read through page ten of *The Duct Tape Murder* before I decided that the Campbell book wasn't going to make me feel any better. Her anti-hero—the guilty man—was connected to his crime by far less circumstantial evidence than connected me to Ted's beating. I didn't relish the thought of reading along as the police tracked him down.

And then the telephone rang.

When the call came shortly after ten o'clock, I was going to ignore it and let the answering machine pick it up. So, before I had a chance to scramble for the receiver and turn off the answering machine, the tape captured Denise screaming, "Drew! Pick up the goddamned phone! *Now!!* This is an emergency!!"

"What's wrong?" I asked breathlessly. My dash for the phone left me sprawled between the couch and the answering machine, with the phone tucked precariously under my chin.

"Anna Franco was just here!" she screamed in response. "She was asking about Frank."

"But how—?"

"Frank was *right* about last night." It sounded as if she was on the verge of tears. "Our cab must have been followed when I picked him up at Benedick's."

"What did she do? What did she say?"

She didn't answer me. "Can I come over? I don't feel safe here."

She was at my apartment in ten minutes. Miraculously, this time the doorman decided to buzz me to see if he should let her up.

When I opened the apartment door, she flew into my arms, crying. I shared an open bottle of cabernet sauvignon with her and calmed her enough so she could tell me what happened.

"Remember how I told you that I pretended to be a drag queen to get into Benedick's last night?" I nodded. "Well, Anna must have heard about that and believed it, because when she pushed her way into my apartment, she tried to pull my wig off."

"Ouch."

"No kidding. Anyway, she was in a rage about Frank being gay—

well, she didn't say *gay,* actually; she called him a *friggin' faggot,* but you know what I mean—and about how she was going to get back at him and everyone else who's ruining her life. And she kept tugging on my hair. And swearing like a sailor . . ."

"That's Anna Franco. Quite a lady. Did she mention me?"

"Not by name. She probably figures that she scared you off. But after she finally figured out that I wasn't really a drag queen, she wanted to know about the *other* woman who was spotted coming into my apartment last night . . ."

"The other . . . ?" I started to ask, until I remembered. "Belle Bacall."

"You got it." She poured herself another glass of wine. "She wanted to know whether or not *Belle* was a real woman, too, so of course I said yes. I figured it would be safer for everyone that way." I nodded my agreement. "After that, she started to calm down. She said that Frank was following her orders, or something like that."

"Yeah. She told Frank she wanted him to start dating someone else—a woman, that is—so that she could call off the engagement and avoid a scandal."

"Oh, I remember that. That's when you were playing matchmaker. But she doesn't consider calling off the engagement to be scandalous?"

"She figures that it's a lot less scandalous than admitting that your fiancé's a *friggin faggot.* And she's probably got a point. Especially in those circles."

I noticed that Denise's glass was almost empty again, so I poured while she talked.

"And do you want to hear another interesting thing? While she was ranting, she said something about giving up Paulie because she had to get engaged to Frank."

"Paulie? Big Paulie Macarini?"

"I don't know. I mean, she was just ranting. But it would make sense, wouldn't it?" Denise paused to take a gulp of wine. "Whatever. That woman is one hundred percent nuts, Drew. Totally, completely out of control. I'm scared."

"You can stay here tonight."

"Thanks. But you'd better watch yourself, too. There's no telling what she's capable of doing."

"I know." I leaned back and shut my eyes, wishing it was that easy to close out all the very bad things that were happening in my very

real life. Unfortunately, reality quickly oozed into the darkness behind my closed eyelids, and they flashed open.

"Wait a minute." Panic stirred once again in my body. "Did you
say that Anna knew that you passed yourself off as a drag queen to
get inside Benedick's?"

"Yeah." Her eyes, too, were now closed.

"*Inside* Benedick's?" I took a few deep breaths as I tried to control my growing panic. I had to keep a clear head. "Did you do the
drag thing outside when you were waiting for a cab or anything? Or
maybe when you were waiting on the sidewalk to get in?
Somewhere that you could have been seen?"

"No." Her eyelids suddenly flickered open. She understood, too.
"No, I didn't."

"You know what this means?" I hurriedly reached for the telephone.

"Yeah," she said as I dialed. "I know exactly what it means." She
stood up, wandered over to the window, and parted the blinds just
the slightest bit. "It means that someone in Benedick's tipped Anna
Franco off."

"Right." The phone started ringing at Benedick's. "It means that
Frank's being watched by someone in his own club."

"I've got news for you, Drew," she said, peering out the window.
"Frank's not the only one who's being watched."

"Oh, no. Don't tell me Big Paulie's out there again tonight."

"Okay," she said, and she fell silent.

This was insane. My life was completely out of control. I couldn't
even catch a break when I was locked in my own apartment.

So much for my plans for a quiet evening.

Someone finally answered the ringing phone at Benedick's, and
I was put on hold as someone else was dispatched to find Frank. I
sat on the couch, stupidly unable to think of any options whatsoever and only in the most tentative control of my panic. Denise left
the window and started pacing nervously, back and forth, across
the small living room. My apartment had never felt so small, and it
was growing smaller with every long passing minute.

"I can't believe this," I said to her as I waited on hold. "Every day
in this city, a hundred guilty people escape undetected, but even
though I haven't done anything wrong, I've got the Mafia and the
police after me. It isn't fair."

"Mmmmhmmmm . . ." mumbled Denise, and it occurred to me

that my complaints were falling on deaf ears, since she was even more innocent than me, and yet nevertheless had just had her hair yanked by Crazy Anna Franco.

"Well, it isn't fair," I felt compelled to add one more time, and then Frank was finally on the line.

"We've got a problem. Anna went to Denise's apartment tonight."

"Ah, Christ." He sighed. "I *told* you someone was out there. Did Anna know you were there?"

"No. She knew about Denise—well, she thought she was a drag queen, but . . ."

"A drag queen?"

"Yeah. The ruse she used to get into Benedick's last night. Someone there must have overheard her and they thought—"

"That means someone here at the club—"

"Yeah. One of your friends isn't your friend."

"I'm coming right over. Where are you? Your place?"

I quickly dismissed that idea. "Don't come over. That Paulie guy is watching the building again tonight."

"Godammit." I heard a banging sound . . . a fist pounding the desk in frustration, I assumed. Finally, and with much more composure, he said, "You've got to get out of that apartment. We have to talk."

"Yeah, we do. Tell me something, though. Big Paulie and Anna . . . were they . . . ?"

"I don't know. Maybe. Nobody really talks about it, but I wouldn't be surprised. When our fathers decided we were going to get married, that was the end of the discussion."

I sighed. Now I wasn't just being tailed by a mob thug; I was being tailed by a mob thug who very well might have a personal grudge against Frank and, by extension, his homosexual lover.

"So, how am I going to get out of this building?" I finally asked.

He didn't have any answers, of course. If there were easy answers, I would have thought of them myself. I looked to Denise for help, but she just shrugged.

Then a thought came to me.

"I have an idea, Frank. Let me call you back when I get it squared away."

* * *

What happened next I'd seen in a dozen movies and television shows, and it always looked so deceptively easy that I couldn't believe it didn't have a lot of hitches in real life. Didn't everything else in the previous few days?

But, no. It really was that easy.

I slowly walked the short block down West Eighty-sixth Street to the subway entrance at the intersection with Broadway, then descended the stairs to the southbound platform. I wasn't disappointed when, twenty seconds later, Big Paulie Macarini—his face partly hidden in the previous day's *Daily News*, already yellowing and stained from whatever trash basket he had retrieved it from— pushed through the turnstile and stood ten yards away from me down the platform. We played our roles well; both of us watched but pretended not to notice each other.

A few minutes later, the Number One train to lower Manhattan entered the station with a deafening roar. The doors opened and I boarded the sixth car, taking care to grab a pole in the center of the aisle for balance when the train pulled out of the station. Through the glass in the doors between the cars, I saw Big Paulie do the exact same thing, positioning himself one car away from me where he could keep the eye not hidden in the *News* on me.

I leaned against the pole and gazed vacantly across the tunnel at the well-lit northbound platform. I didn't look at the platform behind me, or my fellow passengers, or Big Paulie in the next car. Then, as the garbled voice of the conductor squawked over the intercom that Seventy-ninth Street would be the next stop, I waved wildly at the unseeing passengers on the opposite platform.

Two tones signaled that the doors to the subway cars were about to close, and then the train pulled out of the station.

I caught a glimpse of Big Paulie as he stopped searching for the phantom I was waving to on the northbound platform and realized that I was no longer holding on to the pole in the center aisle of the sixth car. Perhaps he would actually enter the car to see if I had taken a seat.

I hadn't. I was back on the southbound platform, saying a silent good-bye to the mobster whose next stop would be Seventy-ninth Street.

I went back through the turnstile and climbed up the flight of stairs to the street, where Denise was waiting with a cab.

"How'd it go?" she asked.

"It's just as easy as it looks on television. Certainly easier than the next stage of this operation."

"We should call first."

"Nah. We'll be much better off if we catch him off-guard." I told the cab driver, "Seventy-fourth and Fifth."

At the corner of Fifth Avenue and East Seventy-fourth Street stood an apartment building towering over Central Park. Since this was the East Side of Manhattan, where the residents tended to compensate for their personal affluence with public understatement, the original owners of the building hadn't felt it necessary to name the structure. They didn't have to. The street address alone was instantly recognizable to many New Yorkers. It was home to as many of the rich, powerful, and famous as the Upper West Side's Dakota. And it was home to even more people who were merely rich and powerful.

Our cab pulled to the curb in front of the nameless building. A white-gloved doorman appeared and opened the rear door, sniffing disapprovingly as Denise and I—neither of whom were obviously rich, powerful, or famous—stepped onto the sidewalk.

I tipped him a dollar anyway.

This nameless building was David Carlyle's home. And, as I expected, he was in. He even seemed happy to see us.

At first.

His mood didn't considerably darken until I asked if it was all right if Frank met me at his apartment.

"What does this place look like?" He gestured around the opulent blue living room, full of expensive first editions and artwork. "Apalachin?"

I called on my deepest reserves of patience and diplomacy. "David, I have to talk to Frank. It's literally a matter of life and death."

"The problem with writers is that they use the term *literally* too liberally." He probably thought that remark was clever. "Andrew, you're in quite enough trouble right now without making things worse. Let's not even mention that you'd be dragging Denise and me into this . . ."

"I'm already in it." Denise absentmindedly patted a tender spot on her scalp. "Look, David, what Andrew is saying is true. Tonight some woman attacked me . . ."

"Attacked you?" David gasped. His hands fluttered to his neck.

"It wasn't just 'some woman.' " I hoped that expanding on Denise's comments would show David why it was imperative that I see Frank. "It was Anna Franco, Frank's former fiancée and the daughter of Crazy Tommy Franco."

"I need to sit down," said David, who was becoming noticeably paler. "No—first I need a drink. *Then* I need to sit down."

David made us all drinks—very strong drinks, although I suspected that his was the strongest—and we sat in the living room. I gave him the quickest version of events of the previous few days, and by the time I finished, he was shaking.

"So, can I call Frank and invite him over?" I asked again, since it appeared that I had him in a weakened position.

"I really don't think that's a good idea. Look around you! There are hundreds of thousands of dollars worth of artwork in this apartment. Almost three hundred thousand dollars worth of Warhols alone!"

"Frank isn't going to steal your collection," I said, with a bit more impatience than I intended. "This is important, or I wouldn't ask."

"Denise?" David looked at her, seeking guidance and, I suspected, support.

"He seems like a nice guy," she told him in a soft voice, crisis once again having brought her to a pro-Frank position. "That doesn't mean that I like what he does or anything, but I think he's sort of sweet. You'll like him."

David was clearly uncomfortable, but finally—after making me swear that I would never ever ever ever mention his complicity to either Max Abraham or the police—begrudgingly allowed me to invite Frank over. I called Benedick's and, as quickly as possible, gave Frank the address, after making him promise to do everything possible to ensure that he wasn't followed.

"If I don't show up, it's because I'm being tailed," he assured me.

When I returned to the living room, David was making another round of strong drinks. "Denise said you made an interesting observation earlier tonight."

"What's that?"

"You said something about hundreds of guilty people going free while you're being hounded by the Mafia and the police. Something like that."

"Oh, yeah." I recalled the comment but didn't remember it as a particularly interesting observation.

David smiled, and I realized that his vodka and tonic was loosening him up considerably. "Have you read the Margaret Campbell book yet?"

"I haven't exactly been in the mood."

"Well, you should. It's very well written, and maybe you'll learn something."

"Learn something? About what?"

"About how to think like a guilty man."

"But I'm not—"

"*I* know you're not guilty of anything worse than bad judgment. But the police certainly have their doubts, and the Mafia certainly has its doubts, and your own lawyer seems to have his doubts. . . . And for some strange reason, you keep playing into everyone's hands by walking around Manhattan with a big target on your back."

"But I didn't do anything!"

"What matters is the perception. And the perception that everyone has—excluding the three of us and your friend Frank—is that you *have* done something. So, since thinking like an innocent man clearly isn't working, perhaps you should start thinking like a guilty man."

"But won't that make things worse?" I asked, determined to play the innocent man to the end.

Both David and Denise laughed. Loudly. At my expense.

"I'm trying to conceptualize how things could get worse for you, Andrew," said David. "I'm drawing a blank."

"Maybe you should just read the book, Drew," said Denise. "It can't hurt."

"Yes," David agreed. "If nothing else, at least you'll be more familiar with one of PMC's best-selling authors. Maybe I'll even let you meet her some day."

"Oh, good," I said without enthusiasm. "Anything for the company . . ."

"The company that pays you," he reminded me. "The company that publishes your books."

The conversation continued in that vein for the next forty-five minutes or so. David and Denise joined together as a tag team whose goal was not to present me with an easy way out of the web I had become entangled in, but rather to point out my many character deficiencies that had led me to this point. Among them were most of the Seven Deadly Sins, some broken commandments, and, of course, the old standbys—naïveté and stupidity—which, I was assured, were not the same thing, even though I evinced both traits in abundance.

All in all, it was almost enough to make me go back to the Upper West Side and seek out Big Paulie for the beating I seemingly deserved and would probably still get.

I was saved when the phone rang. It was David's doorman—the doormen in David's building *never* let strangers past the lobby—calling to tell him that Frank had arrived.

Minutes later, Frank knocked at the apartment door. I opened it, greeting him with a short hug, which would have been longer if not for a disapproving stare from one of David's matronly neighbors who was navigating her way past us in the hallway.

"David," I said, as I ushered Frank into the apartment, "this is Frank."

David Carlyle was certainly predisposed to dislike Frank, but he had also spent several decades refining his appreciation of the physical beauty of men. So, when he caught his first glimpse of Frank as he entered the living room, David forgot his better judgment and stammered out a "Hello" that sounded to my ear more like a "Thank you for gracing my apartment with your presence."

"Nice to meet you," said Frank, who then proceeded to make David very nervous by eyeing a Warhol displayed in the entryway.

"You weren't followed, were you?" I asked, not only because it was an important and relevant question, but also because Frank's art appreciation was starting to make David squirm and I wanted to draw his attention away from it.

"I told you I wouldn't come here if I was followed." He was annoyed that I had even asked the question. It did the trick, though; he took his eyes off the walls and, with a grin, said, "Guess what! I've got good news. I think I found a way to make up to you for what happened with Hanover's."

"I told you that you don't have to do anything. Really. And anyway, I think we should try to figure out what we're going to do about this mess we're in."

He ignored my concerns and went straight to his good news. "Well, I did anyway. You know who Gary Vine is?"

Of course I did. He was the host of "Gary Vine: Six 'til Nine," the New York metropolitan area's most listened-to morning talk radio show and, in the wake of the recent syndication of his show, now heard—I was assured every morning—on seventy-nine stations coast-to-coast, a national radio celebrity rivaling Howard Stern and Don Imus.

"What about Gary Vine?" I asked cautiously, not quite sure of the pertinence.

Frank smiled broadly. "Monday morning he's gonna say that he read your book and he loved it. On the air."

"Huh?" I was stunned.

"Yeah!" He beamed, obviously quite proud of himself. "He'll want to talk to you, of course. Are you okay with that?"

I turned to look at David, who stood behind me, mouth agape.

"That will . . . that will push sales through the roof," David finally stammered. "Gary Vine has a *fanatical* cult following! He can put you on the best-seller list!"

"How did you do this?" I asked Frank. "How do you know him?"

"I just know him," Frank replied, pointedly not answering my question, for which I suppose I was grateful. "He's doing it as a favor to me."

"So, he really liked my book?" I asked, as my ego began to inflate.

Frank laughed. "He hasn't read a book in twenty years. But he trusts my judgment. So, you can talk to him Monday morning, right?"

"Right. *Right!*"

Despite the fact that Gary Vine hadn't actually read my book, my ego remained inflated. In fact, I was almost euphoric. Gary Vine— *the* Gary Vine—was going to interview me and say good things about *The Brewster Mall* on his nationally syndicated radio show. On seventy-nine radio stations coast-to-coast. The book would be sold out by midafternoon on Monday, I'd make a lot of money and, as David noted, I might very well end up on the best-seller lists.

But I was held back from the full feeling of euphoria by a queasy feeling in my stomach, a feeling that told me that there was a dark lining to this silver cloud.

"Champagne!" said David, suddenly bustling with energy and forgetting every reservation he had ever had about Frank. "This calls for champagne."

I was surprised that David didn't start pulling Warhols off the wall and handing them to Frank, so quickly did his doubts seem to vanish with the news about Gary Vine. Denise, too, was swept up in the exhilarating atmosphere of the room. In fact, only my subconscious—and a small part of my subconscious, at that—wasn't joining the party. It was holding back until it knew what the price would be for this piece of good news.

Which didn't mean that I couldn't drink a lot of champagne in the meantime, of course.

Later, after a great deal of champagne and celebration, it was Denise who brought us back down to earth when she asked, "So, now what happens, anyway?"

"Gary Vine makes Andrew a best-seller!" bubbled David, missing her point.

"I mean about the police and the gangsters."

David's bright smile immediately sagged, then disappeared altogether.

"I was afraid you were going to ask that question. I don't know." I turned to Frank. "Here's where we are now. The police know that the guy who beat up Ted works for your father, and they know that you were at the diner with me. And my lawyer says I'm in a lot of trouble."

"That's not good," said Frank, noting the obvious.

"Actually, he says I'm screwed."

"That's worse."

"It's just a case of pulling everything together," added Denise pessimistically. "It's only a matter of time."

"Not now," David moaned under his breath. "Not with the Gary Vine show. Of all times, not now . . ." We ignored him.

"Yeah," I agreed with Denise. "Between the police and Big Paulie, I feel like everything is closing in on me."

"I know," said Frank quietly. "I just wish we could buy some time."

"I wish we could get out of New York," I said. "I've never felt so claustrophobic before."

The four of us sat in silence, lost in our now decidedly less happy thoughts. We had traveled one hundred-eighty degrees away from Gary-Vine–induced euphoria to cops-and-robbers–induced dread.

Then, with a snap of his fingers, David abruptly broke the silence. "Tuesday!"

"What about Tuesday?" I asked.

"I can get you out of town on Tuesday, I think, if you can hold out until then. Glenda Vassar has been having a few . . . er . . . *problems*, and she's had to cancel the last leg of her book tour. So I've got a handful of stores on the West Coast who are expecting an author who won't be showing up next week."

"But Vassar writes mysteries. Our readership is nothing alike."

He waved me away. "Andrew, at this particular stage of your career, you *have* no readership. Now, let me get Angela Keenan on the phone and see if she can work you up a quickie book tour." Before we had a chance to react, he started hunting though an end table drawer for his telephone directory.

"That's impossible, David," I said. "There's not enough time."

"If Gary Vine is going to interview you and plug your book on Monday, then PMC had better be ready to take advantage of it. Ah! Here's her number."

As he dialed, I asked him, "So, what does this get me, anyway?"

"You get out of town for a few days. And you sell some books and make some money. If you can stay out of trouble until Tuesday morning, that is."

"Without Frank?"

"Without Frank."

Next to me on the couch, Frank shrugged. "He's right, Andrew. Right now, the important thing is to get away and let things cool down a little bit."

"I suppose . . . but . . . maybe you could go away with me."

"*No!*" shouted David, Frank, and Denise in unison.

"Well, this won't resolve anything." I felt defeated. "All it does is drag out the suffering."

"What it does," said David, as he half-listened to the ringing phone on the other end of the line, "is give us all a little more time to think. And . . ." He stopped, then addressed the receiver. "Angela, this is David Carlyle. Please call me at home as soon as you get this message. It's very important." He hung up and returned his attention to me. "And things have been moving so fast for you that you need some time to think, Andrew. Trust me: A few days on the West Coast will be refreshing, and they'll give you a little bit of perspective."

"And," said Frank, weighing in, "maybe I can take care of a few things while you're gone, so that you don't have to worry about them."

I didn't like the sound of that. But I didn't ask exactly what he thought he could take care of, because I didn't really want to know. I already knew far too much.

"Then it's resolved," said David, interpreting my silence as agreement. "Andrew will spend next week on the West Coast and we'll see how much of this untidiness can be tidied up in his absence."

I started to object but then thought better of it. Even *I* had to acknowledge that I hadn't been doing a very good job of controlling my life in recent days, so maybe it was time to let others take over its management. And if my closest friends all felt that it would be for the best if I disappeared for a while, who was I to object?

"I'd better get going," Frank said a few minutes later. "It's getting late."

I glanced at my watch and was shocked to see that it was already 4:00 A.M. I nodded at Denise. "You ready to go, too?"

She was.

"You'd better give me a head start," said Frank. "Just in case."

Oh, yeah. Just in case . . .

I kissed him good-bye at the door, and he assured me that everything would be all right.

"Don't worry about things," he said, as the door started to close. "They aren't your problems. Let me take care of them."

And then he was gone.

Denise and I gave him a fifteen-minute head start, then we, too, left David's apartment. Minutes later, as our cab cut through Central Park, she said, "I know things have been crazy, Drew. But they're going to work themselves out."

"I suppose . . ." Everyone kept telling me that, but I couldn't quite believe it.

She sensed my anxiety. "After Gary Vine plugs you, you'll be so busy signing books that you won't have time to get into trouble."

I smiled slightly at the thought of my impending brush with fame. "Maybe it wasn't a completely horrible day."

"Not at all. Your career's about to take off!"

"Thanks to Frank."

"Yeah," she conceded, not altogether happily. "Thanks to Frank."

The cab dropped her off in front of her West Eighty-ninth Street apartment, and I had the driver wait until she was safely inside. When she flashed her apartment lights, I told the driver to take me to Eighty-sixth and Amsterdam. We were there two minutes later.

The doorman wasn't at his post, so the lobby door was locked. As I fished through my pocket for the key, a voice called out.

"Westlake!"

I didn't have to look. I knew that voice. And I knew that I was going to have to get the front door unlocked and get into my building before the body that went with the voice reached me.

I didn't make it.

7

Words Better Left Unsaid . . . Especially When Other People Are Listening

My keys fell to the sidewalk as Big Paulie Macarini, suddenly behind me, slapped my arm away from the door and spun me around. He was still wearing the same expensive suit he had been wearing earlier in the night, though it was now rumpled and creased. His face was distorted with apoplectic rage.

"Think you're funny?" He shoved me against the locked door. "I ought to kill you for pulling that fuckin' stunt."

"Sorry," I said instinctively. It was the only thing that my panicked mind could think to say.

He pulled me away from the door, only to violently shove me against it again. As the reinforced glass rattled in its molding, I started to reevaluate whether or not I'd done the right thing when I lost him on the subway.

Big Paulie held me against the door with one hand. I saw that the other one was balling up into a fist, and I didn't think I was going to like what was about to happen. Immobilized by fear and his grip on my chest, the only evasive action I could think to take was to close my eyes and wish him away.

And then I felt the strangest sensation, as if I was sliding backwards in slow motion. I heard Big Paulie mutter an epithet, and the pressure on my chest was relieved, but still I continued to slide blindly until the back of my head gently, if inelegantly, came to rest on cold ceramic tile. It was only then that I dared to open my eyes.

"You okay, Mr. Westlake?" The doorman was now towering above me. "Did he get anything?"

"No." I lifted my head and looked down at the rest of my body, the top half in the entryway and the bottom half on the sidewalk, to reassure myself that Big Paulie hadn't torn off a limb as a souvenir before taking flight.

"This neighborhood's going to hell," said the doorman, a middle-aged gray-haired man named George who loved to chat with the tenants, which he proceeded to do. "You're just lucky I got off my break when I did, 'cause he looked like he was gonna kill you. I thought I heard someone yelling your name, then I heard all that banging against the door. I thought it was just some kids messing around, but then I come out and I see you getting mugged . . ."

He stopped talking long enough to notice that I was trying to struggle to my feet, so he bent down and put an arm around my shoulders, helping me up off the cold tile.

"Thanks, George."

"Yeah, you're lucky. He could have killed you. This neighborhood's going to hell, I tell you. To hell."

"Yeah," I agreed, now standing on wobbly legs. "Hell . . ."

He brushed a trace of dust off the back of my jacket. "I'll call the police for you."

"Don't bother."

"No bother, sir," he said insistently, and before I could stop him, he was dialing 911 from the phone at the lobby desk.

"It's late." I tried to act as if I didn't want to inconvenience the police, because I couldn't let George know that I had my own very personal reasons to avoid filing a police report on Paulie Macarini. He dismissed my objection, noting that I had an obligation to be a good citizen and report the crime. Before I had a chance to object again, he told the dispatcher about the "attempted mugging."

"They'll be here soon, Mr. Westlake." He smiled as he cradled the phone. "I'll call up to your apartment when they get here."

"Thanks."

I started to shuffle toward the elevator and almost made my getaway before he stopped me cold with, "You know that guy? The guy that was beating on you?"

"No, of course not. Why do you ask that?"

"Well, like I said, I thought I heard him yell your name. Just before all that noise. And then I came out here and I saw you getting pushed around, and—"

"I didn't know him." I doubted he would believe me but hoped he would appreciate that I had my own reasons for telling him that. "I don't know what you heard, but no one yelled my name. He just came at me out of the blue."

"It sure sounded like your name, Mr. Westlake." He wasn't getting the hint.

"Well, I didn't know the guy." With that, I pulled a twenty-dollar bill out of my pocket and slipped it to him. "I don't want the police to waste their time looking for the wrong person, so maybe you should just keep that to yourself."

"What's this for?" He was apparently determined to miss every hint.

"It's for you, George," I said, slightly exasperated. "For helping me out when that *stranger* attacked me."

If hints and bribes weren't enough, I hoped that calling Big Paulie Macarini a stranger one more time would sink in. And if that wasn't enough, well . . . things really couldn't get much worse for me, could they?

Free of George at last, I took the elevator up to the seventh floor, let myself into my apartment, and, since I still had a police report to file before I could go to bed, made a half-pot of coffee. As the coffee brewed, I saw that the red light on my answering machine was flickering, so I hit the play-back button.

It wasn't a new message. It was the captured sound of Denise's terrified voice from earlier that evening. I sat in the dark and listened again to the tape.

"Drew! Pick up the goddamned phone! *Now!* This is an emergency!"

And then I settled back into the couch and decided to let myself have a good cry.

A full hour later, a uniformed officer from the New York Police Department was in my apartment. I gave him my statement and the entire experience was over in a mercifully short period of time.

The closest our conversation came to causing me anxiety was when he asked, "Were there any witnesses?"

"The doorman," I said, reluctantly. "George."

"I already talked to him. His account is the same as yours—"

Good, I thought. George got the hint after all.

"—except that he thought he heard someone call out your name prior to the assault."

So, he didn't get the hint after all. Well, *that* was a waste of twenty dollars.

"He's mistaken." I tried to seem casual about it. "And I told him that he was mistaken. If someone had yelled my name, I think I would have noticed." I attempted to add a dismissive smile to my comment, but my dry lips wouldn't cooperate and I ended up giving the officer something resembling a grimace.

"Yeah," he said, seemingly convinced despite my grimace. "I've been there. When you work at night, sometimes your mind plays tricks on you."

And that was that. After he left, I crawled onto the couch, determined to get a few hours of sleep before whatever new drama Saturday would bring arrived. But before I could even close my eyes the phone rang.

"Good morning!" said David, his voice chipper despite his own lack of sleep.

"It's six forty-five. This had better be good."

"It is. I just got off the phone with Angela Keenan. She's already up! At *this* hour! On a Saturday! Can you believe it? In light of the Gary Vine publicity, she thinks she can ship you off on the tail end of the Glenda Vassar tour next week."

"Good. I really would like to get out of town." Truer words have never been spoken.

"There's one slight hitch that you should know about. I'm sure I'll be able to resolve it before next week, but you should be aware that this might cause some internal problems in PMC. Nothing *too* serious, and nothing that should directly affect you, but I could still end up getting some heat for it."

"You're such a martyr. What is it?"

"Margaret Campbell is trying to claim the rest of Vassar's tour. We'll have to exercise some tact and diplomacy, of course."

"Of course."

"We're planning on giving you Tacoma, Portland, and San Diego, and giving her Phoenix and Sacramento. She will not be happy about that. But Gary Vine is carried by affiliates in the cities we're sending you to, so it makes sense."

"I don't care where you send me," I said. "Just get me out of this city as soon as possible."

David must have heard something new and disturbing in my voice. "What's wrong?"

I told him about Big Paulie Macarini.

"You've got to get out of that apartment," said David, alarmed and afraid for me. "If you stay there, you'll be killed."

"I'll be fine," I said with more hope than certainty.

"Nonsense. You're staying with me. Pack a few bags and I'll send a car over."

"But—"

"Andrew! Don't be foolish! Be ready in an hour."

The fight was out of me. I knew he was right, and I knew that the longer I stayed in my apartment, the more likely it was I'd have an-other unpleasant encounter with Big Paulie . . . or maybe another, less agreeable gangster. I told David to have the car pick me up at eight o'clock.

I showered, shaved, dressed, packed, and was in the lobby a few minutes before eight o'clock.

So were Brogan and Mueller.

"Oh, c'mon!" I said in frustration when I saw them.

"Good morning," said Brogan, seconded by a cheerful nod from Mueller. "Sleep well?"

"Why do you ask?" I glanced at the lobby desk, and was relieved to see that George's shift had ended and his replacement—yet an-other doorman who I didn't recognize—had arrived. Maybe, just maybe, I'd be able to make this short and sweet.

"I hope you don't mind," said Brogan, "but I've asked the local precinct to keep an eye out for any unusual incidents that involve you." He paused for a beat. "Say, if you were mugged outside your apartment building, for instance."

Of course. It couldn't have been as easy as filing a simple police report for a crime that would never be solved, could it?

"I don't know what else I can tell you. This is New York City. It happens."

Brogan pointed to the two full duffel bags I was carrying, the closest thing I had to luggage. "Where you heading?"

"I've got a book tour," I said, playing around a bit with my date of departure. "The West Coast."

"Where? What cities?"

"Uh . . ." I struggled until one of the cities popped into my head. "San Diego. And a few others. Maybe Sacramento. I honestly can't remember."

"Which flight?" Damn. Why couldn't *anything* I say be taken at face value?

"I'm not leaving today. Early next week. But this mugging has me shaken up, so I'm going to stay at a friend's place until it's time for me to leave town."

"Which friend?"

"David Carlyle." Brogan and Mueller nodded.

"Can you give us his address and phone number, in case we have to get in touch with you?" asked Mueller. I recited the information, and she jotted it down in a small notepad. As she wrote, I saw a black luxury car pull to a stop in front of the building.

"I think my car is here. So, if you'll excuse me . . ."

"In a minute," said Brogan gruffly.

"But—"

"He'll wait." Then—to ensure it—he motioned to the doorman. "Would you mind telling the driver of that car out there to wait a few minutes for Mr. Westlake?" The doorman went off to do as he was told.

Brogan got straight to the point. "In the police report, your doorman said that he heard someone yell out your name before the mugging"— Damn! Again! —"but he also said that you insisted that he was mistaken. That seems strange, don't you think?"

"Yeah. It does seem strange. I don't know why he thought he heard my name, because I was out there on the street and *I* certainly didn't hear it." For additional weight, I added, "The officer who took the report thought that George might have been hearing things. He's old, you know."

Brogan's left eyebrow arched. "Hearing things?"

"I don't know. He was working the night shift . . ."

"What's the night shift got to do with it?"

"I . . . I don't know. I'm just repeating what the officer told me. All I know is that I didn't know the guy."

"I didn't say that you did," Brogan said dryly.

The thought of calling Max Abraham suddenly occurred to me, but given his lack of faith in me and my future, it just as quickly passed. I was going to have to get through this using only my own dulled, sleep-deprived, and generally confused wits. So . . .

"Well, that was the implication."

"I don't imply things," tossed back Brogan. "I just look for the truth."

"Well, then," I said, rolling my eyes in an exaggerated display of skepticism in their objectivity, "here's the truth, the whole truth, and nothing but the truth. I was at David Carlyle's apartment on Fifth Avenue last night until after four o'clock, then I took a cab home. And then I was attacked at the front door. I didn't get a very good look at the guy, but I got enough of a look to know that I don't know him."

"What was he wearing?" Mueller asked.

"I don't really remember," I said, as I vividly recalled Big Paulie, dressed in a wrinkled, expensive suit and about to inflict serious bodily injury.

"The doorman said he was wearing a suit," said Mueller, and I once again silently damned George for his talkativeness.

"Could be. It all happened so fast . . ."

"We don't see many common street thugs wandering around the Upper West Side in suits at four-thirty in the morning," said Mueller.

"I wish I could help you," I said, trying to hold back my frustration and at least appear to be helpful and innocent. "But I can't. I don't know what muggers wear. And I didn't dress him."

"Mmm-hmm," she hummed cynically through closed lips.

"Can I ask you a question?" My frustration was finally beginning to break through the surface. "Why are you following me? I haven't done anything."

Brogan looked at Mueller; Mueller looked at Brogan. And then Brogan said, "We're not following you, Andy."

"An*drew*."

"An*drew*. If we were following you, you'd never know it. We'd be two blocks down Amsterdam with binoculars. We'd be behind the fire door down the hall from your apartment, listening. We'd have a guy bundled up and sleeping on cardboard on the church steps across the street. You'd never know we were here."

"Thanks. Because I wasn't paranoid enough already. Can I go now?"

"Sure," said Brogan. "We didn't mean to hold you up. Thank you for your time."

And then he and Mueller smiled at each other, and they looked like hunters who had at long last trapped their prey, and I couldn't get away from them fast enough.

Fifteen minutes later, I was back at David's apartment. He greeted me and pointedly avoided any discussion about Big Paulie as he showed me to one of the guest bedrooms.

"Get some sleep," he said as he began to close the door. "We'll talk when you're rested."

"Wait," I said an instant before the door was fully closed. "You should know something."

The door opened again slightly, and his face appeared in the crack.

"The police were at my building this morning."

"To take a report?"

"I mean later." The sliver of his face that I could see dropped. "Brogan and Mueller—the ones who were at the office the other day—were waiting for me when I was leaving. I told them that I'd be staying here for a few days."

Now he fully opened the door and walked back into the bedroom, shaking his head.

"What do they know?"

"I don't think they believe me," I replied, an obvious understatement. "The doorman told the police that he heard someone yell my name before he saw me getting roughed up, so they think I know who did it."

"And *did* someone yell your name?" I nodded yes, and he shook his head again. "I don't suppose you told them that you knew who it was."

"No." I realized that my mouth was dry again. "I told them that the doorman was mistaken."

He shook his head yet again and glanced at the floor. "So, what you're telling me is that you lied to the police."

"Well, if I told them it was Paulie Macarini, things would only get worse." I paused. "I think."

His lifted up his head and looked me in the eye. "I don't know about that, Andrew. Why don't you get some sleep, and we'll talk about it later."

He left. Without undressing, I fell on top of the soft bed and buried my head in an oversized pillow. For several long minutes, my brain continued to play out the encounters with Big Paulie Macarini and Brogan and Mueller, but then I was pleasantly surprised to feel the onset of sleep approach and I let myself go.

I awoke to pale sunlight filtered through the partially closed curtains. My tired eyes searched the room until they found the red numbers of the digital alarm clock on the nightstand, which told me it was a few minutes past noon. My sleep—devoid of my real-life nightmares—had been so restful that quite a bit of time passed before I recalled the exact reason why I was waking up in that particular bed.

The bad memories pushed to the surface at the same time that I heard voices, muffled by the closed bedroom door, engaged in conversation somewhere else in the apartment. I knew that I had matters to attend to, and I knew that those voices were most likely talking about me and my predicament, but I couldn't bring myself to leave the comfort and peace of the bed. I pulled the pillow over my head, holding it tightly in place with my arms, and tried to drown out the rest of the world.

That worked for maybe another two minutes, until it occurred to me that if someone was trying to suffocate me or muffle the sound of a gun shot, they'd hold a pillow over my head in precisely the same manner. Understandably disturbed by that thought, I hurled the pillow to the foot of the bed and staggered to my feet.

The bedroom was off an azure hallway, which I followed until I reached the empty living room. The voices were silent now, so I couldn't navigate through sense of sound. I smelled coffee, though, so I followed the aroma to the kitchen.

David and Denise, sitting silently at the table, looked up at me as I shuffled into the room.

"Good morning," Denise said.

"That's a look," David said.

"Huh?" I said.

"Your hair, Andrew," he said with a slight smile.

I bent down to look at my outlined reflection in the glass window of the microwave. Stray tufts of hair sprouted in all directions. I decided they were the least of my problems.

"Coffee?" asked David.

"Please."

As David filled a ceramic mug, I asked Denise, "What are you doing here?"

"I'm your new roommate."

"Huh?"

"David and I decided that it wasn't safe for me to stay at my apartment, either. After all, they know where I live, too. And if they don't know it already, it won't take them long to figure out that you and I are friends."

"I'm trying to minimize the potential carnage," added David, setting the steaming mug in front of me. "Lower the body count, as it were."

"What about Frank?" I asked. "Shouldn't he move in, too?"

"No," David snapped. "I must admit that I've come to *somewhat* like Frank, despite everything. But I don't think it's in anyone's interest for him to move in here. He can take care of himself."

"But . . ."

"This isn't a negotiable point, Andrew. If I'm not mistaken, last night we reached somewhat of an agreement about the immediate future. You're going to lay low until PMC sends you to the West Coast, and Frank is going to keep his distance."

"But . . ."

"When you get back from the West Coast, we'll see where things stand." He smiled, trying to temper his words. "It's only a week. You'll survive. And hopefully, by then everything will have been resolved."

"Maybe I should call him."

"Not a good idea," replied David. "The police know that you're staying here, and since they already more than suspect that you're in collusion with Frank, I wouldn't be surprised if they've tapped the phones. Let's not give them any more material to hang you with, okay? It's only a week."

Only a week . . . I sipped my coffee and brooded, thinking about exactly how long a week could last and how much could happen. After all, it had been less than eight days since I had put on my Belle Bacall drag for the first time, and since then . . . Well, besides falling in love with Frank, I didn't really want to think about "since then" too much, even though I knew that it all related directly back to falling in love with Frank.

I sat at the kitchen table and tried to tell myself everyone else was right and I was wrong. That loving Frank was unwise. That it made no sense. That I should move on.

I could adopt David's attitude and "*somewhat* like" Frank; appreciate his physical beauty and sweeter qualities, but mitigate them with the knowledge that he was hopelessly mobbed up, closeted, and likely to remain that way. After all, a lot of bad things had happened to me since Belle Bacall danced in a dark corridor at Benedick's on Halloween night.

But every time I tried to force common sense upon myself, a memory rose to the surface. His tears when he thought I was going to walk out on him . . . his coital awkwardness and post-coital bliss . . . the way he tracked down *Allentown Blues* . . . even his double take through the cab window when he first realized I was a man.

And those memories—none more than eight days old, none fresher than the bad ones I suppressed—forced common sense right back out of my brain and up into the ether.

David broke my introspective mood. "I spoke to Max Abraham about your predicament."

"Is he ready to drop me as a client yet?"

"Almost," David replied too quickly. "He wasn't at all happy that you lied to your detective friends."

"It would have been better if I'd admitted that I recognized a mobster?"

"He didn't say. In any event, he wholeheartedly agrees that you should leave town for a few days. At least then, upon your return, you can claim a spotty memory."

I nodded agreement. And I silently hoped that someday I would be able to forget parts of the previous week.

David, Denise, and I spent the rest of the day cooped up in the apartment, idly watching television and making the smallest of small talk, when David wasn't on the phone with Angela Keenan and other Palmer/Midkiff/Carlyle employees making detailed arrangements for my visit to the West Coast and ordering another printing of *The Brewster Mall*. Every now and then he'd attempt to involve me in the details—telling me about the rush shipment of my book that was now en route from a distribution warehouse to a Barnes & Noble outlet in Tacoma, for instance—but I only half-listened.

I was safe, true. And I was about to realize a professional dream. But I couldn't stop thinking about Frank.

In the late afternoon the skies darkened, and soon a cold, early-November rain began to fall. I watched it from inside the sliding glass door to the small cement terrace outlined by a wrought-iron fence, which overlooked Fifth Avenue and, beyond it, Central Park. Twelve stories below me, the sidewalks were drab and empty, except for dark umbrellas hiding the occasional pedestrian from my range of vision. The street, though, was colorful and busy, full of the softly lit interiors of passing buses and the bright yellow cabs throwing shimmering beams from their headlights onto the watery streets, where they blended with reflected reds, ambers, and greens of the traffic lights.

I raised my head and looked across the leafless treetops of Central Park to the Upper West Side skyline, partly obscured by the low, dark clouds. The facades of the buildings lining Central Park West seemed to be so far away . . .

Frank was out there. Somewhere.

Turning slightly to the left, I found the Dakota and the stoplight that marked the intersection of Central Park West and Seventy-second Street, both of which were almost lost in a cloud.

Frank was there. I felt it. And I felt that if I kept staring at the hazy, indistinct outline of that intersection, the skies would brighten and I'd catch a glimpse of him.

The wind abruptly changed direction, blowing sheets of rain against the window and distorting my vision. Still, I stood and stared, transfixed, until my breath fogged the glass and all I could see was a haze.

I finally stepped away from the window and turned to face the seating arrangement in the living room. David now dozed in his favorite chair, lightly snoring, and Denise slept silently on the couch. Both of them had succumbed to the gray, rainy weather and their own exhaustion. An old and mediocre movie, the sound muted to an almost inaudible level, flickered its black-and-white images across the television screen. I sat and tried to concentrate on the film, but my concentration was shattered within seconds when a pinstriped movie gangster pulled out his tommy gun and mowed down a half-dozen rivals.

"Oh, Christ," I muttered to myself, and in response, both David and Denise stirred slightly. I held my breath, and they returned to their slumber.

I watched the movie gangsters for a little while longer, and then I knew I had to call Frank. I wasn't quite sure of the reasons why, but I knew that if I didn't call him—if I stayed in hiding in that apartment, listening to the rain falling on the terrace and drumming against the glass—things would be intolerable. Or, I should say, *more* intolerable.

But I also knew that I couldn't call him from David's apartment. Even if the phones weren't tapped, I feared the effect of David's paranoia, which was beginning to approach the level of my own. So, taking care to be as quiet as possible, I left the living room, found my loafers in the bedroom and slipped them on, then went into the bathroom and slicked back the stray tufts of hair that still stuck out from my head. On my way back through the living room, I grabbed my jacket off the coatrack, lifted David's keys out of his coat, and slipped gently out the front door.

I made my way from canopy to canopy down Fifth Avenue, avoiding the rain until I found a pay phone a block away from David's building. The phone stood unprotected on the sidewalk near the curb, but the rain was now light enough that I felt confident a short call wouldn't drench me. I dropped a quarter into the coin slot and dialed Frank's number. He answered on the third ring.

"Hi," I said.

"Where are you? I've been trying to call you—"

"I'm staying at David's. I'll tell you about it later."

"Okay." He sounded put out by my secrecy. "But if you're gonna be there Monday morning, you'd better give me the phone number, so I can pass it on to Gary Vine's show."

I recited David's number.

"So, what's up?" he asked when I finished.

"I have to tell you something," I said impulsively, as I was overwhelmed with a single thought. "I have to tell you—"

A car horn suddenly blared and I stopped speaking, leaving my thought unfinished. As I waited through two more short blasts from the driver, impatiently stuck behind a slow-moving bus, I started to rethink what I was about to say. My self-confidence wavered.

"What do you have to tell me?" he asked, and I realized the street noise had subsided.

I stared at the phone, feeling a trickle of rain flowing past my ear and into my collar, and tried to regain my courage. But the harder I tried, the more elusive it was.

"Andrew?"

"I—"

I faltered again, and was saved when the phone clicked and Frank said, "That's the other line. Hold on a second."

I stood there in the rain, working to rebuild my nerve as he took the other call. When he got back on the line, he seemed agitated. "Something's going on, so you'd better make this fast."

I continued to struggle and was about to give up when the impulse burst out. It wasn't born of courage, and it wasn't born of self-confidence. It was born of rashness and impulse and desire and honesty. And I said it.

"I love you."

He was silent, and I was left to my own thoughts, one of which— never before verbalized—was now exposed. That single trickle of water had now become several, and I realized that I had underestimated the rain. As I waited for Frank to react, I felt a raw breeze pick up, gusting down Fifth Avenue.

Finally he said something, even if it was only, "What did you say that for?"

I wondered the same thing. "I just wanted you to know. That's all."

Again he fell silent, and again I felt wet and cold.

And stupid.

And even more stupid, when he replied, "That's nice." Followed by a pause; followed in turn by, "Really, it is. It's a nice thing to say. But—"

Frank was probably simply sitting on his couch, merely feeling a bit uncomfortable, but I envisioned him holding the phone at arm's length, staring at it in shock and panic.

"Sorry," I said, hoping to minimize the damage. "I just felt like I had to say it. I didn't mean to scare you."

"Don't worry about it. You just caught me by surprise, that's all.

Maybe you should have waited. But . . . but it's okay. Don't worry about it."

Stupid, stupid, stupid!

"I'm going away for a while," I said quickly, hoping to steer the conversation to safer ground. "To the West Coast. David got me those readings. But I'll be back soon."

"It's probably for the best." He sounded stiffer than he had before. Or was that just my imagination? "Things are sort of hot right now. We should let them cool down."

"Yeah. You don't have to tell me twice. I had a bit of a run-in with Big Paulie last night."

"Big Paulie? Macarini? Where?"

"Outside my building. He wasn't happy that I lost him on the subway."

"You okay?"

"He shook me up." Which was a slight understatement. "But you should probably know that the police are looking into it and . . ."

"Shit! I really don't want to talk about this now . . . but . . . *shit!* Why'd you call the cops?!"

"I didn't. The doorman did."

"Shit!" In less than one minute, the tone of his voice had changed from gentle to concerned to agitated. "Andrew, you gotta promise me something. If anything like this ever happens again, don't call the fuckin' cops, okay? You tell me. And don't call me. *Tell* me. I'll take care of things."

"Yeah, well, I didn't want the police to get involved. But now they *are* involved, and they seem to know that it was no ordinary mugging."

Even through the wind and rain and street noise, I could hear him sigh. This was not one of my better phone conversations on any level. Finally, he said, "I'll take care of things. Just make sure that you stay away from the cops. Okay? I really don't want to talk about this anymore. Not now."

I agreed. It was an easy thing to agree to. It was less easy to guarantee that the cops would stay away from me.

There was another brief moment of silence, until he said, "I'd like to talk, but like I said, something's going on. I'd better get off the line."

"I've got to go, too," I said quickly, glad that this disaster of a conversation was drawing to a close. "I guess I'll talk to you when I get back."

"Yeah. Call me."

"I—" I stopped myself before the dreaded *L* word popped out of my mouth again, and started over. "I'll be thinking of you."

"Yeah. Take care." A click told me that he'd hung up.

Yeah?

I walked back to David's building, no longer going through the pretense of trying to stay dry. I ran the word over and over again in my head, until I finally rationalized that the only thing that mattered was that Frank liked me enough to take risks for me.

And that was *all* that mattered.

I hoped.

David and Denise were still sleeping when I slipped back into the apartment. I took a shower to warm up, then crawled back into the bed in the guest room where—after tossing, turning, regretting my confession to Frank, and analyzing the many meanings of his *yeah* for hours in the grayness of the rainy early evening—I finally fell asleep.

I slept through the night and rose early Sunday morning to the sound of David Carlyle on the telephone, attempting to smooth some very ruffled feathers.

"Darling, please, you know that we love you at PMC. We'd do *anything* for you. But this is a—"

Although I couldn't make out the individual words, even at a distance I could hear David cut off in midsentence by an enraged female voice barking out of the receiver. David, cradling the phone, mouthed the words "Margaret Campbell" to me, and I instantly understood.

"Has this been going on long?" I whispered to Denise, who sat on the couch amid the scattered sections of the Sunday *Times* and watched the conversation in silent amusement.

"Maybe fifteen minutes. If I'm following this correctly, she doesn't seem to mind losing Tacoma, but she's quite pissed off about San Diego."

I went to the kitchen to get coffee. When I returned to the living room, it was once again David's turn to speak.

"I understand, Margaret. Really, I do. But this is a once-in-a-lifetime shot for this young man, and . . ." He stopped as her voice erupted once again, and when it subsided he said, "Oh, now, don't say that. You don't even know him! He's not like that at all!"

I caught David's eye and pointed at myself. He nodded.

Great. Now not only were the police and the Mafia out to get me, but I was also being targeted by one of the nation's best-selling authors. Great.

"Get all caught up on your sleep?" Denise asked as David continued to defend me and my virtue and, apparently, my matrilineage, in the background.

"I hope so." I pushed the *Times* Metro section to the floor and took a seat next to her on the couch.

She put a hand on my leg. "It'll get better, Drew. It really will."

I slipped my arm around her shoulders and, without really believing my words, said, "I know it will."

"Margaret!" said David sharply into the telephone. "You can't threaten another writer with physical harm!"

I sighed and buried my head in Denise's lap.

When he hung up the phone some minutes later, David said, "Well, I guess you see that we have a little problem here."

"Uh-huh."

"She's insisting that she's going to San Diego, whether we like it or not. Maybe Portland, too, but certainly San Diego. Apparently, she sells well out there. Or maybe she just wants to get some sun." A thought hit him, and David picked the phone back up. "Might as well make Angela earn her mediocre salary. Maybe she can place you in another bookstore."

"Maybe," I mumbled as Denise patted my head.

As David dialed and Denise patted, I caught a glimpse of a newspaper headline out of the corner of my eye. And I didn't like what I saw.

"Ah, no." I picked my head up off Denise to get a better look, hoping that my skewed vision had misread it.

But, no, I hadn't misread it. There, on the front of the Metro section, in a large font and bold type, was the news that ALLEGED CRIME FIGURE SHOT IN QUEENS AMBUSH.

"We were going to hide it from you," Denise said, watching me as I scanned the headline, my head perched on her knees. "But we figured that you'd hear about it anyway, so . . ."

"Well, I wish you would have hidden it, at least until I'd had enough coffee to wake up."

"I'll remember that for the next time."

I gave her a sour look, then grabbed the newspaper section and sat back on the couch to read the article. The alleged organized crime figure—*alleged* in this case being an extremely cautious term—had been gravely wounded outside a Queens "social club" by a shot fired from a passing car. And, of course, no one—including the victim—saw anything.

The article, based largely on unattributed comments from the police and federal agents, continued to speculate that the shooting of alleged Stendardi family lieutenant Anthony "Tony C" Corelli most likely represented a dramatic escalation in the simmering battle between the Stendardi and Morelle crime families, which had already claimed at least seven lives. And the closing paragraph included a tearful "no comment" from the victim's alleged-organized-crime-figure son, who was guarding the front door of the family homestead from inquisitive reporters and law enforcement officials.

"This is bad." I wondered if this could have been the "something" that Frank referred to in our conversation the previous afternoon. "I shouldn't leave New York."

"Why?" asked Denise. "What are you going to do? Single-handedly stop mob warfare? Geez, Drew, I guess I didn't realize how strong your super powers really are."

"Thanks for the sarcasm. Just what I need right now."

"Sorry. But I don't know what you could hope to accomplish by staying in New York right now. If anything, I think it's even more important now that you get out of town."

"But what if Frank needs me?"

"Frank doesn't need you. You'd just be in his way. This is *his* life, not yours. And anyway, he's got the entire Morelle family to watch out for him."

"Stendardi."

"Huh?"

"Frank's father is in the Stendardi family. Not the Morelle family."

"This is something I don't care to know. This is also something that I wish *you* didn't know."

"Well, I *do* know it. I should call him."

I managed to wait until David was off the phone, then grabbed it out of his hands and dialed, ignoring their protests.

"Oh, hi," Frank said when he answered. He sounded tired.

"Are you all right?"

"Yeah. I don't know if you've heard, but—"

"How could I *not* hear? What's going on?"

"It's bad. See, this is why I was supposed to marry Anna . . ." His voice trailed off. "I guess that's out of our hands now, though, huh?"

"Yeah. I guess so."

"Anyway . . . I really don't like to talk on the phone, Andrew. You know what I mean? It's not exactly private."

"Oh . . . right. Of course."

"So, we'll talk when you get back from your book tour."

"Can I meet you—?" I started to ask, but he cut me off.

"No. I'm gonna be very busy today."

"Well . . ." For a brief moment I wanted to protest, but there was a finality to his words that stopped me. So, despite my regrets, I gave in. "Okay, then. I'll, uh . . . I'll talk to you when I get back."

"Good," he said. That was it. *Good.*

"I'll miss you."

There was a pause, and then . . .

"Fuck you." With those two words, he hung up the phone.

What? *What?!!*

Denise was the first one to speak. Her voice sounded to me as if it was coming from miles away.

"Drew, honey, what's wrong? Are you all right?"

"He—" That was all I could get out before my vocal cords stopped working, choking off the rest of my words. And so I sat, stunned, unable to communicate, unable to focus my eyes and my thoughts, and unable to think of anything except Frank's harsh words.

I heard David say, "I'll get him some water." I heard Denise again ask me, "What's wrong?" But I was incapable of breaking my trance to answer.

The water eventually came and I drank, but it really didn't help much. Eventually, I found the presence of mind to rise from the couch and stumble back to my bedroom, where I fell onto the bed, buried my head in a pillow, and tried to block out the rest of the world.

Denise must have followed me into the bedroom, for no sooner had I wrapped the pillow around my head when I heard her muffled voice.

"It's okay if you don't want to talk about it right now. But I'm—*we're*—here for you. Okay? Whenever you feel like talking."

I pulled the pillow off my head and saw that she was already making her retreat out of the bedroom.

"Denise, wait!"

She stopped and turned to face me, smiling slightly. "Feeling better?"

"No. I feel like shit."

"So, what did he say? What was so bad?"

I took a deep breath and tried to keep my thoughts focused. "When I told him I was going to miss him, he said 'Fuck you.' "

"Oh! That's not good."

"No. It's not good at all." With my index finger, I motioned for her to come closer, and when she was within whispering range I confessed, "I don't want David to know this, but I sneaked out yesterday afternoon when you guys were napping and I called him. That didn't go well, either."

"What happened?" She sat on the edge of the bed.

I hesitated briefly as a phone started ringing somewhere in the apartment; then, when the ringing stopped and I was certain that David was occupied with the call, said, "I—I really screwed up. I said the *L* word."

"Oh, Drew," she said, with a light tone of admonishment in her voice as she put her hand to her brow. "I don't suppose the *L* word in question is *like?*"

"No."

She sighed. "Why did you have to go and do that? Take it from me: Nothing scares a man away faster than the premature use of the *L* word. And Frank is having enough trouble dealing with all this as it is. What are you trying to do? Scare him to death?"

"That's not what I was *trying* to do. But I think I did it anyway."

She brushed loose strands of hair off my brow. "That's what his 'Fuck you' was probably all about, Drew. You scared him. He's got this self-image as a tough guy, and now you've come along and confused him. And then you get all mushy and he doesn't know how to deal with it."

"Maybe . . ."

"Don't forget where he's coming from. He's—well, if he's not in the Mafia, then he's the next closest thing. And you're—well, let's face it. You've been out of the closet since you were a teenager, which was sometime during the Coolidge administration, if I remember my ancient history. You've had a lot of time to adjust. He hasn't."

"I suppose . . . I just hope I haven't chased him away."

"The telephone hasn't exactly been your friend. So try to stay off it, okay? You guys have some things you have to work out, and I think you should work them out in person."

"Ah!" said David, who was suddenly standing in the bedroom doorway. "You're functional again. Good, because you have a call." He walked to the bed and handed me the cordless phone, then hovered over me, waiting to hear every word.

"Hello?"

"Hi." It was Frank. I could hear traffic in the background. He was calling from a pay phone out on the street. "Can we talk?"

"Sure." I was nervous but nevertheless gushing with happiness to hear his voice again. "I'm sorry about—"

"No, no. Not on the phone. I don't think David has a private line either, if you know what I mean."

Yeah, I knew what he meant. "So where?"

"The park. Can you meet me at the entrance to the zoo in twenty minutes?"

"Sure."

"Good." And then, as abruptly as before, if with far less hostility, he hung up.

I stepped out onto Fifth Avenue into an eerily silent Manhattan, blanketed with thick, gray clouds and unseasonably chilled by a stalled cold front. The weather, combined with the prematurely leafless trees of Central Park, made it feel more January than November.

Walking briskly, I reached the entrance to the Central Park Zoo before Frank. He arrived minutes later.

"You weren't followed, were you?" I looked past his shoulder at a man who was idly strolling along a walkway in the distance.

"These days," he said, with a nod in the direction of the stroller, "I take that as a given. The only thing I never know for sure is if it's the NYPD, the feds, or the wise guys."

I found none of those options especially reassuring, but I was finally learning not to ask questions about the wrong topics. And anyway, there was another important topic that needed to be addressed.

"I want to apologize for . . . for . . . you know." He looked at me out of the corner of his eye but offered me no assistance, let alone a blanket amnesty for my sins of the heart, so I regrouped my thoughts and averted my eyes. "I like you, Frank. I guess that's no surprise. But I didn't mean to scare you. I can take this—"

"Andrew," he said, but I wanted to finish while my thoughts were still clear.

"—just as slowly as you'd like. No pressure." I finally looked at him. His brown eyes were locked on my face. "Okay?"

He didn't say anything for a while, but continued to stare into my eyes. Finally, he spoke.

"Let me explain a few things to you." It was his turn to avert his eyes. He paused and lit a cigarette, then stared off into the distance as he continued. "We can't talk on the phone. You know what I'm saying? I've already let it go a lot further than I should have, and sometimes it's my own fuckin' fault, but I want you to realize that you can't say the things on the phone that you've been saying. You can't tell me you love me, and you can't tell me you'll miss me. Because you're not just telling me. You're probably telling the cops, too."

"The cops already know that I know you. I'm sure of it."

He took his eyes off the bare trees and locked them again on mine. "That's nice, Andrew. But that's really not what I'm talking about, is it? What I'm talking about is cops tapping my phone and making a nice little tape of me and you talking cute—talking like boyfriends or something—then taking it around the city and playing it for people who I don't think you want to hear it. That'd be real nice, wouldn't it? Frank DiBenedetto's son, caught on tape talking with his boyfriend." He paused and took a drag off his cigarette. "If that happens, I hope that your life insurance policy is paid up."

"Why would the police pass a tape like that around? What possible value could it be to anyone?"

"To make trouble. That's the value of it. To flush out Tommy Franco, 'cause when he hears about Frank DiBenedetto's gay son who almost married his daughter, he's gonna want to do something about it. And it'd humiliate my old man, too. Believe me, if my phone is tapped, and I think it is, whoever's tapping it—the cops, the FBI, whoever—would find a lot of uses for that information."

"But how is that different than what Anna Franco's already seen for herself? Christ, Frank, she walked in and saw us having sex!"

"The difference is this." He exhaled a thick white cloud of smoke. "She's not gonna say anything because, if she does, then she's gonna be humiliated, too. That's why I know she'll keep her mouth shut unless I fuck up. Paulie Macarini, too. But the cops won't have the same consideration."

The wind picked up, and I closed my light jacket against it. I glanced back over Frank's shoulder. The man who had been strolling in the distance was still there, although he was now sitting on a bench.

"Sorry," I said. "I guess you're right."

"I'm sorry, too. That's why I said 'Fuck you' to you this morning on the phone. I hope you understand. But it was for the benefit of anyone who's been listening in on us. I have to protect myself, Andrew . . . we have to protect each other."

I smiled at him. He started to take my arm but stopped abruptly and laughed nervously as he jerked his hand away.

"It's okay."

"I've gotta go." He looked back over to the west side of the park and absently dropped his cigarette on the dead grass, grinding it out with his heel. "I've got things I have to do."

"Yeah. Me, too."

"I'll listen to you on Gary Vine's show tomorrow morning. Maybe he can put you on the best-seller list."

"I won't forget. Thanks again for that."

"No problem. Well . . . I'll see you when you get back."

I didn't respond. And I didn't move. He took a half-dozen steps away from me, then turned.

"For what it's worth," he said, so muted that I could barely hear him over the breeze, "I'll miss you, too. Have a nice trip."

He grinned shyly, then turned and walked away. I watched him slowly disappear into the park. He didn't look back.

It was only when he was completely out of sight that I allowed myself to smile.

And it was only when I finally began to walk back up the path to Fifth Avenue that I realized that the man on the park bench had disappeared, too. That's when I stopped smiling.

I woke up on Monday at 6:15 A.M. to Gary Vine's deep voice as he trashed a recently released major motion picture with his trademark venom.

"I mean, what do they think we are? Morons?" he snarled, to a chorus of laughter and sycophancy from the team of acolytes who shared airtime with him. "What were they thinking? Ladies and gentlemen, take my advice: Do not see this movie. This movie sucks. The people who made this movie should be ashamed of themselves." He paused, audibly taking a drag off a cigarette, then continued on his tirade. "It's not an inexpensive thing, going to the movies. Let me tell you, it would have been more honest if these jokers had just stuck a pistol in my back and taken my wallet. It probably would have been cheaper, too."

More laughter and sycophancy from the acolytes.

And, nervously, I tried to quash my sudden fear that Gary Vine would fearlessly ignore his assurances to Frank and turn on my book, trashing it as effortlessly and thoroughly as he was now trashing this movie.

I heard a knock on the bedroom door, followed by David's voice calling out, "Are you decent?"

"No."

"Good." The door opened. He was carrying a cordless phone. "Mr. Vine doesn't seem to have liked the movie very much."

"Let's hope that he gets it all out of his system before he decides to talk about *The Brewster Mall.*"

As Gary Vine broke for a commercial, Denise appeared in the doorway, wrapped in a terry-cloth robe and still stretching sleep from her limbs.

"Has he mentioned the book yet?" she asked.

"Not yet. He's too busy destroying a one-hundred-twenty-million-dollar movie."

The commercials ended and we continued listening to the radio host's diatribe on the movie, followed by a few jokes loaded with sexual innuendo directed at one of his female sycophants, followed by news on the half hour, followed by more sexual innuendo directed at yet another sycophant. I stayed under the covers, afraid to move lest I miss his review of my book. David paced and Denise sat at the foot of the bed. And all of us hung on every word that came out of Gary Vine's mouth.

Finally, at six thirty-seven, the cordless phone rang. David answered it, then handed it to me.

"Mr. Westlake?" The voice was surprisingly youthful.

"Yeah."

"This is Brian, from 'Gary Vine: Six 'til Nine.' We'll be putting you on the air in approximately eight minutes. Are you ready?"

"Yeah." Suddenly, my mouth felt dry and tacky.

I listened to the show as it played over the phone line for those eight long minutes until I heard Vine's voice say, "I read an interesting book over the weekend."

"Another Dick-and-Jane book?" asked one of the sycophants irreverently.

"That's enough out of you, Billy," Vine said with what sounded like surprisingly good humor.

"Or was it just a Dick book?" asked Billy, pushing for another laugh and, when he didn't get it, nevertheless foolishly forging ahead. "We know that you like the Dick books, Gary."

I cringed in the ensuing silence, less at the childishly bad humor than at the thought of how it would affect Gary Vine's notoriously volatile mood. I was right to cringe.

"I said that's enough." This time his voice was icy.

"Oh, no," I muttered. "Why does he have to provoke him now?" For the briefest of moments, I considered hanging up the phone.

"Especially the Dick books with pictures." Billy was on a roll. All downhill. And I was afraid that he was going to drag me down with him.

I spoke pleadingly into the phone's silenced mouthpiece. "Please don't do this to me, Billy."

"Anyway," Vine continued, the frost still in his voice, "the book is called *The Brewster Mall*, published by PMC here in New York, and it was a fun, well-written book. The author is this guy . . . uh . . ."

"Pretty memorable writer, huh?" It was, of course, Billy again.

"That's it, Billy. I'm turning off your microphone." The other sycophants laughed.

I pulled the blanket over my head. Denise patted my leg sympathetically.

"Now," Vine continued, his voice slightly warmer, "the guy that wrote this, his name is Andy"—I winced—"Westlake, and he really did a first-rate job. Very, very good. It's all about the goings-on at a mall out in Jersey, and I couldn't put it down."

Tentatively, I poked my head out from under the blanket. David and Denise were forcing smiles, hopeful that Gary Vine's good humor would continue through the end of the segment.

"We've got Andy Westlake on the line now. Good morning, Andy. Welcome to the show."

Suddenly, I was no longer hearing Gary Vine's voice distilled through the radio, but directly though the telephone line.

"Good morning," I said nervously. I wasn't about to correct his *Andy.*

"Fascinating book. I really enjoyed it. What inspired you?"

My mind raced, but I couldn't remember the inspiration . . . or even if there had been an inspiration. "Uh . . . er . . ."

"Waldenbooks!" hissed David.

Oh, yeah. "Well, Gary, it all started when I did a book signing at a mall in Jersey City. I only sold three books, so I figured I had to find some other way to make my trip pay for itself."

He laughed, and David and Denise nodded their encouragement.

"So, now, tell me . . . After doing the research for this book, have you figured out how to get those security tags off the clothes without being caught?"

"Sorry, no. That's why I steal all my clothes from the Salvation Army Thrift Store."

"I steal mine from Victoria's Secret," the host cracked. "But that's my own problem. And I'll deal with it."

I took advantage of his gang's laughter at their boss's wisecrack to gather my thoughts. But none were coming. Until something just tumbled out.

"It's not important where you steal them from, Gary. The only important thing is that your undergarments flatter you."

He laughed, and I finally felt a huge weight lifting. "So . . . wait, let me get this straight, Andy. Are you trying to tell me that you steal your underwear from the Salvation Army? No offense, but . . . but that's sort of gross and disgusting."

"No, no. I can assure you that my underwear does *not* come from the Salvation Army. Next question? Maybe about my book?"

"Okay, let's get down to brass tacks here, Andy. What kind of underwear do you wear? Boxers or briefs?"

Again, my mind went blank for a few beats, but finally came up with the crowd-pleasing answer with what appeared to be impeccable timing:

"What underwear?"

That was it. I got a howling laugh from Gary Vine and his acolytes. This was easy. I was on a roll. I was a natural. I felt relaxed and comfortable, and I was ready to chat with him about my book and shopping malls and underwear for another hour.

"Thanks for joining us, Andy," he said abruptly, and my phone line again went dead. That was it. My thirty seconds of fame. Over the radio I heard him continue. "That was Andy Westlake, author of *The Brewster Mall* and, apparently, a man who does not wear underwear. I want all of you to go out and buy this book. It only costs twenty bucks, or something like that, so you can afford it. And I don't want to hear any excuses. Just buy this book instead of spending your hard-earned money on a piece of crap like that stupid movie."

I turned off the phone. "How was I?"

"Surprisingly good," said David. "Considering that all you talked about were undergarments, instead of your book. But that's not really the point. The point was to get your name out. I think we're going to be all right."

We were. Gary Vine continued on to list my upcoming appearances in Tacoma, Portland, and San Diego—which I now hoped had been confirmed, although it was questionable because Angela Keenan had started screening her calls and ignoring the frequent messages from David—and concluded with, "Buy this book, folks. *The Brewster Mall*, by Andy Westlake. You won't be disappointed."

He abruptly segued into a political discussion and David turned the radio off.

"Congratulations," he said, offering me his hand. "You escaped unscathed. It appears that you're going to sell some books and make some money."

"It sure sounds that way. I really owe Frank for this."

"Uh . . . well, yes," said David uncomfortably. "I suppose you do.

But let's not forget that there would be no book to plug without your talent."

Denise put an arm around David's waist. "Come on, David. Let's cut Frank a little slack. He came through for the book, which means he not only came through for Andrew, but he also came through for you."

"Well, then," said David, as he slipped out of Denise's grasp and backed out the bedroom door, "I'll have to remember to pay up on my protection money the next time he comes around."

When he was gone, Denise shrugged. "Deep down, I think David really likes Frank."

"*Way* deep down."

She smiled. "So, is it true that you really don't wear underwear?"

I threw a pillow at her.

By virtue of having lasted longer than anyone else, Angela Keenan was PMC's star publicist. Only twenty-five years of age, she was still a few years away from realizing that her energy and Type A personality were tailor-made for one job and one job only: underpaid publicist for a smallish publishing house. I just hoped that I wasn't around on the day when Angela realized that. It wouldn't be pretty.

Her inability to delegate—or, more to the point, her inability to trust anyone else to do things correctly—had led her to have her hands in almost every aspect of the house's promotional efforts. She personally negotiated with bookstores, she personally made sure that all the details were ironed out, she personally made the travel arrangements, and she personally was waiting for me when I arrived at work that morning.

She was tall and thin and a bundle of nervous energy, her long dark hair in perpetual motion. Outside the office, she chain-smoked as she juggled two cellular phones and a beeper; inside the office, she chain-chewed nicotine gum as she juggled two cellular phones, a beeper, and three regular phone lines, not to mention any other method of communication she could get her hands on. If smoke signals were still an effective means of communication, she would have had a perpetual bonfire burning.

When I arrived at my cubicle, she had already appropriated the phone on my desk, which she chattered into as she repeatedly pressed the redial button on one of her cellular phones. In front of her, an assortment of papers fanned across the desktop.

"Good morning," I said.

She held up her index finger, both acknowledging and silencing me, and continued speaking into the phone.

"Well, when is it aired in San Diego? Uh-huh . . . Uh-huh. It was on just before seven in New York, so you should tune in at six-thirty or so . . . Well, turn it on now, then. Listen, Henry, this is the sort of free publicity that most people would kill for. Do you know how many people listen to Gary Vine's show . . . ? No, Henry, it's a one-shot deal . . . Just listen to the show. All I can tell you is that Vine's show reaches—" She flipped through the papers and found the one she wanted. "Okay, here are the numbers from August: ninety thousand daily listeners in the San Diego area. That's ninety thousand, Henry. Nine-Oh."

She fell silent for a moment and let Henry speak, rolling her eyes at me as if to say "I'm going to wear him down yet." I just wished I knew who Henry was.

She glanced at her watch, then stopped him. "Henry, it's six twenty-five on the West Coast. Just turn on your radio and listen, okay? Trust me on this. You can't lose . . . Uh-huh . . . Well, can I add one thing . . . ? Yes, I think you *do* have to hear it, Henry. Last year, Gary Vine pushed a book by a first-timer that no one thought was going to sell more than a few thousand copies, at best. Do you know what the name of that book was? It was a little book by Roger Kane called *Pennsylvania Avenue*. And I don't have to tell you how long it sat on the best-seller lists, do I?"

She listened again, still pressing the cellular phone's redial button, while I stood, transfixed by her assertiveness and persistence and energy. I would never want to do Angela Keenan's job, but I was glad that she was willing to do it on my behalf.

"Henry," she said, when she found another opportunity to cut him off, "we're wasting time here. Just listen to the Gary Vine show and make your own decision, okay? But let me leave you with something to think about. I know that Glenda Vassar is very popular, but she'll have to be rescheduled. She's not coming . . . Well, if you *must* know, she had a breakdown . . . Yes, she'll be fine. She just needs to rest . . . Oh . . . ? Margaret Campbell called you directly? Really? Well, I can always get you Margaret at another time, Henry.

With Westlake, though, we've got to strike while he's hot. And he *will* be hot now that Vine has plugged his book . . . Uh-huh . . . Okay, then, call me back."

She hung up the phone and looked up at me with a smile, all the while still pressing that redial button. "That was Henry Baylor. Barnes and Noble, San Diego. He's skittish about new authors. And, as you heard, Margaret Campbell called him personally."

"I hear that she isn't very happy that she's not getting San Diego."

"Apparently not. She's like a vulture, swooping down on the carcass of Glenda Vassar's book tour, fighting for every scrap." She unwrapped a stick of nicotine gum with her free hand. "Nice interview on the Vine show, by the way. If you can't give him lesbians, give him underwear."

"Thanks."

"So, let's talk about you."

"That's my favorite subject."

"Good. I hate shy authors." She popped the gum in her mouth and continued, firing off my itinerary in a staccato voice. "You fly out of Newark tonight on the seven-twelve for Sea-Tac Airport. Tuesday you'll read at Barnes and Noble in Tacoma. You fly to Portland Wednesday morning, then read at Powell's that night. Thursday, you're flying from Portland to San Diego, and—unless Henry screws me—you'll be signing at his Barnes and Noble that evening. All the signings are scheduled for seven P.M., and you'll want to select a few excerpts to read. Oh—and prepare for a brief Q and A after the reading. Your hotel rooms have all been booked and there will be people meeting you at each airport. Any questions?"

"I don't suppose you've written this down for me . . ."

She selected a sheet of paper off the desk and handed it to me. "Here you go. Now, I know you've done some signings before, but . . . Well, let me put it this way: You're not doing the Jersey City Waldenbooks anymore. I think this Gary Vine thing will be big, Andrew, and I'd advise you to be prepared for crowds. I've prepared—" She stopped, found yet another piece of paper, handed it to me, and continued. "I've prepared a list of tips that should help you get through this with minimum hassle. Read it. And I've left you my cell phone and beeper numbers, in case you have any problems."

I looked at her list. Seventeen bulleted tips, ranging from "Keep the line moving" (number five) to "Don't accept dinner invitations from strangers" (number sixteen). Somehow, she managed to restrain herself from including, "Remember to wash behind your ears."

Still pressing the redial button, Angela gathered the papers from my desk. "I'd better get back to my office. Beep me if you need me."

I didn't beep her. Her very presence exhausted me, and I needed all the energy I could get. Still, there was no way to avoid her. An hour later she called to tell me, "Henry Baylor heard Vine's show. He's in. You're going to San Diego."

"That's great."

"Yeah," she said, and immediately moved on. "Now I've got to work up your East Coast tour."

The day was busy—*very* busy—and the wonderful thing about that was that it lessened the troubles weighing me down. Of course I thought of Frank—as well as the police and the mob and the rest of the unpleasantness—throughout the day, but the knowledge that I was about to escape New York allowed me to defer my worries.

Somewhat.

Even Denise noticed my lighter mood when she rode in the cab with me to Newark Airport to see me off.

"You look much better already. I think this will be good for you."

"I'm going to miss Frank. But I have to admit that it'll be nice to have a few days when I don't have to look over my shoulder."

"To stress relief." She lifted her bottled water.

"To stress relief." I touched her bottled water with my can of ginger ale.

The cab exited the New Jersey side of the Lincoln Tunnel, and I turned to take one last look at the Manhattan skyline. Like my problems, it seemed overwhelming . . . but already so far away.

8

Bestsellers

When I landed at Seattle-Tacoma International Airport, I was greeted by a cardboard sign bearing my name, held above the bobbing heads of my fellow passengers and *their* greeters outside the gates. I followed the sign until I saw a man in his late twenties, his pale, gangly appearance further softened by owlish glasses.

"Looking for me?" I extended my hand as he slightly lowered the sign.

"Mr. Westlake?" he asked in nasal tones. Although the sign was now at shoulder level, he still held it as if prepared to thrust it back into the air if I turned out to be an impostor.

"That's me."

"*Andrew* Westlake?"

"Yes," I answered and, anticipating his next question, added, "The novelist. That's me."

He tucked the sign under one arm and took my hand. "I'm Chris Cason. On behalf of the Barnes and Noble stores of the Seattle/Tacoma area, welcome to the Pacific Northwest." He flashed a nervous smile.

"Thank you. On behalf of the people of *my* planet."

Chris Cason drove a beat-up Chevy Cavalier with an interior smelling vaguely of stale Mexican food, most likely the result of an ill-fated trip through the drive-thru window at Taco Bell. When he started the engine, exhaust fumes backed up into the passenger compartment. The commingled stale Mexican food and exhaust odors left me feeling nauseous, so I cracked the window despite the chill.

As he drove, he told me in great detail about his dreams of writing a novel. I managed to refrain from telling him that it was an affliction that struck approximately one of every three Americans, and ninety-seven of every one hundred bookstore employees. For someone who had published only his second novel and was on his first real book tour, I realized I was becoming a bit jaded.

For his part, Chris was slightly ahead of the game, since he had recently finished chapter three of his work, "a horror/erotica hybrid, with a neo-Marxist point of view" thrown in for good measure. He prattled on about his work-in-progress for quite a while, which was good because it gave me an opportunity to daydream about Frank.

My daydreams took two forms. In one, Frank was taking advantage of my absence by slipping into a chalk-striped suit and, with a smoking semiautomatic in each hand, prowling the dark alleys of New York City, brutally but efficiently mowing down cigar-chomping wise guys. In the other, Frank paced nervously through his sprawling apartment, overwhelmingly concerned about my well-being and feeling his heart stop at every blast of a taxi horn from the street below.

Neither daydream was especially comforting. But they were both very vivid.

"And so," I finally heard Chris's voice drone, "the Ant Women finally kill off the scientist—see, he's sort of their oppressor—but his brain, and this is where I'm stuck, his brain is still alive."

I tuned him out again and returned to my daydreams.

The Cavalier finally pulled into the circular drive in front of a nondescript Marriott hotel and came to a stop. I pulled the two duffel bags packed with my clothes out of the backseat.

As I stepped out of the car, my nose wrinkled involuntarily.

"What's that odor?"

"Odor? Oh, that's the paper mill." He shrugged. "You get used to it after a while."

Wonderful. A book tour filled with olfactory delights.

"When should I pick you up tomorrow?" he asked. "The reading is scheduled for seven, but I'd be happy to show you some of Ta-coma during the day."

"I'll call . . ." I said, not realizing that my voice was trailing off as I caught a glimpse of a dark Chrysler idling in the parking lot of a truck stop across the street. From behind the night-darkened win-dows, I could see the orange glow of a lit cigarette and the white puff of exhaled smoke as it escaped through the cracked-open win-dow. It wasn't really possible that I'd been followed to the West Coast, was it?

"Mr. Westlake?"

"Huh?"

I looked down to see Chris stretched across the front seat, hold-ing a piece of paper for me through the open passenger side door. I wondered how long I had been staring at the Chrysler . . . *and* I wondered if I was becoming too paranoid. I stole another glance at the car, then looked back down at my escort.

"It's my business card. So you know how to get in touch with me tomorrow. I'm in the store by nine, usually."

"Thank you." I took the card and slipped it into my shirt pocket, then absently waved a silent good-bye. I grabbed the duffel bags and walked toward the entrance to the Marriott lobby, making a point of not looking back.

I checked into the hotel and was given a small room on the fifth floor, into which the hotel management had somehow managed to cram two queen-sized beds separated by a night stand, a small desk, a chair, two floor lamps, and a dresser/entertainment center. I pulled open the heavy curtains to reveal a rain-drenched view of the highway I had just traveled.

And the Chrysler in the parking lot.

I closed the curtains.

I was perfectly aware that I was probably paranoid. To the extent I was targeted by anyone, it would be when I was in New York City. On a West Coast book tour—in Tacoma, Washington, no less— there was no reason for anyone to be shadowing me. No reason whatsoever. And with that logic at work, I began to calm down.

Minutes later, the phone rang.

"Hello," I answered, and there was no response.

I hung up, then walked back to the window. I peeked out of a finger-width opening just in time to catch a glimpse of a raincoat-clad man walking swiftly through the downpour, away from the phone booth outside the truck stop and straight to the Chrysler, where he opened the passenger door and slid in.

The digital clock on the nightstand read 11:17 P.M., which meant that it was 2:17 A.M. in Manhattan. Still, I picked up the telephone and dialed.

"Do you have any idea what time it is here in New York?" asked David Carlyle.

"Actually, I do. My body is still on East Coast time, too, remember? But . . . well . . . maybe I'm just paranoid, but I think my—uh—*problem* has followed me to Tacoma."

After his panic attack ended, David made all the arrangements from New York, so that calls from the hotel room couldn't be traced. First, he got me a room at another motel. Then he sent a cab to meet me at the side door of the Marriott, where the chances that I'd be spotted making my getaway would be somewhat reduced. Still, I ducked down in the backseat as the cab pulled out onto the highway and passed the Chrysler.

The cab driver left me at a seedy motel seven miles away from the Marriott. I registered using the name Nicholas Hafner and paid thirty-five dollars in cash for the room for one night. The sleepy-eyed clerk never even bothered to raise a tired eyebrow.

With the least bit of luck, I thought, as I surveyed the sparse, threadbare room, only David and I knew where I was at that exact moment. I called him to tell him briefly what name I had used to register—he found it "amusing, if evident of lingering bitterness"—then, without removing a single item of clothing, due to both exhaustion and health concerns, I crawled on top of the lumpy bed and tried to fall asleep.

It wasn't that easy, of course. I was finding the possibility that people you don't know are out there, intent on causing you physical pain and/or suffering and/or extermination, was a major cause of insomnia. No less a cause, too, was the probability that Frank was in danger.

Still, I must have drifted off at some point during the night because, when the telephone rang at 7:30 A.M., it woke me out of a troubled sleep. The phone rang four times, in fact, before my brain could understand what was happening and force my body into action.

" 'lo," I said groggily.

"Good morning." It was David. "You seemed to survive the night."

"Barely." I glanced at the curtains covering the window. A slight trace of light penetrated them at the edges. "Hmm . . . I guess it *is* morning, isn't it?"

"How did you sleep?"

"Here? At the Bates Motel? As well as could be expected."

"Sorry to hear that. I'm hunting down a home phone number for your escort from Barnes and Noble now, so hopefully you'll be rescued soon. If not, the store will be open at nine, so I'll get him then."

"Wait a minute." I remembered that Chris's card was still in my shirt pocket. I pulled it out, but he hadn't written down his home telephone number. "Sorry. I thought I had a phone number, but I don't."

"No problem. I must say that your recent scrapes have allowed me the opportunity to hone my skills as a halfway decent amateur detective. Maybe this will be my next career."

"I'll warn Miss Marple."

"I'll track your escort down," he said, ignoring me. "Though why I feel the need to rescue you escapes me at the moment."

"Thanks. I love you, too."

I hung up the phone and made my way to the tiny, mildewed bathroom. It didn't have a tub or shower, so I settled for splashing lukewarm water over my haggard face.

I was still in the bathroom when the phone rang again. I gingerly wiped my face with my sleeve, then walked back to the nightstand and picked it up.

"Yes, David," I said.

"I found him. Chris Cason will pick you up in an hour. Can you be ready?"

"Ready enough, I suppose. But I'll need to find a shower."

"I have confidence in your industry."

"Thanks, David. And don't worry. I'll be fine."

"I have an awkward question to ask you," I said as Chris's Cavalier began to drive off the motel's battered concrete driveway. "Do you think we could swing by your place, so that I could take a quick shower?"

"I suppose . . ." It was, I imagined, one of the odder author requests he had heard. Fortunately, he didn't ask for an explanation.

I cracked the window to minimize the Mexican-food-and-exhaust nausea again, and we drove in silence for several minutes. Finally, he asked the question I knew he had been dying to ask since David first woke him from his sound sleep.

"Why did you stay in that motel last night? I *did* drop you off at the right hotel, didn't I?"

"You did," I said. "But . . . somehow, they screwed up the reservation. So I had to find something else."

"Oh." He clearly didn't believe me, and even more clearly imagined that the truth was tawdry and disreputable. If he only knew . . .

The Cavalier turned into a generic suburban apartment complex, then mazed through a series of identical driveways linking a series of identical buildings until Chris slid it between two identical Ford Escorts in front of his building.

"This is where I live," he said, smiling with obvious pride that he had managed to achieve the Great American Dream of becoming just like everyone else. Well . . . except for his fantasies about ant women.

I opened the door and stepped out onto the wet pavement, gratefully taking in several breaths of the fresh air.

"Let's go. I'm really looking forward to this shower."

When I was finally clean and feeling slightly more human, Chris gave me a mini-tour of Tacoma—which is to say I saw everything there is to see in Tacoma, including the paper mill—after which he drove me to a few bookstores. At each stop, I jumped out of the car, waved down the manager or assistant manager, and signed their handful of stocked copies of *The Brewster Mall.* And I breathed in a lot of paper mill fumes.

Finally, minutes before noon, my escort apologized and said that he had to return to work.

"No problem. I completely understand." My reading wasn't until seven, but I figured that there were worse things in the world than having to kill several hours in a bookstore. Violent death, for instance; or, a bleaker alternative, killing several hours in the Bates Motel.

When we entered the store, he pointed to a huge display of my books under a hastily made sign with large lettering reading, "To- NIGHT: ANDREW WESTLAKE, AUTHOR OF THE BREWSTER MALL, A GARY VINE BOOK SELECTION!!!" Gary Vine's name was spelled out larger than mine, of course, but it was hard to feel resentful.

"We're expecting a big crowd," he said. "The phones have been ringing since yesterday. And Gary Vine mentioned your appearance here again this morning."

"Really?" I tried hard not to burst out in immature glee. News like this was almost enough to make me forget that the Mafia and the police were both an unpleasant part of my life. Almost.

"Really! I just wish he hadn't taken that gratuitous shot at Margaret Campbell."

"Huh?"

"Yeah. I guess he heard that the two of you were competing for the Glenda Vassar tour. Anyway, this morning he called her a talentless hack."

"That's not good."

"Oh, I agree! Margaret Campbell is one of our best sellers! I certainly don't think it's fair to call her 'talentless.' " He paused, then added, "I don't think he should have called her a hag, either."

"A hag? I thought you said he called her a hack."

"He did. A hack *and* a hag."

Ten minutes later, after Chris left me alone in the manager's office to make some personal phone calls, I reached David. After assuring him that I was still all right, I said, "You must not be having the greatest of days, huh?"

"Oh. So you've heard."

"Yeah. How mad is she?"

"Let's just say that—after her first call to me at seven fifty-three this morning—she's mad enough to have not spoken to me since. Nor has she taken any of my calls. Then again, after her seven fifty-three call, I'm not so sure I have the stamina to talk to her again today. Or for the rest of my life, for that matter."

"Well, she can't blame you or PMC for the things Gary Vine says, can she?"

"One wouldn't think so. But . . ."

"Maybe I could ask Frank to get Vine to tone it down."

"No!!" snapped David. "One way or the other, we'll weather the Margaret Campbell storm. But I do not want you to call Frank. Absolutely not! That would ruin the entire purpose of sending you to the West Coast!"

"But—"

"Andrew! This is supposed to be your Frank vacation. This is supposed to be a cooling off period for you, so that maybe you won't end up in the trunk of a car in the immediate future. At least, within the next two weeks. And need I add that everyone *except* you agrees with this strategy? Me, Denise, Max Abraham, and even Frank himself?"

"So, what you're trying to say . . ."

"Listen to me carefully. It's not what I'm *trying to* say. It's what I *am* saying. Do. Not. Call. Frank."

"Okay . . . okay," I agreed, infusing each of the four syllables with as much reluctance as I could muster. We said our good-byes and I hung up the receiver.

I sat, alone and uncomfortable, in the silence of the manager's office for several long minutes, staring at the telephone and willing myself not to call Frank. For once, common sense won out.

Obscurity. It was something every writer struggled to escape, and yet it could also come as such a great comfort. As obscure as I was in Manhattan, I was even more obscure in the stacks of the Barnes & Noble store in Tacoma, where the police and the Mafia didn't know my name or face and only Chris Cason and, perhaps, the mysterious man in the dark Chrysler could pick me out of a lineup. Even Gary Vine's tens of thousands of local listeners wouldn't recognize me.

And that afternoon, killing time in the bookstore in anticipation of my reading and signing in the early evening, I welcomed the comfort of obscurity.

Chris opened his trunk so I could retrieve my copy of *The Duct Tape Murder*. Oh, first he insisted that I could have just read one of the store's shelved copies, but he finally conceded my point that authors made no money on books that were read but not purchased. Libraries, of course, were a necessary evil. But considering that morning's Gary Vine fiasco, I felt an obligation to read my own copy of the Campbell book, rather than soiling a fresh copy. I figured the fact that David had given me the book, and that neither he nor I had actually paid for it, was really beside the point.

I found a chair in a quiet section of the store's second floor and started reading.

It was a typical Campbell novel in many ways. Which isn't to say that I thought she was a hack—far from it—but, as is the case with so many prolific authors, its style was evocative of every other Campbell novel that had ever been published. What set *The Duct Tape Murder* apart from the others was that she altered her usual plot—an innocent protagonist desperately trying to clear his or her name—by making the lead character a guilty man desperately trying to clear his name.

I found the theme every bit as unsettling on the surface as I had when I made earlier stabs at reading it, but the geographical distance between myself and my worst problems gave me a comfort level that finally allowed me to read past page ten.

And so I read . . .

Margaret Campbell's antihero LaMarca—the readers never learned his first name—was a minor nonviolent criminal who, in the course of a petty after-hours burglary, was surprised by the store owner. After a struggle, LaMarca overpowered the store owner and tied him up and gagged him with duct tape, thinking he would buy just enough time to escape. He cleaned up evidence of his presence—fingerprints and the like—and left, making a quick 911 call from several blocks away to alert the authorities of the duct tape–bound victim. By the time the police arrived, however, the victim had suffocated.

There was no initial evidence implicating LaMarca in the crime, especially after the death of the only witness. But his overwhelming guilt forced him back to the scene of the crime, where he began to arouse the suspicion of the police. Armed with his voice on the 911 tape and fingerprints from the pay phone he had used to make the call, the authorities began shadowing him as they tried to build a case. LaMarca soon realized that he was the prime suspect and struggled to throw the police off his trail . . . even if that meant attempting to implicate a dangerous drug dealer.

The cat-and-mouse-and-dangerous-drug-dealer game played out over several hundred pages until . . .

When I finished page 248 and closed the cover it was five thirty-

seven, and Chris Cason suddenly appeared to ask me if I wanted
something to eat before the reading.

"No," I replied. "I've lost my appetite."

He shrugged, smiled, and walked away.

I cracked the novel open again and flipped to the last page.

> *I looked up at Harry Browne, his two-hundred-sixty-five-pound
> frame blocking the lone, bare lightbulb.*
>
> *"I didn't —" I started to say, but my strength had ebbed and I
> couldn't get the other words past my lips.*
>
> *"You fucked up, LaMarca," he said harshly. "You fucked with the
> wrong man."*
>
> *I wanted to agree with him. I wanted to take everything back. I
> wanted to go back to the day when I had first broken into Hutner's
> Hardware and had my ill-fated run-in with Gordon Hutner. But I
> couldn't. And now there was no more time to regret any of the stupid
> things I had done to bring me to this point. There was only time to pray
> for the salvation of my soul.*
>
> *I heard a click, and squinted. The drug dealer held the pistol close to
> my temple, ready to fire a final, unnecessary shot to finish what he must
> have felt was taking too long.*
>
> *"Drop it, Browne!" I heard someone—no, it seemed to be several
> someones—shout. "Police!" Harry looked down at me, sneered, and
> muttered "Damn!" The staccato of a volley of gunshots erupted, and he
> slumped to the floor. His pistol fell heavily onto my chest.*
>
> *I heard someone call for an ambulance. I wanted to tell them not to
> bother, that it was already far too late, but the words wouldn't come.*
>
> *I heard another cop tell me to hang in there, that Harry Browne
> couldn't hurt me anymore, the way he'd killed the guy who owned that
> hardware store.*
>
> *So, my last uncomfortable thought before I died was that I had got-
> ten away with murder.*
>
> *May God have mercy on my soul.*

At 7:05, I began my reading. On an empty stomach.

I selected part of Chapter Three, a seven-page stretch of text
with minimal dialogue that dealt primarily with the budding romance between Mercedes, the fortyish manager of The Gap, and
Phil, the twenty-something manager of Banana Republic. My audience—standing room only, I was happy to note—laughed at all the

right places, including the barbed comments about how a merger between the two of them would create a mall monopoly on khakis. And there was no perceptible boredom. In fact, the closest I came to losing my decidedly heterosexual audience was when two male clerks stole a quick kiss in the men's room at J. C. Penney, oblivious to the security cameras.

"Any questions?" I asked, finishing the reading.

The members of the audience looked at each other, wondering who would be the first to speak.

"Wasn't Glenda Vassar supposed to read tonight?" asked one older woman finally.

Chris stepped out from behind me. "There was a change of plans. I apologize, but Mr. Westlake was kind enough to fill in on short notice."

"Next?" I asked nervously.

A middle-aged hippie stood up. "Is it true that you don't wear underwear?"

I blushed. "Next?"

"What's Gary Vine really like?" asked a young, unkempt man.

"Uh . . . I haven't met him yet."

"Have you met Howard Stern?"

"No."

"How about—?"

"We really should let someone else ask a few questions." Chris pointed at a young woman—she couldn't have been older than twenty—who was tentatively raising her hand.

"I have a question?" she said, which was really quite unnecessary since she inflected her voice in that annoying way that turns every statement into a question. "For Andrew Westlake? How long did it take you to write your book?"

I smiled. "Slightly more than one year. Which is fast for me. My first book took . . . Well, I suppose it took me ten years."

"And I have another question? Would you mind taking a look at my manuscript?"

"Uh . . ."

I inelegantly slid out of that corner, answered three or four equally irrelevant questions, then—as I stayed planted behind the table—the crowd queued up to buy my book and receive an official Andrew Westlake signature.

The Glenda Vassar fan was the fifth person in line. She tossed me a grandmotherly smile. "Well, as long as I'm here . . ."

"Thanks." I scrawled my signature in her book. "I agree that she's a great writer."

"Oh, yes. I'm so disappointed that she's not here tonight." She patted my hand. "But I'm sure that you're acceptable."

I smiled and nodded, damned by faint praise.

The ninth person in line was a very attractive man in his late twenties who, as he presented me with my book, smiled boyishly and leaned close to my ear. "By the way, I loved your first novel."

"*Allentown Blues?*" I asked, shocked, looking up into his dark blue eyes. "You must be one of the twelve people in the world who bought it!"

"It struck close to home." Still smiling, he tossed a wave of dark brown hair off his forehead and gave me a better view of his mesmerizing eyes. "I'd love to get *that* autographed, too."

"Just mail it to me. I'd be happy to . . ."

"I was thinking that maybe we could meet later for a drink and you could sign it then."

I was starting to think that might not be a bad idea. But it also might not be a good idea. There was the minor complication of Frank, after all.

"Where are you staying?" he asked, and I realized that was the best question I had been asked all night. Where *was* I staying? Certainly not at the Bates Motel again. Maybe it was time to get over my paranoia . . . and maybe it was safe enough and innocent enough to meet my adorable fan for a drink and some conversation. It would have to be of a higher level than a discussion about ant women and living, disembodied brains, after all, which was the only alternative I saw in my immediate future.

"I'm at the Marriott," I said finally. "And, yeah, I suppose there's no harm in meeting in the hotel bar for a drink later. Ten o'clock?"

"Sounds good."

"And how should I make out this inscription?" My pen was still poised over the blank page.

"Patrick," he replied. "I'm Patrick. Waverly."

I scribbled out my message and handed the book back to him. "There you go, Patrick Waverly. I'll see you at ten."

The fourteenth person in line made me nervous. He was tall, imposing, taciturn, and slightly hostile. As I signed the book, I tried to compare him to the shadowy figure I had seen outside the Marriott, but I couldn't make a positive ID.

The nineteenth person was formed by the same mold.

So was number twenty-seven. And forty. And fifty-two.

By the time I had sold my fifty-eighth and final book—which Chris told me was a number "beyond excellent"—I decided I was getting paranoid. They couldn't *all* be after me, after all. Maybe Gary Vine fans were just a bit surly.

I glanced at my watch and saw that it was almost nine.

"Chris, would you mind driving me to the Marriott?"

"Are you sure you can get a room tonight?"

"Uh . . . yeah. I called earlier, and the mix-up has been resolved."

Twenty minutes later, the Cavalier pulled into the circular driveway. I was happy to note that the Chrysler was *not* parked across the street, nor was it parked in the Marriott's lot.

Paranoia, I told myself. That's all it was.

Back in my room, I checked for waiting messages—there were none—then took a quick shower and changed into a heavy crewneck sweater and jeans. Eighteen minutes later I walked into the hotel bar. Patrick Waverly was already waiting for me.

"I'm surprised you actually showed up," he said, as his ever-present smile dimpled his cheeks.

"No, you're not." I settled onto the stool next to his. "I have the feeling you're not exactly lacking in self-confidence."

He didn't reply—well, besides broadening that damned smile—so I added, "Did you bring the book?"

"Oh! Yeah!" He rummaged around for a moment until he produced a copy of *Allentown Blues* from an oversized coat pocket. I took it from his hands and opened it, hunching over the bar as I wrote, *Patrick: It's been my pleasure to meet you and discover that you have such exquisite taste in fiction. —Andrew Westlake.* Yes, I knew that the word *exquisite* had a David Carlylish ring to it, but it seemed to fit so I used it anyway.

"How long are you in Tacoma for?" Patrick asked after I returned the book.

"I'm out of here tomorrow morning. Next stop, Portland."

"Too bad." He slid his body slightly closer to mine, and it occurred to me that Patrick Waverly was very likely looking for something more than an autograph and some innocent face-time with one of his favorite authors. "I would have enjoyed showing you the sights."

"I saw the sights," I said with a slight, nervous stammer. "All three of them."

"So, what's it like to live in New York?"

"It's not for everyone. But I like it."

"I've never been there. Would you recommend a visit?"

"*Everyone* should visit New York City at least once in his life. Not everyone should stay."

"Are you seeing anyone?" He changed the topic with an abruptness that caught me by surprise.

"Uh . . . sort of."

"Just my luck," he said, still smiling and once again sweeping away the hair that fell across his forehead. He slid back a few inches, as if to signal that he respected my relationship. "So, what's his name?"

"Frank."

"Have you been together long?"

"No. Only . . ." I stopped as the accelerated nature of my relationship with Frank occurred to me. "Wow, it's only been a little bit more than a week. Unbelievable!"

"What's so unbelievable about it?"

That simple question was almost all it took. I was a stranger in a strange city, Patrick Waverly seemed eager to listen, and I needed to pour my heart out to someone. So I gave Patrick a condensed version of my life with Ted, segued into my first encounter with Frank at Benedick's, and left it dangling.

"That's it?" he asked. "Happily ever after?"

"Well, like I said, we haven't even been together for two weeks."

Patrick stared thoughtfully at his drink, then shrugged. "Hey, if it works for you, Andrew, that's great. As long as you're prepared for the bad times when they happen."

"Oh, Frank and I have already been through some bad times," I said.

"Tell me about them."

I didn't really mean to tell Patrick Waverly almost everything, but somehow, it came out. It's true that I needed to unburden my soul, but every time I reached a natural end point, he asked another question that propelled me deeper into the story. And so, over the next forty-five minutes, he learned about Crazy Anna Franco,

Hanover's Book Store, Gary Vine, Big Paulie Macarini, Max Abraham, Brogan and Mueller, and every other little piece of insanity that had occurred in my life in recent days.

When I finished my monologue, he shook his head. "Amazing."

"To say the least."

"You should write a book about it."

"I don't write nonfiction. For that matter, I don't seem to live it, either."

"Well, I hope I didn't pry too much. I didn't mean to."

I laughed. "I guess I needed to get it all off my chest. I'm the one who should be apologizing. I hope I didn't bore you."

"Bore me? With *that* story?"

We were the only customers in the bar, so I suggested calling it a night. He gave me a hopeful smile, but I disarmed it with a playful punch to the shoulder. "I really don't think you want to become a player in this particular melodrama, Patrick."

"No." He didn't seem to be disappointed in the least. And who could blame him? "I suppose not. But I don't have to work tomorrow, so maybe I'll take a drive down to Portland and catch you there."

"You really are a glutton for punishment, aren't you?"

"A masochist. That's me." He paused. "It's only a two-and-a-half, three-hour drive. And I wouldn't do it if I didn't think I'd enjoy it. Plus, I'm still waiting to hear the answer to the 'Do you wear underwear?' question."

I smiled. "You'll have to wonder."

"Okay, then. I'm a patient man." He returned my smile, and, of course, his cheeks dimpled. "Maybe I'll see you tomorrow."

We parted in the hotel lobby. When I returned to my room, I clicked on the television and watched one of the generic late-night talk shows. For some reason, baring my personal trials to Patrick *had* made me feel better, and it *had* made me feel less of a need to call David or Denise or even Frank for some late-night hand-holding, so I managed to sit through a half-hour of mediocre television with only a modicum of angst. And I couldn't deny that the thought that an attractive young man would have slept with me if given half a chance was just the sort of ego boost I needed.

Thank heavens for the handful of people who actually find writers fascinating and sexually attractive, I thought.

* * *

Another day, another flight, another new city. Two days into my book tour and I was already growing weary, even though—with the mysterious Chrysler, the Bates Motel, *The Duct Tape Murder*, and my introduction to Patrick Waverly—the first thirty-six hours had been far from boring. The assistant manager from Powell's, a Chris Cason clone, was waiting for me in the Portland airport with yet another hand-lettered and -held sign.

Another brief tour of the city, another series of drive-by autographs, another hotel room, another trip back to another bookstore, another standing-room-only crowd composed of 80 percent Gary Vine fans and 20 percent Glenda Vassar fans who only learned at the last moment that her appearance had been canceled . . . Oh, and Patrick Waverly, of course.

Another batch of stupid questions, another batch of books sold and, finally, another hotel bar. Oh—with Patrick Waverly, of course.

"So, how did I sound?" I asked.

"Great." He seemed pleased that I had honored him by allowing him to be my own personal sycophant. In fact, he was doing me the favor. He provided me with much-needed companionship in these unfamiliar West Coast cities, without which I would have locked myself in my hotel room, raided the mini-bar, and worried about Frank. Not to mention the fact that he was very cute and obviously attracted to me. Even though I was quite sure I didn't have it in me to cheat on Frank, I appreciated the flirtatious aspect of our acquaintanceship. As many people have said before—some of whom even meant it—there's no harm in looking.

"I love the part about the two guys getting caught by the security camera in the men's room at J. C. Penney."

He caught me off-guard, until I remembered that we were discussing my reading. "That's the voyeur in you trying to come out."

"You could tell?"

We laughed and ordered a second drink. That's when I felt a stern tap on my shoulder. I made a half-turn to face a short woman who looked unhappy and vaguely familiar peering at me through pinched eyes and reading glasses. I struggled to place her face until I remembered that she had been standing unhappily at the back of the crowd at my reading. She hadn't bought a book.

"Hi," I said, forcing myself to be chipper despite her stern expression. "How are you tonight?"

"I. Am. Well." The clipped words forced themselves from her lips. "All things considered."

"Didn't like the reading?" All my insecurities began to bubble to the surface. "I'm sorry. I'm not very good at these things . . ."

She looked me—and then Patrick—up and down with distaste.

"Well . . . can I buy you a drink?" I offered.

"Bourbon," she replied. "Neat."

The bartender returned with drinks for Patrick and me. I ordered the bourbon. When he set her drink down, the woman grabbed it from the bar and asked, "Can I speak to you?" It sounded more of a command than a question.

"Sure." I motioned for her to take the empty barstool next to me.

"Alone." She nodded unhappily at Patrick.

I watched as she began walking to a nearby table without waiting for my answer, then looked back at Patrick, shrugged an apology, and followed her.

"So, what can I do for you?" I asked, as I sat across from her at the small round table. The reflection from a small candle in the center of the table added even more fire to her facial features.

"Do you know who I am?"

"Should I?"

"I'm Margaret Campbell."

I felt my stomach free-fall. "Uh . . . uh . . . I . . . uh . . ."

"I don't know what this is all about, Westlake, but if PMC has decided to start playing favorites with its authors, then you can tell that son-of-a-bitch David Carlyle to find himself a new best-seller. I'll be at another house so fast it'll make your head spin!"

"Uh . . . I . . . I . . ."

"PMC owed me this. They screwed me once by giving Portland and San Diego to Glenda Vassar, and they screwed me again when they gave them to you. This should have been *my* tour, and don't you forget it! PMC has screwed me over in some of my best territory. Not only that, but they've managed to get that ridiculous Gary Vine to promote you and *insult* me!"

"Oh, but PMC didn't have anything to do with that. That was just Gary Vine . . ."

"Was it? PMC sent you to Tacoma, Portland, and—on this I

could just scream—*San Diego,* knowing that I wanted them. Three days later Gary Vine was pushing your piece of crap and calling me a *hag!* And *talentless!* You're the hero because you went on the air and compromised your dignity by talking about underwear with that freak, but *I'm* the talentless hag! Pardon me if I don't buy into the 'coincidence' argument."

"But . . . but . . . that *was* just coincidence. PMC didn't . . . wouldn't . . . they wouldn't tell Gary Vine to call you a talentless hack."

"Thanks. I forgot that he called me a hack, too."

I mentally kicked myself. "I'm sure it was nothing personal."

Despite her short stature, she still managed to look down her nose at me. "This is nothing *but* personal, Andy."

"An*drew.*"

"Whatever. What you call yourself really doesn't interest me. Because tomorrow morning you're flying back to New York, where I'd advise that you go immediately to Saint Patrick's Cathedral and start praying that *The Duct Tape Murder* sells at least as well as I was anticipating it would. Because if it doesn't, I'm going to make sure that your stupid little shopping mall book is the last thing you ever publish."

"I'm supposed to fly to San Diego tomorrow," I protested.

" 'Supposed to' being the operative phrase. But you won't be going to San Diego because *I'm* going to San Diego. I was fortunate enough to book my own Portland appearance at Border's this afternoon, but I'm not doing my own scheduling for San Diego. Not at this late date."

"But—"

"I've already worked things out with Henry Baylor at Barnes and Noble. As of this evening, there's been a change of plans. You're out and I'm in. The way it should have been in the first place."

I glanced back at Patrick, who was watching from the bar and no doubt wondering what the heated discussion was about. And I wasn't so sure that I wasn't wondering that myself. When I looked back at Margaret Campbell, she was already taking one last gulp of her bourbon and gathering her purse.

"Margaret," I pleaded, as she stood, "can't we discuss this?"

"That's *Ms. Campbell* to you. We are *not* peers. And there's nothing more to discuss." With that, she stood and marched away.

I walked back to the bar, feeling every bit as beaten as the night when Big Paulie Macarini had returned my books from Hanover's.

"That," I said, "was Margaret Campbell."

"The mystery writer?"

"One and the same. Basically, she told me that she didn't think it would be a good idea for me to go to San Diego. And I have to agree. After five minutes with her, I think I'd rather take my chances with the Mafia."

He placed a hand on my arm. "Don't say that, Andrew. You're too good a guy to get tangled up in that stuff."

"Too late. I'm already tangled."

His hand squeezed my arm. "You could always go back to Tacoma with me."

For a brief moment I felt a flicker of temptation. I saw myself and Patrick, a golden couple living a quiet life in the Pacific Northwest, safe from harm. I'd write books and he'd do, well, whatever it was that Patrick did. And thoughts of Frank would never enter my mind.

Except that they would. The moment I thought of *not* thinking of Frank, I was, of course, thinking of Frank. And the flicker of temptation died a mercifully quick death.

I shook my head. "Sorry, Patrick, but . . . I can't."

"I know."

Since I had two queen-sized beds again, and since it was too late for me to let him drive back to Tacoma with a clear conscience, and because I reasoned that I could use the company, I *did* invite Patrick to spend the night. But first I emphasized and reemphasized the word *platonic.*

We ordered a bottle of wine from room service, then—while he relaxed—I called David. "The shit hit the fan with Margaret Campbell."

"So she told me a few minutes ago," he said. "And I'm still shell-shocked. Was she very vulgar with you?"

"No."

He sighed. "That must be a facet of her personality that she's reserved exclusively for me, then. Anyway, Andrew, you have to go to San Diego. Margaret doesn't have the authority to make decisions

like this. Those are reserved for the publisher. At least, the last time
I looked, the publishers still had that authority."

"Do I get a bodyguard?"

"Maybe you can take along the cute boy who was sitting next to
you at the bar."

I gasped. "How did you—?"

"Margaret. Although, truth be told, she didn't call him a cute
boy. Actually, she said he was probably a hustler. But I assume that
she *meant* 'cute boy.' "

"He's just a guy," I said, glancing out of the corner of my eye to
catch a glimpse of Patrick before adding, in a whisper, "And he has
to go home tomorrow."

"So, he's still with you, eh?" Oops. "Well, it's too bad it's such a
short-lived fling—"

"It's not what you think—"

"—but maybe you're getting over Frank at last."

"David—"

"I can dream." Changing course, he said, "Don't you worry
about Margaret. I'll deal with her, and I'll sic Angela on the bookstore. You just worry about selling books. They're flying off the
shelves, Andrew, and I've been hearing only the best reports from
your tour."

I sighed. "If you're sure I should go to San Diego . . ."

"I'm sure. Now, it's very late here on the East Coast, so why don't
you call it a night? Call me tomorrow when you get to the bookstore."

"All right."

"And say good night to the cute boy for me," he said as he hung
up.

"David Carlyle says good night," I told Patrick, cradling the phone.

"How does he know I'm here?"

"Welcome to my life. Everyone has spies, and there are no private moments."

"So it seems." For once he didn't smile. "How do you feel about
that?"

"The frightening thing is that I'm beginning to accept it as the
natural order of life."

Soon the wine arrived. It wasn't going to win any awards, but it
did the job. I had just enough to loosen up, but not so much that I
would let myself do something that I'd later regret with Patrick.

And, for the second night, I managed to keep my obsession with Frank in check and avoided calling him.

My bags were packed. I was showered and dressed. A car was waiting downstairs to whisk me off to the airport for my next confrontation with Margaret Campbell in San Diego.

I was waiting only for the late-rising Patrick to finish his shower.

I had already rehearsed our farewell scene. There would be my thanks for his company, his thanks for my companionship, a vague promise to get together again sometime soon, and a semi-chaste kiss . . . all of it tinged with the excitement of a mutual flirtation. Then we'd head off in our separate directions—possibly to meet again, more likely to not meet again.

As the shower continued to run, I gathered his clothes together and laid them out on one of the beds. That's when his wallet fell out of his pants pocket. I reached to the floor to pick it up and was suddenly face-to-face with a gold badge. Identification from the Federal Bureau of Investigation.

"Son of a bitch," I muttered. I grabbed my bags and angrily—but silently—exited the room, leaving the shield open and exposed on top of his pile of clothes.

After discovering Special Agent Patrick Waverly's—or whatever his real name was—duplicity, I was enraged. To the point where I eagerly looked forward to a confrontation with Margaret Campbell in San Diego. To the point where I eagerly looked forward to returning to Manhattan and taking on the Mafia.

In short, I was really getting tired of being crushed against the rocks by waves not of my own making. And if the Mafia, the New York City Police Department, the Federal Bureau of Investigation, the publishing industry, and best-selling author Margaret Campbell didn't like it, then they were perfectly welcome to try to stop me.

I still had a head of steam when my plane landed in San Diego. Yet another clone of Chris Cason waited for me nervously in the airport.

"Mr. Westlake?" he asked timidly. "I'm here to drive you to your hotel. But Mr. Baylor—the manager—would like you to call him before you go over to the bookstore."

"Fuck Mr. Baylor." The Chris Cason clone looked like he was going to cry.

When I got to the hotel—my third Marriott with exactly the same room layout in as many days—I punched in the number for Barnes & Noble. When the phone was answered, I said, "This is Andrew Westlake calling for Henry Baylor."

Less than a minute later, I heard Henry Baylor's hearty and entirely insincere greeting. "Andrew! Welcome to San Diego!"

"Let's cut the crap, Henry. I know Margaret Campbell is planning to do a reading at your store tonight. But I don't intend to be dumped."

"I . . . I understand that, Andy—"

"An*drew*."

"Right. Andrew. I understand your situation, Andrew. But can't we work something out?"

"I don't see how."

"I'll think of something," he said. "You aren't due here for six more hours, so I'm sure I'll find some way to accommodate you."

"Good luck." I slammed down the phone before picking it back up and punching in the phone number for David's office.

"I just had a run-in with Henry Baylor," I told him angrily. "He's planning on trying to accommodate both Campbell and me."

"More power to him, I suppose." Then, with concern in his voice, he asked, "Are you all right? You don't sound well."

"I'm just . . . I'm just pissed off at the world, all right?"

"Talk to me."

"It's just . . . not . . . fair." I got the last word out before the tears of rage, frustration, and fear poured out.

"What's wrong?"

I regained my composure. "On top of everything else, the FBI is following me."

"Oh, dear. Have you called Max?"

"No, I have not called Max. I just found out this morning, and I've been on planes since then. That cute boy? From the hotel last night? He was a federal agent." I explained to David how I found his badge, and how I had spent more than twenty-four hours with "Patrick Waverly," including a long period of time in which—at his prompting—I did nothing but outline every single moment of my relationship with Frank DiBenedetto Junior, not neglecting to mention the facts that we had been discovered in a more-than-compromising position by his fiancée and that Frank had been behind Ted's beating.

"You stay in your room," he said. "I'll have Angela hound Henry Baylor to make sure he keeps his word. And I'll update Max."

"Thanks," I said. "And you'd better let Frank know about it, too."

"I really don't think—"

"Please, David?" I begged. "He has to know."

"I'll see what I can do."

I glanced at the clock on the nightstand. It was 12:45 P.M.

"I need a drink," I said.

"I think you should stay in your room until you hear from me," he replied. "Maybe this West Coast trip wasn't the best idea. I don't want you to do anything to make it worse."

"David, things just keep getting worse no matter where I go or what I do. If I'm not in my room, I'll be in the bar." Before he could answer me, I hung up.

I was relieved to see that I wasn't the only one in the Marriott bar. When I walked in, there were a handful of businessmen who had either decided to call it a day or certainly would after another drink, and there was one lonely, middle-aged woman holding up the far corner and flirting ineffectually with the dark-eyed bartender.

I sat and, when the bartender happily tore himself away from the woman, ordered a Bloody Mary.

I felt the iciness before I heard the voice.

"You again." Margaret Campbell was suddenly behind me. "I thought I'd made myself clear . . ."

"Oh, you did." I made a point of not turning to look at her. "But I've gone through too much grief in the past two weeks, and I've decided that enough is enough."

"I'm calling Henry Baylor," she said, whipping a cellular phone from her purse.

"Be my guest."

She dialed, announced herself, then disconnected without saying good-bye. "He's at lunch."

"Or so they tell you."

"I don't think I like you very much, Westlake."

I waved to the bartender, who once again smiled at the opportunity to get away from the woman at the end of the bar.

"The lady needs a drink."

"It's too early."

"Bourbon," I instructed the bartender. "Neat."

While her drink was poured, she mounted the stool next to mine. "Well, I shouldn't do this, but if you're buying . . . Can I ask you why you're doing this? Do you think this will buy my affection?"

I laughed. "Somehow, I can't see that happening. But let me put it this way: After what I've been through lately, I find your honesty refreshing."

She took her drink out of the bartender's hand—he sighed and wearily walked back down the bar to talk to the woman—and asked, "Tired of the kiss-ass book tour circuit already?"

"I wish that was the worst of my problems. But unless you've lived the lives of your characters, you couldn't begin to know."

She took a sip and raise one eyebrow. It arced over the rim of her eyeglasses. "Why don't you try me?"

"Sorry, but the last time I told my sad tale of woe, I ended up getting burned."

"That's life, Westlake. The only consolation is that, if it's that bad, you can change a few names and make a best-seller out of it."

I smiled, then glanced out of the corner of my eye and was surprised to see that she was smiling, too.

"Let's just say I think you'll find it telling that people have been telling me for a week to read *The Duct Tape Murder*. Not as literature, but as a how-to guide."

"Hmm . . ." She took another sip of her bourbon. "That sounds bad, all right. But maybe you should try reading it for literary merit, too. I don't think it's as bad as *some* people"—an unmistakable reference to PMC—"think it is."

"I read it. It was good. It scared me, but I have to agree that it was good."

An hour and two more Bloody Marys later, I told her everything, which was much the same as I related to Patrick Waverly but which now, of course, *included* Patrick Waverly. Or whatever his name was.

"Fascinating," she said when my narrative came to a close.

"Any thoughts about what I should do?"

She thought for a moment. "Well, there's the obvious option of breaking off your relationship with Frank. But that doesn't sound like it would be very easy for you. Although now that you've told everything to the FBI, Frank might dump you first." A knot formed in my stomach. "Or have you taken out." The knot tightened.

"Taken out?" I asked, knowing full well what she meant.

"Killed," she said, even though she really didn't have to. Oblivious to my internal pain, she paused to light a cigarette, then continued. "The other option, I suppose, is for you and Frank to simply disappear. Go away somewhere, where the Mafia and the authorities can't find you."

"Does such a place exist?"

"Yes." She took another sip. "But only in fiction."

Despite a nap and a shower, I was still a bit woozy when I stepped into the hotel lobby several hours later. Margaret was already there, perched in the middle of an uncomfortable-looking couch and talking animatedly to a short, balding man with a sweaty brow.

"Westlake!" she said when she saw me. "This is Henry Baylor. From Barnes and Noble."

I took his hand. It was warm and damp. He wasn't finding comfort in our joint appearance.

"So, what's the verdict, Henry?" My tongue still felt a bit thick from the afternoon cocktails. "How are we gonna handle this thing?"

"Uh . . . I thought, maybe, that a joint reading . . . uh . . ." Henry stammered.

Margaret looked at him with clear distaste.

"Our books are nothing alike, Henry. Our readership is nothing alike. Our personalities are nothing alike." I nodded at each of her points and relished each fresh coating of sweat that flowed down his brow.

"Please . . ." he rasped. "You've got to show up!"

"Why?" asked Margaret.

"Yeah, why?" I added.

"Because it's the professional thing to do," he said. "And you're professionals, aren't you?"

Margaret looked at me, and I looked at Margaret, and finally we both looked at Henry Baylor.

"Professionalism is highly overrated," she said finally. Then, wearily, she rose from the couch. "But I'll do this joint appearance thing if it will help sell some books." She took three heavy steps toward the front door, then turned. "Westlake?"

"I suppose." I sighed. "But only to sell books."

"Thank you!" gushed Henry. "Thank you!"

"Don't push it, Henry," said Margaret, with a style that would have done Bette Davis proud.

I sold only thirty-two books that night—Margaret Campbell easily doubled my total sales—but my West Coast book tour finally had drawn to a close. And not soon enough.

New York City held its own problems, of course, but at least I would be in the place where I belonged.

9

When Bad Things Happen to Stupid People

I breathed a sigh of relief when the cab pulled up in front of my apartment building late the next afternoon. There was no sign of Big Paulie Macarini, any other gangsters, the police, the FBI, or even Interpol, which—given the way things had been going recently—I was expecting at any moment.

Maybe, I allowed myself to think, the worst part of the nightmare had ended.

No sooner had I double-locked my apartment door behind me—taking care to ignore the copies of *The Brewster Mall* still heaped in the corner—than I called David. After assuring him that my flight was fine and that a hit crew hadn't been waiting for me, I cut to the chase.

"Did you talk to Frank?"

"Er . . . no," he confessed. "But I talked to Max Abraham, and he—"

"But you didn't talk to Frank?"

"I didn't have time. I couldn't reach him."

"Well, I've got to talk to Frank."

"But—"

I hung up on David and dialed Frank's phone number.

"It's Andrew," I said when he answered.

"Welcome home." It sounded as if he was glad to hear my voice.

"Can we talk?"

"Let's meet."

"Benedick's?"

"I don't think so. Lately, everything that happens there seems to become public record." He paused to think for a few beats. "Meet me on the Staten Island Ferry. The nine o'clock boat. We can talk there."

The subway train down to the South Ferry station ran slow, and I barely made the nine o'clock boat, running through the lower-level doors just as they were being pulled shut. On the top passenger level I found Frank sitting along one of the long wooden benches to the side of the ferry, sipping Budweiser out of the can.

"Here." He offered me a beer of my own, which was sitting in a pool of condensation on the bench.

"Thanks."

We sat in silence next to each other on the bench, staring out at the vast darkness of the New York Harbor through a grimy window. During rush hour, the huge orange ferry boats were always packed full of Staten Islanders traveling to work in Manhattan in the morning and home again in the evening, but at this late hour on a Friday night, our boat was uncrowded. I took advantage of the sparse number of riders to reach over and hold his hand. He started to pull away instinctively, then relaxed and let our fingers intertwine.

As much as I hated to break the spell, there was something I had to say. "I screwed up, Frank."

"Again?" A slight grin appeared at the corner of his mouth.

"Again."

"How's that?" He didn't take his eyes off the black harbor.

"I talked too much. To the wrong person."

He didn't reply for a long time, but we would have an hour together as the ferry made its round trip, and I could afford to wait. Finally, he asked, "Who did you talk to?"

"I thought he was a friend. But he turned out to . . . *not* be a friend."

"Cop?"

"Fed."

His shoulders hunched; then, as they relaxed, he let out a sigh that was heavy with disappointment. His fingers let go of mine and he brought the beer to his lips. He still didn't look at me.

"He was with the FBI," I continued. "He pretended to be a fan, and ... and I felt the need to talk to someone."

"How do you know he was a fed?"

"His wallet ..." I started to say, before I realized that the very fact that I had my hands on Patrick's wallet was going to require an even greater explanation. Which wasn't going to be particularly pleasant, either, but ... "I let him sleep in the extra bed in my hotel room, and in the morning when he was in the shower, his wallet fell out of his pants and ... that's when I saw the badge."

He turned to look at me. The face was blank and his words were measured but harsh.

"Every morning for the past couple of weeks I've been waking up and wondering what the hell you've done to me. I mean, I had a business, I had a fiancée ... Things weren't great, okay, but things were stable. And then you walked into my life, and all of a sudden I'm with another guy ... you know, *sexually* ... I've got people listening to my phone calls and gossiping about me ... I've got people blackmailing me ... I've got the police and the feds checking me out. And to make matters worse, you're wandering around the country *helping* the same people who are making my life a living hell!" He paused, took a sip of beer, and collected his thoughts for a moment. "Oh, and on top of that, you're letting strangers sleep in your hotel rooms, which would be bad enough if it was innocent—which I'm not altogether sure it was—but it's doubly bad when you're having fuckin' pillow talk with the fuckin' FBI."

His diatribe over, he swiveled his head and again stared out the window.

"Frank," I said, and I heard a catch in my voice. "Nothing happened. I just—"

He tossed a dismissive wave in my general direction. I stopped talking.

We sat like that for several long minutes, not speaking and not looking at each other. The lights of Ellis Island and the Statue of Liberty broke the dark loneliness of the harbor as the ferry quietly passed, but I was too intent on looking inward to see them. I saw nothing but the darkness.

"This isn't going to work," he said finally, breaking the silence.

"Frank, don't say that."

"Our worlds don't fit together. We're too different."

"But . . ."

"I'm not happy, Andrew." Judging from the hardness of his expression, I thought that was probably an understatement. "Part of it is that we don't have much in common. And part of it is that you don't understand the situation I'm in. I don't think you appreciate what it does to my life when you talk about these things with strangers . . . when you babble about having sex with me over the telephone . . . when you start telling me that you love me when other people can hear . . ."

With those words, and quite out of the blue, it was my turn to be pissed off.

"Hold on there," I said, a bit too loudly to be appropriate. I tried to moderate my tone with only occasional success. "This isn't only about Frank, okay? Don't give me shit about how *I've* made *your* life miserable. Since the night I met you, I've been roughed up twice. I've been investigated by the police . . . and remember, I never asked you to have Ted beaten up. In fact, I was appalled. And most of all I've been scared out of my mind because everywhere I go, someone—Mafia, police, FBI, whatever—is out to get me. So don't give me that poor-Frank routine. *You* are the cause of *my* problems, not the other way around."

Drained, I leaned back on the bench and finished my beer.

He didn't respond, and I had nothing left to say except that, despite it all, I loved him. I didn't say it, but I should have. Maybe.

We rode the rest of the way to Staten Island, then back to Manhattan, in silence. Neither of us had the inclination to speak or the nerve to walk away.

It was a few minutes before ten o'clock when the boat docked back at Manhattan's Whitehall Terminal. We walked down the winding ramp to the street level, together physically but emotionally far apart.

"I'm going to the club," he said when we reached the sidewalk. It was a declaration, not an invitation.

"Take care." I turned toward the subway entrance.

"We'll talk soon."

"Yeah."

There weren't many people on the subway platform. Which was good, because that meant that no one saw the mist in my eyes as I waited for an uptown train.

*   *   *

"Oh, here we go again." Denise sighed when she heard the tone of my voice. It had only been an hour since Frank and I parted, probably forever. The reality had yet to set in, let alone the healing.

"Yeah. I think it's over." I told her about our trip on the ferry and the events preceding it. Especially Patrick Waverly.

"I'm sorry, Drew," she said. "But maybe it's for the best. You have to admit that the past few weeks have been a bit . . . uh . . . dramatic."

"Dramatic. That might be an understatement."

"Maybe. But let's face it, Drew, you and Frank were mismatched from the start. You had almost nothing in common except a mutual attraction, and mutual attractions don't last forever. Trust me on that. I mean . . . the guy wasn't even gay!"

"Oh, I think he was gay. Well . . . sort of."

"With you, maybe. Which wouldn't make him the first heterosexual to experiment, would it?"

"It just seems like we've gone through too much to have it end this way," I said, not answering her question and still trying to rationalize the relationship.

She sighed again. "I'm not saying that you didn't go through a lot, Drew. But we all go through a lot every day. We're New Yorkers. It's our lifestyle."

We're New Yorkers. Right. And everyone knows that the average New Yorker's day is spent dodging bullets while being indiscreetly watched by cops and robbers, all while streaking up the New York *Times* Best-seller List as an overnight—literally—success story, thanks to an on-air endorsement from an extremely popular radio shock jock.

Right. I was living a New York life, right down to the tapped phone and the bruised ribs.

Right.

"I really don't think you can compare *my* past two weeks with the lives of any other New Yorkers," I told her. "You have no idea . . ."

"I'm forcing myself to be sympathetic. Don't make this harder than it has to be."

"I loved him, okay? So will you let me grieve?"

She paused for moments that seemed like hours . . . then began circling for the kill.

"He was a good-looking guy," she said. "Very handsome. Sexy. Is *that* what you loved?"

"There was more than that. And you know it."

"Was it a wounded puppy thing you had going? Did you love the thought of saving Frank from himself? From his fiancée? From the Mafia? From his heterosexuality?"

"Denise, that's not fair."

She continued, ignoring me. "Did you love it that he could do things for you? Did you love being in Hanover's window? Did you love what Gary Vine said about you?"

"You're starting to piss me off."

Again, I was ignored. "Did you love it—oh, I know you'll deny it, but still—did you love it when Ted was beaten? Did you feel avenged?"

"Denise!"

"Did you, Andrew?" Her voice was remarkably calm, given her devastating words.

"Denise, I . . . I . . ." I was torn between slamming down the phone and breaking into tears.

We were both silent for a long time, listening to each other's shallow breath. My eyes were pinched closed. My head pounded.

Finally, her voice—now far less confrontational, although not quite sympathetic—came back through the line.

"Sorry. I don't mean to hurt you, Drew. Really. But you have to take a deep look inside yourself and think about what you were looking for with Frank, and why you're so damned certain that you're in love."

"I just am," I whispered. "I just am."

I didn't know how to offer Denise a better explanation when I could barely understand it myself. As much as I hated to admit it, she was close to the mark on a few things. But it wasn't just physical attraction and rescue fantasies; it wasn't what he could do for me and what I could do for him. There was the excitement, of course, but also something deeper, more profound, in the way he had put his trust and faith in me . . . when, that is, he *had* trust and faith in me. Now, though . . .

I had been silent for too long, and Denise was again filling the vacuum.

"Think about what love is. It's not just sexual attraction, and it's not just the desire to save someone. It's more than that. And if it's a real love, it really should be mutual."

"You're not much of a romantic," I said, my voice still hushed.

"Oh, but I am. I *am* a romantic. But I'm also a realist. Along with everyone *except* you, I watched your relationship with Ted deteriorate for months while you sat there, oblivious, behind your rose-colored glasses. And it wasn't pretty when you were forced to take those glasses off."

"You saw my break-up with Ted coming?"

"Me and the rest of the world, honey. For months."

"Why didn't you warn me?"

"That isn't my job, Drew. You're thirty-five years old, and you're a gay man in Manhattan. You're supposed to be well-versed in the art of human interaction by now. But if you don't pay attention to the *other* person in the relationship, and if you focus only on your own desires, you're not doing your job."

"It sounds like you're trying to tell me that I'm self-absorbed." I forced a self-deprecating laugh in an awkward attempt to lighten the moment, which so desperately needed lightening.

"To the point of annoyance sometimes," she said, adding her own light touch with, "so join the club," before dipping back into sobriety. "I don't mean to sound cruel, you know, but this thing with Frank had disaster written all over it. You would have seen it, too, if you had just stepped back a bit to think things through. Just be glad it only lasted a few weeks."

"I suppose we were just too different . . ."

"Better to nip it in the bud now than later. Nothing good would have come of it. And I really don't have the energy to hold your hand through another Ted-style meltdown."

Again, the phones fell silent for a time period approaching awkwardness. When it became clear that Denise had nothing left to say, I took the initiative.

"Thanks for being honest. It still hurts, but I think you've helped put things in perspective."

"It wasn't easy. So, I suppose I should thank you for listening. Most self-absorbed people would have hung up on me."

We forced ourselves to laugh.

"So . . ." she said, "tell me about this Patrick Waverly. He sounds nice. Maybe you could start dating *him!*"

It was an appropriate point to end the call.

* * *

The next morning, as most of New York coped with yet another cold and rainy Saturday, Max Abraham debriefed me. He kept me waiting in that tastelessly mismatched outer office for half an hour. I reached the point of boredom with his outdated collection of magazines before he popped his head out of his office and motioned me in.

"Have a seat," he said. "Sorry to keep you waiting, but I was on an important conference call." He gestured to his casual attire and smiled. "Actually, in the spirit of full disclosure, I suppose I should tell you that I was making some last-minute arrangements to get away to Fort Lauderdale for the weekend. My flight leaves in two hours, so we're going to have to make this snappy."

"No problem."

"So . . ." he said, before taking a lengthy pause as he read over notes he had scratched on a loose piece of paper in my folder. Finally, he looked up. "David tells me you had an encounter with the FBI while you were in California."

"Washington, actually. And Oregon."

He jotted down the correction. "Tell me about it."

I sketched out my encounter with Patrick Waverly for him, from our first meeting through my abrupt exit from the Portland hotel room. Outside of a few grunts and hmms, Abraham was silent.

" . . . And that's it." I ended the story.

"You say Waverly kept questioning you about Frank DiBenedetto and all these related . . . uh . . . incidents, correct?"

"Yeah."

"May I ask why you felt compelled to answer his questions?"

"I guess I needed to talk."

He jotted again, then looked me straight in the eye and asked, "Did you have a sexual relationship with this Waverly?"

Despite my innocence, I blushed and stammered. "No! Not at all."

He raised one skeptical eyebrow. "You're sure?"

"I think I'd remember."

He raised another skeptical eyebrow.

"I'm telling you the truth, Max. I did *not* sleep with that man."

More jotting. Then, "Tell me about the car outside the hotel in Tacoma."

I did, adding that I realized that I might have been paranoid.

"In your situation," he said, "I think a little paranoia is a helpful thing."

"Yeah."

He closed the folder and leaned back in his chair.

"Here's the way I see it, Andrew. If this Waverly is, in fact, a special agent—and you can be certain I'll find that out, even if he wasn't using his real name—then it's probably good that you told him everything. First of all, since he never identified himself as a federal agent, not a word you said to him can be used in court. And by telling the truth, you've cleared yourself from being directly implicated in the Langhorne assault and other Mafia activities. If the feds were trying to build a case against you, then you did yourself a big favor by admitting your knowledge but denying your complicity."

"That's good!" A smile momentarily crossed my face. Until he continued.

"Yes. *That* is good. But there's a downside. Two downsides, actually. First of all, you've admitted that you've lied to the police about your knowledge of the assault, other specific crimes, and general organized crime activity. That tends to be frowned upon by the authorities. I don't think they can pin a charge on you, but you've made yourself vulnerable. Second, we have to think about the very real possibility that everything you said to Waverly could get back to the New York mob families. Maybe it already has."

"What?" The thought that the New York City Police Department might learn of my impromptu confession was bad enough, but the thought that the Stendardi and Morelle families might learn of it sent chills through my body.

Max Abraham shook his head as he watched my eyes widen. "Well, I'm not saying that it *will* happen . . . just that it *could* happen. You don't know if this Waverly fellow was really a special agent. Maybe he carried a badge as part of a fantasy . . . or maybe he's in the Mafia and carried the badge for protection. Or maybe he's a rogue agent. Or maybe someone he works with is being paid off by the mob. Or maybe—"

I put my hand up, palm forward, to stop him.

"I get the point. My problems aren't over."

"Sorry."

"Does it help any that Frank and I broke off our . . . uh . . . relationship last night?"

"You did? That was a wise—and far overdue—move." He paused, then added, "But I don't think it much matters. You're not out of the woods yet, Andrew. Not by a long shot. All it gives you is an excellent and long-delayed opportunity to separate yourself from Frank DiBenedetto."

No, I wasn't out of the woods. And, no, I didn't welcome that opportunity.

I spent most of the rest of the restless weekend mourning the end of my relationship with Frank. In a reprise of my post-Ted Sturm und Drang, I roosted in the window frame, staring vacantly into the steady rain.

And then there were those other concerns, of course. They didn't help matters.

The worst they could do to me, I reasoned, was kill me. How long could it take? Maybe I'd never know what hit me, or maybe the life would seep out of me slowly over minutes or hours. But if they killed me, the torture would only last a finite amount of time. It would be cruel, yes, but nowhere near as cruel as the torture I was now enduring as I waited for whatever would come next, which could come at any moment of any hour of any day . . . or maybe even not at all. The Mafia, the NYPD, and the FBI—not to mention the publishing industry—had me dangling on a hook in a meat locker.

Waiting . . .

For some inexplicable reason, I still held out hope that Frank would come to his senses. He would see the light, realize that we were meant to be together forever, apologize profusely, beg my forgiveness, and whisk me away to that fictional place where our long lives together would never again be troubled.

Not unlike my hope after Ted left me, really. Except that, with Frank, the stakes were much higher.

The weekend passed until the Sunday afternoon haze began to darken as it approached evening. I realized that I had to get out of my apartment. The four walls offered no solace, the telephone wasn't ringing, and I needed to hear another human voice. I couldn't call Denise or David. I had used them up, squandered the precious resource of their friendships by repeatedly seeking their guidance and then ignoring it. I didn't think I could bear to hear them give the very same advice once again, and I was confident that they couldn't bear to listen to me whine about the gross unfairness of my life.

I needed to hear new voices . . . voices of people who didn't know who I was. I had no intention of telling my story to yet another stranger—Patrick Waverly had cured me of that impulse—and, in fact, I had no intention of even talking to another stranger. My only goal was to reassure myself that there was still a world out there in which I could function.

A world After Frank, if you will.

I changed into khakis, a polo shirt, and topsiders and, suitably dressed, set off for a preppy Upper West Side gay bar near my apartment where I could be assured of finding a crowd late on a Sunday afternoon. I wasn't disappointed.

As I stepped in through the front door, a dozen hopeful faces turned in my direction. My expression, finely honed over seventeen years of gay bar experience, said that I wasn't interested in making a new friend that afternoon. So, one by one, the faces turned away, resuming their conversations or staring into the mirror behind the bar. All except one young man with carefully styled blond hair, apparently a student in his Columbia University sweatshirt, who kept stealing glances as I walked past him toward the distant, less-crowded end of the bar.

I found an open space, waved the bartender over and ordered a drink. Instinctively, I looked back at the Columbia student and, caught staring, he nervously averted his gaze. Good, I thought; go back to the dorm and study, and leave me alone.

The bartender traded me my drink for an excessive amount of money and an excessive tip, and I settled in at the bar. I was quite content to eavesdrop on the conversations of others . . . who was going back into the closet for the Thanksgiving holiday at home, who was so sick of his job at Bloomingdale's that he was going to quit, who was spending December in South Beach, who was upset because his best friend slept with his ex-lover . . .

It was the tonic I was looking for, evidence of other lives being lived. In silence, I gloried in the minor details of minor lives and looked forward to the day when my life, too, was once again little more than a jumble of minutiae.

I ordered another drink and continued to eavesdrop. Half an hour must have passed before I was rudely interrupted as I finished my second drink.

"Bad day?" I turned to see the Columbia student standing behind me.

"So-so," I replied, unfriendly but not quite ill-mannered.

"Just wondering. You haven't smiled or said a word since you walked through the door."

"I guess I'm in a quiet mood this afternoon."

He looked awkwardly at the floor, not moving but at least not speaking. The bartender, noting my need for a refill, began to freshen my drink.

"I'm Rich," the Columbia student finally said.

I sighed. "I'm Andrew. Nice to meet you. I don't mean to be rude, but—"

"Did you ever notice how cliquish this place is?"

Of course I had. It *was* a gay bar, after all. But I didn't say that, because that would have meant agreeing to a conversation. Instead, I said, "Not really."

"Maybe it's me." He wasn't getting my hint. "I haven't been out in a while, but my boyfriend and I just broke up, so . . . well, I'm trying to force myself to get back into circulation."

"I've been there," I said without elaboration. "You'll get over it and back into the swing of things."

"How long does it take to feel comfortable again?"

"You're asking me that question like I'm Dear Abby." I had already said far more than I intended to say. "Yeah, I've been around a lot longer than you have, but that doesn't make me the voice of experience. If I were that smart, I wouldn't keep screwing up my own love life."

A tiny grin worked its way onto his lips. Despite myself, I had given him an invitation to converse. "It sounds as if you're trying to get over someone, too."

I rolled my eyes. "Rich, you seem like a nice enough kid, but take my advice and steer clear. You're right, I *am* trying to get over someone. And I will get over him, with time. But it does take time." I paused, then added, "We'll both survive."

He backed away a few steps. "Sorry, Andrew. I didn't mean to bother you."

"I know. No apology necessary."

"For what it's worth, you seem like a nice guy. I hope you get over him quickly. I'm starting to believe that no man is worth this anguish."

He vanished back into the crowd before I could tell him that he was wrong; that some men *were* worth the anguish. Whether or not Frank was one of those men, though, remained to be seen.

The conversation with Rich the Columbia student ruined the pleasure I had found in listening in on the conversations of others. I wanted to be revived through the idle details of ordinary lives, but now the only words I heard centered on the inevitability of heartbreak. Still, I stayed at the bar for several more hours, drinking too much and growing more embittered, until I realized that it was well past the time to go home.

An unmarked police car was idling at the curb, waiting for me, when I arrived back at my apartment building. I didn't realize it was an unmarked car, of course. Not at first. Not until a window rolled down as I passed and I saw Detective Mueller's face looking back at me.

"Good evening, Andrew," she said, unsettlingly cheerful. "Do you mind if Detective Brogan and I ask you a few questions?"

"Yes." I turned my back to her.

I heard two car doors open and close.

"Don't be a fool," said Brogan's voice over the traffic. "Just answer a few questions and we'll be on our way."

I spun around to face them. My voice slurred slightly. "I don't know what you want from me! I didn't have anything to do with what happened to Ted! I'm not a criminal! I'm just . . . I'm just a writer!"

"We believe you, Andrew," said Mueller. I was surprised to see Brogan nod sympathetically as he stepped from the curb to the sidewalk. I wondered if the alcohol was playing tricks with my brain. "But I'm not sure that you don't know who *did* do it."

Brogan took over. "Until we solve this case, we're going to keep pursuing the few leads we have." He paused, then unnecessarily added, "And you're the one person who can tie this together for us."

"Tell us what you know," Mueller implored. "If you know that Frank DiBenedetto and Vince Castellano did this, then tell us. The sooner you do, the sooner we can close the case and put this behind us."

It suddenly occurred to me that Rich the Columbia student was right: No man was worth this anguish. I was taking far too much flack protecting a closet case of a man who didn't want to see me anymore, and who had the gall to blame *me* for his problems. I had a brief, fleeting impulse to confess everything to Brogan and Mueller, then and there on the sidewalk, and wash my hands of Frank forever.

But, no, I couldn't do that. It would take more than too much liquid courage to push me to that point.

"Andrew . . ." said Mueller, sensing my confusion. "Please tell us what you know."

"I don't know anything. I don't know any of these people. I'm as horrified by this crime as anyone, but I had nothing to do with it."

"Okay." Mueller sighed, making no effort to mask her frustration. "If that's your story . . ." She began to turn away from me, then stopped and turned back. "I *do* believe that you had nothing *directly* to do with the Langhorne assault, Andrew. Maybe if you give us a statement to that effect, Detective Brogan and I can get authorization from our superiors to close your end of the case."

I stood on the sidewalk, weaving slightly and wondering if I was in the right condition to make a decision. True, I'd had too much to drink . . . but still, the decision seemed to be such an easy one.

I wasn't directly involved, was I? And yet here I was, left open as a target by the ungrateful Frank. Now Detectives Mueller and Brogan were giving me an opportunity to wiggle off the hook and return to what might pass as a normal life, free of police investigations and other legal complications.

The decision seemed so easy . . .

"Okay. You want a statement? I'll give you a statement."

They had me sit in the backseat of the unmarked car and handed me an official form attached to a clipboard.

"Here's what I need," said Mueller. "In your own handwriting, state that you were not present at the assault on Theodore Langhorne, nor did you instruct any other person to carry out the assault."

I quickly wrote out the words in a lazy drunken script, and with each letter that flowed from the pen I felt a bit closer to the light at the end of my long, dark tunnel.

Brogan added, "And you should write that you have no additional knowledge of the identity of the perpetrators, before or after the fact. Except for what you've learned from us, of course."

The pen faltered. What was it Max Abraham had said about denying my complicity but admitting my knowledge? What was it he had said about lying to the police? I struggled with the thoughts, but my brain wouldn't cooperate.

"Do you have a problem, Andrew?" asked Mueller.

"No." I grit my teeth and willed the pen to finish the sentence. When I was done, I asked, "Is that it?"

"One more thing, just to be on the safe side," she said. "You'd better put in a sentence stating that, to the best of your knowledge, you don't know Frank DiBenedetto or Vince Castellano."

I looked up at her.

"We don't want to have to keep dragging you through this. Obviously Detective Brogan and I are certain that DiBenedetto ordered Castellano to assault Mr. Langhorne. If you tell us in your statement that you don't know them, then that's one less reason for us to bother you."

I sighed. It didn't feel right. It felt like a setup. It felt like something Max Abraham would strongly advise me not to write.

"It's true, isn't it? You *don't* know DiBenedetto or Castellano, do you? That's what you keep telling us."

"Of course not," I muttered, surprised at the casualness of the lie.

"Then just write that down and we'll be on our way."

Maybe, I thought, I should call my lawyer. But no . . . he was in Fort Lauderdale and unreachable.

"C'mon, Andrew. It's just one more sentence. And it means that you'll most likely never see us again."

I swallowed hard.

"That's okay," she added. "If you don't want to state that, you don't have to. Detective Brogan and I only want to find the people who were involved in this crime. We didn't think you were involved. Maybe we were wrong." She turned to her partner. "How many years in prison on a first-degree assault conviction?"

"Seven . . . ten, maybe," Brogan replied calmly. "It depends on the judge. At least seven."

Seven years in prison. For what? To protect Frank? No man was worth this anguish.

"Seven years," Mueller repeated. "That's a long time for a young man."

I knew they were playing mind games with me. But they were also clearly winning. I raised the pen again and wrote that, to the best of my knowledge, I didn't know Frank DiBenedetto or Vince Castellano, and at least the latter was the truth. Then, before I could think twice, I skipped over the fine print and signed and dated the statement.

"That wasn't so hard, was it?" asked Brogan.

I heard myself say, "No." But I was thinking, "Yes."

A bad hangover and a queasy stomach were my souvenirs when I woke up Monday morning. I vaguely remembered the conversation with Rich the Columbia student and my growing anger with Frank, but I was almost finished with my shower before I remembered Brogan and Mueller and the statement I gave them.

My hangover intensified and my queasy stomach churned. I knew that I had made a very big mistake.

And all I could do was wonder just how big a mistake it was.

I didn't have to wonder for long. When I got to the office, I found Brogan and Mueller already waiting for me.

"Good morning," said Brogan, without a smile. "Coffee?"

"Yeah." My voice was heavy with depression at the sight of them. "So, what brings you to PMC?"

"We're just following up on a few things," said Mueller as she rifled through a file folder. "We're trying to close out this Langhorne case."

I rolled my eyes. "C'mon! How many times do I have to—"

"Recognize either of these people, Mr. Westlake?" She pulled a photograph from the folder and held it in front of me. I *did* note that she was no longer calling me Andrew, and I considered that to be a bad sign.

Did I recognize the people in the photograph? Of course I did. The people in the photograph were me and Frank, walking side by side as we exited the Staten Island Ferry Terminal in Manhattan at 9:56 P.M. on the previous Friday night.

For once, I managed to keep my mouth shut.

"That's you, isn't it?" asked Mueller. "So, who's that other guy?"

I sighed.

"Mr. Westlake?" Brogan bent over slightly to look me directly in the eyes. His face was just inches from mine. I noticed for the first time that his breath smelled of stale cigarettes. "Why don't you identify this other person for us?"

"I'd like to call my lawyer."

"Short time, no see," said the slightly sunburned Max Abraham as he was escorted to a PMC conference room thirty-seven minutes later. "And don't think I'm ecstatic about that."

David, Brogan, and Mueller were already there, along with an ashy-faced PMC counsel who had been serving as my substitute lawyer until Abraham arrived, although—unless I was unexpectedly charged with copyright infringement—his usefulness was limited. He left wordlessly when Abraham—a *real* lawyer—entered the room.

Abraham sat next to me and asked to see the photograph. Mueller slid it across the conference table.

"Yes, that's my client." He held the photo at various angles against the fluorescent light, as if there was some doubt that could be explained by a trick of the eyes. "Yes, that's him. So, what is your question?"

"The question is," said Brogan, "who is the fellow walking next to him?"

One of Abraham's overgrown eyebrows hiked itself in my direction. "And what did he tell you?"

"Nothing," said Brogan. "Nothing at all."

The lawyer allowed himself a faint smile. He was no doubt pleased with my rare moment of discretion. "And why should you assume that my client knows this man?"

Brogan chuckled. "C'mon, Mr. Abraham. Your client knows who he is. I'm sure that even *you* know who he is. So, why are we playing this game?"

"Game?" said Abraham, sounding not at all puzzled. "I don't play games, Detective." He looked back at the picture. "I can't say that I *do* know this man. Maybe . . . but I can't be sure." He slid the photo back across the table to Mueller. "In any event, it's irrelevant whether or not I know who that is, and it's irrelevant if my client knows who that person is. That photograph—and, for the sake of argument, I'll assume for the time being that it *hasn't* been doctored—that photograph documents no illegal act. It documents no crime. In fact, it doesn't even document that my client and Fr—" I winced, and Abraham caught himself "—*that other fellow* even know each other. They are just two men walking near each other, Detectives. They aren't even talking."

Brogan sat back in his chair—a motion quickly followed by Mueller—then smiled. "Let me help you out a bit here, Mr. Abraham. That man in the picture is Frank DiBenedetto Junior."

"Oh, my!" exclaimed David, in mock surprise so patently mock that it was embarrassing.

"Frank *who?*" asked my lawyer.

Brogan, enjoying the game, was now close to laughter. "Frank DiBenedetto Junior, sir. The son of Frank DiBenedetto Senior." Abraham still betrayed no trace of recognition, so Brogan, relishing his role, added, "The Stendardi family *capo.*"

"If you say so," said the lawyer with a dismissive wave. "So . . . let's get back on track here, shall we? It seems to me that you want to question my client because he chose to take a ride on the Staten Island Ferry. Do I have this right?"

Brogan corrected him. "He took a ride on the Staten Island Ferry with a known organized crime figure."

"And Mr. Westlake was . . . what? Was he supposed to check the credentials of everyone who rode the ferry that night?" My lawyer leaned forward toward the detectives and stage-whispered, "In case you haven't heard, that ferry goes to Staten Island. I'd be more shocked to learn that there were *no* organized crime figures aboard."

At that, Brogan finally broke down and let out an audible laugh. Max Abraham indulged him with a smile and an almost imperceptible wink.

"You're good, Abraham," said Brogan. "No wonder you can get away with charging a zillion dollars an hour. It'll almost be worth arresting your client just to have the opportunity to watch you in court."

The lawyer glowed. Everyone smiled. Goodwill filled the room. In fact, I seemed to be the only one who had even heard the phrase "arresting your client."

"Excuse me," I finally said to Brogan, breaking the spell of the Max Abraham Admiration Society. "Did I hear you say something about arresting me? For what?"

"Lying about your involvement in the Langhorne case in a

sworn statement," Brogan replied. "That's perjury, and it's only for starters. And I think you'll agree that I'm being generous in supposing your involvement came *after* the crime was committed."

Max Abraham turned to me. "A sworn statement?"

I looked at my hands. "Last night they stopped me in front of my apartment building. I had been out. I had a few drinks ... well, more than a few. They told me that if I gave them a statement, they'd leave me alone."

He shook his head, but then zeroed in on Brogan. "It's a bullshit charge and you know it."

"Bullshit? I don't think so. I don't do bullshit charges."

"Let me see the statement." He took his reading glasses out as Brogan gave him a copy of my drunken handwriting, reviewed it, then pronounced, "There are no inconsistencies between this statement and my client's statements to you."

"But this picture clearly shows—" Brogan began.

"We've been through this before. The photograph proves nothing. Everything here is circumstantial."

"So ... so, wait!" I was afraid they were both going to forget all about me once again. "What's going to happen to me?"

"Nothing," Abraham replied. "Just sit still. He's bluffing. Your sworn statement and your comments to the police are consistent."

"But if your lawyer's wrong," said Brogan, "you could be looking at spending some time in jail."

I slumped back in my chair and moaned, "I can't believe that Frank did this to me."

They all looked at me—Brogan and Mueller grinning, Abraham and David aghast—and it took a moment for my brain to register the words that had just tumbled out of my mouth.

I *had* said that, hadn't I? I had just confirmed that I knew Frank, after repeated denials, including a statement to the police.

"How'd you like to take a little ride with me and Detective Mueller, Andrew?" said Brogan.

"Not much." I looked at Abraham, but the lawyer had his head buried in his hands.

"That question was just rhetorical," Brogan said as he pushed his chair away from the table and stood. Mueller also rose, and I felt my own body lift itself out of my chair, dully prepared for whatever came next.

Max Abraham's face finally reappeared. "You had to sign a statement, didn't you?" He sighed. "I'll have you out of there in two hours. But *please*, don't make another statement or say another word to the police. *Please!*"

You hear horror stories all the time about jail. Well, let me tell you, the stories don't do justice to the reality . . . especially if you're a much-less-than-street-smart, much-less-than-scary person who has never so much as gotten a parking ticket, and who probably would have cried if he had.

And what made things worse were the long days of waiting. Oh . . . okay, it didn't really take days. From the moment I was booked through the moment I was released on my own recognizance amounted to three hours and sixteen minutes, but it *felt* like it took days. Then again, cowering in a dirty jail cell and praying not to get gang-raped isn't exactly the most carefree way to pass time.

But eventually I was free. David—and a PMC car—were waiting for me when I emerged back into the sunlight. I joined him in the backseat.

"Meet anyone interesting?" he asked.

"Fuck you."

"You're welcome."

David leaned forward, about to tell the driver our destination, when a hand holding a badge appeared in front of the driver's face. The driver looked at the badge, then back at David, giving him a what-can-I-do? shrug.

David returned the shrug, then hit a button and slowly lowered the rear window until it stopped. The hand and badge reappeared, this time at his window.

"Can I help you?" David asked with a sigh, looking up through the window.

"FBI," was the reply, and I felt my stomach churn as the realization hit that things really *could* get worse than they already were. "Please step out of the car."

As his hand gripped the handle to open the door, David leaned over to me and murmured, "Well, at least he's very cute."

He didn't have to tell me that. Because I had already recognized the voice.

We got out of the car. Special Agent Patrick Waverly stood on the sidewalk, pocketing his badge, his deep blue eyes hidden behind dark sunglasses.

"So," I said, "we meet again. Imagine my joy."

He grinned sheepishly, then motioned to a man—obviously another agent in his suit-and-sunglasses costume—leaning against a mailbox twenty yards down the sidewalk.

"What about him?" I asked.

"He's my partner. And he doesn't have to know. Okay?"

"Oh!" gasped David, as he realized who was standing in front of him. "Oh!"

"David," I said, "this is Special Agent Patrick Waverly." I spat out his title with contempt. "Patrick, this is my boss, David Carlyle."

"Oh!" David gasped again, but he nevertheless shook Patrick's hand.

"Can we talk?" asked Patrick.

"I think I've talked enough. Let's leave the rest of our talking for a time when my lawyer is present."

He scuffed his shoes against the sidewalk. "Yeah, I guess I deserve that. I didn't really mean for things to . . . to lead you . . . to . . ."

"Whatever," I muttered, unable to look him in the eye—or sunglasses, for that matter. "What's done is done. You got what you wanted."

"Let's take a walk around the block, Andrew. I really need to talk to you."

"Sorry. But like I said, I want my lawyer present."

He threw up his hands in frustration, then shook his head sadly.

"Should I call Max?" David asked, fumbling as he tried to pull his cellular phone out of a jacket pocket.

I didn't reply, and none of us moved. We simply stood there, looking at or near each other, posed in an uncomfortable streetside tableau.

"Never mind, Andrew," Patrick finally said. "I understand. I really do. But . . ." He looked up and down the sidewalk, then took a few steps toward me until he was in the range of quieter conversation. "Can I say a few things to you? You don't have to say a word. Just listen."

I nodded a weak agreement.

"I feel bad about what I did in Tacoma and Portland, okay? I just

wanted to talk to you, find out how much you knew about organized crime in New York and whether or not you were involved,
and get out. I didn't intend to get . . . well, I didn't intend to get so
close to you on a personal level." He laughed self-consciously. "Short
but sweet, huh?"

I shrugged indifferently. David moaned, still in shock.

"It was my job, Andrew. I want you to know that. After Tacoma,
my work was done. As far as I'm concerned, the FBI has no further
interest in you. Not even your buddy DiBenedetto, really. He might
be guilty of some crimes, but nothing that excites me all that
much." He paused and waited for a reaction, but I held a stoic expression, so he added, "I got what I wanted in Tacoma, but I went
to Portland because I *wanted* to go to Portland. I enjoyed your company, and I think you're a great guy who doesn't deserve to be
caught up in all this crap. That's why I tracked you down here."

"Thank you," I said, with what I hoped was a frosty edge to my
voice.

"So . . . I'm sorry that I didn't level with you. I should have, but I
had a job to do. And . . ." He stopped himself, blushing.

"What?" I asked, my curiosity piqued by the blood rushing to his
face.

He looked down. "And if you had wanted to, I would have."

"Would have what?"

"Slept with you that night in Portland."

"Oh!" gasped David.

Now it was my turn to blush, and—despite myself—I felt a smile
of self-satisfaction break through. None of us—especially David—
could look at anyone else while we shuffled our feet, jangled coins,
and looked at the upper floors of the surrounding buildings until
we regained our composure.

"Anyway," Patrick finally said, "what's done is done, I suppose. I
just hope that you can forgive me someday, because I'd like to keep
in touch."

I magnanimously offered my hand to him. He took it and shook
forcefully.

"What's done is done," I agreed. "I wish things had been different, but thanks for your honesty."

"I'd better get going." He released my hand. "You're probably
not inclined to get together with me socially just yet, and it doesn't
really matter, because I'm only in New York for a few more days

wrapping this thing up. But . . . uh . . . call me if you're ever back in the Pacific Northwest." He took a business card from his breast pocket, adding his home and beeper phone numbers before pressing it into my palm.

"Thanks. Of course you already know how to find *me*."

He smiled and pivoted, beginning his slow walk down the sidewalk and calling over his shoulder, "Anytime. Anywhere."

I watched him saunter away for the first ten feet or so; then, feeling the eyes of his partner on me, realized that I was wearing a dopey grin. It was a good time to leave.

"Ready, David?" I asked.

"Oh!"

David eventually recovered on the drive back to his Fifth Avenue apartment.

"So *that* was the agent!" he said, clearly wanting to know even more than he already knew.

"That was the agent," I confirmed but said nothing more. He wasn't satisfied, of course, but he asked no further questions.

The car deposited us in front of his apartment building.

"Are you staying here for a while?" he asked as we stood on the sidewalk. "It seems to me that you might be well-advised to stay away from your apartment for a few nights. I have a feeling that some of the wrong people might hear about your arrest."

"There are no 'right people' to hear about it," I observed. "Thanks, but I think I'll stick close to home. At this point, there's no sense in trying to hide. Everyone seems to know where I am at all times, so I might as well face this on my home turf."

"If you're sure . . ."

"I'm sure."

"Well, if there's any trouble . . ."

"Thanks."

He walked into his building, somewhat relieved, I suspected, that he was getting a respite from my melodrama. I crossed Fifth Avenue and began cutting through Central Park to the West Side in the fast-fading late-afternoon sunlight.

I was halfway across the park when paranoia began to creep up on me once again. Didn't that kid on the bicycle pass me five minutes ago? Was it mere coincidence that the couple behind me was following the same paths? Why did I keep hearing rustling in the bushes? Why was that woman staring through binoculars in my direction?

By the time I broke out of the park at Central Park West, I was almost running and my body was soaked in cold sweat. I didn't feel any better when I realized that I had exited the park at Seventy-second Street. The Dakota apartment building—the place where John Lennon got whacked—loomed in front of me, more imposing and frightening than ever in the blue-black twilight. I involuntarily jerked my head to the left and saw Frank's apartment building, which held its own secrets.

I kept moving.

When I arrived home, I slipped into shorts and a sweatshirt, put on a mellow compact disk, poured myself a drink, and made a quick call to Max Abraham to assure him that not only had I survived my first—and, I hoped, only—stint in jail, but that I had also encountered Special Agent Patrick Waverly immediately upon my release.

"Well, at least you had the good sense to keep your mouth shut this time." He was still very unhappy that I had given a statement to the police, and I couldn't blame him. "One word of advice, though: Don't trust him. Just because he says he likes you on a personal level doesn't mean that he really does. And just because he says that you're clear from his perspective doesn't mean that you are."

Okay. *That* was a reassuring conversation.

I called Denise.

"Whatcha doing tonight?" she asked.

"I'm going to get drunk. You're welcome to join me, but it might not be a pretty sight. Then again, we hard timers don't care if we're pretty or not."

"I don't believe that for a second. You will always care about appearances. I'm just trying to get you to look beyond those appearances."

"Oh, here we go again," I moaned playfully.

"Sorry. I'll save the lecture for another time. How's next Tuesday sound?"

"Tuesday's bad. I've got flagellation class that night."

"Another book tour?"

"Ha. Ha." I sipped from my drink then said, "Maybe you *should* come over. I've had such a fascinating day."

"Uh-oh. I don't like the sound of that."

"Then you'll come over?"

"Give me a half hour."

"Okay. Bring wine." I thought better of that request and re-ordered. "Brings *lots of* wine."

When Denise arrived at my apartment—bearing a large bottle of chardonnay and a large bottle of cabernet sauvignon—I quickly poured two glasses to the brim and recapped my Monday for her: the early-morning interrogation by Brogan and Mueller that led to the midmorning meeting with Max Abraham that led to the late-morning arrest; the living hell that was my holding cell; and, finally, the encounter with Special Agent Patrick Waverly.

Soon she was outdrinking me.

"Just keep telling yourself that it's almost over." She patted my hand. "Pretty soon there'll be no more Frank, no more arrests . . . life will be back to normal, and maybe you'll abandon me here in New York when you move to Seattle with Agent Pat."

"Tacoma. But it's not going to happen."

"He gave you his home phone number, didn't he?" I nodded. "Let me see."

I pulled Patrick's business card out of my wallet and gave it to her.

"Let's call," she said.

"No! Why do you want to call?"

"I wanna hear his voice." I noticed that she had a slight slur to her own voice. "I'm a very good judge of character. I can tell what he's like from his voice."

"Let's *not* call." I grabbed the business card out of her fingers. "You've got an obsession about fixing me up with Patrick, don't you?"

"At least he's on the right side of the law, Drew. Although I have to hand it to you. In the past two weeks, you've found yourself a gay mobster and a gay FBI agent. It takes a special talent." She stopped to yawn; as she stretched her arms, her empty wineglass was knocked off the coffee table, landing without incident on the carpet. "Oops. Sorry."

"Maybe it's time for you to go home," I said as I picked the glass up off the floor and carried it to the kitchen sink. When I turned around, I saw that in the twenty-five seconds it took me to say those words and complete the task, she had fallen asleep on the couch.

"Or you can stay right here."

The phone rang, startling me, and I grabbed it after the first ring, before it could disturb Denise.

"Hello," I said softly into the receiver.

"Hi." It was Frank.

"Hi." *This* was a surprise. Slowly, I eased myself into a sitting position, wedged between the couch and the wall. "I didn't expect to hear from you."

"I know." It sounded like Frank, too, had been drinking. "I feel bad about the other night."

"Me, too." I wanted to be angry but I couldn't. I was instantly forgiving, and I was too thrilled to hear his voice again.

"Well . . . I'm sorry. I've been thinking about what you said, and what *I* said, and . . . Well, I know that it isn't your fault."

"Thanks." Denise stirred on the couch, so I patted her head gently with my free hand. "I didn't mean to screw things up, y'know."

"I know. I keep forgetting that you aren't . . . uh . . . quite the type of person I'm used to dealing with."

"Backatcha," I replied. He laughed. "Anyway, you'll be happy to know that the feds are going to keep their hands off." Mindful of Abraham's advice, I added, "Or, so they tell me."

"And how did you hear this?"

"My gay FBI agent tracked me down."

"Take a word of advice from me: Don't believe them when they tell you shit like that."

"Don't worry about that. I'm adopting a new philosophy: Trust no one."

"That's a good philosophy." He paused, and I heard the sound of ice cubes clinking in a glass. "Anyway . . . can we move on? Can we forget that the other night ever happened?"

"I'd like that." Of course, as long as the NYPD had a picture of us together on the Staten Island Ferry, it would be difficult to forget that the night ever happened. But I could at least try to pretend.

"Good. 'Cause I've been thinking about things since last night, and I've decided that I really want you . . . I really want to be with you."

With those seven words, Frank took my breath away. With those seven words, he forced me to forgive him the ferry and Hanover's and Crazy Anna and Big Paulie and Ted's beating and everything else that could possibly be construed as bad or dangerous or criminal.

"I really want to be with you." I couldn't remember hearing those words from Ted. Ever. Or anyone else.

But as divine as the words were to hear, it struck me as wrong that I should hear them. It took a while for reality to seep in through the string section that was serenading me in my head, but when it did . . .

"Frank!" I said too loudly, and Denise stirred again. "Are you sure you should be talking like this on your telephone? I mean, what if our conversation isn't private?"

"Fuck 'em." I realized he was more drunk than I had thought. "Fuck 'em all, Andrew. I really want to be with you, and let the chips fall where they may."

So, this was the latest in my long line of dilemmas: Should I accept Frank's words—words I so desperately wanted to hear and believe—at face value? Or should I chalk them up to alcohol and assume they meant nothing? My head and heart once again offered a split decision.

I decided that a test might be in order, and I had some fresh material—material that he hadn't had a chance to adjust to—that would provide a good gauge of his sincerity.

"Frank," I said warily, hoping he'd do the right thing, "before we go any further, I have something to tell you."

"Yeah?"

"Yeah." I swallowed hard, wishing my wineglass was full. "The police came to see me today and—"

"Fuck *them*, too!"

"Right. Anyway, the police came, and . . . uh . . ." I swallowed again. "And they have a picture of the two of us from Friday night, when we were getting off the ferry."

He was silent at first, and I began to fear the worst . . . until he said, "Good. I'm glad they have a picture of us. Tell them I want a copy to frame."

The right answer! Frank came up with the right answer! Even though it was probably the alcohol talking, Frank came up with the right answer!

"Well . . . I'm glad to hear that," I said, trying hard to hide the ecstasy in my voice. "You're sure that doesn't bother you?" Left unsaid was my concern that it might bother him in the morning after he sobered up.

"Takes the burden off me. Let them run it in the fuckin' newspaper for all I care. On the front page. Let me tell you, Andrew, it's like I had some sort of epiphany after last night." It always sounded foreign to me when someone like Frank used a word like *epiphany*. "I don't want to risk losing you again, and if that means we have to move to Alaska and change our names to stay together, that's what I'll do."

"Wow." That was all I could think to say.

"Yeah. Wow. And sorry I've been such an asshole. I think I was having some trouble coming to terms with all this."

"Don't worry about it," I said, instantly deciding to forgive him not only his *real* undesirable personal aspects but also all heretofore unknown or idly speculated negative personal aspects, including any serial killings, mass bombings, or votes cast for Jesse Helms.

I just had to make sure I didn't slip and tell him that I loved him again. At least for a while.

In all fairness to him, and in the spirit of his epiphany, I also had to confess that I had been arrested that afternoon, and that his name had come up once or twice or fourteen times. He all but laughed it off.

"Perjury? That's what Catholic schoolgirls get arrested for in my old neighborhood. Don't worry about it, Andrew. They're just using you to try to get to me, but neither of us are going down. Sorry you had to see the inside of a cell, but I can pretty much guarantee that they won't send you back."

"I like your confidence," I said, wanting to believe that *pretty much* meant *absolutely*.

"Yeah, well, it comes with experience." I didn't need to be reminded of that, of course, but—at this point—it really didn't seem to matter.

"So, when can we get together again?" I asked, going for broke. "Tonight?"

Huh? Frank DiBenedetto was full of surprises on this telephone call. And for once they were all good surprises.

I glanced at the clock radio sitting atop a battered end table. It was only ten-thirty.

"I . . . well . . ." I glanced at Denise, asleep on the couch, and wavered. But Denise had managed to pass many nights on the couch, and experience showed that she wouldn't wake until morning. And she was an adult. I could count on her to know how to let herself out. "Okay. I'll be there by eleven o'clock."

"One thing, though: You might want to . . . er . . . you might want to send your cousin Belle over."

"But . . ."

"Trust me, Andrew: This isn't a case of regression. It's a case of not making our lives any more difficult than they have to be."

Well . . . one more time couldn't hurt, could it?

10

Scenes from an Italian Restaurant

The Belle Bacall drag—the drag that wouldn't die and, for that matter, wouldn't even retire gracefully—came back out of the closet. I was becoming quite practiced at playing dress up, so I was appropriately outfitted in less than ten minutes. Then I rifled through Denise's purse until I found makeup and lipstick, and five minutes later the transformation was complete. I tossed a change of male clothing into one of my duffel bags for my later comfort—I had learned that, when it comes to apparel, women really do have it much more difficult than men—and left a note for Denise on the coffee table.

Once again, the doorman paid no attention to me as I passed his station in the lobby. Outside, I hailed a cab, remembering only at the last moment to use my Belle Bacall voice before giving the driver my destination.

The doorman at Frank's building was much more observant than my own. He eyed me suspiciously as I entered the black marble lobby, and his "Can I help you?" had the unsubtle undertone of, "Go away, you freak."

But I wouldn't be deterred.

"Yes," I drawled, realizing a bit too late that my alcoholic buzz was doing my drag no favors. "I'm here to see Mr. DiBenedetto."

"And your name?"

"Belle Bacall."

The doorman rolled his eyes but dutifully called up to Frank's apartment. Moments later, he nodded unhappily to me. "You may go up. Mr. DiBenedetto is expecting you."

"Thank you," I replied, and gratuitously added, "Have a good evening."

He turned away, clearly annoyed by my very existence.

Frank was waiting at the door to his apartment when I stepped off the elevator. He leered drunkenly, his smile crooked. "Looking good."

"Thanks, but I don't think your doorman agrees."

"Then I guess it's lucky that we don't have to please him, isn't it?"

"I guess it is," I agreed as I started to push past him into the apartment. He stopped me in the entryway and closed the door gently behind me.

"Wait a minute. I have a surprise for you."

Frank produced a remote control from his back pocket and aimed it at the CD player as he led me into the living room. With a click, the Bee Gees began singing.

Unfortunately, they began singing "More Than a Woman."

"Oops," he muttered. "Wrong track."

I laughed. "I thought maybe you wanted this to be my Belle Bacall theme song."

"Yeah . . ." He smiled and tossed the remote on an end table. "What the hell. This works, too."

He picked up an almost-empty tumbler from the glass coffee table, with just a trace of amber liquid at the bottom, and sloshed around a few partially melted ice cubes.

"Drink?"

"Desperately."

"Scotch okay?"

"Perfect." I was wholly unconcerned with how the various adult beverages I had consumed would mix.

Frank talked as he poured the drinks. "Hell of a couple of days, huh? A real roller-coaster."

"Yeah," I agreed as I started to undergo the physical transformation from Belle to Andrew once again. "I'd just as soon have missed it all . . . until your phone call, of course."

"Of course." He handed me my drink and collected discarded

pieces of clothing while I rummaged through the gym bag for a pair of jeans and a green polo shirt.

"Bear with me just a second," I said as I changed. "I just didn't want to be stuck here without clothes appropriate for my real sex."

He smiled. "That's okay. I told you that I want you *as a man*. No matter what. That was my epiphany."

I was beginning to wonder if Frank had come across the word *epiphany* in some sort of vocabulary-building article in *Reader's Digest*. That would have explained its very recent overuse. But I was in such a happy mood that I decided that I'd forgive him his "epiphanies" . . . well, another three or four of them, anyway.

"How do I look?" I asked after my male clothes were finally on my male body.

"A little . . . foofy."

"Excuse me?"

"Well . . . you're still wearing makeup."

"Oh."

I went back to the bathroom and washed off the makeup, then returned to the living room.

"So, what brought all this on?" I asked. "What made you suddenly realize that our relationship was worth taking this risk?"

He sank into the black sectional. "I was sick to my stomach for three days. I lost my appetite. I couldn't sleep. I thought I was sick, but then I started to realize that maybe it was love."

I couldn't help but ask, "And are you sure that you *weren't* sick?"

He smiled boyishly. "I'm sure."

"Good. Because I never want to go through that again."

Frank's smile vanished, and he looked at me with uncertainty.

"Is something wrong?" I asked.

"No." He paused. "Well . . . maybe."

"Spill."

He nervously lit a cigarette and sat, patting the cushion next to him to indicate that I should join him.

"I have to get something off my chest," he said. "It's about this gay thing. I haven't really been honest with you."

"Oh?"

He cast his eyes to the floor. "I haven't been honest with myself, either. I *did* think you were a girl when I first met you—shows how stupid I can be, huh?—but I knew what I was doing when I opened a gay bar. Shit, I could've just gone into salvage, y'know?"

"You were looking to meet a man?"

"Looking . . . hoping . . . I don't know. Maybe nothing would have happened. *Probably* nothing would have happened." He took a long drag off his cigarette, exhaling the smoke away from me, then continued, his voice rising slightly in an anger that seemed self-directed. "You have to understand where I come from, Andrew. I don't come from where you come from. And I'm not talking about the difference between Brooklyn and Allentown. I'm talking about the difference between being a DiBenedetto and being, well, almost anyone else. I've heard about guys who've been fuckin' shot for things like this."

"I understand, Frank—"

"No, Andrew. I'm not sure that you can. I'm not even sure that *I* understand it." Now his words were soft, regretful. "All I know is that I wasted a lot of time and spent a lot of years beating myself up, trying to please other people and be something I'm not. I thought it would go away . . . I thought I could force it to go away. And then . . . and then I met you, and I didn't want it to go away anymore."

I put my arm over his shoulders. "I'm glad."

He smiled. "And I'm glad that you're not really a girl. That would have *really* fucked up my head."

And so we sat and talked—*really* talked, like we did when we first met but hadn't done since—for hours. We confessed insecurities and the secrets of our childhoods and we talked about our dreams and even, vaguely, about our future together. Most importantly, we managed to steer clear of anything that could threaten the new-found happiness growing out of Frank's "epiphany," even extremely important things such as the Mafia, my arrest, and the FBI. It was as if, by unspoken agreement, we felt that those things had already consumed too much of our time and energy, and no longer needed our attention.

It was only when I had an occasional thought about how unhappy Max Abraham would be to learn that I was sitting on Frank DiBenedetto's couch, drinking scotch and enmeshing my legs with his, that I felt the slightest tinge of danger.

The talk and the scotch and the leg-enmeshing evolved over the course of the hours into hand-holding, hair-stroking, body-hugging, button-undoing, thigh-caressing, and deep, passionate kissing, until we reached the point where there was no place for talk and scotch. And leg-enmeshing would only have been redundant.

I slipped my hand up under his shirt, feeling the light cover of hair over his flat stomach, and let it slowly work its way up until I felt the hard definition of his muscled chest through a heavier cover of curls and, just beyond it, an erect nipple. I let one finger delicately circle it, and Frank let out a low moan.

"That feels good," he whispered. His eyes, which had been closed, fluttered open. "Let's go to the bedroom."

" 'kay," I agreed, more than willingly. Sex in Frank's living room was fine, but we'd already done it here once and I was looking for a new challenge.

He took my hand and led me to the bedroom off the hall, three-quarters full with a king-sized bed covered by a navy blue comforter, then playfully threw me down on my back. I sank deeply into the comforter as he lowered his body onto mine, and I could feel the stiffness of his erection through his jeans as he rubbed against me.

I could have stayed like that forever; just the two of us, slowly blending our bodies in an unhurried yet passionate and unbroken series of embraces and caresses. There were no sexual acrobatics and there was no rush. There was just a steady, rhythmic, and intense union of two human bodies as they became one.

After a while our clothes came off, not at any specific point but rather over the course of half an hour, item by item. As each piece was discarded, probing hands and hungry mouths quickly rediscovered the flesh that had been hidden. When I felt his mouth finally find my penis, my body let out an involuntary shudder.

"What's the matter?" I heard his voice ask from somewhere Down There.

"Nothing's the matter," I said, smiling, then laughing. "Everything's perfect."

He gagged a few times, but once he relaxed, he had no problem taking me into his mouth. He was getting much better with very little additional experience. His wet lips and smooth tongue moved steadily, if inexpertly, along the shaft, until—fearful that I was about to explode—I grabbed his shoulders to move him off me.

"Too close," I gasped, almost afraid that I had been too late. But the tingling sensation—the sensation that almost always warned me that I was going to climax when I could no longer do anything about it—eventually faded.

I rolled him off me and onto his back, finding that nipple again

and tonguing it slowly, eliciting another deep moan from Frank before I worked my mouth slowly down his torso. As my tongue
lapped at his rippled stomach, I reached a hand out blindly and
felt for his erection. When my fingers found it, the silky skin was
hot to the touch. I wrapped my hand around it and stroked gently.

"Uh . . . ah!!!" he shouted, after a dozen strokes. A hot stream of
semen coated my neck and shoulders; more sprayed out across the
dark blue comforter, his body, and almost everything else within a
three-foot radius.

"I'm sorry," he mumbled breathlessly, his chest heaving as he
gasped for air. "I didn't mean for it to happen so soon . . ."

I glanced at the clock. It was 5:45 A.M. We had been fooling
around for almost six hours. This was "soon"?

"Don't worry about it, Frank." I bent down to kiss him. "I'd
hardly call that a premature ejaculation."

I slid a leg over him and straddled his narrow hips and his still-
hard penis, and that often-unreliable tingling sensation came back
as I quickly worked to catch up. Within a minute I ejaculated, then
slumped to the mattress next to him. He turned to face me, smiling
sweetly.

"I think," I remember saying before I fell asleep, "that I'll call in
sick to work tomorrow."

The next morning I managed to wake up long enough to call
PMC and leave a message that I wouldn't be coming in. I called my
apartment, too, but Denise was already gone. I considered trying to
reach her back at her own apartment, then thought better of it.
There would be enough hell to pay about Frank from everyone I
knew in the future, and I saw no reason to rush the wrath of the
gods and goddesses.

I fell easily back to sleep, nestled close to Frank's warm body.

We woke past noon and immediately fell back into action, continuing to unlock the secrets of each other's bodies. Unhurried
hours passed quickly, until I caught sight of the alarm clock on the
nightstand out of the corner of my eye and selfishly decided that
we should put an end to our lovemaking before we lost the entire
day. And at that point, after hours of sexual intimacy, it didn't take
long to reduce our erections to spent, flaccid tissue.

"How are you doing?" I gently stroked a hand across his chest, feeling the curls bristle under my fingers. "Still enjoying this?"

"Oh, yeah." His eyes were shut tight. "Yeah. I think that . . . I'm glad that . . . you know."

"I know."

I let several minutes pass, reveling in our new mutual comfort with each other. It was as if the Bad Things had never existed. Then, finally, I lazily rose on one elbow and said, "I think I'll take a shower."

"Towels are in the bathroom closet." His eyes were still closed. "Second shelf."

I crawled over his body and walked into the bathroom, leaving the door ajar. After splashing some water on my face, I examined my reflection in the mirror that filled the wall over the sink. I was good-looking enough, I knew, even with my hair in wild disarray after eighteen hours of sex and sleep, but still . . . still I couldn't see in my face or body whatever it was Frank saw. I was certainly no Frank DiBenedetto.

I looked closer, staring deep into unexceptional, slightly blood-shot hazel eyes. Still nothing.

An involuntary tremble ran through my body as I realized what I was doing. I knew what those feelings of self-doubt meant. I remembered. I had been there before. With Ted Langhorne.

Those feelings of self-doubt meant that I had fallen completely and irrevocably in love, to the point where the other person seemed so perfect that I couldn't understand why I was chosen as the lucky man to receive his affection. Nothing about me seemed adequate anymore, especially when compared to him.

I broke eye contact with myself and tried to remember that he was tied to the Mafia, which was considered slightly-less-than-perfect by many people. Also, I doubted that he had read many great books.

Still, I avoided looking in the mirror. Rationality had very little to do with my mental state at that particular moment.

The shower ran slightly warmer than I was used to, but I adjusted. As I lathered, taking care to make sure that certain areas were *exceptionally* clean, I heard the phone ring distantly somewhere in the apartment, and I decided that—unless his call changed my plans—I would try to convince Frank to go out to a gay dance club

that wasn't Benedick's that night. So that I could show him off, of
course. Frank was the type of man who should be shown off. He
was my trophy mobster.

The shower curtain suddenly ripped open and Frank's face appeared. I started to smile, until I noticed the alarm etched on his
face. My first thought was "Crazy Anna." But, no, it was worse.

"It's my father!" His voice was tight with panic.

"He's coming here?"

"He *is* here. That was the doorman. He's on his way up."

"Shit." It was becoming apparent that we'd no longer be able to
have sex in Frank's apartment, ever again, if only for the fact that I
found the post-coital visiting hours very disturbing.

Frank held one hand to his brow, wet with sweat and shower
spray, and took a deep breath. "Okay, we've got to think. What can
I do?"

"Umm . . ." I wanted to be helpful, but my brain had slipped into
paralysis, too.

He looked down at himself. Dried semen caked the hair on his
stomach and chest. That could be covered, of course. But adding
to that the naked man in his shower, the rumpled, semen-spotted
bed, and the discarded clothes—male and female—in the living
room, it was going to be impossible for him to play the role of the
innocent heterosexual son. This was the Crazy Anna Franco Crisis
squared.

"First thing you should do," I said, trying not to panic, "is throw
something on. Then you'd better get the clothes out of the living
room. Maybe if you keep him out of the bedroom and the bathroom . . ." And that's when I had my revelation. "Wait!" I said. "Wait
a minute . . ."

I heard his voice long before I saw him. It was deep and smooth,
not the Cagney/Brando voice I was expecting. That's what I get for
watching too much television.

"I see I caught you at a bad time," Frank Senior said, out in the
living room with his son.

"I don't know what you mean," Frank Junior replied, an awkward nervousness to his voice.

"Ah, to be young again . . ." The Mafia *capo* let his baritone trail
off wistfully.

I stared at myself in the mirror. This time, the stare wasn't one of self-doubt. It wasn't an intense stare. It was a careful stare.

Their voices faded, then grew stronger, then faded again as they moved around the living room. My stare remained constant, probing, searching for the slightest imperfection in my face and body. I couldn't find any. I was ready for my close-up.

For effect, I flushed the toilet and ran the sink for a brief moment, then cracked the bathroom door. A white-faced Frank Junior stared back at me. And then I heard the smooth baritone again.

"Come out and say hello, Anna." He stepped into view—a handsome, olive-skinned, graying man in an expensive black suit—and smiled. The smile faltered for a second, then recovered. "You're not Anna." He might have been surprised, but he was the most collected person in the apartment.

The father looked at the son, questioning him through the smile. The son's nervousness was apparent in the wet rings that appeared under the arms of his sweatshirt, which had been thrown on so hastily it was inside-out.

"That's not Anna," Frank Senior said again. His smile disappeared.

Frank Junior's voice trembled. "I can explain. I've wanted to tell you, but—"

The elder DiBenedetto cut him off. "I'm . . . I'm a bit embarrassed, Frankie. I don't know what to say. You caught your old man by surprise."

"Sorry . . ." said *my* Frank. "I know you're probably disappointed, but . . ."

Frank Senior's smile returned, wider than ever. His teeth sparkled unnaturally as he beamed at me, and I recognized his son's captivating smile in his. He turned his face to Frank Junior. "Disappointed? Nah. Not in my kid. So, aren't you going to introduce us?"

Frank Junior gulped audibly. The sweat mark now extended almost to his elbow.

"Sure. This is my father. And Pop, this is my friend, Belle."

"Pleased to meet you, Mr. DiBenedetto." Somehow I managed to stay calm enough to keep in character. "Frank's told me so much about you."

"My pleasure." He took my hand and gently raised it. I was afraid he was going to kiss it. He didn't, but still he held it for an uncomfortable period of time. "But please, call me Frank."

"Frank," I repeated.

"I like your accent. Southern?"

"On my father's side." I had no idea why I said that. It just popped out.

"You look a little like that actress. Demi Moore."

"Uh . . . thank you."

"So!" Frank Junior suddenly slapped his hands together. "What brings you here, Pop?"

"In the neighborhood," he said, finally—and seemingly reluctantly—letting go of my hand. "Some problems with . . . *something*. Thought I'd pay you a surprise visit."

"Well . . . it *is* a surprise!"

"Good." He nodded at his son. "Can I speak to you in private?"

Frank gave him an exaggerated shrug, and the two men walked into the kitchen. As they turned the corner, Frank gave me a look of abject terror. I hurried back to the bathroom to make sure that no whiskers had sprouted through my makeup or some other disaster hadn't occurred. I couldn't find anything.

They talked in the kitchen for several minutes, then returned to the living room where I sat on the couch, pretending to read a magazine. I waited until the last moment to look up as they approached, afraid of what I'd see in their eyes.

But there was no hint of a problem. Quite the contrary, in fact. Even my nervous new lover seemed to be gaining confidence, although he was now calming himself with a cigarette. Frank Senior excused himself to use the "little boy's room" and, when he was gone, I motioned for his son to sit next to me.

"What's going on?" I whispered.

"He wanted to know about me and Anna." He was also whispering. "I told him it was over, that it wasn't going to work out between us. He wasn't exactly thrilled—he thought that'd be a good way to keep Tommy Franco happy—but he says he can live with it."

"See? One problem solved. And it wasn't nearly as difficult as you thought."

"Don't make this sound so easy. It wasn't. It still isn't." The toilet flushed, and he glanced at the bathroom door. "And it won't be."

Now the sink was running.

I patted his hand. "Hang in there. And remember, I love you."

He was about to reply when the door jerked open and Frank

Senior filled its frame, casually tossing a balled hand towel on the vanity.

"So, Belle," he said, stepping forward into the living room, "not Italian, I assume."

"Er . . . no. I hope it doesn't matter."

"We're just . . . sort of seeing each other," said Frank Junior awkwardly.

"It's the Nineteen-nineties," his father replied. "I think we've moved past that."

"Oh," I said. "Good." As if that was my biggest problem. As if!

"So . . . ?" Frank Senior made a rolling gesture with one hand. I didn't understand, so he continued. "If you don't mind me asking, what's your background? Irish? You look Irish."

It occurred to me that I had no idea which Old Country claimed the name Bacall. So I decided to let him make the choice.

Which proved to be a mistake.

"My last name is Bacall. Why don't you tell me?"

"Bacall," he repeated. "Any relation?"

"To who?"

"*Lauren* Bacall." As if he could have been asking about someone else.

My mouth once again moved faster than my brain. It was a bad habit of mine. "Yes. I'm her niece." I paused, then added, "But her friends and family call her Betty." I just had to keep piling it on, didn't I?

"No shit! She's your aunt?" He shook his head in awe. "Pardon my language. I'm just . . . well, I already knew that it was an honor to meet you, but now . . . let's just say you've blown me away." I doubted that someone with a career like Frank Senior's used the phrase "blown me away" lightly.

"Yes," I said, more to fill a conversation gap than to add substance. "She's my Aunt Betty, all right."

My Frank struggled to catch up. "That's right, Pop. That's how I met Belle. She was visiting her aunt and . . . and . . . we met over in Central Park."

"Lauren Bacall lives around here?" The son pointed out the window at the Dakota. "No shit." He didn't excuse his language again, but rather sat next to me and leaned close. "Do you think . . . ? Do you think I might meet your aunt someday? I've been a fan since . . . forever."

"You never know." I finally realized that I'd gone too far.

"Is she seeing anyone?"

"Pop!"

"It's okay, Frankie. Your mother's been dead for ten years, and the official mourning period has ended." He returned to me. "Is she?"

I wanted to pull the name of a celebrity from thin air to play the role of Aunt Betty's boyfriend, but I didn't. I knew I'd feel guilty if Harrison Ford or Norman Mailer got whacked because of my lies. "I don't think so."

"I've got an idea, then," he said, with frightening enthusiasm. "How about if the four of us—"

"Pop!"

"Oh, I don't think she's in town . . ." I babbled. "I think she . . . uh . . . left this morning . . . for . . . uh . . . Hollywood." Where else?

The father looked at his watch, a huge gold monster clamped to his hairy left wrist. "It's almost six o'clock. Call your aunt and see if she's home. If she is, tell her to meet us here. Or leave a message to meet us at Viggio's at nine o'clock. If she isn't . . . well, I'll still take you kids out, and I'll link up with her some other time. How's that sound?"

I looked at my Frank, and he looked at me. In all four of our eyes, panic mixed with resignation, with a dash or two of fear thrown in for good measure.

"Uh . . . okay," I said finally.

"You'd better call her right now, so she doesn't make other plans." His enthusiasm made him almost seem boyish. It also made him extremely frustrating.

I walked to the telephone and dully picked it up, unsure of exactly how I was supposed to get Lauren Bacall on the phone, let alone explain to her that I was her niece, I was living with her, and it was imperative that she dine at Viggio's at nine o'clock because one of New York City's better-known Mafioso wanted to meet her.

I dialed the first seven numbers that came to mind.

"Hello?" answered Denise in a singsong voice.

"Uh . . . er . . ."

"Who is this?"

"Is she home?" asked Frank Senior.

"Who was *that?*" asked Denise. "Who's—?"

"No," I replied. "She's not home. I got the machine."

"Drew? Is that *you?* Why are you—? Are you dressed as Belle Bacall again? What's going on?"

I ignored her. "Hi, Aunt Betty. It's Belle."

"What the hell are you doing?" asked Denise.

"It's six-o-five, and I don't know if you've left for . . . uh . . . Hollywood or not, but I wanted to leave you a quick message."

"This had better be good, Drew."

"I'm having dinner tonight at nine o'clock at Viggio's with my new boyfriend, Frank"— the boyfriend blushed —"and his father, and—"

"His *father!!*" Denise screamed so loudly that I covered the receiver with my hand so that the mobster wouldn't hear her. "Are you insane?!"

"—and this *nice* Mr. DiBenedetto is a huge fan of yours and he'd love to meet you. So, if you can make it, I hope you'll join us. If you're not already in Hollywood, that is."

"Drew, you are getting yourself into so much trouble."

"Bye!" I hung up on her.

Denise was right, of course. This was just the latest thing to go careening out of control. I wondered if letting her know where I was going to be and who I would be with was wise.

I need not have wondered. Of course it wasn't.

After the phone call, the father excused himself, telling us that he'd see us at nine o'clock in a voice that made it clear that a cancellation wouldn't be accepted without a note from a physician. Frank and I spent several hours deep in thought, each of us hoping to come up with the brilliant idea that would extricate us from the increasingly complex web in which we had entangled ourselves, and both of us quite clearly coming up with nothing.

I considered calling Denise but decided to leave well enough alone. There was nothing to be accomplished in furthering her anger. Ditto David.

"Lauren Bacall," I muttered. "I had to make Lauren Bacall my aunt."

Frank shook his head. Then he laughed.

"What?"

"Aunt Betty?"

And I had to laugh, too. We both needed it. There had to be

humor in here somewhere, and we were determined to find it, no matter how deep we had to dig.

Nine o'clock. Viggio's, a dark Italian restaurant, just off Canal Street in Lower Manhattan's Little Italy.

The sort of restaurant that derives its atmosphere on three sides from dusty empty Chianti bottles suspended by dusty plastic grape-vines stapled to trellises nailed to the wall, and on the fourth side from styleless murals of the Leaning Tower of Pisa and Venetian canals. The sort of restaurant that derives its charm from surly, heavily accented waiters and surly, clipped-voiced customers.

That was the bad news. The good news was that there was little chance that we'd accidentally run into my Aunt Betty there.

We were led to a table in the rear of the restaurant where Frank's father sat, back to the wall, at a large table covered with a stereo-typical red-and-white-checked tablecloth. A small candle burned inside a blue glass holder, and an unwrapped basket of bread sat in the center of the table.

"Son," he said, in greeting. He took my hand again and, rather charmingly, added, "Belle. And *bella* you are."

Frank and I offered our own greetings and sat.

"Did you hear from your aunt?" he asked hopefully.

I offered a thin smile. "Sorry. No. She wasn't home when I got there. She must have flown to the West Coast."

"That's a shame. But there will be other times. Right?"

The *right?* wasn't a hopeful question. I heard it as a demand.

"I'm sure of it."

Frank Junior kicked me under the table. I was going to kick him back, but my shoe fell off.

"What's good here, Pop?" Frank was playing with his menu and desperately trying to change the subject.

"Everything."

A short, dark, middle-aged man in a white shirt and black tux-edo pants appeared at our table.

"Good evening, Mr. Dee," he said with a light Italian accent. "Good to see you again, sir."

"Ay, Viggio," said Frank Senior, patting his arm. "I'd like you to meet my son, Frankie." They shook hands. "And this is his friend, Belle Bacall."

Viggio smiled at me and said, plastically, "What a beautiful woman. Thank you for gracing my restaurant with your presence."

I smiled back. It was a forced smile, but it was still a smile.

"Viggio owns this place," the father explained needlessly. "He's had it for—what's it been now? Five years?"

"Six."

"Six," Frank Senior agreed, before gesturing at me. "Belle here is Lauren Bacall's niece, Viggio."

"Really!"

"Yes. In fact, Ms. Bacall may be joining us for dinner."

Viggio broke into a wide, proud grin. "At my restaurant? Miss Lauren Bacall?"

"Oh, I wouldn't count on it," I stammered. "I think she's filming something right now." At the last moment I remembered to add, "In Hollywood."

"Once," said the restaurateur, pointing at a distant black-and-white head shot mounted on the wall near the tiny bar, "Tony Bennett came here for lunch."

"I really wouldn't count on it," I said again.

"If she comes, I'm sure we can get a photo for your wall," said Frank Senior.

"That would be nice," said Viggio. "But we'll see what happens."

"I'd like a drink," I said, jumping the gun.

"Are you sure that's wise?" asked Frank Junior, almost imperceptibly shaking his head. "After all, you have to take care of your voice." I knew what he meant, but . . .

"You sing?" the father asked me.

"Uh . . ." I was sure that non-singers had reasons to take care of their voices, but at that moment I was drawing a blank.

So was Frank. In fact, it seemed as if the entire restaurant had fallen silent, waiting for my answer. I could hear the seconds tick by loudly as I sat, my brain idling.

I sighed. "Yes. I sing." Under the table, I delivered a sharp kick to my lover's shin, before adding pointedly in his direction, "But that doesn't mean I can't have a glass of wine. Or two."

The Franks ordered drinks, too, and Viggio went off to fill the order. I heard the rustle of the front door opening and saw Frank Senior eye the newcomers with suspicion before relaxing, deciding that they posed no threat to him. I stole a glance over my shoulder at the front door.

He was right. The newcomers didn't pose a threat to Frank Di-Benedetto. They posed a threat to me.

David Carlyle and Denise Hanrahan stood just inside the front door.

"Oh . . ." I muttered.

Frank Senior ignored my sudden distress, but his son didn't. He looked at me, then glanced at the door.

"Oh . . ." he muttered.

"I really loved your aunt in *Key Largo,*" the older man said, turning his attention from nothing back to me. "That's the movie when I think I fell in love with her."

"Pop . . ."

"It's true, Frankie. It's true. No disrespect meant to your beloved mother, God rest her soul, but, well, Lauren Bacall! I dragged your mother to see her on Broadway many times." He paused and shrugged. "She liked *Applause,* but not *Woman of the Year.*"

I felt strangely disconnected from the conversation about my alleged aunt. I never suspected that I'd be in the presence of a real fan, or else I would have chosen a less excitable drag name. Teri Garr, maybe. Or, better yet, I would have kept my mouth shut when Frank Senior asked if we were related.

Thankfully, Viggio was back with our drinks. When Frank's father turned to talk to him—repeating his *Key Largo* line, I might add—I looked for Denise and David. I found them with no trouble. They were alarmingly close . . . if you consider the next table alarmingly close.

Over their menus, they looked at me with an incredible mixture of contempt and concern. My head waved what I hoped would be read as a silent *go away,* but it didn't seem to work. I turned away from them, only to see my Frank giving them the same sign. They paid no attention to him, either.

"Chardonnay for the *bella* Belle." Frank Senior set my glass in front of me. "A fine drink for a woman."

I tried not to resent the remark.

My glass of wine was gone in three minutes.

When Viggio reappeared, I ordered an entrée from the menu by pointing, since I didn't want to mangle the Italian pronunciation. The Franks pronounced their orders flawlessly. Behind me, I heard David also master the pronunciation, while Denise obviously pointed. Denise and I were apparently bound together forever, if only because we wouldn't embarrass each other in Italian restaurants.

The front door opened again, and again the older DiBenedetto tensed. This time, though, he didn't relax quite as quickly; it was more of the slow deflation of bellows than a sudden sigh of relief. Yes, he was relaxing, but I couldn't help but swivel to see what sort of person had walked into the restaurant to pose the hint of a threat.

I scanned the restaurant.

Of course.

I saw the new patrons. It was Special Agent Patrick Waverly and his partner, the man I saw standing silently on the sidewalk the day before. They were dressed casually and acting very much unlike FBI agents—more like slightly obnoxious Wall Streeters unwinding after a day of merging and acquiring—but even my untrained eye noted that they didn't belong here. Still, they could pass. I hoped.

While I was watching Patrick, he quickly scanned our table. His eyes passed right over me, but why shouldn't they? I was Belle Bacall, Lauren Bacall's singing niece. I wasn't Andrew Westlake.

His eyes rested for only a split second on the Franks before turning to the bar to place his drink order. The Franks probably never even noticed.

I did.

So did David, the only other person in my circle who had seen Patrick Waverly. Behind me, I heard him utter, "Oh, dear," before muttering to Denise.

She, in turn, said, "*That's* him?" I didn't look but hoped she wasn't pointing. And I blushed, despite myself.

"What's going on?" Frank Junior whispered into my ear. He had heard them, and most likely saw me redden.

I glanced at his father, who was thankfully distracted again by Viggio and in the midst of an intense conversation about where to find the best calamari in the New York City metropolitan area. A restaurant in Bay Ridge was the leading contender.

"Remember that FBI agent I mentioned?" I whispered.

"Oh, no . . ."

"Oh, yes. Oh yes, indeed."

Frank drained his glass.

"A wonderful night," said Frank Senior, apropos of nothing, when he again graced us with his attention. "Too bad your aunt couldn't join us, but still, I'm having a wonderful night."

And, yes, the irony did occur to me that the only person I knew in the restaurant who wasn't sitting on pins and needles was also the only person who had most likely killed other people. The rest of us—the ones with consciences—were left to stew in the juices of guilt by association.

"I have to go to the mmm . . . er, ladies' room," I announced suddenly, removing the napkin from my lap and grabbing my purse.

As I passed her table, Denise wordlessly rose and followed me into the hallway discreetly labeled RESTROOMS AND PHONES.

"Drew," she hissed behind me once we were alone in the hall. "Wrong door."

I looked back at her. She was opening a door closer to the dining room, while I—through force of habit—was opening the door decorated with a male cutout. Oops.

I followed her into the ladies' room and locked the door behind us.

"I can't even begin to think of what to say to you." She wasn't pleased. "You have a death wish, don't you? Am I gonna have to burn those Belle Bacall clothes? Is that the only way to get you out of them?"

"I know, I know . . . I didn't know what to do. Frank's father walked in on us, and doing the Belle Bacall act was the only way I could think of to get out of it. But now . . . well, he thinks I'm Lauren Bacall's niece. And then Patrick walked through the door, and . . . I'm in so much trouble!"

"You've got that right."

"But what are you doing here?"

"Believe it or not, David and I care about you. Probably more than you care about yourself. Although I don't know why. We came down here because . . . well, let's face it, that was one strange phone call you made to me this afternoon."

"Yeah. And things have just gotten stranger. What's Patrick doing here? Do you think he's following me?"

"I doubt it. Too obvious."

"Well, what, then?"

"Did you ever hear the phrase 'ongoing investigation'? You

know that the FBI has been watching the father. That's the only reason you met Agent Pat in the first place. Why does it surprise you that they're watching him in this restaurant?"

A thought occurred to me.

"Go get David's cellular phone."

"Why?"

"Please?" I didn't want to tell her why, because I was pretty sure that she'd try to talk me out of it . . . and I wasn't altogether convinced of the wisdom of my idea myself.

She left the bathroom, returning less than a minute later with the phone.

"He says to hurry," she said, handing it to me. "He's expecting a call."

"This won't take long." I knew full well that David wasn't really expecting a call. I had already fished Patrick's business card out of my purse, and I punched the number to his beeper into the keypad of David's phone. It rang, and after a series of tones I entered David's phone number. If I was lucky, at that very moment Patrick was excusing himself from the bar to use the pay phone.

I was lucky. Two minutes later David's cell phone rang.

"Patrick?" I said, answering the ring.

"Uh . . . yes . . ." He didn't recognize my voice.

"It's Andrew Westlake."

"Oh, hi . . . I don't mean to be rude, but I really can't talk right now."

"Me, either. I'm just calling to ask you and your partner to leave the restaurant, if there's any way you can."

"How do you . . . ?"

"I'm here. And you're making me nervous. And I think that DiBenedetto has made you out, too."

"You're . . . ?" His voice dropped to a whisper. "You're not here. You can't be. Where?"

I could envision him as he stood at the phone, furtively scanning the handful of patrons looking for my familiar face.

"I'm in the ladies' room right now. But . . ."

He made the connection. I had told him about the night I first dressed in drag and met Frank, and now it all came together for him. "That was you? The woman at the table?"

"Uh-huh."

He laughed, despite himself.

"So, can you . . . leave?" I asked again.

"Well . . ." He paused, then, "I should talk to you first."

"We're talking."

"Not here." I realized he meant that he didn't want to chat on a public phone in front of several potential eavesdroppers.

"Okay. I'll wait for you in the ladies' room."

A moment later there was a quiet rap on the door, and I let him in.

"Fancy meeting you here," I said as I locked the door behind him. It was getting crowded.

"Look at you!" He grinned as he looked me over. "You look like Demi Moore!" He saw Denise. "Is she . . . ?"

"She's with me," I said. "Well . . . I mean, she's with me, but not with my party. She's with the party that's following me. Patrick Waverly, this is Denise Hanrahan."

"Hi," they said uncomfortably to each other.

"Denise and my friend David came down here to make sure I wasn't getting into too much trouble."

"And are you?"

"That goes without saying," Denise said humorlessly.

"So, anyway," I said, "do you think there's any way that you and your partner could clear out?"

"This is official business, Andrew. I need to know why Frank DiBenedetto is here tonight."

"I'll tell you why. He's here because he wants to meet Lauren Bacall."

"Huh?"

I recounted the story to him. To Patrick's credit, he actually found it amusing.

"Does that satisfy you?" I asked, when it was ended. "Can you leave now?"

"Well . . ."

We fell mute at the sound of a knock on the door and remained silent as the knock was repeated. Finally, we heard my Frank's hushed voice.

"Andrew? Denise? What's going on?"

"We'll be out in a minute," I hissed back.

"Let me in."

"No."

"Andrew . . ."

Denise and Patrick stood openmouthed, both silently pleading with me to keep the door locked.

"Andrew, I need to know what's going on."

I gave in and unlocked the door. I felt mental daggers from Denise and Patrick pierce my back, but I shrugged them off.

Frank crowded into the bathroom, nodding pleasantly at Denise, then eyeing Patrick with confusion.

"What's *he* doing in here?"

"I had to talk to him," I replied. "That's all."

"I don't like this, Andrew."

"I don't either," added Patrick icily.

"That makes three of us." Denise took David's cell phone from my hand. "I'm going back to my table."

As she began to squeeze past me, Patrick unhappily said, "Well, I suppose you forced my hand, Andrew. I'd better be leaving, too."

"Sorry," I said, suddenly feeling guilty.

"Let's just say that we're even now." He held the bathroom door for Denise and they stepped out into the hall.

Frank and I were left alone.

"So?" he asked accusingly.

"I was trying to convince him to leave. That's all."

"I believe you," he said, although a trace of suspicion still hung in his words. "Still, it's a bit dangerous to risk being seen with a federal agent in a place like this. That's all."

"But nobody knows . . ."

"Sure they do. My old man can pick out a fed a mile away. He had your buddy's number the minute he walked through the door."

That surprised me. "He didn't seem to notice."

"He noticed. He just didn't care a whole lot. He's out having a nice quiet dinner with his son and his son's girlfriend—and, hopefully, Lauren Bacall—and the feds can't lay a hand on him. When he's watching that front door, he's not looking for shields. He's looking for Crazy Tommy Franco and people like that."

"I thought I was doing a good thing here."

"I know. But you've gotta trust me when I tell you that my father can take care of himself."

"Sorry." I bent forward to embrace him. He returned the embrace, leaning back against the white porcelain sink. "I guess I have a lot to learn."

We were interrupted by yet another knock. Before either of us had the chance to answer the door, which I hadn't bothered to lock after Denise and Patrick left, it swung open to reveal Frank Senior.

"There you are!" he exclaimed. "I was beginning to worry about you. You two lovebirds can't keep your hands off each other, can you?" At that, Frank and I scrambled out of each other's arms. "C'mon! Your dinner's getting cold."

Special Agent Patrick Waverly and his partner were gone when we returned to the table. I glanced at Denise and David, who pointedly would not look in my direction as they picked through a limp antipasto.

The next half hour passed in relatively comfortable small talk sprinkled between generous portions of veal and pasta. We were nearing the end of our dinner—almost home free—when Viggio approached the table to inquire if everything was to our satisfaction.

"Excellent," replied Frank Senior, taking it upon himself to speak for us all. "You outdid yourself, my friend."

"Thank you, Mr. Dee. It's always a pleasure to serve you and your delightful guests." He leaned closer to the older man. "If I may request a favor . . ."

"Try me out."

"When I heard that Miss Lauren Bacall might be joining your party, I mentioned it to a friend of mine, and he . . . well, sir, this friend knew of a photographer, and he mentioned it to that man, and now . . ." He shrugged a *what can I do?* although he had obviously done quite enough already, in my opinion.

Frank Senior furrowed his brow. "But she couldn't make it."

"I informed the gentleman of that. And, of course, I would never have allowed him to take a photograph without your approval, Mr. Dee. But still, he thought that maybe a picture of you and Miss Lauren Bacall's niece . . . She's a singer, no?"

Oh, no. Fortunately, I felt quite confident that the alleged organized crime figure seated to my left would summarily dismiss the idea.

So why wasn't he summarily dismissing it? Why was he thinking it over?

"I don't know 'bout this, Viggio," he said finally. "The newspapers print a lot of lies about me."

"I understand, sir. And nobody who knows you would ever believe such lies. Of course, I would love the publicity for my struggling little *ristorante,* but I would never allow anyone to do something that would hurt you." Viggio inserted a contrived pause, then added a coda to his performance. "But I thought that maybe a photograph like that would help undo some of those lies by showing you with a beautiful woman who's—how shall I put this?—who's not of the usual crowd. And who is related to a very famous movie star."

No, I certainly wasn't of the usual crowd, although I wasn't related to a very famous movie star, either. Which was all the more reason I telepathically urged Frank Senior to just say no. I could only hope that Viggio's manipulations were as obvious to him as they were to me.

"Why not?" he finally said. And I muttered a curse, prompting Frank Junior to once again kick me under the table. "But tell them just one picture. That's all. Any more and I'll shove the camera up—" He remembered that a lady was at the table and abruptly stopped.

"I really don't photograph very well," I stammered.

"You look beautiful, Belle," Frank Senior replied, smiling.

"But I'm very camera shy. I'll probably roll my eyes up or wrinkle my nose, and it'll look like you had dinner with a carnival sideshow."

"Yeah, Pop. I really don't think—"

But Frank Senior wasn't listening to us. He was still listening to Viggio's seductive words, words that promised him a photographic association with a famous actress that, by extension, could make him seem less Mafia *capo* and more man about town. The fact that Viggio wanted the picture taken for purely selfish promotional reasons seemed to have escaped him.

The photographer was escorted to our table, was graciously allowed four shots, took our names down, and left. It was relatively painless. I made sure to smile bewitchingly for the camera.

Only when he was gone did I think to look at David and Denise. They were, of course, horrified. I had a strong feeling that the incidents of tonight were the beginning of the end of our friendships.

I ordered another drink to dull the pain.

I woke early Wednesday morning in Frank's bed with a horrible what-have-I-done? feeling. It wasn't just the fact that I went to Viggio's, and it wasn't just the bathroom conference with Patrick, and it wasn't just the photographer . . . It was all of them rolled together, along with a myriad of other smaller, disquieting incidents. It was Crazy Anna and Big Paulie and Margaret Campbell and the police and my arrest and Max Abraham and Ted and Nicky. It was the panic of recognition that my life was out of control.

But when I moved a few inches and felt the warm body sleeping soundly next to me, everything else fell into perspective. It was a skewed perspective, granted, but nevertheless it was a perspective.

I called in sick to work again. I didn't want to have to face David.

I scanned the newspapers. The photograph wasn't in any of them, which pleased me until I remembered that it probably wouldn't have made their deadlines. Which meant that there was always tomorrow, or the next day, or even some time in the indefinite future. It wasn't as if a photo of an alleged organized crime figure and the alleged singing niece of an actress was time sensitive.

When Frank finally crawled out of bed, it was late in the morning.

"I hate to do this," I said, "but I think I'm gonna head back to my place. You want to go slumming with me?"

"I should go to the club," he said, wiping sleep from his eyes. "What time is it?"

"Almost eleven o'clock."

"Oh. Early." He rubbed his eyes again and yawned. "Sure. I'll go over to your place for a while."

We walked. It took us almost half an hour, but it felt good to stretch my legs and breathe the crisp mid-November air. In my duffel bag I carried the hated Belle Bacall costume. I was fairly certain I'd be throwing it out in the trash at my earliest opportunity.

The message light on my answering machine was blinking furiously when we got back to the apartment. I didn't really want to listen to it, but I faced the inevitable and tapped the playback button.

Tuesday, 9:25 A.M.: Denise calling, to find out where I had gone while she was sleeping.

Tuesday, 11:38 A.M.: Denise calling, to see if I was home yet.

Tuesday, 12:07 P.M.: David calling, to see how I was feeling.

Tuesday, 12:10 P.M.: Denise calling, to tell me that she's just realized what I must have done the night before, and that I'm a stupid bastard. Also, that she wanted her makeup back.

Tuesday, 5:45 P.M.: Denise calling, to tell me that she's home from work and that I had better call her.

Tuesday, 6:07 P.M.: Denise calling, to tell me that she can't believe that I'm going to dinner with those gangsters, let alone while dressed in drag, and if I thought that there was any way that she'd allow herself to get involved in my psychodrama, I had another think coming.

Tuesday, 6:27 P.M.: David calling, to say that he'd just heard from Denise, and that I was almost certainly insane and should be hospitalized for my own protection.

Wednesday, 12:38 A.M.: Denise calling, to see if I was home yet.

Wednesday, 9:48 A.M.: David calling, to tell me that, although he didn't forgive me, he was still concerned about my well-being, and avoiding him by calling in sick wasn't going to resolve anything, and he needed me at work because Margaret Campbell was in town and asking for me.

Wednesday, 10:48 A.M.: Denise. She didn't get a chance to leave a message before the tape ran out.

"It's nice to know that your friends care, though, isn't it?" asked Frank.

"I suppose . . . Sorry if they sounded . . . uh . . . harsh about you and your father."

"Don't worry about it." Their nasty comments had rolled off his back. When you grow up with the knowledge that other people innately want to garrote you and your family, I suppose that old sticks-and-stones adage is easier to appreciate. "I've heard worse. Anyway, they were much harder on you. For what it's worth, I don't think you're insane."

"Thanks. I need to hear that sometimes."

The phone rang. I didn't want to answer it. I knew that it was either David or Denise.

"Want me to get it?" asked Frank.

"Not especially," I said with resignation. I picked up the phone and mumbled, "Hello?"

"Look who's home!" It was David, and he sounded surprisingly happy to hear my voice. "We were beginning to worry about you!"

"I can take care of myself. So, what can I do for you? I'm sick, remember?" I coughed twice, unconvincingly.

"Of course you are. A chest cold, right? When I last saw you, your chest seemed quite . . . er . . . full."

"You're a funny man. You should do stand-up."

"That's my next career. For now, though, I'm merely senior management at that publishing house where you occasionally work. Which brings me to the reason for my call. Apparently, you have a fan in town, and she wants to say hello."

Ah! Now I understood why David was pleasant. He wasn't alone.

The phone was passed, and a Southern-accented woman's voice said, "Hello, Westlake. Feeling any better?" It was Margaret Campbell.

"Much. What brings you to New York?"

"I'm taking a look at the cover art for my next book. Which is crap, by the way. The artwork, that is, not the book." In the background, I heard David groan.

"Well, I'm sorry I'm not—" The feel of Frank's hand as it slid inside the back of my pants broke my train of thought. "I mean, I, uh . . . I'm sorry I'm not going to get a chance to see you."

"I'm in town until Saturday. Maybe we can still get together."

"Sure," I said, not really meaning it. I was glad I had the opportunity to unburden myself to her, but I saw no point in furthering our acquaintance. In my mind, she belonged on the West Coast, along with Special Agent Patrick Waverly. The very fact that my West Coast demons had followed me home to Manhattan only served to heighten my apprehension.

"By the way, I read your book." Now she had my interest. Talk about me usually did that. "I thought it was great. Y'know, I was predisposed to dislike you, Westlake. But you can write. It's fluff, of course, but it's good fluff."

"Uh . . . thanks!" Coming from one of the nation's best-selling writers, that was noteworthy praise. I hoped David had heard that. I'd be demanding a huge advance for my third book.

She must have read my mind. "If you want, I'll blurb your next novel. Or the paperback, if these cheapskates at PMC open their wallets." I heard David groan again.

"That would be great!" I said as Frank tightly clasped a buttock.

"Good, then," she said. "I'm staying at the Mayflower Hotel on Central Park West, near Columbus Circle. You know where that is?" I did. "Great view of the park. Give me a call and we'll sip some bourbon together."

"I will," I promised, not really thinking that I would. We said our good-byes, and then David took the phone again.

"Will I be seeing you?"

"Soon enough."

"I'd really like to see you, Andrew. And not just for . . . the reasons that we don't need to go into right now. We've had a number of inquiries from the media and bookstores about *The Brewster Mall* in the wake of the Gary Vine plug, and I've got to get you out promoting it. Gary Vine can't do it alone, you know."

"I'll come in tomorrow. Just . . . take it easy on me, okay?"

"Take it easy on yourself," he said, ending the conversation.

Frank's hand was still down the back of my pants, squeezing. "Are you trying to tell me something?" I asked.

He was.

Frank left for Benedick's later that afternoon, when the sky was beginning to turn dark. I begged off, reasoning that a quiet night at home for a change might do me good.

When Denise called—and I knew she would—her anger had mellowed. Slightly.

"You're such an asshole," she said when I picked up the phone. "But I still want to see you."

We agreed to meet at Renaldo's, the Italian restaurant on Broadway. When she joined me at the bar twenty-five minutes later, her first words were, "You look good in men's clothes. You should try it more often."

"I'm burning my drag," I said, loud enough to be heard over the Sinatra record that played in the background. "I never want to wear a dress again."

An older man sitting a few stools away from me moved over a few additional stools.

"That was crazy, what you did last night," she said. "You know that, don't you? And what the hell was going on with that photographer?"

"The paparazzi follow me wherever I go. I am, after all, Belle Bacall." She didn't smile, so I explained. "That bastard Viggio tipped off a freelancer that Lauren Bacall was going to be there having dinner with Frank's father, but the photographer decided to settle for us. That's it."

"And you allowed that?"

"I didn't have a choice. More to the point, Frank's father allowed it. As a favor to Viggio, that's all. He wasn't exactly thrilled with it." She still didn't react. "But what does it matter? So what if a picture of Belle Bacall ends up in the *Post* or the *Daily News*? After last night, I've sworn off drag."

"I've heard that before."

"I mean it this time. Belle Bacall, age thirty-five, dead after a freak boiler explosion. Survived only by her Aunt Betty."

"I hope you mean it. I really do."

"I do." I paused. "Are you still mad at me?"

"Yes," she admitted. "A little bit. But I'll get over it. Just remember, though, when David and I get mad at you, it's only because we're worried. You keep doing stupid things to screw up your life. I've said this before, and I'm afraid that I'll have to say it again, but the world doesn't revolve around you. You merely exist in it. You don't get to write your own rules as you go along."

"I know," I said sheepishly. "For what it's worth, I haven't exactly been finding the past few weeks a laugh riot. It used to be so easy, this relationship thing. Go out dressed like a man, meet another man dressed like a man, have a few dates, sleep together—oh, okay, sleep together and *then* go out on a few dates—and see what happens from there. I'll admit that I had a habit of screwing things up through my own self-involvement . . ." She was pleased to hear me echo her words from earlier in the week. "But at least the rules were straightforward and uncomplicated. Now, the only way I can be with the man I truly love is to pretend I'm someone else."

"That's not what you want, though. If you have to dress in drag to be seen with Frank, then it isn't right for you."

I waved her comment away. "No, I don't want the situation. But I do want the man. Desperately. More than anyone I've ever wanted before."

"Even Ted?"

My answer came easy. "Yes. Even Ted."

"Hmmm," she muttered, more surprised than upset. I suppose my years of talking about Ted as some sort of God—even after he left me—had left her unprepared for the thought that someone could ever replace him, let alone surpass him, in my heart.

"And," I added, "you have to admit that Frank's been making great strides in coming out. Three weeks ago it had never entered his mind. Now, he says he doesn't care what people think, that he only wants to be with me."

"So he says. If he doesn't care about what people think, then what was the deal last night?"

"Baby steps, okay? Give the guy some room to take a few baby steps."

She sighed. She still wasn't happy, but she realized that there was nothing she could do about the situation.

And she was right.

She was helpless. Every bit as helpless as I was.

Okay, so I admit it: I thought a night off from each other would do me good.

But by the time I walked back to my apartment from Renaldo's, I felt an ache that had nothing to do with my physiology. I called Benedick's, and after the usual interminable wait, I was put through to him.

"Hey," he said. "How ya doin'?"

"I miss you."

He laughed. "Same here. I miss you, too. Why don't you come down to the club?"

"Why don't you leave the club and come here?"

"Sorry. Gotta lot of work to do. You remember work, right?" Oh, good—a joke at my expense, from the man who was responsible for the situation. Still . . .

"Well . . ." My watch told me it was just minutes past ten o'clock. Even though I knew that I should stay home and make an effort to get to work fresh and on time, I didn't think I could fight that ache.

"C'mon," he pleaded. "Come down here and see me." His voice dropped to a whisper. "My office door has a lock on it, y'know. We'd have privacy. Anna and my father would never set foot in here."

He wasn't fighting fair. Was it really true that he had been a homosexual for less than three weeks?

Fifteen minutes later I was freshened up and waiting for the subway.

When I reached his office I found that he did, indeed, have a lock on the door. Unfortunately, Frank was locked inside, and I was locked outside in the dark hallway.

"Can you give me a few minutes, Andrew?" he asked, cracking

the door open after I knocked. "I've got a few business things I have to take care of."

I didn't know what type of business he meant—club business or illegal business—and I didn't want to know. I went to the bar and ordered a drink, watching the time anxiously as the minute hand on my watch approached eleven o'clock, then passed it. I resigned myself to the probability that I wouldn't arrive at Palmer/Midkiff/Carlyle well rested and refreshed after all.

Quite some time later, Frank and Barry Blackburn walked out to the bar. In the three weeks since I'd last seen him, Barry's frosted blond hair had been cut short and dyed jet black, and he had added a pierced eyebrow. He now looked even more like a rodent than before.

"Hi, bud." Frank slapped me a bit too manfully on the upper arm. "How's it going?"

"Great," I said, responding to his quasi-heterosexual buddy act with open affection. He flinched but quickly relaxed, apparently remembering his recent and sincere proclamations of love.

"Hmmm," sneered Barry Blackburn, standing to the side of us but speaking only to me. "Looks like the club needs stricter admissions standards."

I ignored him—after a decade of snide shots, there wasn't much new he could say to me—but Frank rose to my defense.

"Andrew's a friend of mine, Barry. And he's a good customer. Maybe you should watch your mouth."

"Sorry, Frank. I didn't realize you were friends." He turned to me but wouldn't look me in the eye. "And I apologize if I offended you, Andrew. I don't think I've seen you in here since that night you were dressed in drag."

I didn't like it that he remembered. I could only hope that he wouldn't remember my drag name.

"Belle Bacall, wasn't it?" Shit! He remembered.

I forced a thin smile. "I can't remember, Barry. Something like that."

He smiled. He knew. I didn't think he had any understanding of how destructive that information could be, but he definitely knew my drag name.

"Let's go back to the office," Frank said, tapping me on the shoulder. As I followed him, I glanced back. Barry Blackburn watched us with a malevolent grin. I didn't like any of this at all.

When we were back in Frank's office and the door was locked, I asked, "So, what were you talking about with Barry?"

"Bar business. Holiday promotions, New Year's Eve . . . that sort of thing."

"I don't trust him."

"So you've said." He was standing behind me and wrapped his strong arms around my waist. "How's about we don't talk about Barry Blackburn anymore, okay?"

"Okay."

I reached back and found his lean hips, pulling them tightly against me. His breath gently brushed my neck, and one hand found its way beneath my shirt and T-shirt and . . .

There was a knock at the door.

"Just once, could we not be interrupted?" I whined.

"Who is it?" Frank called out.

"Barry. Would you like me to come back later?"

"Do you mind?" Frank asked me.

I shrugged. "The moment has passed."

He unlocked the door and let Barry into the office.

My archenemy sized us up, curving the pierced eyebrow, as he entered.

"What is it?" asked Frank, annoyed.

"Just stopping by to say good night," he said, an excuse that rang hollow. Not that I really expected Barry to say, "I wanted to see what you guys were up to, so I can spread gossip about it."

"Good night," Frank said.

"Good night, Andrew." Barry Blackburn was taunting me, but I wasn't going for the bait. I nodded cordially.

He left, taking my romantic mood with him.

"I think I'll head home," I said. "It was good to see you again—I needed it—but it's late, and I need my sleep." That wasn't merely an excuse. It *was* late, approaching midnight. I had essentially wasted two precious hours of sleep that I didn't have to waste in pursuit of someone who would still be available tomorrow.

"If you wait a few minutes," said Frank, "I'll give you a lift in the van. Save you the subway ride."

"The van?"

"Not mine, really. It belongs to the business. But I've gotta pick up some stuff tomorrow morning."

I considered it. It was tempting. But it was also midnight, and—if I knew Frank—his "few minutes" would likely turn into an hour.

I kissed him gently. "Not tonight. I really have to go."

He shrugged. But at least he kissed back.

When I stepped outside Benedick's, I realized that the night had turned much colder. For the briefest of seconds I considered taking Frank up on his offer of a ride, then thought better of it. A ride home would result in an invitation to come up to my apartment, which would result in hours of passionate sex, which would result in another lost work day, which would result in more hours of passionate sex . . .

I wasn't doing myself any favors by thinking it through, so I stopped thinking about it and started walking toward the subway station.

"Westlake." A hissing voice from a shadowy stairwell startled me. My eyes followed the sound and found Barry Blackburn.

"What is it, Barry?" I asked, annoyed.

He stepped out of the shadows. I could make out his weasly features in the glow of a streetlight. The gold ring in his eyebrow glittered.

"You and Frank?"

"What about me and Frank?"

"I heard the rumor. But I didn't believe it."

"I don't know what you're talking about." In fact, I didn't know what he was talking about. I found it hard to believe that gossip about my awkward, tentative relationship with Frank was making the gay club circuit.

He laughed, either to himself or at me or both, and let out a low whistle. "Andrew Westlake and Frankie DiBenedetto. How about that?"

I felt a chill that had nothing to do with the cold temperature. Did Barry really just call Frank 'Frankie'?

"I'm still not sure I follow you," I said coyly. "What have you heard about me and Frank?"

Again, he didn't answer me. "So, Frankie DiBenedetto's a closet case, huh?" There was that Frankie again.

I neither confirmed nor denied but struck from a different angle. "Is that the way you should talk about your employer?"

He shrugged off my thrust. "He doesn't employ me. He gets the benefit of my services, and I get the benefit of his space. If Frankie decides to kick me out, I'll have another club like *that.*" He snapped his fingers for emphasis.

"Good for you." I turned and started to walk away.

"So, how is he?" he asked my back. "Pretty hot, I'll bet. Those closet cases usually are . . . until they sober up."

Barry Blackburn's needling was having its desired effect. I was growing angrier with every syllable he uttered. But I refused to look back. I refused to give him the satisfaction of knowing he had succeeded.

And why, I wondered, as I commuted back uptown, was he calling Frank 'Frankie'?

When I returned to my apartment I was still puzzling over that question. True, the only other people I had heard refer to him as Frankie were mob types, but Barry Blackburn couldn't possibly be in the mob. Could he? Wasn't it more likely that he used the name to show familiarity? Or to belittle Frank? Or because he was a pompous twit who cared little for calling people what they preferred to be called?

I wanted to believe he was just a pompous twit. That belief was what finally allowed me to put aside my concerns and fall asleep. My last drowsy thought was that, the next day, I'd make sure that Frank threw Barry Blackburn's sorry ass out on the street.

At the very least, he was guilty of gross disrespect of the man I loved, which I considered to be a capital crime.

Then again, Barry Blackburn wasn't the sort of man to settle for the very least.

11

The Long Good-Bye

picked up a copy of the *Post* on my way to the subway the next morning. It didn't take long to find the Page Six gossip column item. It would have been hard to miss, since it was printed directly beneath the photograph.

Spotted: Alleged importer/exporter **Frank DiBenedetto** and his son, **Frank Jr.**, at Viggio's Ristorante in Little Italy on Tuesday night. No surprise there. The surprise was their dinner guest: songstress **Belle Bacall**. Sources tell Page Six that Belle's aunt, legendary actress **Lauren Bacall**, was supposed to join the happy threesome but canceled at the last minute to catch the red-eye to L.A. That was news to the actress's publicist, who not only claimed that her client was in Manhattan spending a quiet evening in her lavish Central Park West apartment, but that she doesn't have a niece named Belle. Was someone getting wise with the wise guys?

"Not good," I said aloud, shaking my head. No one on the subway platform bothered to acknowledge me.

So, I repeated the words into the phone to Frank when I got to my office.

"Not good."

"Not at all," he agreed.

"Who would have dreamed that they'd drag the real Lauren Bacall into this? Why does the tiniest detail have to spin out of control?"

"Maybe you should think your drag name through a bit more the next time." I supposed he was trying to be helpful.

"There won't be a next time," I said with finality.

Frank was silent and reflective for a moment. "My old man is gonna blow up when he sees it. It makes him look like a fool. And he doesn't like it when he looks like a fool." Controlled panic grew in his voice as he continued. "Then he's gonna wonder who you really are. And he'll find out. He will. Too many people know about this Belle Bacall creation of yours."

"Yeah. Like Barry Blackburn. Speaking of which . . ." I related the previous night's encounter to Frank.

"That bastard! I'd better not see him in Benedick's again or I'll have his legs broken." Which was most likely not an idle threat.

"Break one for me."

As much as I wanted to indulge in fantasies of Barry Blackburn's excruciating pain, Frank was still preoccupied with the Belle Bacall crisis at hand. "Thanks for reading me the article, I guess. I'd better get off the phone, though. I think I'm gonna have a lot of music to face today."

He agreed to keep me updated as the story unfolded from his end, and I hung up at the exact moment that David appeared in my cubicle.

"Did you see this?" I pushed the *Post* across my desk at him.

He sighed. "Yes, I've seen it. It's . . . unfortunate."

"Maybe it'll blow over."

"You're cute when you're optimistic." He set a pile of loose manuscript pages on my desk and added, "But maybe you'll be proven correct. In that event, I hope you won't mind if I put you to work."

I didn't mind. Work helped take my mind off everything that had gone wrong, and it kept me from speculating about the complications that still awaited me. And the manuscript wasn't half bad, either, if you like light mysteries featuring cat-loving sleuths with meddlesome mothers.

I was speed-reading toward the denouement several hours later when the phone rang.

"Drop everything," ordered David. "I need to see you in my office."

Were Detectives Brogan and Mueller visiting me again? Did Max Abraham hear that I was still seeing Frank and have a stroke? Was Frank Senior waiting for me, red-faced and homicidal at the mockery of being photographed with a man in drag? There were so many options, and none of them were good.

But when I reached David's office, I learned that he had summoned me for something that hadn't even crossed my mind.

"Ninety minutes ago," he said, "federal agents raided Hanover's Book Store. I was just called about it by a reporter looking for a comment."

"Wow." I thought about Special Agent Patrick Waverly.

"Indeed. The FBI is calling it one of the largest offensives against organized crime ever. They've arrested thirteen people—including one Tommassino Franco, by the way—and confiscated all the firm's financial records. Apparently, more arrests are expected." He paused and smiled. "Now are you willing to believe me when I tell you that Hanover's is a Mafia front?"

I nodded. "Tommassino Franco. That's Crazy Tommy Franco?"

"One and the same."

"Did they arrest Anna Franco?" I could take slight relief if she was off the streets.

"Not that I've heard, but I only know what the reporter told me. This is a big story, Andrew. They also raided a few other businesses, including Viggio's. I wouldn't be surprised if Benedick's will be a target, too . . . if the FBI hasn't already been there."

I hadn't thought of that. "But Benedick's is a legitimate business," I said defensively. "It's not a front."

"Hmmph," David sniffed, unimpressed.

I felt a knot in my stomach. What if David was right? What if Frank had been fooling me, and I had been fooling myself?

"Can I use your phone?" I asked.

"No. I know what you want to do, and I'd just as soon not have my private office phone number show up on the FBI's caller ID screen. If you insist on being a fool, then I recommend using a pay phone."

Three minutes later I stood on the street corner, anxiously trying to feed a quarter into the pay phone, dropping it three times on the sidewalk before my shaking hand found the coin slot.

" 'lo," said Frank, answering quickly and, just as quickly, the words streamed out of my mouth in an unintelligible jumble.

"Hanover's. Crazy. Benedick's. Tommy. Raid. FBI."

"I know," he said, interpreting my babble. "I just heard about it. But there's nothing I can do about it now, except keep my head down."

"We can run."

"Run? Where? Cuba? I can't run. If they're coming to get me, they're coming to get me."

Coming to get him? "But Frank, Benedick's is legitimate, isn't it? Why would they want you?"

He didn't answer.

I found myself fighting a rising dread. "They're not investigating you. And that's because Benedick's is legitimate." If Frank wasn't going to convince me, I was determined to convince myself.

"You're panicking, Andrew. Don't. Everything's cool." He laughed. "You're so innocent sometimes."

"Innocent, yes. That's not a bad word, you know."

"I know. We're all innocent in our own ways and our own circumstances."

I didn't like the turn this conversation was taking, but at least its more philosophical level was having a calming effect on me. And if Frank wasn't panicked, then I supposed I shouldn't panic, either.

I decided to shift gears.

"Heard anything about the item in the paper?"

"No. But the Hanover's thing has sort of overshadowed it. I will, though. I will."

"What are you going to say?"

"I don't know yet. Maybe I'll plead ignorance. Or maybe I'll come clean, and tell the world about us."

"That'd be great," I said, gushing, forgetting about all the other things that were arguably more important. "Then we'd be free to be together."

"It's never gonna be that easy," he said cautiously. "Things would change for both of us. Forever. So be careful what you wish for, Andrew."

He was right, of course. I knew he was right. It didn't take a Rhodes scholar to figure out that the minute the various families that made up the New York Mafia learned that I was Frank's lover, our lives would change forever. People like me—people who think of themselves as creative and harmless observers—didn't stand a chance against ruthless criminals intent on righting what they perceived to be an emasculating wrong.

But I was in love. Every second of my future might be spent looking over my shoulder, but I was in love and I wanted the world to know about it.

"I love you," I said. "And I want you to come out. I don't care what happens, as long as there are no more lies and no more deceit."

He took his time before responding but still could do no better than, "We'll see what happens."

It wasn't the enthusiastic "Yes" I hoped for, but it wasn't a "No," either. In that nonanswer I read progress.

What can I say? Deep down, I'm an optimist. And I'm cute when I'm optimistic.

Although most of my concentration was gone, I finished the cat-loving sleuth manuscript late in the afternoon. It was close enough to quitting time that I decided to leave work early. Emotionally, I had put in more than a full day. No . . . emotionally, I had put in more than a full *life*.

Darkness was approaching when I left the building and stepped out onto the bustling sidewalk. That's why I didn't notice him at first.

But I did notice him.

Big Paulie Macarini stood to one side of the front door, leaning casually against the granite facade. He made no effort to conceal himself and fell into step several yards behind me as I began my walk up Sixth Avenue, pushing through pockets between my fellow pedestrians as the undulating mass of humanity advanced north. Several times each block, I stole a look behind me, only to see Big Paulie keeping pace.

We crossed West Fortieth Street and I saw my opportunity. I took advantage of the last flickering vestiges of a DON'T WALK sign as it cautioned pedestrians of the imminent red light and bolted to my left, racing across Sixth Avenue in front of a lineup of cabdrivers engaging their gears. I heard Big Paulie shout, then curse at the knot of people clogging the corner and blocking his pursuit. But his voice was soon drowned out by the cacophony of a half-dozen cabbies blaring their horns at me, which was followed in turn by the cacophony of several dozen more cabbies blaring their horns at *them.*

I couldn't allow myself the luxury of looking back. If he hadn't made it across the intersection, I needed every extra inch of advantage I could get. And if he *had* made it across the intersection, then I *really* needed every extra inch of advantage I could get.

So I ran, weaving through the crowds and traffic. It was only when the congestion of Broadway and the Times Square foot traffic forced me to stop that I realized I didn't know where I was running to. Not my apartment, certainly. But was anywhere else necessarily any safer?

Trapped in the middle of a dense pack of tourists, I looked around for Big Paulie. I didn't see him, but that didn't mean he wasn't there. Or, for that matter, that he wasn't inches from me, hidden behind a hefty vacationer from Kansas.

Having nowhere else to go, I followed the flow of the crowd as it inched its way toward Times Square. There was safety in numbers, I kept telling myself, even if the numbers constituted a claustrophobe's worst nightmare. I passed through Times Square, and by the time I reached Fiftieth Street, the solid wall of people started to break up. Which was good, because by that point I never again wanted to see another human being.

There was still no sign of Big Paulie. That was the good news. The bad news, though, was that as I flipped through my mental Rolodex of friends, I rejected every potential haven as too risky. Benedick's: out. Frank: out. Denise: out. David: out. The very fact that it occurred to me to pay a visit to Ted and Nicholas underscored my desperation.

Soon I was at Columbus Circle, the point where the southwest corner of Central Park touched Broadway as the boulevard began its northwestern slice through the Upper West Side. To the east of the circle, Fifty-ninth Street took the much more prestigious name of Central Park South. Ahead of me, Eighth Avenue became the elegant Central Park West as it continued northward.

Central Park West . . .

That's when I suddenly realized that there was still one place I could hide while I collected my thoughts.

*   *   *

The Mayflower Hotel was a few blocks north of Columbus Circle on Central Park West. I called Margaret Campbell from a house phone in the hotel lobby.

"Westlake! What a pleasant surprise. Come on up."

"Great view," I said when I walked into her room several minutes later. It was true; the suite itself was utilitarian and unexceptional, but she had a great view of Central Park from her upper floor. Across the park, the lights of the pricey high-rises on the Upper East Side flickered. To the right, the solid wall of hotels lining Central Park South glowed steadily.

"That's why I always stay here. The park keeps me calm and helps me remember that this city isn't all glass and concrete." She held an open bottle of bourbon in one outstretched arm. "Join me?"

"I need it."

"You look like you need it." Even though I wasn't expected, she seemed to be waiting for me. A conveniently spare glass was quickly produced, and she poured the brown liquor over ice. "Wanna tell me about it? I hope it's not more of your Mafia saga."

"I'm afraid so. Where would you like me to start? With my New York *Post* photo op, or my meeting with the FBI agent in the ladies' room?"

She laughed throatily and handed me my drink. It was clear that she wasn't on her first bourbon of the day.

"What *Post* photo? We can get to the FBI agent in the bathroom later—I do want to hear that one—but first, tell me about your picture. I hope they got your best side." She scanned the room absently. "Was it in today's paper? I think I have a copy around here somewhere."

I spotted the unopened *Post* buried under an unopened *Times* on an end table. I flipped to the Page Six article and pointed to the photograph.

She squinted at the picture, not quite sure what she was supposed to see. It was only when she read the item that her eyes grew big and she excitedly tapped her finger on Belle Bacall's glamour shot.

"You? Oh, Westlake!" She burst into cackles of laughter. "I must say you look stunning!"

I told her the story, as well as about my encounter with Patrick in Viggio's ladies' room and the rest of my Mafia saga. She wrinkled her nose when I told her about the Hanover's raid, furrowed her brow when I told her that I'd encouraged Frank to come out, and otherwise punctuated the saga with colorful facial expressions.

"So, why is this Big Paulie character tailing you again?" she asked when I concluded my story at the point where my main character wandered into the Mayflower Hotel seeking sanctuary.

"I don't know. I didn't stick around long enough to ask him. Probably the Francos sent him after me because Frank and I stayed together, despite Anna's ultimatum. Avenging their honor and all that. Or maybe it has to do with the raids. I honestly don't know. But I wish he'd stop."

"You've got to get out of New York."

"I tried that last week, remember? It doesn't make a difference. This black cloud follows me wherever I go."

"Well, much as I enjoy your company, you can't hide in my hotel room forever. Especially since I'm checking out in two days." She paused and groaned. "To tell you the truth, Westlake, I'm a bit disappointed in myself. I'm supposed to be the best-selling grande dame of the American mystery, at least according to *People*, but I can't think of a single damned way to get you out of this mess."

"I wasn't expecting that. I got myself into it and I'll get myself out. Somehow."

It was six o'clock. I wanted to see how the Hanover's story was playing out on the news, so I asked permission to turn on her television. Permission was granted.

The Channel Seven News logo appeared on the screen. And here's how it ran as the top story:

"A series of raids by agents from a variety of law enforcement agencies today closed numerous businesses and resulted in dozens of arrests, including that of a well-known radio host," said the perky anchor as the theme music faded out. The screen filled with videotape of several men, heads bowed and wrists handcuffed as they were led to police vans.

"Good evening, I'm Suzette Chan. Their target was organized crime, and by the end of the day, Federal Bureau of Investigation sources were calling the raids their most successful and well-coordinated effort ever. Twenty-eight people have been arrested, including popular radio host Gary Vine and alleged organized crime kingpin Tommassino Franco."

"Gary Vine!" I gasped. As if on cue, his picture appeared on the screen.

"Good," said Margaret. "I hate that bastard." She thought to add, "Nothing personal. I hated him before he screwed me last week. Not that I thought he was mobbed up. I just hated him."

Suzette Chan continued. "No word on the specific charges have been released as of this hour by law enforcement authorities, but Channel Seven News has learned that most, if not all, of those arrested will be charged with violating the federal Racketeer Influenced Corrupt Organizations law."

A warehouse in Brooklyn flashed across the screen.

"Nine businesses were padlocked and their financial records seized by federal agents, including a Brooklyn construction company, a midtown Manhattan bookstore, and a Greenwich Village nightclub."

Oh, no.

But the screen now showed a different bar. I sighed in relief . . . until the camera cut to the facade of Benedick's and I inhaled the remainder of that sigh.

"Let's go live to Lance Mitchell, who's at Benedict's on West Street. Lance?"

Great. Benedick's was not only the Channel Seven News team's featured mob joint, but Suzette Chan couldn't even get the name right.

"Is that—?" Margaret began to ask. I cut her off with a sad nod.

"Thanks, Suzette," said the toothy Lance. I wasn't sure, but I thought I recognized him from the club's grand opening party. "I'm standing in front of Benedick's, a former West Street warehouse that opened three weeks ago as Manhattan's hottest gay nightclub. Tonight, federal agents have locked it tight and carted off the club's financial records. The reason? Benedick's is suspected of being a front for the Stendardi crime family."

The camera cut to stock footage from some other gay club. Channel Seven News apparently didn't let a tiny detail like accuracy stand in the way of a lurid story.

Lance, in a voice-over, said, "Benedick's owner, Francis DiBenedetto Junior, was unavailable for comment, and sources tell us that he still hasn't been charged in this ongoing investigation."

I gasped as the *Post* photo flashed onto the screen. Belle Bacall refused to die.

"But if his name sounds familiar, that's because his father—
Frank DiBenedetto Senior—has long been suspected of holding an
influential position in the Stendardi organized crime family hierar-
chy. The elder DiBenedetto also hasn't been charged, but authorities insist that many more charges will be coming in the next few
days as they attempt to eradicate organized crime in New York City.
Reporting live from West Street for Channel Seven News, I'm
Lance Mitchell."

To add insult to injury, the *Post* photo stayed on the screen well
into the beginning of the next story. It might still be there; I wouldn't
know. Because the moment Lance Mitchell signed off, I stabbed at
the remote control and turned off the television.

"No matter what anyone says, it isn't always fun being me," I announced.

"Oh, no," replied Margaret. "I quite agree."

"So, what do I do now? I mean, what do *we* do now? Me and
Frank?"

She reached for the bourbon. "This calls for a war council."

David Carlyle and Denise Hanrahan were the easy ones to reach.
They agreed to come to the Mayflower Hotel as quickly and discreetly as possible.

When I finally reached Max Abraham, he was decidedly not interested in coming to the hotel. After a few choice words, he advised me that, in his opinion I was in a hopeless position and that I
should turn myself in to the police. After a few more choice words,
he told me that, as a favor to David, he would plead attorney/client
privilege if anyone asked him where I was hiding, but that was as far
as he was going to stick his neck out for me. And after a few more
final choice words, he hung up on me.

That left Frank.

I tried calling his apartment but, not surprisingly, he wasn't
home. Still, I left a message for him to call my apartment—leaving
the Mayflower's number would have been counterproductive to
the concept of a hideout—if he happened to check his answering
machine tape.

David and Denise arrived separately but within minutes of
each other, just before seven o'clock. Margaret, delighted to be
cast in the role of the gracious host, greeted them both with a kiss

on the cheek and ushered them in. In recognition of the gravity of the situation, the bottle of bourbon was safely stowed in a dresser drawer.

I got straight to the point. "So, what am I going to do?"

"You know how I feel," said David. Denise silently nodded her agreement. "Wash your hands of Frank. He was damaged goods before, and he's even more damaged now. In a few days this Paulie fellow will stop following you around, and your life will return to its usual semblance of normalcy."

"But I love Frank! I'm not just going to leave him. Not at a time like this."

"You can see him on visiting days," David replied, exasperated. "Andrew, you've constantly failed to take this situation seriously. Look what's happened: You've got Mafia thugs chasing you all over Manhattan, the police and the FBI know your name quite well . . . and all this for what? For a man who's very likely going to spend the next seven-years-to-life breaking rocks and selling his body for cigarettes."

"David . . ." It was a warning.

"Sorry," he said, calming down. "Still, my point is valid. I know that Frank's important to you, but how important are you to Frank? He gets everything he wants, and you get to keep putting on that damned dress and getting into trouble."

"I mean more to him than you think."

"Do you? Well then, where is he? Why isn't he here? Why isn't he trying to hunt you down?"

"In case you hadn't heard, he has a few problems of his own right now."

"Indeed. But that's my point, Andrew. You have problems, and all you can think about is him. He's got problems, and all he can think about is him, too. It sounds a little one-sided."

"You're wrong."

"He's not wrong, Drew," said Denise.

"Great. The tag team is up and running."

"*Goddamn it!*" Denise suddenly roared, red-faced, as she rose to her feet. Her anger shocked me in its intensity. "Andrew, we're your friends! I can't force you to obey us, but at least you could give us the courtesy of listening. None of us have to be here, you know. We could leave you to fend for yourself. At this point, frankly, I'd love to do just that, you ungrateful son of a bitch."

"Sorry." I mumbled an apology. Denise did have a way of making me feel like dirt.

"You'd better mean that. And you'd better start listening to us."

"I will."

"Okay." She folded her arms triumphantly across her chest. "Now, David outlined a very good plan, and I think you should give it some serious consideration. You have to accept the fact that you've reached the point where you can't charm your way out of this situation. In fact, there's almost nothing you can do that won't make it worse."

"So, you all think I should cut Frank off."

Denise and David nodded.

"Margaret?"

Margaret took her time answering, pausing to light a cigarette and take in the calming view of the darkened park one more time before finally gracing us with the official opinion of the grande dame of the American mystery. According to *People*, that is.

"They make a good argument for taking that course of action, Westlake. I've heard nothing but your side of the story until tonight, and you make a compelling case for following the dictates of the heart. But Denise and David make a more compelling case for following common sense." She paused, took a drag from her cigarette, and added, "Sorry, hon, but if I were forced to choose, I'd have to side with common sense. That way, at least you'll have a chance to live long enough to fall in love again."

So that was it. Everyone I trusted was in this hotel room, with the exception of the missing Frank and the fed-up Max Abraham, and the verdict was unanimous: drop Frank and get on with my life.

It sounded easy.

It sounded logical.

It tore my heart out.

"Margaret," I said softly, "maybe it's time to break out that bottle of bourbon."

Periodically I called my apartment to check my answering machine tape. There were no messages. More to the point, there were no messages from Frank.

My friends—and, yes, they were most definitely my friends, because only friends would have talked to me the way they did—

helped talk me down gently over the next few hours. We talked about the fleetingness of love and the remarkable healing powers of the soul. It wasn't a cure for my heartbreak, but it was a balm.

I had gotten over Ted, hadn't I? I'd get over Frank, too. And, probably, whoever came after Frank. We all agreed, me and my friends.

The fact that I didn't want to get over Frank was left unsaid. That wasn't a cure for my heartbreak, either.

David and Denise and, now, Margaret were in the midst of the umpteenth variation of you're-a-good-looking-guy-and-a-published-author-and-you-have-a-lot-to-offer-the-right-man when I excused myself much later to check my answering machine.

I had two messages. Finally. Pessimistically, I punched in the code and heard, "Hi, it's Frank. Well . . . I suppose you heard what's going on, that Benedick's was closed. Not a good thing. But . . . well . . . There were other things tonight, too. I told my old man about us. It wasn't very cool, but I did it. For us. Now, though . . ."

"Oh, you guys should hear this," I said, forgetting in ten seconds the hours of intervention they had expended on my behalf. "Frank told his father that he's gay!"

I heard them issue a collective groan.

". . . I've got to go away for a while. Alone. I don't want to fuck up your life." Frank's voice was such a monotone that the meaning of his words took a second to hit me. But when they did . . . "It's not just the gay thing with my old man. That's part of it, but it's the legal thing and, well, Anna and her father." His voice cracked. "I really wish I could talk to you, Andrew. I wish you were home right now. I don't want to leave a good-bye message on your tape. But I suppose it's better than not saying good-bye at all, right? . . . So . . . anyway . . . hopefully, I'll . . . ah, shit. Just take care of yourself, okay?"

The message ended.

No. It couldn't end like that. It couldn't! Stunned, I almost hung up before an atonal mechanical voice prompted me to wait for the second message.

"Hi, it's me again. You probably already know that I'm not home, but I forgot to tell you how to reach me if you get this message before I leave. I think you'll understand why I can't give you the phone number here, but leave your number on my beeper and I'll call you back. If you can." He recited his beeper number. "I really hope I hear from you. But if I don't, remember that I love you. And I will. Always."

David, Denise, and Margaret had logic on their side. Still, if logic ever really stood a chance, it didn't after that.

I beeped Frank and punched in the Mayflower Hotel's switchboard number, followed by the room number.

"I'm afraid to ask," said David.

"And I'm afraid to find out." Yes, I was still every bit as head-over-heels in love with Frank as I'd ever been, but my joy at hearing from him was tempered by the content of his message. He was going to go away, and I wasn't. And I didn't think I liked that plan very much.

While I waited for Frank to return my beep, I filled in the others. "It's a good news/bad news situation. The good news is that he called me, and he told his father about me, and he left me his beeper number. The bad news is that he's leaving New York for a while. And he says that he has to go alone."

"I'm sorry, Drew," said Denise, wrapping a protective arm around me. "I think it's for the best, but I know how you must feel."

I nodded my agreement, conveniently forgetting to tell her that I was planning to talk Frank out of his plans. She would find out soon enough.

He called back fifteen minutes later. I excused myself and took the call on the bedroom extension.

"Where are you?" I asked.

"I'm at a friend's place in Brooklyn. But I can't stay here long. I just got word that Crazy Tommy Franco's out on bail, and he's looking for me. They say he wants revenge for Anna's humiliation. That's sort of the main reason I have to leave town for a while."

"But I want to see you . . ."

"I really don't think that's gonna be possible, Andrew. The problem is, it's not even gonna be all that easy for me to get out of town. From what I hear, this situation has made Franco even nuttier than usual. He's got his entire crew out hunting me down. And word is that his order is 'Shoot to kill.' He thinks I've dishonored him and his entire family."

Yes, Frank had managed to top me with his personal drama once again. But it did occur to me that if they knew about *him* . . .

"What about me? Big Paulie Macarini tried to follow me from work this afternoon. Are they after me, too?"

"Probably. But only to get to me. By tomorrow, when I'm out of the picture, I doubt they'll be concerned with you. Just lay low and keep your nose clean for a few days and it'll blow over." He laughed. "Remember how we were so concerned with the picture in the newspaper? Well, guess what? That wasn't what did it. That was just icing on the cake. I have to admit that I wasn't brave enough to bring the subject up to my father, either. I just confirmed it when he brought it up to me."

"So how . . . ?"

"Barry Blackburn. It turns out that bastard's been on the Morelle family payroll for years. He's, like, best friends with Anna, and he's been telling her everything that's been happening in Benedick's. So much for all her talk about 'friggin' faggots,' huh? When she walked in on us that day, it wasn't a coincidence. It was because Barry tipped her off that he thought I might be fooling around. After he saw us together last night, he couldn't wait to call her. And she couldn't wait to call her father, of course, but by then Crazy Tommy was sidetracked by the feds for a few hours. Good thing, too, I suppose, or else we'd both be dead by now."

Yes, that was a good thing. But I couldn't help but say, "I told you Barry Blackburn was no good."

"From what I hear, he'll be getting his just desserts soon. My old man might be unhappy and disappointed in me, but what *really* sets him off are snitches."

I didn't want to know any more than he'd already told me about that. I already knew too much. And anyway, I had to finally ask the question that needed to be asked.

"When will I see you again?"

"Andrew . . ."

"I'd like to know. And I'd like to know why I can't go with you."

He sighed. Clearly, he had been hoping that I'd let him slip away without making a scene. He was wrong.

"You can't go with me because it's too dangerous. Right now, nobody's very happy with me here in New York. You've got your friends, but I don't really have anyone."

"Will you be gone long? When will you be coming back?"

"I can't answer those questions."

I lowered my voice in case eavesdroppers were listening on the other side of the bedroom door. "You can't just leave me like this. I need to see you again before you go."

"I don't see how that would be possible."

"Please," I begged. "Make it possible."

There was a long pause. I didn't know if that meant he was frustrated with my selfish persistence or seriously mulling it over. And I didn't really care. I knew that I couldn't end it like this, with a short and furtive telephone conversation.

Finally and reluctantly, he said, "Well, I do have to come back through Manhattan on my way out of town. I suppose we can get together for a few minutes." His tone changed, taking control. "But *only* for a few minutes. That's it. If you have any plans to try to talk me out of this or take you with me, you'd better forget about them right now."

"Okay," I agreed, and part of me meant it. "I'm at the Mayflower Hotel. You know where it is?"

He did. He said he'd be at the room by two-thirty.

Denise, David, and Margaret were surprisingly understanding when I related my conversation to them and told them that Frank would be coming by, even though that meant that they would have to keep vigil with me for another several hours. Maybe it was the security they felt, hidden away in the hotel, or maybe it was a desire to see through the imminent end of my ill-starred relationship. Whatever the reason, I needed and welcomed their support. This wasn't quite Ted's goodbye note written on a paper towel, but it was the next worst thing.

The next few hours dragged by, but finally, only minutes late, there was a light rap on the door. I flew out of my chair and yanked the door open, only to be stopped by the security chain. I unhooked the chain and tried again, and this time Frank flew into my arms.

As the door swung closed, I buried my face in his chest and his strong arms wrapped around me. In agony and ecstasy, we whispered each other's names and our bodies coiled.

"Ahem." David broke the spell, and we awkwardly pulled apart.

"I was going to tell you to get a hotel room, but since this *is* a hotel room, that would seem redundant."

"Hello, David," said Frank, blushing. "Hi, Denise." He greeted them tentatively, unsure if they were going to be supportive or if they considered him to be the enemy.

"And this is Margaret Campbell," I said, pointing. "Margaret, this is Frank."

Frank threw her a short wave, and Margaret greeted him with, "Nice to finally meet you. I've heard so much about you, I already feel as if I know you."

"She's the author I told you about from my West Coast trip."

"You sure like to talk, don't you?" he replied. I was unsure if that meant I was in trouble again until he burst into a wide smile. "At least this one isn't from the FBI. Are you?"

"I'm afraid not. I didn't meet the height requirement."

Denise stepped forward. "Frank, I just hope you know that I wish you all my best. I really do. Anything I've said or done that didn't seem that way was because I was concerned about Drew. It wasn't personal."

"I know. I never took it personally. I know that I come with baggage, and I can't blame you for looking out for your friend."

She smiled, then reached over and kissed him. "Good luck."

"Thanks."

Then it was David's turn. "I second what Denise said. In another time, under other circumstances, you and Andrew would have been the perfect couple. But . . ." He shrugged, then tried for a more positive approach. "It seems our Andrew got something out of this relationship, despite all the negative consequences. I hope you did, too, Frank."

"I did." He put an arm around my waist. "I really did. Andrew meant . . . Andrew *means* a lot to me. He always will."

"Good, then." David offered his hand. "I wish you the best. And if you ever decide to write your memoirs, please give me a call."

And then it was my turn. I looked deep into his eyes and wistfully murmured, "Frank . . ."

"Don't ask me to stay, Andrew. Please. And don't ask me to take you with me. I can't."

I tried to speak but couldn't. My eyes welled up, and the first trickle of a tear slowly edged its way down my cheek.

"You'll be all right," he said, barely keeping control of his composure. "And some day, maybe, we'll meet again."

I fell against him, my watering eyes dampening his neck, and we held each other tightly. The wild ride on the roller coaster had finally come to an end, but we had grown addicted to its thrills and terror and neither of us wanted to get off. We wanted to ride again. We wanted to experience the excitement of self-discovery and the suspense of the unknown once more.

I felt his heavy lashes flutter against my forehead, and he turned slightly to gently kiss me.

"I've got to go." His hand stroked the back of my head.

I tried one more time. "Stay. Please."

"No. But you'll hear from me again, Andrew. I promise."

And that was that. I finally realized it was over, and all I would accomplish by pleading and whining and begging would be to lose the last fading traces of my dignity. I pulled away from him, hoping that a few inches of physical distance would accomplish what words wouldn't. It didn't, but it also didn't make it any more difficult to say good-bye.

"I'll walk you outside," I said.

"Andrew," said Denise from somewhere behind me. "I think you should stay here."

"I know what I'm doing." My voice was hoarse with swallowed emotions. I couldn't look at her. "I'll be fine."

Frank said a final good-bye to Denise, David, and Margaret and we left the room. We didn't talk again until we reached the lobby.

"I meant it," he said as we walked through the lobby and outside into the cold November night. "You *will* hear from me again."

"Soon?"

He smiled sadly. "Probably not. But someday. Just don't believe everything you read in the newspapers about me, okay?"

"Okay," I said, even though I wasn't really sure what he was getting at. If he wanted me to believe that he didn't have mob connections, I was far past that point. Hadn't he realized that I didn't care about that anymore?

We stood on the sidewalk and he took my hands in his.

"This is it, Andrew. Good-bye."

"Good-bye, Frank." I leaned into him and kissed him. To his credit, he didn't object.

Frank backed away from me for a few steps, then turned and

walked across Central Park West. I watched, hoping he'd turn around and rush back into my arms, but he just kept walking until he reached his van.

I heard the door slam shut and the engine turn over. The headlights flicked on, and the van slowly pulled out onto the deserted street. I waved as it passed, not knowing if he could see me or was even looking for me, and the van turned the corner toward Broadway.

And that, I thought, was the end of my relationship with Frank DiBenedetto. Despite my best efforts at self-control, I walked to the corner to take one last look at his vehicle's taillights as it idled at a red light at the end of the short block. The directional light indicated that he was going to turn right, north on Broadway. Most likely he was headed for the George Washington Bridge and, beyond it, New Jersey and the rest of the world.

Behind me, I heard another vehicle approach on Central Park West, then slow to a crawl as it cruised through the intersection.

"There he is," I heard a man report through a cracked-open window. My back was to him, but his voice carried in the still night. I thought he was talking about me until I heard him add, "He's making a right onto Broadway. We'll catch him there."

I looked back and saw a large black sedan drive away up Central Park West, accelerating to beat an amber light before it turned red.

My head turned back in the direction of Broadway. The light was still red; Frank's van still idled there, waiting.

I started to run.

I caught Frank just as the light turned green and he began to make a slow turn onto Broadway. I banged furiously on the passenger side window of the rolling vehicle, which first startled him and then, when he realized it was me, annoyed him. Still, he stopped in front of a fire hydrant when he completed the turn.

"Let's not do this," he said, unrolling the window. "I'm sorry, Andrew, but I have to go."

"No! That's not why I'm here! You're being followed!"

His brow creased. "Followed?"

"Two guys in a big car. They drove by after you pulled away, and they spotted you." I looked up Broadway, but I didn't see the other car.

"What did the car look like?"

"Black. Or dark. Big, though."

"That doesn't help me mu—"

At that moment, the big, dark car pulled out of the next cross street, blocking Frank's route. The front doors opened and two very large, very young men stepped out. Their hands were hidden suspiciously in their jackets.

"Get in!" He unlocked the door and, as I tried to scramble through, put the van in reverse and careened wildly back into the intersection. Then—with total disregard for traffic signals—he drove forward in a wild arc until the van was southbound on Broadway. I thought I heard the sound of a gunshot, but I was too preoccupied with making sure that I didn't fall out and end up under the wheels to fully concentrate on outside noises.

"Shit!" he yelled. "How did they find me?"

"I think they went the wrong way down a one-way street." I slammed the door shut. "Can they do that?"

"I don't think they care. They're trying to kill us, remember? Normal rules don't apply."

Frank braked the van in the middle of the next intersection and made a hard right turn, speeding down West Sixtieth Street. I slid down in my seat, willing myself not to look.

The gunmen in the dark sedan, confused by the broken pattern of cross streets around Lincoln Center, fell behind us.

Although we had a red light at the intersection of Amsterdam Avenue, Frank continued to speed through without even attempting to slow the van. I saw a wide sweep of headlights bounce off a corner building and heard the brakes on a taxi squeal as it swerved to avoid us.

"Maybe you should slow down," I said timidly.

"If those guys catch us, we're dead, Andrew. Just hang on. Don't look, if it makes you nervous."

"I already tried that."

He turned left when we reached West End Avenue, heading south again.

"Maybe we should ditch the van," I recommended.

"Huh-uh." He ran another red light. "We're better off in here."

"But they know what the van looks like."

"And they know what we look like. Would you rather try to outrun them on foot?"

I shut up. I was out of my league.

At Fifty-seventh Street, Frank turned right abruptly, and I was thrown against the dashboard. Ahead of us was the entrance to the Henry Hudson Parkway, and he made yet another right against the light. We were heading north again, making a reckless, high-speed loop of Manhattan's West Side.

"Can I ask a question?" I asked, without waiting for permission. "If they're looking for you on the Upper West Side, why don't we keep going south? To the Lincoln Tunnel, maybe. Why are we driving back to the Upper West Side?"

"I have to meet people. At Seventy-ninth Street. Can you make your way home from Seventy-ninth and Riverside Drive?"

"Sure." His answer didn't satisfy me, but there was clearly no purpose served in pursuing it. At least on the parkway there would be no more traffic lights to run. I could take a measure of relief in that small comfort.

As the van raced past the Seventy-second Street exit, I saw headlights approach on the entrance ramp.

"We might have company." I craned my neck and tried to see the car more clearly.

Frank, too, was watching the car in his rearview mirror. "Damn. I think that's them."

He passed the exit to Seventy-ninth Street, giving it a look of regret, and sped up. The next exit was at Ninety-sixth Street. By the time we reached it, the other car was close behind and we were all but certain it was following us.

"Watch out for this exit," I said. "It's short."

"I know. That's what I'm counting on."

He barely touched the brake pedal as he swerved into the exit lane, pulling the steering wheel hard to the right. The van skidded and tires squealed as it kicked up gravel, and my head hit the dashboard again.

I closed my eyes and prayed that Frank could keep the van upright. When I opened them, we were making another hard right turn onto Riverside Drive. As we rounded the corner, I glanced back and saw the big, dark car fishtail to an inelegant stop on the narrow shoulder of the parkway beyond the exit, the driver caught by surprise by Frank's sudden turn.

"Good job," I said, or rather tried to say, as I caught my breath.

"Thanks." He smiled slightly to himself. "But I only bought us a few blocks' worth of a lead, so we'd better count on some other lucky breaks." He glanced at his watch. "Shit, it's after three. I'm supposed to be leaving soon."

"It can wait for a few minutes, can't it?" I silently hoped it couldn't, and that Frank would have to stay in Manhattan.

"I hope so." He braked slightly to avoid driving through the car slowly traveling in front of us. "But I don't have a lot of time to play with. I still think I should drive straight down to Seventy-ninth and—"

He stopped talking. I looked over at him and saw that his eyes were transfixed on the car ahead of us. As his eyes should have been.

I couldn't see the passengers in the front seat, but in the back seat sat Crazy Anna Franco, carefully studying the sidewalks and side streets. She was looking for us, not knowing that we were hiding in plain sight directly behind her.

"This is bad," he muttered. "Sooner or later, they're gonna realize that we're here."

"Maybe they'll turn."

He ignored me. "What was I thinking? The minute I went to the hotel, those guys were probably on the phone. The Upper West Side is probably swarming with Morelle guns right now!"

"Maybe they'll turn," I said again, weakly.

We followed Crazy Anna's car in silence for a few more blocks until Frank muttered an indistinct expletive under his breath.

"What?" I asked.

"Those other guys. They've caught up to us."

I looked in the side-view mirror and saw the car that had chased us down the parkway speeding toward us. We were caught in a Mafia sandwich.

"Hold on!" Frank shouted, and the van abruptly shot to the left. My head cracked painfully—this time against the window, instead of the dashboard—and the buildings blurred in front of me as we sped into the turn. I could vaguely hear the sound of squealing brakes and vehicles colliding. I hoped that one of them wasn't the van.

It wasn't. I was reassured of that when I heard Frank snicker.

I rubbed the back of my head. "You mind telling me what just happened?"

"Just what I hoped would happen. The second car couldn't see

that Anna's car was in front of the van. When I turned, Anna's driver hit the brakes and the car from the parkway ran into it." He
glanced over and saw my look of concern. "Don't worry, Andrew. It
was just a fender bender."

"It's not that. It's that . . . I don't want to play this game anymore. We could have been killed."

"What do you think I've been trying to tell you?" Yes, that was
true. *Everyone* had been trying to tell me that.

We were on West Eighty-fourth Street nearing Broadway, only a
few blocks from my apartment.

"You can drop me off here." I realized I was more shaken by
what was happening than I had realized. There was nothing like a
few hard blows to the head to clarify matters. It no longer seemed
an adventure. Now, it just seemed dangerous and stupid.

"I'll take you home. If you think it's safe, that is."

Anything would be safer than another two minutes in that van.

It was 3:08 when Frank brought the van to a stop on Amsterdam
Avenue just twenty feet from the corner of West Eighty-sixth Street,
where my apartment building stood beckoning safety and peace.
There was no sign of anyone waiting for me. That was a good thing.

"I'm running late," he said, "so I hope you won't mind if I don't
come up . . ."

I laughed. I was going to miss him. *God,* I was going to miss him.

And somehow, despite ourselves, our good-bye kiss ended up
spilling over into the back of the van. Looking back at it, I want to
blame it on an adrenaline rush from the chase. But, truthfully, it
was far more likely that magnetism between us that was alterna-
tively our salvation and our curse.

We sat in the dark, holding each other and listening to our shallow breaths. I felt his hand start to unbutton my shirt and put my
hand on his to help him. My feet kicked off his sneakers and then
my own. I heard the gentle grind of a zipper, then felt his pants go
slack as he lowered them from his hips.

Still, though, it didn't feel sexual. It was the ultimate in intimacy,
a divine union of two bodies that meant far more than sexual grat-
ification. Frank and I were taking our togetherness to an entirely
new level, one at which clothes were obstacles to intimacy.

"I should go," he said unconvincingly.

"Yeah."

Neither of us meant it.

I was stripped to my T-shirt, underwear, and sweat socks, writh-
ing under a similarly clad Frank on a musty moving pad in the back
of the van, and he was struggling to remove his T-shirt when . . .

The rear doors of the van swung open, spilling light into the
van. Instinctively, I looked at my watch. It was three-fifteen.

In the noise and confusion, my first thought as I looked at the
silhouettes framing the doorway, backlit by bright headlights, was
that the police were going to arrest us on a morals charge. My second thought was that I didn't need the hassle or the new notch on
my arrest record. And my third, and most insightful, thought was
that these weren't police officers after all.

Frank's instinct, of course, was to assume from the start that we
were looking at more trouble than a comparatively simple morals
charge. He was right.

The chase hadn't ended with the collision at West Eighty-fourth
Street and Riverside Drive. It couldn't have been that easy. That
was nothing more than an insignificant interruption, and if we had
been thinking more clearly we would have realized it. Instead, we'd
set ourselves up as easy targets. Easy targets who were only half-
dressed, at that.

Four burly men piled into the back of the van. I still saw no
faces, just their silhouettes in the headlights. They dragged me out
onto the street and I was suddenly, strangely, self-consciously aware
that I was dressed only in my underclothes.

"Andrew!" I heard Frank yell. I couldn't find him in the confusion. I spun around and was face-to-face with Big Paulie Macarini.

"What—? Where—?"

"Get down on the ground, asshole." He punctuated his command with a shove to the gutter. In my disoriented state, I went
down easily, sprawling in the fetid New York City street water.

Big Paulie's heel jabbed into my back. "I really, truly want to
blow your fuckin' brains out. You fucked with me one too many
times."

Near my head, the feet of several men scrambled together, as if
performing a particularly violent slow dance. I noticed that two of
the feet wore sweat socks. I tried to call out Frank's name but
couldn't catch my breath. And then they were gone.

"You're a dead man, Westlake," said Big Paulie. "I'm gonna look
forward to putting a bullet in that pretty little head of yours."

I closed my eyes and did my best to calm myself. I was so frightened, in fact, that I didn't even take Big Paulie's "pretty little head" comment as a compliment. I felt the slimy, fetid water in the gutter ooze through my clothes and into my skin. Somewhere in the distance, I heard men's voices and car doors slam. None of the voices were Frank's.

And where in hell's name were the witnesses? It suddenly occurred to me that I was being assaulted twenty feet from a major Manhattan intersection and not a single person seemed to see anything except Frank, the mobsters, and me.

Big Paulie ground his heel into my back again. "I really, truly want to blow your fuckin' brains out. I should do this city a big fuckin' favor." I felt his hand grab the back of my neck and tried to prepare for what seemed like the inevitable. But Big Paulie didn't shoot; instead he hauled me to my knees. "Get up. We're gonna take a little ride."

I stood slowly, trying to regain control of my shaking legs. I was coated with a grayish-brown grime, but when I tried to brush it off, it just spread. I looked hopefully at the windows to my apartment— there was a shower there, and fresh clothes, and, most importantly, no big men with guns—but hope wasn't doing me any good at that moment.

Big Paulie led me in the direction of a late-model Buick parked behind the van. As we passed the van's still-open rear doors, I asked, "Can I get my clothes?"

"You ain't gonna need 'em."

The stark inevitability of my immediate future gave me the courage I needed to ask, "What did you do with Frank?"

"Shuddup," he snarled, and he pushed me into the back seat of the Buick.

12

Things that Happened after 3:17 A.M.

Wedged between Big Paulie on my left and an equally bulky and humorless thug on my right, I was pinned in the back seat of the Buick. But at least I could now see what was going on, and the initial shock was wearing off. My sheer terror had been reduced to a more manageable intense fear.

In front of us was another car, a Chrysler, and I recognized the back of Frank's head through the rear windshield. My car followed the Chrysler as it pulled away from the curb and turned left onto West Eighty-sixth Street, leaving the van behind, doors still ajar.

"Are you going to kill us?" I turned and asked Big Paulie. It was something I thought I had the right to know.

"Fuck you," he said. I guess I didn't.

The cars rolled down Eighty-sixth Street back toward Riverside Drive in the early morning darkness. They stopped for a red light at West End Avenue and then proceeded on the green, finally turning left on Riverside Drive and coming to a stop behind the fender bender that Frank had caused to his great, if misplaced, satisfaction just minutes earlier.

Big Paulie grabbed my arm. "C'mon."

I stepped out onto the pavement. The Chrysler also emptied, and Frank joined me. The asphalt was cold beneath my feet.

"Now what?" I asked, shivering.

"I really don't want to know," Frank said.

"Miss Franco wants to say hello," said Big Paulie unpleasantly, taking each of us by the upper arm and leading us to the first car in line, where Anna Franco still sat in the back seat.

When she saw us, her dark expression grew darker.

"I can't even begin to tell you how much I want to hurt you," she said. "I'd like to cut your skin off, one tiny piece at a time, until you'd both be begging to die. I'm only sorry that my father insists on getting it over with quickly."

Big Paulie violently shoved Frank in the chest, knocking him back a few steps. "You hurt Miss Franco. That pisses me off."

Frank was gasping for air but managed to get out, "Yeah, well, she's all yours now, Paulie."

Big Paulie took two threatening steps toward him but stopped at the sound of Anna's voice.

"It ain't worth it, Paulie. Just get me out of here." She paused, then added, "And make sure that before you kill those freaks, you cut off their dicks and shove 'em down their throats, so people will know what happens to people who make me mad."

Things had been bad enough, but that was something I *really* didn't want to hear.

"You need a ride back, Miss Franco?" asked another one of the goons, holding open the door to one of the undamaged cars.

"Yeah. I sure don't want to be in the same car with those friggin' cocksuckers." She stepped out of the back seat onto the pavement and turned to us. "I won't be seeing you again, Frankie, so have a nice trip to hell."

Frank leaned toward me and whispered, "We've got to get out of here."

I agreed. Then again, we were dressed in only our underwear, and it was very cold, and we had no weapons, so I hoped Frank was formulating a very good plan.

He disappointed me.

"On the count of three, we make a run for it," he hissed in my ear. "Head for Seventy-ninth. One . . ."

Out of the night, two more black cars pulled alongside the others lined along Riverside Drive.

"Two . . ."

I noticed confusion falling over the faces of the Morelle family members. They weren't expecting these new arrivals. They didn't recognize them. I placed a hand on Frank's arm to stop his count-down.

"FBI," boomed a voice from one of the cars over a loudspeaker. "Don't move! Put your hands up where we can see them."

Instinctively, my hands went up. Not that I could very well hide anything. No one else, though, seemed to know quite how to react.

"I *said,* put your hands up! *Now!* Get out of the cars and put your hands where we can see them."

Federal agents were now beginning to crawl out of the black cars, guns drawn. In the distance I heard sirens.

"This is our chance," Frank whispered again. "On three."

"Run away from the FBI? Are you crazy?"

"One—"

"Frank, don't . . ." I stopped when I saw Patrick Waverly get out of one of the black cars. He saw me and shook his head, smiling slightly.

"Two—"

The sirens were getting closer now.

"Three."

I turned to look at Frank, but he was already ten feet away, dart-ing down Riverside Drive's wide, dark sidewalk in his socks. I caught myself admiring the beauty of his muscular calves before it occurred to me that he was fleeing.

"Stop right there!" commanded the loudspeaker, but Frank kept running. And then all hell began to break loose.

"Get him!" Anna screamed from the back seat of her car, spot-ting Frank as he sprinted away. "Kill him!"

Some of her thugs, clearly confused and rattled by her com-mands, began reaching for their guns. That, in turn, unleashed a volley of FBI fire. Although the feds were firing warning shots into the air above their heads, the gangsters reacted as if their lives were in danger and shot back. And so . . .

Well, that's how these things escalate.

When the first government bullet crashed into the stone wall separating the sidewalk from Riverside Park a mere foot from where I was standing, I ran after Frank. The agent on the loud-speaker yelled at me, but worse things had happened lately. Really.

Frank had a one-block lead, but I closed it and we entered Riverside Park side by side at the Seventy-ninth Street entrance, which ran alongside the Henry Hudson Parkway access ramp. Our evening's adventures around the Upper West Side once again had brought us back to where we had been before.

The gunfire ended quickly, but I could still hear sounds of confusion and shouting amid the sirens, and I wasn't confident that Frank and I had truly escaped. Maybe, like before, we had merely postponed the inevitable for a few more minutes.

"What time is it?" asked Frank, panting from fear and exertion.

I glanced at my watch. "Just past three-thirty."

"I'm supposed to be leaving now. Maybe I can still catch them . . ."

I had no idea where we were going. None whatsoever. We were running through a passageway under the parkway, which made no sense if he was really trying to escape, because the only thing on the other side was the Hudson River.

And then I understood. He was running straight for the Seventy-ninth Street Boat Basin, one of the Upper West Side's more secluded recreational attractions . . . and the perfect place to leave town without being spotted.

"The Boat Basin?" I asked. "We're going to the Boat Basin?"

"*I'm* going to the Boat Basin. You're going home to bed."

I stopped him as we entered the open-air rotunda directly beneath the traffic circle that funneled vehicles on and off the parkway. "What do you mean?" I demanded, panting from the run. "I was almost executed by the Mafia out there, and I ran from the FBI. *And* I almost had my dick sliced off! Whether you like it or not, I'm in this far too deep to go home and get on with my life."

"But this isn't your life, Andrew."

"It *wasn't* my life. But it is *now*."

"Andrew . . ."

Frank almost certainly had more to say, but the sound of heavy footsteps was abruptly upon us as a shadowy figure rushed into the rotunda.

"Go!" Frank yelled, grabbing me as he turned to run toward the Boat Basin. I tried, but strong arms were suddenly wrapped around my thighs and I reeled forward. In desperation, I reached out for Frank in the murky darkness but only succeeded in sending him tumbling to the stone floor under my weight.

I began scrambling to free myself. Beneath me, I felt Frank also trying to claw his way out of the pile of bodies. But the man on the top had us pinned.

"Hold it right there," he finally commanded. "Don't move."

Frank and I both surrendered, giving up the struggle. I heard Frank, sprawled under me, sigh deeply in defeat.

The pressure eased on my body as the man shifted his weight off me. Still, Frank and I stayed prone on the ground.

"Get up, Andrew. You, too, Frank."

I turned and looked up. Patrick Waverly towered above me.

"That . . . that was *you?*" I stammered.

He smiled. "What, you didn't believe I was a *real* federal agent? Not for nothing, Andrew, but the Bureau didn't hire me for my good looks."

I rolled off Frank and looked at him. He returned an accusing scowl, and all I could think to do was mouth, *I'm sorry.*

"Patrick," I said, turning to him. "Can't you let us go? Look at me! Haven't I been through enough?"

He smiled. "You are a mess."

"Didn't you see me back there? Anna Franco wanted to kill me! And she wanted to cut my dick off and stuff it down my throat!"

"Hmmm. Now *that* wouldn't be a very nice thing to do." Compared to Frank and me, he was so clean and calm, even in the face of a shoot-out with the Mafia and a chase through Riverside Park, that I reluctantly found myself envying him. "If it makes you feel any better, we did more damage to them than they did to us."

"It does," I admitted. "But can't you let us go? Just look the other way?"

"I'm not supposed to let Frank leave town. He probably didn't tell you that, did he?"

I looked at Frank, who nodded sheepishly.

"That's why he's trying to slip out on a boat, instead of just crossing the George Washington Bridge or heading for Westchester like anyone else would do. He knows that we're not just watching the airports and train stations. We're watching the bridges and tunnels, too. Our investigation is complete, but we're still making arrests. A lot of them." He paused, then added, "It's lucky for you that we are, too, otherwise we wouldn't have been tailing Macarini tonight and the two of you would be heading for the Fresh Kills Landfill about now. Sans penises."

"Thanks," I said. "But as a favor to me—"

Patrick interrupted me. "Frank's indictment will be handed down tomorrow, Andrew. He already knows that." He saw the concern in my face. "Don't worry, Andrew, it's minor stuff. Bullshit. If it were up to me, it wouldn't have happened. But if we're going to bust up the Mafia, we've got to take down everyone we possibly can."

"Is this true, Frank?"

"Yeah." His reply was so quiet that I almost didn't hear it.

"C'mon, Patrick," I begged, brushing off Frank's misdeeds as even more insignificant than Patrick made them sound. "Let us go. Who are you trying to be, Inspector Javert?"

"It depends." He took a few steps toward us. "Which of you is Valjean?"

I sighed. I couldn't believe that, with all the people out there who were after us, the adorable and adoring fan with the dark blue eyes from Tacoma was the man who was going to be our undoing.

"What do you want from us, Patrick?" I asked.

"The usual All-American stuff." He casually brushed a mop of hair off his forehead. "Apple pie, motherhood, respect for the law . . . That last one gets a bit tricky, though, at times." He smiled, dimpling his cheeks, then slowly turned away from us and raised his arms, until we were looking at his tapered back. "I'm not looking at the two of you. If I were in your position, I'd take advantage of that unprofessional lapse in my judgment. And, since you both know that I'm not the only federal agent in Riverside Park tonight, if I was in your position, I'd certainly leave at once." He glanced over his shoulder to me and winked. "Before the real Javert wannabes show up."

"Thanks," I said, relieved, smiling, and winking back.

Frank and I started to edge away.

"Move faster," Patrick called after us. "That's an official order."

"One last thing," I said back to him. "Would you call my friend Denise and tell her that I'll be away for a while?"

"Denise from the ladies' room? Sure."

"Do you need her phone number?"

"I don't need it. I can find anyone." He looked over his shoulder and winked again. "Anytime. Anywhere. And don't you forget it."

His soft laughter echoed in the rotunda as Frank and I hustled through the passageway under the Henry Hudson Parkway. On the other side, we descended a short flight of stairs back into Riverside Park and, just feet beyond the park, we finally reached the Boat Basin.

* * *

They were still waiting for Frank in the darkness. A small cluster of men, led by his father, was framed against the inky Hudson River and, beyond it, the dirty gray silhouette of New Jersey.

"You're late," Frank's father said gruffly when we approached. He eyed us up and down before asking the obvious. "Trouble?"

"Just the usual." Frank didn't have to explain further. His father had certainly heard the gunshots and the sirens.

Which was just as well. Frank Senior didn't seem to care about the explanation. He looked at me with disdain. "Who's this?"

"This is Andrew. From . . . uh . . ." Obviously, Frank didn't want to be forced to mention the Belle Bacall incident if he didn't have to. "It's Andrew. I told you about him."

"Oh, yeah." The elder DiBenedetto was very unhappy with my presence. He turned to me. "You'd better get along home, son. Frankie's got to get moving."

"I'm going with him," I said.

Frank Senior looked at Frank Junior, who agreed.

"That's right, Pop. Andrew's in over his head, too, and he's coming with me."

The older man sighed heavily and turned, waving for us to follow him. He unlocked the chain-link gate to the docks and we trailed him as he walked along the creaking boards suspending us over the water, until we reached a small motorboat tied up at the last rotting wooden piling.

"Get on the boat," he commanded, and we obeyed. Once we were aboard, he handed Frank a thick envelope. "This should get you by for a while."

"Thanks." Frank Junior pocketed the envelope without taking a second look at it. He had no choice but to trust his father.

"Don't blow it all at once," the father continued, then, indicating me, he added, "And don't feel that you have to pay for anyone else. Understand?"

Frank looked at me and smiled, as if to say *ignore him.* I smiled back.

Frank's father climbed back up on the dock, then waved for his men. They approached slowly and carefully, and when they drew nearer, I saw that they were carrying a heavy, unwieldy bundle.

When they reached the end of the dock, Frank Senior said, "Unwrap it. Let's get this over with and get out of here. Too many damned people in this park tonight."

I watched in growing horror as the bundle was unwrapped to reveal the body of a man roughly thirty years of age . . . a man with the same general build and coloring of my Frank.

"I think I'm going to be sick," I told Frank, averting my eyes.

"It's okay, Andrew. They didn't kill him. He was already dead."

The men silently rolled the corpse off the dock. It made a light splash as it fell inelegantly into the Hudson and submerged, only to bob to the surface moments later, where it began the casual process of settling into the river.

"In the next few days, when the body surfaces, everyone will think it's me. So no one will be looking for me anymore."

"But won't the medical examiner know that it's not your body?"

He shook his head and laughed. "Andrew, sometimes you are so naïve."

I glanced at the body as it floated inches below the surface of the placid black water, alternately horrified and calmed by the thought that maybe this would put an end to the chase.

"But everyone will think you're dead," I said. "How does that solve anything?"

"It doesn't." He leaned back in the boat and put his arm around my shoulder. "It just buys me time. And maybe time is all I—I mean, *we*—need."

"Time," I agreed. "Time would be good. Time, and you."

He smiled broadly and tilted his head until it came to rest against mine.

"Time, and us," he said.

One of his father's henchmen climbed into the boat and brought the engine to life. We looked back at the dock, but Frank Senior had already retreated into the predawn darkness.

Its lights off, the boat carefully crossed the Hudson River. I wasn't really sure what waited for us on the other side, and I really wasn't sure what I had left behind. But I knew that I only really needed two things: Frank and time.

Frank and time. At least I'd have those things. Everything else could wait.

* * *

Over the next few weeks, the media—especially the tabloids—had a field day with the story. The first headlines dealt with the disappearance of alleged organized crime figure Frank DiBenedetto Junior. Within days, though, they figured out that I was missing, too, and put two and two together. Soon, we were dubbed "The Outlaw Lovers."

Then, the body that wasn't Frank's surfaced in the Hudson, and the FBI admitted that my clothes and wallet were left behind in a van at the corner of Amsterdam Avenue and West Eighty-sixth Street, along with Frank's personal effects. Foul play was suspected, and we became "The Til-Death-They-Parted Lovers," which I sort of liked, in a gruesome way.

Days after that, though, a Riverside Drive dog-walker came forward to tell the world that he saw us running down the street, half-naked, awash in misery. Others—even Ted Langhorne, of all people—were quoted as saying that I was too wrapped up in the romance of romance. And even Frank's father chimed in to confirm that Frank was mortified that he'd fallen in love with a transvestite. I didn't like that, but it was nice of him to acknowledge me.

That's when we became "The Tragic Lovers." It was a trite label, but it stuck.

The media collectively took the angle that Frank and I threw ourselves in the Hudson because our friends and families would never let us be together. We were portrayed as the most recent version of Romeo and Juliet, if the Montagues carried semiautomatic weapons and the Capulets owned time-shares on Fire Island.

Frank's friends and family uniformly told the press that he was a good boy who had never run afoul of the law. That was nice of them.

As for me, well . . . I must admit, the reporters seemed somewhat taken aback that my two closest friends were a bit acid-tongued about my role as half of "The Tragic Lovers." Denise Hanrahan was quoted as saying, "I don't know if I can ever forgive Andrew." I suppose that could be read as the tearful utterance of a bereft friend, but I knew better. She was talking directly to me . . . *and* she called me Andrew.

For his part, David Carlyle referred to his friend, employee, and best-selling author as "a tragic figure, unable to make the right choices." Still, I helped fatten his wallet. Gary Vine might have gone to federal prison for a year and a day for a few minor RICO-related crimes connected to Stendardi family gambling interests, but in the wake of my apparent tragic suicide, my books still flew off the shelves. *The Brewster Mall* finally made the *Times* best-seller list three weeks later, hitting fourth place two weeks after that before it descended slowly, like a floater in the Hudson. It went to trade paper six months later, but by then my tragic ending was out of the news, so it peaked at eleventh place. Not bad, though.

The FBI ended up arresting more than ninety alleged organized crime figures in their anti-Mafia offensive. Only forty-three went to prison, including Paulie Macarini and Anna Franco, who made the big mistake of getting into a shoot-out with federal agents on Riverside Drive. Apparently, Big Paulie and Crazy Anna were never destined to be together. Not for another ten to twenty years, at least.

Frank's father and Crazy Tommy Franco were found not guilty by their respective juries on each of a variety of counts. To the best of my knowledge, they still aren't close friends.

Oh, speaking of items in the news, a few weeks after my apparent tragic suicide, I read that famed gay party promoter Barry Blackburn was beaten into a near-coma one night in the East Village. Community pressure forced the police to classify it as an anti-gay hate crime, which goes to show what the community and the police know. As far as I was concerned, it was an anti-hate gay crime. I still felt bad, but mostly because I wished I'd had the balls to do it myself.

My body was never found. Tragic, isn't it? Well, I was a Tragic Lover, after all. Oh, every now and then a body or part thereof washes up in the New York metropolitan region, and the speculation erupts. But so far it hasn't been my body. Go figure.

Two years later, after the alleged tragedy, Palmer/Midkiff/Carlyle published *Andrew's Life* by first-time author Grant Brewster. *Publishers Weekly* called it "a funny, bittersweet look back through life's many mistakes, many of which Brewster's protagonist makes in spades, before he finally finds redemption in the arms of an improbable lover." Well, okay . . . I wimped out, and the fictitious improbable lover in *Andrew's Life* was a woman. Still, it shows that I can be reflective at times. Poignant, perhaps.

Industry buzz and a wonderful cover blurb by Margaret Campbell put it on the best-seller lists as soon as it hit the bookstores. Grant Brewster is a happy man.

By the way, some folks resented the fact that this Brewster fellow was a bit of a hermit when the book came out. They thought that only writers of literary fiction—Salinger, Pynchon, and the like—had the right to be reclusive. That commercial fiction writers—like Brewster—were public property.

I've got news for them: Grant Brewster is going to stay right where he is in Nowhere, USA, with Kevin DiVincenzo, the man with the dark, curly hair and the bright brown eyes, whom he loves and who loves him in return. Grant and Kevin are going to continue to lead lives of quiet anonymity, tending to the garden, watching old movies, experimenting in the kitchen, and—when the mood strikes them—slow-dancing to "How Deep Is Your Love."

And each morning, after Kevin leaves for his steady and very legal job as the assistant manager of a three-star restaurant, Grant is going to write about worlds that he never again wants to visit.

He's seen enough of the outside world. He was a Tragic Lover. Now he's a Real-Life Lover, and he gets love back.

Finally, he's found something he loves more than the illusion of romance.

He's found the real thing.